OLD MR. TREDGOLD

OLD MR. TREDGOLD

A Story of Two Sisters

MRS. M. O. W. OLIPHANT

AUTHOR OF "CHRONICLES OF CARLINGFORD," "MADAM," ETC.

NEW YORK

LONGMANS, GREEN, AND CO.

1895

OLD MR. TREDGOLD.

CHAPTER I.

THEY were not exactly of that conventional type which used to be common whenever two sisters had to be described—the one dark and the other fair, the one sunny and amiable, the other reserved and proud ; the one gay, the other melancholy, or at least very serious by nature. They were not at all like Minna and Brenda in the '' Pirate,'' which used to be a contrast dear to the imagination. But yet there was a very distinct difference between them. Katherine was a little taller, a little bigger, a little darker, than Stella. She was three years older but was supposed to look ten. She was not so lively in her movements either of mind or person, and she was supposed to be slow. The one who was all light threw a shadow—which seems contradictory—on the other. They were the two daughters of an old gentleman who had been that mysterious being called a City man in his time. Not that there was anything at all mysterious about old Mr. Tredgold ; his daughters and his daughters' friends were fond of saying that he had come to London with the traditionary half-crown in his pocket ; but this was, as in so many cases, fabulous, Mr. Tredgold having in fact come of a perfectly creditable Eastern Counties family, his father being a well-to-do linen draper in Ipswich, whose pride it was to have set forth all his boys comfortably, and done everything for them that a father could do. But perhaps it is easier to own to that half-crown and the myth of an origin sudden and commercially-romantic without antecedents, than to a respectable shop in a respectable town, with a number of relatives installed in other shops, doing well and ready to claim the rights of relationship at inconvenient moments. I do not know at all how fortunes are made "in the City." If you dig coals out of the bowels of the earth, or manufacture anything, from cotton to ships, by which money is made, that is a process which comes within the comprehension of the most limited faculties; but making money in the City never seems to mean anything so simple. It means handing about money, or goods which other people have produced, to other third or fourth people, and then handing them back again even to the Scriptural limits of seventy times seven; which is why it appears so mysterious to the simple-minded.

But, indeed, if anybody had investigated the matter, Mr. Tredgold's progress had been quite easy to follow, at least in the results. He had gone from a house in Hampstead to a house in Kensington, and thence to Belgravia, changing also his summer residences from Herne Bay to Hastings, and thence to the wilds of Surrey, and then to the Isle of Wight, where, having retired from the cares of business, he now lived in one of those beautiful places, with one of the most beautiful prospects in the world before him, which so often fall to the lot of persons who care very little about beauty in any shape. The house stood on a cliff which was almost a little headland, standing out from the line of the downs between two of the little towns on the south side of that favoured island. The grounds were laid out quite regardless of expense, so much so that they were a show in the district, and tourists were admitted by the gardeners when the family was absent, to see such a collection of flowering shrubs and rare trees as was not to be found between that point, let us say, and Mr. Hanbury's gardens at Mortola. The sunny platform of the cliff thus adorned to the very edge of the precipice was the most delightful mount of vision, from which you could look along the lovely coast at that spot not much inferior to the Riviera, with its line of sunny towns and villages lying along the course of the bay on one hand, and the darker cliffs clad with wood, amid all the picturesque broken ground of the Landslip on the other ; and the dazzling sea, with the additional glory of passing ships giving it a continual interest, stretching out far into the distance, where it met the circle of the globe, and merged as all life does in the indefinite Heaven beyond—the Heaven, the Hades, the unknown—not always celestial, sometimes dark with storm or wild with wind, a vague and indeterminate distance from which the tempests and all their demons, as well as the angels, come, yet the only thing that gives even a wistful satisfaction to the eyes of those who sway with every movement of this swaying globe in the undiscovered depths of air and sky.

Very little attention, I am sorry to say, was paid to this beautiful landscape by the family who had secured it for their special delectation. The girls would take their visitors "to see the view," who cast a careless glance at it, and said, "How pretty!" and returned with pleasure to the tennis or croquet, or even tea of the moment. Mr. Tredgold, for his part, had chosen a room for himself on the sheltered side of the house, as was perhaps natural, and shivered at the thought of the view. There was always a wind that cut you to pieces, he said, on that side of the cliff; and, truth to tell, I believe there was, the proverbial softness of the climate of the Isle of Wight being a fond delusion, for the most part, in the minds of its inhabitants. Katherine was the only one who lingered occasionally over the great panorama of the sea and coast ; but I think it was when she felt herself a little "out of it," as people say, when Stella was appropriating everything, and all the guests and all the lovers were circling round that little luminary, and the elder sister was not wanted anywhere—except to fill out tea perhaps, or look after the comforts of the others, which is a *rôle* that may suit a staid person of forty, but at twenty-three is not only melancholy but bewildering— it being always so difficult to see why another should have all the good things, and yourself all the crosses of life.

In the circumstances of these two girls there was not even that cheap way of relief which ends in blaming some one.

Even Providence could not be blamed. Katherine, if you looked at her calmly, was quite as pretty as Stella; she had a great deal more in her; she was more faithful, more genuine and trustworthy; she played tennis as well or better; she had as good a voice and a better ear; in short, it was quite incomprehensible to any one why it was that Stella was the universal favourite and her sister was left in the shade. But so it was. Katherine made up the set with the worst players, or she was kept at the tea-table while the merriest game was going on. She had the reversion of Stella's partners, who talked to her of her sister, of what a jolly girl, or what an incipient angel she was, according to their several modes of speech. The old ladies said that it was because Katherine was so unselfish; but I should not like to brand a girl for whom I have a great regard with that conventional title. She was not, to her own consciousness, unselfish at all. She would have liked very much, if not to have the first place, at least to share it, to have a retinue of her own, and champions and admirers as well as Stella. She did not like the secondary position nor even consent to it with any willingness; and the consequence was that occasionally she retired and looked at the view with anything but happy feelings; so that the appreciation of Nature, and of their good fortune in having their lines thrown in such pleasant places, was very small and scant indeed in this family, which outsiders were sometimes disposed to envy for the beauty of their surroundings and for their wonderful view.

The house which occupied this beautiful situation was set well back in the grounds, so that it at least should not be contaminated by the view, and it was an odd fantastic house, though by no means uncomfortable when you got into the ways of it. A guest, unacquainted with these ways, which consisted of all the very last so-called improvements, might indeed spend a wretched day or night in his or her ignorance. I have indeed known one who, on a very warm evening, found herself in a chamber hermetically sealed to all appearance, with labels upon the windows bearing the words

"Close" and "Open," but affording no information as to how to work or move the complicated machinery which achieved these operations; and when she turned to the bell for aid, there was a long cord depending by the wall, at which she tugged and tugged in vain, not knowing (for these were the early days of electrical appliances) that all she had to do was to touch the little ivory circle at the end of the cord. The result was a night's imprisonment in what gradually became a sort of Black Hole of Calcutta, without air to breathe or means of appealing to the outside world. The Tredgolds themselves, however, I am happy to say, had the sense in their own rooms to have the windows free to open and shut according to the rules of Nature.

The whole place was very elaborately furnished, with an amount of gilding and ornament calculated to dazzle the beholder—inlaid cabinets, carved furniture, and rich hangings everywhere, not a door without a *portière*, not a window without the most elaborate sets of curtains. The girls had not been old enough to control this splendour when it was brought into being by an adroit upholsterer; and, indeed, they were scarcely old enough even yet to have escaped from the spell of the awe and admiration into which they had been trained. They felt the flimsiness of the fashionable mode inspired by Liberty in comparison with their solid and costly things, even should these be in worst taste, and, as in everything a sense of superiority is sweet, they did not attempt any innovations. But the room in which they sat together in the evening was at least the most simply decorated in the house. There was less gold, there were some smooth and simple tables on which the hand could rest without carrying away a sharp impression of carved foliage or arabesques. There were no china vases standing six feet high, and there was a good deal of litter about such as is indispensable to the happiness of girls. Mr. Tredgold had a huge easy-chair placed near to a tall lamp, and the evening paper, only a few hours later than if he had been in London, in his hands. He was a little old man with no appearance to speak of—no features, no hair, and very little in the way of eyes. How he had managed to be the father of two vigorous young women nobody could understand ; but vigorous young women are, however it has come about, one of the commonest productions of the age, a fashion like any other. Stella lay back in a deep chair near her father, and was at this moment, while he filled the air of the room with the crinkling of his paper as he folded back a leaf, lost in the utterance of a long yawn which opened her mouth to a preternatural size, and put her face, which was almost in a horizontal position thrown back and contemplating the ceiling, completely out of drawing, which was a pity, for it was a pretty face. Katherine showed no inclination to yawn— she was busy at a table doing something—something very useless and of the nature of trumpery I have no doubt ; but it kept her from yawning at least.

"Well, my pet," Mr. Tredgold said, putting his hand on the arm of Stella's chair, "very tired, eh—tired of having nothing to do, and sitting with your old father one night ? "

"Oh, I've got plenty to do," said Stella, getting over the yawn, and smiling blandly upon the world ; "and, as for one night I sit with you for ever, you ungrateful old dad."

"What is in the wind now ? What's the next entertainment ? You never mean to be quiet for two days together ? " the old gentleman said.

"It is not our fault," said Katherine. "The Courtnays have gone away, the Allens are going, and Lady Jane has not yet come back."

"I declare," cried Stella, "it's humiliating that we should have to depend on anybody for company, whether they are summer people or winter people. What is Lady Jane to us ? We are as good as any of them. It is you who give in directly, Kate, and think there is nothing to be done. I'll have a picnic to-morrow, if it was only the people from the hotel ; they are better than nobody, and so pleased to be asked. I shan't spend another evening alone with papa."

Papa was not displeased by this sally. He laughed and chuckled in his throat, and crinkled his newspaper more than ever. "What a little hussy!" he cried. "Did you ever know such a little hussy, Kate?"

Kate did not pay any attention at all to papa. She went on with her gum and scissors and her trumpery, which was intended for a bazaar somewhere. "The question is, Do you know the hotel people?" she said. "You would not think a picnic of five or six much fun."

"Oh, five or six!" cried the other with a toss of her head; and she sprang up from her chair with an activity as great as her former listlessness, and rushed to a very fine ormolu table all rose colour and gold, at which she sat down, dashing off as many notes. "The Setons at the hotel will bring as many as that; they have officers and all kinds of people about," she cried, flinging the words across her shoulder as she wrote.

"But we scarcely know them, Stella; and Mrs. Seton I don't like," said Katherine, with her gum-brush arrested in her hand.

"Papa, am I to ask the people I want, or is Kate to dictate in everything?" cried Stella, putting up another note.

"Let the child have her way, Katie, my dear; you know she has always had her way all her life."

Katherine's countenance was perhaps not so amiable as Stella's, who was radiant with fun and expectation and contradiction. "I think I may sometimes have my way too," she said. "They are not nice people; they may bring any kind of man, there is always a crowd of men about *her*. Papa, I think we are much safer, two girls like us, and you never going out with us, if we keep to people we know; that was always to be the condition when you consented that Stella should send our invitations without consulting you."

"Yes, yes, my dear," said the old gentleman, turning to his elder daughter, "that is quite true, quite true;" then he caught Stella's eye, and added tremulously: "You must certainly have two or three people you know."

"And what do you call Miss Mildmay?" cried Stella, "and Mrs. Shanks?—aren't they people we know?"

"Oh, if she is asking them—the most excellent people and

knowing everybody—I think—don't you think, Katie?—that might do?"

"Of course it will do," cried Stella gaily. "And old Shanks and old Mildmay are such fun; they always fight—and they hate all the people in the hotels; and only think of their two old faces when they see Mrs. Seton and all her men! It will be the best party we have had this whole year."

Katherine's ineffectual remonstrances were drowned in the tinkling as of a cracked bottle of Mr. Tredgold's laugh. He liked to hear the old ladies called old cats and set to fight and spit at each other. It gave him an agreeable sense of contrast with his own happy conditions; petted and appealed to by the triumphant youth which belonged to him, and of which he was so proud. The inferiority of the " old things " was pleasant to the old man, who was older than they. The cackle of his laugh swept every objection away. And then I think Katherine would have liked to steal away outside and look at the view, and console herself with the sight of the Sliplin lights and all the twinkling villages along the coast; which, it will be seen, was no disinterested devotion to Nature, but only a result of the sensation of being out of it, and not having, which Stella had, her own way.

"Well, you needn't come unless you like," cried Stella with defiance, as they parted at the door between their respective rooms, a door which Katherine, I confess, shut with some energy on this particular evening, though it generally stood open night and day.

" I don't think I will," Katherine cried in her impatience; but she thought better of this before day.

CHAPTER II.

STELLA had always been the spoilt child of the Tredgold family. Her little selfishnesses and passions of desire to have her own way, and everything she might happen to want, had been so amusing that nobody had chidden or thought for a moment (as everybody thought with Katherine) of the bad effect upon her character and temper of having all these passions satisfied and getting everything she stormed or cried for. Aunt after aunt had passed in shadow, as it were, across the highly lighted circle of Mr. Tredgold's home life, all of them breaking down at last in the impossibility of keeping pace with Stella, or satisfying her impetuous little spirit; and governess after governess in the same way had performed a sort of processional march through the house. Stella's perpetual flow of mockery and mimicry had all the time kept her father in endless amusement. The mockery was not very clever, but he was easily pleased and thought it capital fun. There was so much inhumanity in his constitution, though he was a kind man in his way and very indulgent to those who belonged to him, that he had no objection to see his own old sister (though a good creature) outrageously mimicked in all her peculiarities, much less the sisters of his late wife. Little Stella, while still under the age of sixteen, had driven off all these ladies and kept her father in constant amusement. "The little hussy!" he said, "the little vixen!" and chuckled and laughed till it was feared he might choke some time, being afflicted with bronchitis, in those convulsions of delight. Katherine, who was the champion of the aunts, and wept as one after the other departed, amused him greatly too. "She is an old maid born!" he said, "and she sticks up for her

kind, but Stella will have her pick, and marry a prince, and
take off the old cats as long as she lives.''

" But if she lives,'' said a severe governess who for some time
kept the household in awe, "she will become old too, and probably be an old cat in the opinion of those that come after her.''

" No fear,'' cried the foolish old man—" no fear.'' In his
opinion Stella would never be anything but pretty and young,
and radiant with fun and fascination.

And since the period when the girls " came out '' there had
been nothing but a whirl of gaiety in the house. They did not
come out in the legitimate way, by being presented to Her
Majesty and thus placed on the roll of society in the usual
meaning of the word, but only by appearing at the first important ball in the locality, and giving it so to be understood
that they were prepared to accept any invitations that might
come in their way. They had come out together, Stella being much too masterful and impatient to permit any such step
on Katherine's part without her, so that Katherine had been
more than nineteen while Stella was not much over sixteen
when this important step took place. Three years had passed
since that time. Stella was twenty, and beginning to feel like
a rather *blasé* woman of the world ; while Katherine at twenty-three was supposed to be stepping back to that obscurity
which her father had prophesied for her, not far off from the
region of the old cats to which she was supposed to belong.
Curiously enough, no prince had come out of the unknown
for the brighter sister. The only suitor that had appeared
had been for Katherine, and had been almost laughed out of
countenance, poor man, before he took his dismissal, which
was, indeed, rather given by the household in general than by
the person chiefly concerned. He was an Indian civilian on
his way back to some blazing station on the Plains, which was
reason enough why he should be repulsed by the family ; but
probably the annoying thought that it was Katherine he wanted and not her sister had still more to do with it.

" It was a good thing at least that he had not the audacity
to ask for you, my pet,'' Mr. Tredgold said.

"For me!" said Stella, with a little shriek of horror, "I should very soon have given him his answer." And Katherine, too, gave him his answer, but in a dazed and bewildered way. She was not at all in love with him, but it did glance across her mind that to be the first person with some one, to have a house of her own in which she should be supreme, and a man by her side who thought there was nobody like her—— But, then, was it possible that any man should really think that? or that any house could ever have this strange fascination of home which held her fast she could not tell how or why? She acquiesced accordingly in Mr. Stanford's dismissal. But when she went out to look at the view in her moments of discouragement her mind was apt to return to him, to wonder sometimes what he was doing, where he was, or if he had found some one to be his companion, and of whom he could think that there was nobody like her in the world?

In the meantime, however, on the morning which followed the evening already recorded, Katherine had too much to do in the way of providing for the picnic to have much time to think. Stella had darted into her room half-dressed with a number of notes in her hand to tell her that everybody was coming. "Mrs. Seton brings six including her husband and herself—that makes four fresh new men besides little Seton, whom you can talk to if you like, Kate; and there's three from the Rectory, and five from the Villa, and old Mildmay and Shanks to do propriety for papa's sake."

"I wish you would not speak of them in that way by their names. It does not take much trouble to say Miss Mildmay and Mrs. Shanks."

"I'll say the old cats, if you like," Stella said with a laugh, "that's shorter still. Do stir up a little, and be quick and let us have a good lunch."

"How am I to get cold chickens at an hour's notice?" said Katherine. "You seem to think they are all ready roasted in the poultry yard, and can be put in the hampers straight off. I don't know what Mrs. Pearson will say."

"She will only say what she has said a hundred times; but it always comes right all the same," cried Stella, retreating into her own room to complete her toilette. And this was so true that Kate finished hers also in comparative calm. She was the housekeeper *de jure*, and interviewed Mrs. Pearson every morning with the profoundest gravity as if everything depended upon her; but at bottom Katherine knew very well that it was Mrs. Pearson who was the housekeeper *de facto*, and that she, like everyone else, managed somehow that Miss Stella should have her way.

"You know it's just impossible," said that authority a few minutes later. "Start at twelve and tell me at nine to provide for nearly twenty people! Where am I to get the chickens, not to speak of ham and cold beef and all the rest? Do ye think the chickens in the yard are roasted already?" cried the indignant housekeeper, using Katherine's own argument, "and that I have only to set them out in the air to cool?"

"You see I did not know yesterday," said the young mistress apologetically; "it was a sudden thought of Miss Stella's last night."

"She *is* a one for sudden thoughts!" cried Pearson, half-indignant, half-admiring; and after a little more protestation that it was impossible she began to arrange how it could be done. It was indeed so usual an experience that the protests were stereotyped, so to speak. Everything on the Cliff was sudden — even Katherine had acquired the habit, and preferred an impromptu to any careful preparation of events. "Then if anything is wrong we can say there was so very little time to do it in," she said with an instinct of recklessness foreign to her nature. But Mrs. Pearson was wise and prudent and knew her business, so that it was very seldom anything went wrong.

On ordinary occasions every one knows how rare it is to have a thoroughly fine day for the most carefully arranged picnic. The association of rain with these festivities is traditional. There is nothing that has so bad an effect upon the most settled weather. Clouds blow up upon the sky and rain

pours down at the very suggestion. But that strange Deity
which we call Providence, and speak of in the neuter gender,
is never more apparently capricious than in this respect. A
picnic which is thoroughly undesirable, which has nothing in
its favour, which brings people together who ought to be kept
apart, and involves mischief of every kind, is free from all the
usual mischances. That day dawned more brightly even than
other days. It shone even cloudless, the glass rising, the
wind dropping as if for the special enjoyment of some favourite of Heaven. It was already October, but quite warm, as
warm as June, the colour of autumn adding only a charm the
more, and neither chill nor cloud to dull the atmosphere.
The sea shone like diamonds but more brilliant, curve upon
curve of light following each other with every glittering facet
in movement. The white cliff at the further point of the bay
shone with a dazzling whiteness beyond comparison with anything else in sky or earth.

At twelve o'clock the sun overhead was like a benediction,
not too hot as in July and August, just perfect everybody said ;
and the carriages and the horses with their shiny coats, and
the gay guests in every tint of colour, with convivial smiles
and pleasant faces, made the drive as gay as Rotten Row when
Mr. Tredgold came forth to welcome and speed forth his
guests. This was his own comparison often used, though the
good man had never known much of Rotten Row. He stood
in the porch, which had a rustical air though the house was so
far from being rustical, and surveyed all these dazzling people
with pride. Though he had been used for years now to such
gay assemblages, he had never ceased to feel a great pride in
them as though of " an honour unto which he was not born."
To see his girls holding out hospitality to all the grand folks
was an unceasing satisfaction. He liked to see them at the
head of everything, dispensing bounties. The objectionable
lady who had brought so many men in her train did not come
near Mr. Tredgold, but bowed to him from a safe distance,
from his own waggonette in which she had placed herself.

" I am not going to be led like a lamb to that old bore,"

she said to her party, which swarmed about her and was ready
to laugh at everything she said; and they were all much
amused by the old man's bow, and by the wave of his hand,
with which he seemed to make his visitors free of his luxuries.

"The old bore thinks himself an old swell," said someone
else. "Tredgold and Silverstamp, money changers," said
another. "Not half so good—Tredgold and Wurst, sausage
makers," cried a third. They all laughed so much, being
easily satisfied in the way of wit, that Stella, who was going
to drive, came up flourishing her whip, to know what was the
joke.

"Oh, only about a funny sign we saw on the way," said
Mrs. Seton, with a glance all round, quenching the laughter.
The last thing that could have entered Stella's mind was that
these guests of hers, so effusive in their acceptance of her invitation, so pleased to be there, with everything supplied for
their day's pleasure, were making a jest of anything that belonged to her. She felt that she was conferring a favour upon
them, giving them "a great treat," which they had no right
to expect.

"You must tell me about it on the way," she said, beaming
upon them with gracious looks, which was the best joke of all,
they all thought, stifling their laughter.

Mr. Tredgold sent a great many wreathed smiles and gracious gestures to the waggonette which was full of such a distinguished company, and with Stella and her whip just ready
to mount the driving-seat. They were new friends he was
aware. The men were all fashionable, "a cut above" the
Sliplin or even the smaller county people. The old gentleman
loved to see his little Stella among them, with her little delightful swagger and air of being A 1 everywhere. I hope nobody will think me responsible for the words in which poor
Mr. Tredgold's vulgar little thoughts expressed themselves.
He did not swagger like Stella, but loved to see her swagger-
ing. He himself would have been almost obsequious to the
fine folks. He had a remnant of uneasy consciousness that
he had no natural right to all this splendour, which made him

deeply delighted when people who had a right to it conde-
scended to accept it from his hand. But he was proud too to
know that Stella did not at all share this feeling, but thought
herself A 1. So she was A 1 ; no one there was fit to hold a
candle to her. So he thought, standing at his door waving
his hands, and calling out congratulations on the fine day and
injunctions to his guests to enjoy themselves.

" Don't spare anything—neither the horses nor the champagne ; there is plenty more where these came from," he said.

Then the waggonette dashed off, leading the way ; and
Katherine followed in the landau with the clergyman's family
from the Rectory, receiving more of Mr. Tredgold's smiles
and salutations, but not so enthusiastic.

" Mind you make everybody comfortable, Kate," he cried.
" Have you plenty of wraps and cushions ? There's any number in the hall ; and I hope your hampers are full of nice
things and plenty of champagne—plenty of good champagne ;
that's what the ladies want to keep up their spirits. And
don't be afraid of it. I have none but the best in my
house."

The vehicle which came after the landau was something of
the shandrydan order, with one humble horse and five people
clustering upon it.

" Why didn't you have one of our carriages ! " he cried.
" There's a many in the stables that we never use. You had
only to say the word, and the other waggonette would have
been ready for you ; far more comfortable than that old rattle-
trap. And, bless us ! here is the midge—the midge, I declare
— with the two old — with two old friends ; but, dear me,
Mrs. Shanks, how much better you would have been in the
brougham ! "

" So I said," said one of the ladies ; " but Ruth Mildmay
would not hear of it. She is all for independence and our own
trap, but I like comfort best."

" No," said Miss Mildmay. " Indebted to our good friend
we'll always be for many a nice party, and good dinner and
good wine as well ; but my carriage must be my own, if it's

only a hired one ; that is my opinion, Mr. Tredgold, whatever
any one may say.''

" My dear good ladies,'' said Mr. Tredgold, " this is Liberty Hall ; you may come as you please and do as you please ;
only you know there's heaps of horses in my stables, and when
my daughters go out I like everything about them to be nice—
nice horses, nice carriages.   And why should you pay for a `
shabby affair that anybody can hire, when you might have my
brougham with all the last improvements ?   But ladies will
have their little whims and fads, we all know that.''

" Mr. Perkins,'' cried Miss Mildmay out of the window to
the driver of the fly, " go on !   We'll never make up to the
others if you don't drive fast ; and the midge is not very safe
when it goes along a heavy road.''

" As safe as a coach, and we're in very good time, Miss,''
said Mr. Perkins, waving his whip.   Perkins felt himself to be
of the party too, as indeed he was of most parties along the
half circle of the bay.

" Ah, I told you,'' cried Mr. Tredgold, with his chuckle,
" you'd have been much better in the brougham.''   He went
on chuckling after this last detachment had driven unsteadily
away.   A midge is not a graceful nor perhaps a very safe vehicle.   It is like a section of an omnibus, a square box on
wheels wanting proportions, and I think it is used only by elderly ladies at seaside places.   As it jogged forth Mr. Tredgold
chuckled more and more.   Though he had been so lavish in
his offers of the brougham, the old gentleman was not displeased
to see his old neighbours roll and shamble along in that uncomfortable way.   It served them right for rejecting the luxury he had provided.   It served them still more right for being poor.   And yet there was this advantage in their being
poor, that it threw up the fact of his own wealth, like a bright
object on a dark background.   He went back to his room after
a while, casting a glance and a shiver at the garden blazing
with sunshine and flowers which crowned the cliff.   He knew
there was always a little shrewd breeze blowing round the corner somewhere, and the view might be hanged for anything he

cared. He went indoors to his room, where there was a nice little bit of fire. There was generally a little bit of fire somewhere wherever he was. It was much more concentrated than the sun, and could be controlled at his pleasure and suited him better. The sun shone when it pleased, but the fire burned when Mr. Tredgold pleased. He sat down and stretched himself out in his easy-chair and thought for a minute or two how excellent it was to have such a plenty of money, so many horses and carriages, and one of the nicest houses in the island—the very nicest he thought—and to give Stella everything she wanted. "She makes a fool of me," he said to himself, chuckling. "If that little girl wanted the Koh-i-Noor, I'd be game to send off somebody careering over the earth to find out as good." This was all for love of Stella and a little for glory of himself; and in this mood he took up his morning paper, which was his occupation for the day.

2

CHAPTER III.

A PICNIC is a very doubtful pleasure to people out of their teens, or at least out of their twenties; and yet it remains a very popular amusement. The grass is often damp, and it is a very forced and uncomfortable position to sit with your plate on your knees and nothing within your reach which you may reasonably want in the course of the awkward meal. Mrs. Seton and the younger ladies, who were sedulously attended upon, did not perhaps feel this so much; but then smart young men, especially when themselves guests and attached to one particular party, do not wait upon "the old cats" as they do upon the ladies of the feast. Why Mrs. Shanks and Miss Mildmay should have continued to partake in these banquets, and spend their money on the midge to convey them there, I am unable so much as to guess, for they would certainly have been much more comfortable at home. But they did do so, in defiance of any persuasion. They were not entirely igno- rant that they were considered old cats. The jibes which were current on the subject did not always fly over their heads. They knew more or less why they were asked, and how little any one cared for their presence. And yet they went to every entertainment of the kind to which they were asked with a steadiness worthy of a better cause. They were less consid- ered even than usual in this company, which was chiefly made up of strangers. They had to scramble for the salad and help themselves to the ham. Cold chicken was supposed to be quite enough for them without any accompaniment. The *pâté de foie gras* was quite exhausted before it came their length, and Miss Mildmay had to pluck at Mr. Seton's coat and call his attention half a dozen times before they got any champagne; and yet they were always ready to accept the most careless invitation, I cannot tell why. They talked chiefly to each other, and took their little walks together when the young ones dispersed or betook themselves to some foolish game. " Oh, here are the old cats ! " they could almost hear the girls say, when the two ancient figures came in sight at the turn of the path; and Stella would turn round and walk off in the opposite direction without an attempt at concealment. But they did not take offence, and next time were always ready to come again.

That Mrs. Seton should have been ready to come was less wonderful, for though she was old enough to be a little afraid of her complexion, and was aware that damp was very bad for her neuralgia, it was indispensable for her to have something to do, and the heavy blank of a day without entertainment was dreadful to bear. And this was not for herself only but for her court, or her tail, or whatever it may be called—the retinue of young men whom she led about, and who had to be amused whatever happened. Think of the expenditure of energy that is necessary to amuse so many young active human creatures in a sitting-room in a hotel for a whole morning, before lunch comes to relieve the intolerable strain; or even in an afternoon before and after the blessed relief of tea ! They sprawl about upon the chairs, they block up the windows, they gape for something to do, they expect to have funny things said to them and to be made to laugh. What hard work for any woman whose whole faculty consists in a capacity for saying every folly that comes into her head with an audacity which is not accompanied by wit ! " What a fool you do look, Algy, with your mouth open like a little chick in a nest ! Do you expect me to pop a worm into it ? " This speech made them all roar, but it was not in itself amusing, the reader will perceive. And to go on in that strain for hours is extremely fatiguing, more so than the hardest work. Many people wondered why she should take the trouble to have all these men about her, and to undertake the Herculean task of entertaining them, which was a mystery quite as great as the per-

sistence of the elder ladies in going to feasts where they are
called old cats and receive no attention. The lightest of social
entertainments *donnent à penser* in this way. You would have
thought that Mrs. Seton would have welcomed the moment of
relief which ensued when the boys and girls ran off together in
a sort of hide-and-seek among the tufted slopes. But when she
found that she was actually left alone for a moment with only
her husband to attend upon her, the lady was not pleased at all.

"Where have they all gone?" she cried. "What do they
mean leaving me all alone? Where's Algy—and where's Sir
Charles—and all of them?"

"There's nobody but me, I'm afraid, Lottie," said little
Seton, who was strengthening himself with another glass of
champagne; "they've all gone off with the young ones."

"The young ones!" Mrs. Seton cried, with a sort of suppressed shriek. The eldest of the Stanley girls was seated at a
little distance, sedately employed in making a drawing, and
Mrs. Shanks and Miss Mildmay sat resting upon a pile of carriage cushions which they had collected together when the
others went away. The old ladies were much occupied in
seeing that Perkins, the driver of the midge, had his share
with the other servants of the relics of the feast. And was she,
the brilliant, the gay, the lovely Lottie, left with these *débris*
of humanity, deserted by her kind? She rose up hastily and
flourished her parasol with an energy which nearly broke the
ivory stick. "Have you no spirit at all," she cried, "to let
your wife be neglected like this?" Katherine was the one
who met her in full career as she went down the winding
slopes—Katherine enjoying herself very moderately with none
of the stolen goods about her, in sole company of Evelyn
Stanley and Gerrard, her brother. "Where are all my
party?" cried Mrs. Seton. "They will never forgive me for
deserting them. You stole a march upon me, Miss Tredgold." But certainly it was not Katherine who had stolen
the march. At this moment Stella appeared out of the bushes,
flushed with fun and laughter, her pretty hat pushed back
upon her head, her pretty hair in a little confusion.

"Oh, come along, come along!" she cried, seizing Mrs. Seton by the arm, "here's such a beautiful place to hide in; they are all after us, full cry. Come, come, we must have you on our side." Thus, again, it was Stella that was on the amusing side where all the fun and the pleasure was. Evelyn Stanley cast wistful eyes after the pair.

"Oh, Katherine, do you mind me going, too? Hide-and-seek is such fun, and we can walk here every day."

"Do you want to go, too, Gerrard?" Katherine said.

"Not if I may walk with you," said the youth, who was at the University and felt himself superior. He was only a year younger than she was, and he thought that a *grande passion* for a woman advanced in life was a fine thing for a young man. He had made up his mind to keep by Katherine's side whatever happened. "I don't care for that silly nonsense," he said; "it's very well for these military fellows that have not an idea in their heads. I always liked conversation best, and your conversation, dear Katherine——"

"Why, I cannot talk a bit," she said with a laugh.

It was on Gerrard's lips to say, "But I can." He had the grace, however, not to utter that sentiment. "There are some people whose silence is more eloquent than other people's talk," he said, which was a much prettier thing to say.

"Oh, why didn't you come at first?" cried Stella in Mrs. Seton's ear. "They all think you are with me, only that you've got some very cunning place to hide in: and here it is. I am sure they'll never find us here."

"I hope they will, though," said the elder lady, speaking in tones that were not at all subdued. "You need not be so clever with your cunning places. Of course we want them to find us; there is no fun in it if they don't."

Stella stared a little with widely opened eyes at her experienced companion. She was still schoolgirl enough to rejoice in baffling the other side, and liked the fun simply as Evelyn Stanley did, who was only sixteen, and who came crowding in upon them whispering in her delight: "They've run down the other way, the whole lot of them like sheep; they have no sense.   Oh, hush ! hush ! speak low ! they'll never think of a place like this.''

" I shall make them think," cried Mrs. Seton, and then she began to sing snatches of songs, and whistled through the thicket to the astonishment of the girls.

"Oh, that is no fun at all," said Evelyn.

"Hush ! " cried Stella, already better informed, " it isn't any fun if they don't find us, after all.''

And then the train of young men came rushing back with shouts, and the romp went on.   It was so far different from other romps that when the fun flagged for a moment the faces of the players all grew blank again, as if they had at once re-lapsed into the heavy dulness which lay behind, which was rather astonishing to the younger ones, who loved the game for its own sake.   Stella, for her part, was much impressed by this recurring relapse.   How exquisite must be the fun to which they were accustomed, which kept them going !   She was painfully aware that she flagged too, that her invention was not quick enough to think of something new before the old was quite exhausted.   She had thought of nothing better than to go on, to hide again, when Mrs. Seton, yawning, sat down to fan herself, and said what Stella thought the rudest things to her cavaliers.

" Why does Charlie Somers look so like an ass ? " she said. " Do you give it up ?   Because he's got thistles all round him and can't get at 'em.''

Stella stared while the young men burst into noisy laugh-ter.

" Is that a conundrum ? " Stella said.

They thought this was wit too, and roared again.   And then once more all the faces grew blank.   It was her first expe-rience of a kind of society decidedly above her level, and it was impressive as well as alarming to the inexperienced young woman.   It had been her habit to amuse herself, not doubting that in doing so she would best promote the amusement of her guests.   But Stella now began to feel the responsibilities of an entertainer.   It was not all plain sailing.   She began to understand the rush of reckless talk, the excited tones, the startling devices of her new friend. In lack of anything better, the acceptance of a cigar on Mrs. Seton's part, and the attempt to induce Stella to try one too, answered for a moment to the necessities of the situation. They were not very particular as to the selection of things to amuse them, so long as there was always something going on.

Sir Charles Somers sat with her on the box as she drove home, and gave her a number of instructions which at first Stella was disposed to resent.

"I have driven papa's horses ever since I was born," she said.

"But you might drive much better," said the young man, calmly putting his hand on hers, moulding her fingers into a better grasp upon the reins, as composedly as if he were touching the springs of an instrument instead of a girl's hand. She blushed, but he showed no sense of being aware that this touch was too much. He was the one of the strangers whom she liked best, probably because he was Sir Charles, which gave him a distinction over the others, or at least it did so to Stella. This was not, however, because she was unaccustomed to meet persons who shared the distinction, for the island people were very tolerant of such *nouveaux riches* as the Tredgolds, who were so very ready to add to their neighbours' entertainment. Two pretty girls with money are seldom disdained in any community, and the father, especially as he was so well advised as to keep himself out of society, was forgiven them, so that the girls were sometimes so favoured as to go to a ball under Lady Jane's wing, and knew all "the best people." But even to those who are still more accustomed to rank than Stella, Sir Charles sounds better than Mr. So-and-so; and he had his share of good looks, and of that ease in society which even she felt herself to be a little wanting in. He did not defer to the girl, or pay her compliments in any old-fashioned way. He spoke to her very much as he spoke to the other young men, and gripped her fingers to give them the proper grasp of the reins with as much force of grip and as perfect calm as if she had been a boy instead of a girl. This rudeness has, it appears, its charm.

"I shouldn't have wondered if he had called me Tredgold," Stella said with a pretence at displeasure.

"What a horrid man!" Katherine replied, to whom this statement was made.

"Horrid yourself for thinking so," cried her sister. "He is not a horrid man at all, he is very nice. We are going to be great—pals. Why shouldn't we be great pals? He is a little tired of Lottie Seton and her airs, he said. He likes nice honest girls that say what they mean, and are not always bullying a fellow. Well, that is what he said. It is his language, it is not mine. You know very well that is how men speak, and Lottie Seton does just the same. I told him little thanks to him to like girls better than an old married woman, and you should have seen how he tugged his moustache and rolled in his seat with laughing. Lottie Seton must have suspected something, for she called out to us what was the joke?"

"I did not know you were on such terms with Mrs. Seton, Stella, as to call her by her Christian name."

"Oh, we call them all by their names. Life's too short for Missis That and Mr. This. Charlie asked me——"

"Charlie! why, you never saw him till to-day."

"When you get to know a man you don't count the days you've been acquainted with him," said Stella, tossing her head, but with a flush on her face. She added: "I asked him to come over to lunch to-morrow and to see the garden. He said it would be rare fun to see something of the neighbourhood without Lottie Seton, who was always dragging a lot of fellows about."

"Stella, what a very, very unpleasant man, to talk like that about the lady who is his friend, and who brought him here!"

"Oh, his friend!" cried Stella, "that is only your old-fashioned way. She is no more his friend! She likes to have a lot of men following her about everywhere, and they have got nothing to do, and are thankful to go out anywhere to

spend the time; so it is just about as broad as it is long.
They do it to please themselves, and there is not a bit of love
lost."

" I don't like those kind of people," said Katherine.

" They are the only kind of people," Stella replied.

This conversation took place from one room to another, the
door standing open while the girls performed a hasty toilette.
All the picnic people had been parted with at the gate with
much demonstration of friendship and a thousand thanks for a
delightful day. Only the midge had deposited its occupants
at the door. The two old cats were never to be got rid of.
They were at that moment in another room, making themselves tidy, as they said, with the supercilious aid of Katherine's maid. Stella did not part with hers in any circumstances, though she was about to dine in something very like a
dressing-gown with her hair upon her shoulders. Mr. Tredgold liked to see Stella with her hair down, and she was not
herself averse to the spectacle of the long rippled locks falling
over her shoulders. Stella was one of the girls who find a certain enjoyment in their own beauty even when there is nobody
to see.

" It was a very pleasant party on the whole to be such an
impromptu," said Mrs. Shanks ; " your girls, Mr. Tredgold, put
such a spirit in everything. Dear girls ! Stella is always the
most active and full of fun, and Katherine the one that looks
after one's comfort. Don't you find the Stanleys, Kate, a little
heavy in hand ?—excellent good people, don't you know, always
a stand-by, but five of them, fancy ! Marion that is always at
her drawing, and Edith that can talk of nothing but the parish,
and that little romp Evelyn who is really too young and too
childish ! Poor Mr. Stanley has his quiver too full, poor man,
like so many clergymen."

" If ever there was a man out of place—the Rector at a
picnic ! " said Miss Mildmay, " with nobody for him to talk to.
I'll tell you what it is, Mr. Tredgold, he thinks Kate is such
a steady creature, he wants her for a mother to his children ;
now see if I am not a true prophet before the summer is out."

Mr. Tredgold's laugh, which was like the tinkling of a tin vessel, reached Katherine's ear at the other end of the table, but not the speech which had called it forth.

"Papa, the officers are coming here to-morrow to lunch— you don't mind, do you?—that is, Charlie Somers and Algy Scott. Oh, they are nice enough; they are dreadfully dull at Newport. They want to see the garden and anything there is to see. You know you're one of the sights of the island, papa."

"That is their fun," said the old man. "I don't know what they take me for, these young fellows that are after the girls. Oh, they're all after the girls; they know they've got a good bit of money and so forth, and think their father's an easy-going old fool as soft as——Wait till we come to the question of set-tlements, my good ladies, wait till then; they'll not find me so soft when we get there."

"It is sudden to think of settlements yet, Mr. Tredgold. The Rector, poor man, has got nothing to settle, and as for those boys in the garrison, they never saw the dear girls till to-day."

"Ah, I know what they are after," said Mr. Tredgold. "My money, that is what they are all after. Talk to me about com-ing to see over the garden and so forth! Fudge! it is my money they are after; but they'll find I know a thing or two before it comes to that."

"Papa," said Stella, "you are just an old suspicious absurd ——What do they know about your money? They never heard your name before. Of course they had heard of *me*. The other battalion were all at the Ryde ball, and took notes. They thought I was an American, that shows how little they know about you."

"That means, Stella," said Miss Mildmay, "everything that is fast and fly-away. I wouldn't brag of it if I were you."

"It means the fashion," said Mrs. Shanks. "Dear Stella *is* like that, with her nice clothes, and her way of rushing at everything, and never minding. Now Katherine is English, no mistake about her—a good daughter, don't you know—and she'll make an excellent wife."

"But the man will have to put down his money, piece for piece, before he shall have her, I can tell you," said the master of the house. "Oh, I'm soft if you like it, and over-indulgent, and let them have all their own way ; but there's not a man in England that stands faster when it comes to that."

Stella gave her sister a look, and a little nod of her head ; her eyes danced and her hair waved a little, so light and fluffy it was, with that slight gesture. It seemed to say, We shall see ! It said to Katherine, "You might stand that, but it will not happen with me." The look and the gesture were full of a triumphant defiance. Stella was not afraid that she would ever feel the restraining grip of her father's hand ; and then she thought of that other grip upon her fingers, and shook her shiny hair about her ears more triumphant still.

CHAPTER IV.

STELLA, however, courageous as she was, was not bold enough
to address Sir Charles and his companion as Charlie and Algy
when they appeared, not next day, but some days later ; for
their engagements with Mrs. Seton and others of their friends
were not so lightly to be pushed aside for the attraction of her
society as the girl supposed.   It was a little disappointing to
meet them with their friends, not on the same sudden level of
intimacy which had been developed by the picnic, and to be
greeted indifferently, "like anybody else," after that entertainment and its sudden fervour of acquaintance.   When, however, Mrs. Seton left the hotel, and the young men had no
longer that resource in their idleness, they appeared at the Cliff
without further invitation, and with an evident disposition to
profit by its hospitality which half flattered and half offended
the girls.

"They have never even left cards," said Katherine, after
the picnic, "but now that their friends have gone they remember that you asked them, Stella."

"Well," cried Stella, "that is so much the more friendly.
Do you suppose they haven't hundreds of places to go to?
And when they choose *us*, are we to be disagreeable ?   I shan't
be so at least."

She ran downstairs indeed wreathed with smiles, and received them with an eager gratification, which was very flattering to the young men, who opened their eyes at the luxury
of the luncheon and gave each other a look which said that
here was something worth the trouble.   Old Mr. Tredgold, in
his shabby coat and his slippers, was a curious feature in the
group ; but it was by no means out of keeping that a rich old

father, who had begun life with half a crown, should thus fulfil
his part, and the young men laughed at his jokes, and elevated
an eyebrow at each other across the table, with a sense of the
fun of it, which perplexed and disturbed the two young
women, to whom they were still figures unaccustomed, about
whose modes and manners they were quite unassured. Katherine took it all seriously, with an inclination towards offence,
though it is not to be supposed that the advent of two young
officers, more or less good-looking and a novelty in her life,
should not have exercised a little influence upon her also. But
Stella was in a state of suppressed excitement which made her
eyes shine indeed, and brightened her colour, but was not very
pleasant to behold for anyone who loved her. She was half
offended with her father for the share he took in the conversation, and angry with the young men who listened to and applauded him, without remarking her own attempts to be witty.
Her voice, though it was a pretty voice, grew a little shrill in
her endeavours to attract their attention and to secure the loud
outbursts of laughter which had been used to accompany Mrs.
Seton's sallies. What was it about Mrs. Seton which amused
them? She said nothing remarkable, except for rudeness and
foolishness, and yet they laughed ; but to Stella's funniest remarks they gave but a gape of inattention, and concentrated
their attention on her father—on papa ! What could they
possibly see in him ?

It was consolatory, however, when they all went out into the
garden after lunch, to find that they came one on each side of
her instinctively with a just discrimination, leaving Katherine
out. Stella, to do her justice, did not want Katherine to be
left entirely out. When her own triumph was assured she was
always willing that there should be something for her sister.
But it was well at least that the strangers should recognise that
she was the centre of everything. She led them, as in duty
bound, through all the rare trees and shrubs which were the
glory of the Cliff. " This papa had brought all the way from
Brazil, or somewhere. It is the first one that ever was grown
in England ; and just look at those berries ! Wain, the gar-

dener, has coaxed them to grow, giving them all sorts of nice
things to eat. Oh, I couldn't tell you all he has given them—
old rags and rusty nails and all kinds of confectioneries ! ''

'' Their dessert, eh ? '' said Sir Charles. He had stuck his glass
in his eye, but he looked gloomily at all the wonderful plants.
Algy put up his hand to his moustache, under which his mouth
gaped more open than usual, with a yawn. Stella remembered
that Mrs. Seton had proposed to pop a worm into it, and longed
to make use, though at second hand, of that famous witticism,
but had not the courage. They looked about blankly even
while she discoursed, with roving yet vacant looks, seeking
something to entertain them. Stella could not entertain them
—oh, dreadful discovery ! She did not know what to say ;
her pretty face began to wear an anxious look, her colour became hectic, her eyes hollow with eagerness, her voice loud
and shrill with the strain. Mrs. Seton could keep them going,
could make them laugh at nothing, could maintain a whirl of
noisy talk and jest ; but Stella could not amuse these two heavy
young men. Their opaque eyes went roving round the beautiful place in search of some '' fun,'' their faces grew more and
more blank. It was Katherine, who did not pretend to be
amusing, who had so very little to say for herself, who inter-
posed :

'' Don't you think,'' she said, '' Stella, they might like to
look at the view ? Sliplin Harbour is so pretty under the
cliff, and then there are some yachts.''

'' Oh, let's look at the yachts,'' the young men said, pushing forward with a sudden impulse of interest. The bay was
blazing in the afternoon sunshine, the distant cliff a dazzle of
whiteness striking sharp against the blue of sky and sea ; but the
visitors did not pause upon anything so insignificant as the
view. They stumbled over each other in their anxiety to see
the little vessel which lay at the little pier, one white sail
showing against the same brilliant background. Whose was
it ? Jones's for a wager, the *Lively Jinny*. No, no, nothing
of the sort. Howard's the *Inscrutable*, built for Napier, don't
you know, before he went to the dogs.''

Stella pressed forward into the discussion with questions which she did not know to be irrelevant. What was the meaning of clipper-rigged? Did raking masts mean anything against anyone's character? Which was the jib, and why should it be of one shape rather than another? The gentlemen paid very little attention to her. They went on discussing the identity of the toy ship with interest and fervour.

"Why, I know her like the palm of my hand," cried Sir Charles. "I steered her through that last westerly gale, and a tough one it was. I rather think if any one should know her, it's I. The *Lively Jinny*, and a livelier in the teeth of a gale I never wish to see."

"Pooh!" said the other. "You're as blind as a bat, Charlie, everyone knows; you wouldn't know your best friend at that distance. It's Howard's little schooner that he bought when poor Napier went to——"

"I tell you it's *Jinny*, the fetish of Jones's tribe. I know her as well as I know you. Ten to one in sovs."

"I'll take you," cried the other. "Howard's, and a nice little craft; but never answers her helm as she ought, that's why he calls her the *Inscrutable*."

"What a strange thing," cried Stella, toiling behind them in her incomprehension, "not to answer your helm! What is your helm, and what does it say to you? Perhaps she doesn't understand."

This, she thought, was *à la mode de* Mrs. Seton, but it produced no effect, not even a smile.

"You could see the figure-head with a glass," said Captain Scott. "Where's the glass, Miss Tredgold? There ought to be a glass somewhere."

"Jove!" cried Sir Charles. "Fancy a look-out like this and no telescope. What could the people be thinking of?"

"You are very rude to call papa and me the people," cried Stella, almost in tears. "Who cares for a silly little cockle-shell of a boat? But it is a good thing at least that it gives you something to talk about—which I suppose you can understand."

" Hullo ! " said the one visitor to the other, under his breath, with a look of surprise.

" If it is only a glass that is wanted," said Katherine, " why shouldn't we all have a look ?   There is a telescope, you know, upstairs."

Stella flashed out again under the protection of this suggestion.   " I'll run," she said, being in reality all compliance and deeply desirous to please, " and tell one of the footmen to bring it down."

" Too much trouble," and " What a bore for you to have us on your hands ! " the young men said.

" Don't, Stella," said Katherine ; " they had better go up to papa's observatory, where they can see it for themselves."

" Oh, yes," cried the girl, " come along, let's go to papa's observatory, that will be something for you to do.   You always want something to do, don't you ?   Come along, come along ! "   Stella ran on before them with heated cheeks and blazing eyes.   It was not that she was angry with them, but with herself, to think that she could not do what Mrs. Seton did.   She could not amuse them, or keep up to their high level of spirits, and the vacancy of the look which came over both their faces—the mouth of Algy under his moustache, the eyes of Charlie staring blankly about in search of a sensation —were more than her nerves could bear.   And yet she was alarmed beyond measure, feeling her own prestige in question, by the thought that they might never come again.

Papa's observatory was a terrace on the leads between the two gables where the big telescope stood.   Was it a pity, or was it not, that papa was there in his shabby coat sniffing at the ships as they went out to sea ?   He had an extended prospect on all sides, and he was watching a speck on the horizon with much interest through the glass.   " Perhaps you young fellows have got some interest in the shipping like me ? " he said.   " There, don't you see the *Haitch* and the *Ho* on the pennant just slipping out of sight ?   I have a deal of money in that ship.   I like to see them pass when it's one I have an interest in.   Put your little peeper here, Stella, you'll see her yet. They pay very well with proper care. You have to keep your wits about you, but that's the case with all invest-ments. Want to see any particular ship, eh? I hope you've got some money in 'em," Mr. Tredgold said.

"Oh, papa, take your horrid thing away; you know I never can see anything," cried Stella. "Now look, now look, Sir Charles! Remember, I back you. The *Jenny* before the world."

"Miss Tredgold, put a sixpence on me," said Algy; "don't let a poor fellow go into the ring unprotected. It's Howard's or nobody's."

"Betting?" said Mr. Tredgold. "It is not a thing I ap-prove of, but we all do it, I suppose. That little boat, if that is what you're thinking of, belongs to none of those names. It's neither the *Jones* nor the *Howard*. It's the *Stella*, after that little girl of mine, and it's my boat, and you can take a cruise in it if you like any day when there's no wind."

"Oh, papa," cried Stella, "is it really, really for me?"

"You little minx," said the old man as she kissed him, "you little fair weather flatterer, always pleased when you get something! I know you, for all you think you keep it up so well. Papa's expected always to be giving you something— the only use, ain't it? of an old man. It's a bit late in the season to buy a boat, but I got it a bargain, a great bargain."

"Then it was Jones's," cried Sir Charles.

"Then Howard was the man," cried his friend.

"That's delightful," cried Stella, clapping her hands. "Do keep it up! I will put all my money on Sir Charles." And they were so kind that they laughed with her, admiring the skip and dance of excitement which she performed for their pleasure. But when it turned out that Mr. Tredgold did not know from whom he had bought the boat, and that the figure-head had been removed to make room for a lovely wooden lady in white and gold with a star on her forehead, speculation grew more and more lively than ever. It was Stella, in the excitement of that unexpected success, who proposed to run down to the pier to examine into the yacht and see if any

3

solution was possible. "We have a private way," she cried.
"I'll show you if you'd like to come; and I want to see my
yacht, and if the Stella on it is like me, and if it is pretty inside, and everything. And, Kate, while we're gone, you
might order tea. Papa, did you say the Stella on the figure-
head was to be like me?"

"Nothing that is wooden could be like you," said Sir
Charles graciously. It was as if an oracle had spoken. Algy
opened his mouth under his moustache with a laugh or gape
which made Stella long there and then to repeat Mrs. Seton's
elegant jest. She was almost bold enough in the flush of spirits which Sir Charles's compliment had called forth.

"I wish Stella would not rush about with those men," said
Katherine, as the noise of their steps died away upon the
stairs.

"Jealous, eh?" said her father. "Well, I don't wonder
—and they can't both have her. One of them might have
done the civil by you, Katie—but they're selfish brutes, you
know, are men."

Katherine perhaps walked too solemnly away in the midst
of this unpalatable consolation, and was undutifully irritated by
her father's tin-tinkle of a laugh. She was not jealous, but the
feeling perhaps was not much unlike that unlovely sentiment.
She declared indignantly to herself that she did not want them
to "do the civil" to her, these dull frivolous young men, and
that it was in the last degree injurious to her to suggest anything of the sort. It was hopeless to make her father see what
was her point of view, or realise her feelings—as hopeless as it
was to make Stella perceive how little fit it was that she should
woo the favour of these rude strangers. Mrs. Seton might do
it with that foolish desire to drag about a train with her, to
pose as a conqueror, to—— Katherine did not know what
words to use. But Stella, a girl! Stella, who was full of real
charm, who was fit for so much better things! On the whole,
Katherine found it was better to fulfil the homely duties that
were hers and give her orders about the tea. It was the part
in life that was apportioned to her, and why should she object

to it? It might not be the liveliest, but surely it was a more befitting situation than Stella's rush after novelty, her strain to please. And whom to please? People who sneered at them before their faces and did not take pains to be civil—not even to Stella.

It did her good to go out into the air, to select the spot under the acacia where the tea-table stood so prettily, with its shining white. It was still warm, extraordinary for October. She sat down there gazing out upon the radiance of the sea and sky; the rocky fringe of sand was invisible, and so was the town and harbour which lay at the foot of the cliff; beyond the light fringe of the tamarisk trees which grew there as luxuriantly as in warmer countries there was nothing but the sunny expanse of the water, dazzling under the Western sun, which was by this time low, shining level in the eyes of the solitary gazer. She saw, almost without seeing it, the white sail of a yacht suddenly gleam into the middle of the prospect before her, coming out all at once from the haven under the hill. Someone was going out for a sail, a little late indeed; but what could be more beautiful or tempting than this glorious afternoon! Katherine sighed softly with a half sensation of envy. A little puff of air came over her, blowing about the light acacia foliage overhead, and bringing down a little shower of faintly yellow leaves. The little yacht felt it even more than the acacia did. It seemed to waver a little, then changed its course, following the impulse of the breeze into the open. Katherine wondered indifferently who it could be. The yachting people were mostly gone from the neighbourhood. They were off on their longer voyages, or they had laid up their boats for the season. And there had begun to grow a windy look, such as dwellers by the sea soon learn to recognise about the sky. Katherine wished calmly to herself in her ignorance of who these people were that they might not go too far.

She was sitting thus musing and wondering a little that Stella and her cavaliers did not come back for tea, when the sound of her father's stick from the porch of the house startled her, and a loud discussion with somebody which he seemed to be carrying on within. He came out presently, limping along with his stick and with a great air of excitement. "I said they were only to go when there was no wind. Didn't you hear me, Katie? When there was no wind—I said it as plain as anything. And look at that; look at that!" He was stammering with excitement, and could scarcely keep his standing in his unusual excitement.

"What is the matter, papa? Look at what? Oh, the boat. But we have nothing to do with any boat," she cried. "Why should you disturb yourself? The people can surely take care of——Papa! what is it?"

He had sunk into a chair, one of those set ready on the grass for Stella and her friends, and was growing purple in the face and panting for breath. "You fool! you fool! Stella," he cried, "Stella, my little girl. Oh, I'll be even with those young fools when I catch them. They want to drown her. They want to run away with her. Stella! my little girl!"

Katherine had awakened to the fact before these interrupted words were half uttered. And naturally what she did was perfectly unreasonable. She rushed to the edge of the cliff, waving aloft the white parasol in her hand, beckoning wildly, and crying, "Come back, come back!" She called all the servants, the gardener and his man, the footmen who were looking out alarmed from the porch. "Go, go," she cried, stamping her foot, "and bring them back; go and bring them back!" There was much rushing and running, and one at least of the men flung himself helter-skelter down the steep stair that led to the beach, while the gardeners stood gazing from the cliff. Katherine clapped her hands in her excitement, giving wild orders. "Go! go! don't stand there as if nothing could be done; go and bring them back!"

"Not to contradict you, Miss Katherine——" the gardener began.

"Oh, don't speak to me—don't stand talking—go, go, and bring them back."

Mr. Tredgold had recovered his breath a little. "Let us think," he said—"let us think, and don't talk nonsense, Kate.

There's a breeze blowing up, and where will it drive them to, gardener? Man, can't you tell where it'll drive them to? Round by the Needles, I shouldn't wonder, the dangerousest coast. Oh, my little girl, my little girl! Shall I ever see her again? And me that said they were never to go out but when there was no wind.''

" Not to the Needles, sir—not to the Needles when there's a westerly breeze. More likely round the cliffs Bembridge way ; and who can stop 'em when they're once out? It's only a little cruise ; let 'em alone and they'll come home, with their tails be'ind them, as the rhyme says.''

" And I said they were only to go out if there was no wind, gardener ! '' The old gentleman was almost weeping with alarm and anxiety, but yet he was comforted by what the man said.

" They are going the contrary way,'' cried Katherine.

" Bless you, miss, that's tacking, to catch the breeze. They couldn't go far, sir, could they? without no wind.''

" And that's just what I wanted, that they should not go far—just a little about in the bay to please her. Oh, my little girl ! She will be dead with fright ; she will catch her death of cold, she will.''

" Not a bit, sir,'' cried the gardener. " Miss Stella's a very plucky one. She'll enjoy the run, she'll enjoy the danger.''

" The danger ! '' cried father and sister together.

" What a fool I am ! There ain't none, no more than if they was in a duck pond,'' the gardener said.

And, indeed, to see the white sail flying in the sunshine over the blue sea, there did not seem much appearance of danger. With his first apprehensions quieted down, Mr. Tredgold stumbled with the help of his daughter's arm to the edge of the cliff within the feathery line of the tamarisk trees, attended closely by the gardener, who, as an islander born, was supposed to know something of the sea. The hearts of the anxious gazers fluctuated as the little yacht danced over the water, going down when she made a little lurch and curtsey before the breeze, and up when she went steadily by the wind, making one of those long tacks which the gardener explained were all made, though they seemed to lead the little craft so far away, with the object of getting back.

"Them two young gentlemen, they knows what they're about," the gardener said.

"And there's a sailor-man on board," said Mr. Tredgold— "a man that knows everything about it, one of the crew whose business it is———"

"I don't see no third man," said the gardener doubtfully.

"Oh, yes, yes, there's a sailor-man," cried the father. The old gentleman spoke with a kind of sob in his throat ; he was ready to cry with weakness and trouble and exasperation, as the little vessel, instead of replying to the cries and wailings of his anxiety by coming right home as seemed to him the simplest way, went on tacking and turning, sailing further and further off, then heeling over as if she would go down, then fluttering with an empty sail that hung about the mast before she struck off in another direction, but never turning back. "They are taking her off to America !" he cried, half weeping, leaning heavily on Katherine's arm.

"They're tacking, sir, tacking, to bring her in," said the gardener.

"Oh, don't speak to me !" cried the unhappy father ; "they are carrying her off to America. Who was it said there was nothing between this and America, Katie? Oh, my little girl ! my little girl ! "

And it may be partly imagined what were the feelings of those inexperienced and anxious people when the early October evening began to fall, and the blue sky to be covered with clouds flying, gathering, and dispersing before a freshening westerly gale.

CHAPTER V.

I WILL not enter in detail into the feelings of the father and sister on this alarming and dreadful night. No tragedy followed, the reader will feel well assured, or this history would never have been written. But the wind rose till it blew what the sailors called half a gale. It seemed to Katherine a hurricane—a horrible tempest, in which no such slender craft as that in which Stella had gone forth had a chance for life; and indeed the men on the pier with their conjectures as to what might have happened were not encouraging. She might have fetched Ventnor or one of those places by a long tack. She might have been driven out to the Needles. She mightn't know her way with those gentlemen only as was famous sailors with a fair wind, but not used to dirty weather. Katherine spent all the night on the pier gazing out upon the waste of water now and then lighted up by a fitful moon. What a change—what a change from the golden afternoon! And what a difference from her own thoughts!—a little grudging of Stella's all-success, a little wounded to feel herself always in the shade, and the horrible suggestion of Stella's loss, the dread that overwhelmed her imagination and took all her courage from her. She stood on the end of the pier, with the wind—that wind which had driven Stella forth out of sound and sight—blowing her about, wrapping her skirts round her, loosing her hair, making her hold tight to the rail lest she should be blown away. Why should she hold tight? What did it matter, if Stella were gone, whether she kept her footing or not? She could never take Stella's place with anyone. Her father would grudge her very existence that could not be sacrificed to save Stella. Already he had begun to reproach her. Why did you let her go? What is the use of an elder sister to a girl if she doesn't interfere in such a case? And three years older, that ought to have been a mother to her.

Thus Mr. Tredgold had babbled in his misery before he was persuaded to lie down to await news which nothing that could be done would make any quicker. He had clamoured to send out boats—any number—after Stella. He had insisted upon hiring a steamer to go out in quest of her; but telegrams had to be sent far and wide and frantic messengers to Ryde—even to Portsmouth—before he could get what he wanted. And in the meantime the night had fallen, the wind had risen, and out of that blackness and those dashing waves, which could be heard without being seen, there came no sign of the boat. Never had such a night passed over the peaceful place. There had been sailors and fishermen in danger many a time, and distracted women on the pier; but what was that to the agony of a millionaire who had been accustomed to do everything with his wealth, and now raged and foamed at the mouth because he could do nothing? What was all his wealth to him? He was as powerless as the poor mother of that sailor-boy who was lost (there were so many, so many of them), and who had not a shilling in the world. Not a shilling in the world! It was exactly as if Mr. Tredgold had come to that. What could he do with all his thousands? Oh, send out a tug from Portsmouth, send out the fastest ferry-boat from Ryde, send out the whole fleet—fishing cobles, pleasure boats—everything that was in Sliplin Harbour! Send everything, everything that had a sail or an oar, not to say a steam engine. A hundred pounds, a thousand pounds—anything to the man who would bring Stella back!

The little harbour was in wild commotion with all these offers. There were not many boats, but they were all preparing; the men clattering down the rolling shingle, with women after them calling to them to take care, or not to go out in the teeth of the gale. "If you're lost too what good will that do?" they shrieked in the wind, their hair flying like Katherine's, but not so speechless as she was. The darkness, the flaring feeble lights, the stir and noise on the shore, with these shrieking voices breaking in, made a sort of Pandemonium unseen, taking double horror from the fact that it was almost all sound and sensation, made visible occasionally by the gleam of the moon between the flying clouds. Mr. Tredgold's house on the cliff blazed with lights from every window, and a great pan of fire wildly blazing, sending up great shadows of black smoke, was lit on the end of the pier—everything that could be done to guide them back, to indicate the way. Nothing of that sort was done when the fishermen were battling for their lives. But what did it all matter, what was the good of it all? Millionaire and pauper stood on the same level, hopeless, tearing their hair, praying their hearts out, on the blind margin of that wild invisible sea.

There was a horrible warning of dawn in the blackness when Stella, soaked to the skin, her hair lashing about her unconscious face like whips, and far more dead than alive, was at last carried home. I believe there were great controversies afterwards between the steam-tug and the fishing boats which claimed to have saved her—controversies which might have been spared, since Mr. Tredgold paid neither, fortified by the statement of the yachtsmen that neither had been of any use, and that the *Stella* had at last blundered her way back of her own accord and their superior management. He had to pay for the tug, which put forth by his orders, but only as much as was barely necessary, with no such gratuity as the men had hoped for; while to the fishers he would give nothing, and Katherine's allowance was all expended for six months in advance in recompensing these clamorous rescuers who had not succeeded in rescuing anyone.

Stella was very ill for a few days; when she recovered the wetting and the cold, then she was ill of the imagination, recalling more clearly than at first all the horrors which she had passed through. As soon as she was well enough to recover the use of her tongue she did nothing but talk of this tremendous experience in her life, growing proud of it as she got a little way beyond it and saw the thrilling character of the episode in full proportion. At first she would faint away, or rather, almost faint away (between two which things there is an immense difference), as she recalled the incidents of that night. But after a while they became her favourite and most delightful subjects of conversation. She entertained all her friends with the account of her adventure as she lay pale, with her pretty hair streaming over her pillow, not yet allowed to get up after all she had gone through, but able to receive her habitual visitors.

" The feeling that came over me when it got dark, oh! I can't describe what it was," said Stella. " I thought it was a shadow at first. The sail throws such a shadow sometimes; it's like a great bird settling down with its big wing. But when it came down all round and one saw it wasn't a shadow, but darkness—night!—oh, how horrible it was! I thought I should have died, out there on the great waves and the water dashing into the boat, and the cliffs growing fainter and fainter, and the horrible, horrible dark ! ''

"Stella dear, don't excite yourself again. It is all over, God be praised.''

" Yes, it's all over. It is easy for you people to speak who have never been lost at sea. It will never be over for me. If I were to live to be a hundred I should feel it all the same. The hauling up and the hauling down of that dreadful sail, carrying us right away out into the sea when we wanted to get home, and then flopping down all in a moment, while we rocked and pitched till I felt I must be pitched out. Oh, how I implored them to go back ! 'Just turn back !' I cried. 'Why don't you turn back? We are always going further and further, instead of nearer. And oh ! what will papa say and Katherine?' They laughed at first, and told me they were tacking, and I begged them, for Heaven's sake, not to tack, but to run home. But they would not listen to me. Oh, they are all very nice and do what you like when it doesn't matter ; but when it's risking your life, and you hate them and are miserable and can't help yourself, then they take their own way.''

"But they couldn't help it either," cried Evelyn, the rector's daughter. "They had to tack; they could not run home when the wind was against them."

"What do I care about the wind?" cried Stella. "They should not have made me go out if there was a wind. Papa said we were never to go out in a wind. I told them so. I said, 'You ought not to have brought me out.' They said it was nothing to speak of. I wonder what it is when it is something to speak of! And then we shipped a sea, as they called it, and I got drenched to the very skin. Oh, I don't say they were not kind. They took off their coats and put round me, but what did that do for me? I was chilled to the very bone. Oh, you can't think how dreadful it is to lie and see those sails swaying and to hear the men moving about and saying dreadful things to each other, and the boat moving up and down. Oh!" cried Stella, clasping her hands together and looking as if once more she was about almost to faint away.

"Stella, spare yourself, dear. Try to forget it; try to think of something else. It is too much for you when you dwell on it," Katherine said.

"Dwell on it!" cried Stella, reviving instantly. "It is very clear that *you* never were in danger of your life, Kate."

"I was in danger of *your* life," cried Katherine, "and I think that was worse. Oh, I could tell you a story, too, of that night on the pier, looking out on the blackness, and thinking every moment—but don't let us think of it, it is too much. Thank God, it is all over, and you are quite safe now."

"It is very different standing upon the pier, and no doubt saying to yourself what a fool Stella was to go out; she just deserves it all for making papa so unhappy, and keeping me out of bed. Oh, I know that was what you were thinking! and being like me with only a plank between me and—don't you know? The one is very, very different from the other, I can tell you," Stella said, with a little flush on her cheek.

And the Stanley girls who were her audience agreed with

her, with a strong sense that to be the heroine of such an adventure was, after all, when it was over, one of the most
delightful things in the world. Her father also agreed with
her, who came stumping with his stick up the stairs, his own
room being below, and took no greater delight than to sit by
her bedside and hear her go over the story again and again.

"I'll sell that little beast of a boat. I'll have her broken
up for firewood. To think I should have paid such a lot of
money for her, and her nearly to drown my little girl!"

"Oh, don't do that, papa," said Stella; "when it's quite
safe and there is no wind I should like perhaps to go out in
her again, just to see. But to be sure there was no wind
when we went out—just a very little, just enough to fill the
sail, they said; but you can never trust to a wind. I said I
shouldn't go, only just for ten minutes to try how I liked it;
and then that horrid gale came on to blow, and they began
to tack, as they call it. Such nonsense that tacking, papa!
when they began it I said, 'Why, we're going further off
than ever; what I want is to get home.'"

"They paid no attention, I suppose—they thought they
knew better," said Mr. Tredgold.

"They always think they know better," cried Stella, with
indignation. "And oh, when it came on to be dark, and
the wind always rising, and the water coming in, in buckets
full! Were you ever at sea in a storm, papa?"

"Never, my pet," said Mr. Tredgold, "trust me for that.
I never let myself go off firm land, except sometimes in a
penny steamboat, that's dangerous enough. Sometimes the
boilers blow up, or you run into some other boat; but on the
sea, not if I know it, Stella."

"But I have," said the girl. "A steamboat! within the
two banks of a river! You know nothing, nothing about it,
neither does Katherine. Some sailors, I believe, might go
voyages for years and never see anything so bad as that night.
Why, the waves were mountains high, and then you seemed
to slide down to the bottom as if you were going—oh! hold
me, hold me, papa, or I shall feel as if I were going again."

"Poor little Stella," said Mr. Tredgold, "poor little girl! What a thing for her to go through, so early in life! But I'd like to do something to those men. I'd like to punish them for taking advantage of a child like that, all to get hold of my new boat, and show how clever they were with their tacking and all that. Confound their tacking! If it hadn't been for their tacking she might have got back to dinner and saved us such a miserable night."

"What was your miserable night in comparison to mine?" cried Stella, scornfully. "I believe you both think it was as bad as being out at sea, only because you did not get your dinner at the proper time and were kept longer than usual out of bed."

"We must not forget," said Katherine, "that after all, though they might be to blame in going out, these gentlemen saved her life."

"I don't know about that," said the old man. "I believe it was my tug that saved her life. It was they that put her life in danger, if you please. I'd like just to break them in the army, or sell them up, or something; idle fellows doing nothing, strolling about to see what mischief they can find to do."

"Oh, they are very nice," said Stella. "You shan't do anything to them, papa. I am great chums with Charlie and Algy; they are such nice boys, really, when you come to know them; they took off their coats to keep me warm. I should have had inflammation of the lungs or something if I had not had their coats. I was shivering so."

"And do you know," said Katherine, "one of them is ill, as Stella perhaps might have been if he had not taken off his coat."

"Oh, which is that?" cried Stella; "oh, do find out which is that? It must be Algy, I think. Algy is the delicate one. He never is good for much—he gives in, you know, so soon. He is so weedy, long, and thin, and no stamina, that is what the others say."

"And is that all the pity you have for him, Stella? when it was to save you——"

" It was not to save me," cried Stella, raising herself in her bed with flushed cheeks, " it was to save himself! If I hadn't been saved where would they have been? They would have gone to the bottom too. Oh, I can't see that I'm so much obliged to them as all that! What they did they did for themselves far more than for me. We were all in the same boat, and if I had been drowned they would have been drowned too. I hope, though," she said, more amiably, " that Algy will get better if it's he that is ill. And it must be he. Charlie is as strong as a horse. He never feels anything. Papa, I hope you will send him grapes and things. I shall go and see him as soon as I am well."

" You go and see a young fellow—in his room! You shall do nothing of the sort, Stella. Things may be changed from my time, and I suppose they are, but for a girl to go and visit a young fellow—in his——"

Stella smiled a disdainful and amused smile as she lay back on her pillow. " You may be sure, papa," she said, " that I certainly shall. I will go and nurse him, unless he has someone already. I ought to nurse the man who helped to save my life."

" You are a little self-willed, wrong-headed—— Katherine, you had better take care. I will make you answer for it if she does anything so silly — a chit of a girl! I'll speak to Dr. Dobson. I'll send to — to the War Office. I'll have him carted away."

" Is poor Algy here, Kate? Where is he — at the hotel? Oh, you dreadful hard-hearted people to let him go to the hotel when you knew he had saved my life. Papa, go away, and let me get dressed. I must find out how he is. I must go to him, poor fellow. Perhaps the sight of me and to see that I am better will do him good. Go away, please, papa."

" I'll not budge a step," cried the old gentleman. " Katie, Katie, she'll work herself into a fever. She'll make herself ill, and then what shall we do?"

" I'm very ill already," said Stella, with a cough. " I am being thrust into my grave. Let them bring us together —

poor, poor Algy and me. Oh, if we are both to be victims, let it be so ! We will take each other's hands and go down — go down together to the——''

'' Oh, Katie, can't you stop her ? '' cried the father.

Stella was sobbing with delicious despair over the thought of the two delightful, dreadful funerals, and all the world weeping over her untimely fate.

Stella recovered rapidly when her father was put to the door. She said with a pretty childish reverberation of her sob : '' For you know, Kate, it never was he — that would be the poignant thing, wouldn't it ? — it was not he that I ever would have chosen. But to be united in — in a common fate, with two graves together, don't you know, and an inscription, and people saying, ' Both so young ! ' '' She paused to dry her eyes, and then she laughed. '' There is nothing in him, don't you know ; it was Charlie that did all the work. He was nearly as frightened as I was. Oh, I don't think anything much of Algy, but I shall go to see him all the same — if it were only to shock papa.''

'' You had better get well yourself in the meantime,'' said Katherine.

'' Oh, you cold, cold — toad ! What do you care ? It would have been better for you if I had been drowned, Kate. Then you would have been the only daughter and the first in the house, but now, you know, it's Stella again — always Stella. Papa is an unjust old man and makes favourites ; but you need not think, however bad I am, and however good you are, that you will ever cure him of that.''

CHAPTER VI.

WHEN Stella was first able to appear out of the shelter of her father's grounds for a walk, she was the object of a sort of ovation — as much of an ovation as it is possible to make in such a place. She was leaning on her sister's arm and was supported on the other side by a stick, as it was only right a girl should be who had gone through so much. And she was very prettily pale, and looked more interesting than words could say, leaning heavily (if anything about Stella could be called heavy) upon Katherine, and wielding her stick with a charming air of finding it too much for her, yet at the same time finding it indispensable. There was nobody in the place who did not feel the attraction of sympathy, and the charm of the young creature who had been rescued from the very jaws of death and restored to the family that adored her. To think what might have been! — the old man broken-hearted and Katherine in deep mourning going and coming all alone, and perhaps not even a grave for the unfortunate Stella — lost at sea! Some of the ladies who thronged about her, stopping her to kiss her and express the depths of sympathetic anguish through which they had gone, declared that to think of it made them shudder. Thank Heaven that everything had ended so well! Stella took all these expressions of sympathy very sweetly. She liked to be the chief person, to awaken so much emotion, to be surrounded by so many flatteries. She felt, indeed, that she, always an interesting person, had advanced greatly in the scale of human consideration. She was more important by far since she had " gone through" that experience. They had been so near to losing her; everybody felt now fully what it was to have her. The rector had returned thanks publicly

in church, and every common person about the streets curt-
sied or touched his hat with a deeper sentiment. To think
that perhaps she might have been drowned — she, so young,
so fair, so largely endowed with everything that heart could
desire ! If her neighbours were moved by this sentiment,
Stella herself was still more deeply moved by it. She felt to
the depths of her heart what a thing it was for all these people
that she should have been saved from the sea.

Public opinion was still more moved when it was known
where Stella was going when she first set foot outside the gates
—to inquire after the rash young man who, popular opinion
now believed, had beguiled her into danger. How good, how
sweet, how forgiving of her ! Unless, indeed, there was something—something between them, as people say. This added
a new interest to the situation. The world of Sliplin had very
much blamed the young men. It had thought them inexcus-
able from every point of view. To have taken an inexperienced girl out, who knew nothing about yachting, just when
that gale was rising ! It was intolerable and not to be forgiven. This judgment was modified by the illness of Captain
Scott, who, everybody now found, was delicate, and ought
not to have exposed himself to the perils of such an expedition. It must have been the other who was to blame, but
then the other conciliated everybody by his devotion to his
friend. And the community was in a very soft and amiable
mood altogether when Stella was seen to issue forth from her
father's gates leaning on Katherine at one side and her stick
on the other, to ask for news of her fellow-sufferer. This
mood rose to enthusiasm at the sight of her paleness and at
the suggestion that there probably was something between
Stella and Captain Scott. It was supposed at first that he was
an honourable, and a great many peerages fluttered forth. It
was a disappointment to find that he was not so ; but at least
his father was a baronet, and himself an officer in a crack
regiment, and he had been in danger of his life. All these
circumstances were of an interesting kind.

Stella, however, did not carry out this tender purpose at

4

once. When she actually visited the hotel and made her way
upstairs into Captain Scott's room her own convalescence was
complete, and the other invalid was getting well, and there
was not only Katherine in attendance upon her, but Sir
Charles, who was now commonly seen with her in her walks,
and about whom Sliplin began to be divided in its mind
whether it was he and not the sick man between whom and
Stella there was something. He was certainly very devoted,
people said, but then most men were devoted to Stella. Captain Scott had been prepared for the visit, and was eager for
it, notwithstanding the disapproval of the nurse, who stood
apart by the window and looked daggers at the young ladies,
or at least at Stella, who took the chief place by the patient's
bedside and began to chatter to him, trying her best to get
into the right tone, the tone of Mrs. Seton, and make the
young man laugh. Katherine, who was not " in it," drew
aside to conciliate the attendant a little.

" I don't hold with visits when a young man is so weak,"
said the nurse. " Do you know, miss, that his life just hung
on a thread, so to speak? We were on the point of tele-
graphing for his people, me and the doctor ; and he is very
weak still."

" My sister will only stay a few minutes," said Katherine.
" You know she was with them in the boat and escaped with
her life too."

" Oh, I can see, miss, as there was no danger of *her* life,"
said the nurse, indignant. " Look at her colour ! I am not
thinking anything of the boat. A nasty night at sea is a nasty thing, but nothing for them that can stand it. But he
couldn't stand it ; that's all the difference. The young lady
may thank her stars as she hasn't his death at her door."

" It was her life that those rash young men risked by their
folly," said Katherine, indignant in her turn.

" Oh, no," cried the nurse. " I know better than that.
When he was off his head he was always going over it.
' Don't, Charlie, don't give in ; there's wind in the sky.
Don't give in to her. What does she know ? ' That was

what he was always a-saying. And there she sits as bold as brass, that is the cause.''

'' You take a great liberty to say so,'' said Katherine, returning to her sister's side.

Stella was now in full career.

'' Oh, do you remember the first puff—how it made us all start ? How we laughed at him for looking always at the sky ! Don't you remember, Captain Scott, I kept asking you what you were looking for in the sky, and you kept shaking your head ? ''

Here Stella began shaking her head from side to side and laughing loudly—a laugh echoed by the two young men, but faintly by the invalid, who shook his head too.

'' Yes, I saw the wind was coming,'' he said. '' We ought not to have given in to you, Miss Stella. It doesn't matter now it's all over, but it wasn't nice while it lasted, was it ? ''

'' Speak for yourself, Algy,'' said Sir Charles. '' You were never made for a sailor. Miss Stella is game for another voyage to-morrow.''

'' Oh, if you like,'' cried Stella, '' with a good man. I shall bargain for a good man—that can manage sails and all that. What is the fun of going out when the men with you won't sit by you and enjoy it. And all that silly tacking and nonsense—there should have been someone to do it, and you two should have sat by me.''

They both laughed at this and looked at each other. '' The fun is in the sailing—for us, don't you know,'' said Sir Charles. It was not necessary in their society even to pretend to another motive. Curiously enough, though Stella desired to ape that freedom, she was not—perhaps no woman is—delivered from the desire to believe that the motive was herself, to give her pleasure. She did not even now understand why her fellow-sufferers should not acknowledge this as the cause of their daring trip.

'' Papa wants to thank you,'' she said, '' for saving my life ; but that's absurd, ain't it, for you were saving your own. If you had let me drown, you would have drowned too.''

"I don't know. You were a bit in our way," said Sir
Charles. "We'd have got on better without you, we should,
by George! You were an awful responsibility, Miss Stella.
I shouldn't have liked to have faced Lady Scott if Algy had
kicked the bucket; and how I should have faced your father
if you——"

"If that was all you thought of, I shall never, never go out
with you again," cried Stella with an angry flush. But she
could not make up her mind to throw over her two companions for so little. "It was jolly at first, wasn't it?" she said,
after a pause, "until Al—Captain Scott began to look up to
the sky, and open his mouth for something to fall in."

But they did not laugh at this, though Mrs. Seton's similar
witticism had brought on fits of laughter. Captain Scott
swore "By George!" softly under his breath; Sir Charles
whistled—a very little, but he did whistle, at which sound
Stella rose angry from her seat.

"You don't seem to care much for my visit," she cried,
"though it tired me very much to come. Oh, I`know now
what is meant by fair-weather friends. We were to be such
chums. You were to do anything for me; and now, because
it came on to blow—which was not my fault——"

Here Stella's voice shook, and she was very near bursting
into tears.

"Don't say that, Miss Stella; it's awfully jolly to see you,
and it's dreadful dull lying here."

"And weren't all the old cats shocked!" cried Sir Charles.
"Oh, fie!" putting up his hands to his eyes, "to find you
had been out half the night along with Algy and me."

"I have not seen any old cats yet," said Stella, recovering
her temper, "only the young kittens, and they thought it a
most terrible adventure—like something in a book. You
don't seem to think anything of that, you boys; you are all
full of Captain Scott's illness, as if that dreadful, dreadful sail
was nothing, except just the way he caught cold. How funny
that is! Now I don't mind anything about catching cold or
being in bed for a week; but the terrible sea, and the wind,

and the dark—these are what I never can get out of my mind.''

'' You see you were in no danger to speak of; but Algy was, poor fellow. He is only just clear of it now.''

'' *I* only got up for the first time a week ago,'' said Stella, aggrieved ; but she did not pursue the subject. '' Mrs. Seton is coming across to see us—both the invalids, she says ; and perhaps she is one of the old cats, for she says she is coming to scold me as well as to pet me. I don't know what there is to scold about, unless perhaps she would have liked better to go out with you herself.''

'' That is just like Lottie Seton,'' they both said, and laughed as Stella's efforts never made them laugh. Why should they laugh at her very name when all the poor little girl could do in that way left them unmoved ?

'' She's a perfect dragon of virtue, don't you know ? '' said Algy, opening his wide mouth.

'' And won't she give it to the little 'un ! '' said Sir Charles, with another outburst.

'' I should like to know who is meant by the little 'un ; and what it is she can give,'' said Stella with offence.

They both laughed again, looking at each other. '' She's as jealous as the devil, don't you know ? '' and '' Lottie likes to keep all the good things to herself,'' they said.

Stella was partly mollified to think that Mrs. Seton was jealous. It was a feather in her little cap. '' I don't know if you think that sail was a good thing,'' she said. '' She might have had it for me. It is a pity that she left so soon. You always seem to be much happier when you have her near.''

'' She's such fun, she's not a bad sort. She keeps fellows going,'' the young men replied.

'' Well then,'' said Stella, getting up quickly, '' you'll be amused, for she is coming. I brought you some grapes and things. I don't know if you'll find them amusing. Kate, I think I'm very tired. Coming out so soon has thrown me back again. And these gentlemen don't want any visits from us, I feel sure.''

"Don't say that, Miss Stella," cried Sir Charles. "Algy's a dull beggar, that's the truth. He won't say what he thinks; but I hope you know me. Here, you must have my arm downstairs. You don't know the dark corners as I do. Algy, you dumb dog, say a word to the pretty lady that has brought you all these nice things. He means it all, Miss Stella, but he's tongue-tied."

"His mouth is open enough," said Stella as she turned away.

"Choke full of grapes, and that is the truth," said his friend. "And he's been very bad really, don't you know? Quite near making an end of it. That takes the starch out of a man, and just for a bit of fun. It wasn't his fun, don't you know? it was you and I that enjoyed it," Sir Charles said, pressing his companion's hand. Yes, she felt it was he whom she liked best, not Algy with his mouth full of grapes. His open mouth was always a thing to laugh at, but it is dreary work laughing alone. Sir Charles, on the other hand, was a handsome fellow, and he had always paid a great deal more attention to Stella than his friend. She went down the stairs leaning on his arm, Katherine following after a word of farewell to the invalid. The elder sister begged the young man to send to the Cliff for anything he wanted, and to come as soon as he was able to move, for a change. "Papa bade me say how glad we should be to have you."

Algy gaped at Katherine, who was supposed to be a sort of incipient old maid and no fun at all, with eyes and mouth wide. "Oh, thanks!" he said. He could not master this new idea. She had been always supposed to be elderly and plain, whereas it appeared in reality that she was just as pretty as the other one. He had to be left in silence to assimilate this new thought.

"Mind you tell me every word Lottie Seton says. She *is* fun when she is proper, and she just can be proper to make your hair stand on end. Now remember, Miss Stella, that's a bargain. You are to tell me every word she says."

"I shall do nothing of the sort; you must think much of

her indeed when you want to hear every word. I wonder you didn't go after her if you thought so much of her as that.''

"Oh, yes, she's very amusing,'' said Sir Charles. "She doesn't always mean to be, bless you, but when she goes in for the right and proper thing ! Mrs. Grundy is not in it, by Jove ! She'll come to the hotel and go on at Algy ; but it's with you that the fun will be. I should like to borrow the servant's clothes and get in a corner somewhere to hear. Lottie never minds what she says before servants. It is as if they were cabbages, don't you know ? ''

"You seem to know a great deal about Mrs. Seton, Sir Charles,'' said Stella severely ; but he did not disown this or hesitate as Stella expected. He said, "Yes, by Jove,'' simply into his big moustache, meaning Stella did not know what of good or evil. She allowed him to put her into the carriage which was waiting without further remark. Stella began to feel that it was by no means plain sailing with these young soldiers. Perhaps they were not so silly with her as with Mrs. Seton, perhaps Stella was not so clever ; and certainly she did not take the lead with them at all.

"I think they are rude,'' said Katherine ; "probably they don't mean any harm. I don't think they mean any harm. They are spoiled and allowed to say whatever they like, and to have very rude things said to them. Your Mrs. Seton, for instance——''

"Oh, don't say my Mrs. Seton,'' said Stella. "I hate Mrs. Seton. I wish we had never known her. She is not one of our kind of people at all.''

"But you would not have known these gentlemen whom you like but for Mrs. Seton, Stella.''

"How dare you say gentlemen whom I like ? as if it was something wrong ! They are only boys to play about,'' Stella said.

Which, indeed, was not at all a bad description of the sort of sentiment which fills many girlish minds with an inclination that is often very wrongly defined. Boys to play about is a thing which every one likes. It implies nothing perhaps, it means the most superficial of sentiments. It is to be hoped that it was only as boys to play about that Mrs. Seton herself took an interest in these young men. But her promise of a visit and a scold was perplexing to Stella. What was she to be scolded about, she whom neither her father nor sister had scolded, though she had given them such a night! And what a night she had given herself—terror, misery, and cold, a cold, perhaps, quite as bad as Algy Scott's, only borne by her with so much more courage! This was what Stella was thinking as she drove home. It was a ruddy October afternoon, very delightful in the sunshine, a little chilly out of it, and it was pleasant to be out again after her week's imprisonment, and to look across that glittering sea and feel what an experience she had gained. Now she knew the other side of it, and had a right to shudder and tell her awe-inspiring story whenever she pleased. "Oh, doesn't it look lovely, as if it could not harm anyone, but I could tell you another tale!" This was a possession which never could be taken from her, whoever might scold, or whoever complain.

CHAPTER VII.

"I ONLY wonder to find you holding up your head at all. Your people must be very silly people, and no mistake. What, to spend a whole night out in the bay with Charlie Somers and Algy Scott, and then to ask me what you have done? Do you know what sort of character these boys have got? They are nice boys, and I don't care about their morals, don't you know? as long as they're amusing. But then I've my husband always by me. Tom would no more leave me with those men by myself —though they're all well enough with anyone that knows how to keep them in order; but a young girl like you—it will need all that your friends can do to stand by you and to white-wash you, Stella. Tom didn't want me to come. 'You keep out of it. She has got people of her own,' he said; but I felt I must. And then, after all that, you lift up your little nozzle and ask what you have done!"

Stella sat up, very white, in the big easy-chair where she had been resting when Mrs. Seton marched in. The little girl was so entirely overwhelmed by the sudden downfall of all her pretensions to be a heroine that after the first minute of defiance her courage was completely cowed, and she could not find a word to say for herself. She was a very foolish girl carried away by her spirits, by her false conception of what was smart and amusing to do, and by the imperiousness natural to her position as a spoilt child whose every caprice was yielded to. But there was no harm, only folly, in poor little Stella's thoughts. She liked the company of the young men and the *éclat* which their attendance gave her. To drag about a couple of officers in her train was delightful to her. But further than that her innocent imagination did not go. Her wild adventure

in the yacht had never presented itself to her as anything to be
ashamed of, and Mrs. Seton's horrible suggestion filled her with
a consternation for which there was no words.   And it gave
her a special wound that it should be Mrs. Seton who said it,
she who had first introduced her to the noisy whirl of a " set "
with which by nature she had nothing to do.

" It was all an accident," Stella murmured at last ; " everybody knows it was an accident.   I meant to go—for ten minutes
—just to try—and then the wind got up.   Do you think I wanted
to be drowned—to risk my life, to be so ill and frightened to
death ?   Oh ! " the poor little girl cried, with that vivid reali-
sation of her own distress which is perhaps the most poignant
sentiment in the world—especially when it is unappreciated by
others.   Mrs. Seton tossed her head ; she was implacable.   No
feature of the adventure moved her except to wrath.

" Everybody knows what these accidents mean," she said,
" and as for your life it was in no more danger than it is here.
Charlie Somers knows the bay like the palm of his hand.   He
is one of the best sailors going.   I confess I don't understand
what *he* did it for.   Those boys will do anything for fun ; but
it wasn't very great fun, I should think—unless it was the lark
of the thing, just under your father's windows and so forth.
I do think, Stella, you've committed yourself dreadfully,
and I shouldn't wonder if you never got the better of it.
I should never have held up my head again if it had been
me."

They were seated in the pretty morning-room opening upon
the garden, which was the favourite room of the two girls.
The window was open to admit the sunshine of a brilliant
noon, but a brisk fire was burning, for the afternoons were
beginning to grow cold, when the sunshine was no longer
there, with the large breath of the sea.   Mrs. Seton had arrived by an early train to visit her friends, and had just come
from Algy's sick .bed to carry fire and flame into the convalescence of Stella.   Her injured virtue, her high propriety,
shocked by such proceedings as had been thus brought under
her notice, were indescribable.   She had given the girl a care-

less kiss with an air of protest against that very unmeaning endearment, when she came in, and this was how, without any warning, she had assailed the little heroine. Stella's courage was not at all equal to the encounter. She had held her own with difficulty before the indifference of the young men. She could not bear up at all under the unlooked-for attack of her friend.

"Oh, how cruel you are!—how unkind you are!—how dreadful of you to say such things!" she cried. "As if I was merely sport for them like a—like any sort of girl; a lark!—under my father's windows——" It was too much for Stella. She began to cry in spite of herself, in spite of her pride, which was not equal to this strain.

Katherine had come in unperceived while the conversation was going on.

"I cannot have my sister spoken to so," she said. "It is quite false in the first place, and she is weak and nervous and not able to bear such suggestions. If you have anything to say against Stella's conduct it will be better to say it to my father, or to me. If anybody was to blame, it was your friends who were to blame. They knew what they were about and Stella did not. They must be ignorant indeed if they looked upon her as they would do upon "—Katherine stopped herself hurriedly—"upon a person of experience—an older woman."

"Upon me, you mean!" cried Mrs. Seton. "I am obliged to you, Miss Tredgold! Oh, yes! I have got some experience and so has she, if flirting through a couple of seasons can give it. Two seasons!—more than that. I am sure I have seen her at the Cowes ball I don't know how many times! And then to pretend she doesn't know what men are, and what people will say of such an escapade as that! Why, goodness, everybody knows what people say; they will talk for a nothing at all, for a few visits you may have from a friend, and nothing in it but just to pass the time. And then to think she can be out a whole night with a couple of men in a boat, and nothing said! Do you mean

to say that you, who are old enough, I am sure, for anything——''

" Katherine is not much older than I am," cried Stella,
drying her tears. " Katherine is twenty-three—Katherine
is——''

" Oh, I'm sure, quite a perfect person ! though you don't
always think so, Stella ; and twenty-three's quite a nice age,
that you can stand at for ever so long. And you are a couple
of very impudent girls to face it out to me so, who have come
all this way for your good, just to warn you. Oh, if you
don't know what people say, I do ! I have had it hot all
round for far more innocent things ; but I've got Tom always
to stand by me. Who's going to stand by you when it gets
told all about how you went out with Charlie Somers and
Algy Scott all by yourself in a boat, and didn't come back
till morning ? You think perhaps it won't be known ? Why,
it's half over the country already ; the men are all laughing
about it in their clubs ; they are saying which of 'em was it
who played gooseberry ? They aren't the sort of men to play
gooseberry, neither Algy nor Charlie. The old father will
have to come down strong——''

Poor Stella looked up at her sister with distracted eyes.
" Oh, Kate, what does she mean ? What does she mean ?''
she cried.

" We don't want to know what she means," cried Katherine, putting her arms round her sister. " She speaks her
own language, not one that we understand. Stella, Stella
dear, don't take any notice. What are the men in the clubs
to you ?''

" I'd like to know," said Mrs. Seton with a laugh, " which
of us can afford to think like that of the men in the clubs.
Why, it's there that everything comes from. A good joke or
a good story, that's what they live by—they tell each other
everything ! Who would care to have them, or who would
ask them out, and stand their impudence if they hadn't always the very last bit of gossip at their fingers' ends ? And
this is such a delicious story, don't you know ? Charlie Som-

ers and Algy Scott off in a little pleasure yacht with a millionaire's daughter, and kept her out all night, by Jove, in a gale
of wind to make everything nice ! And now the thing is to
see how far the old father will go. He'll have to do something big, don't you know ? but whether Charlie or Algy is
to be the happy man———''

''Kate!'' said Stella with a scream, hiding her head on her
sister's shoulder. ''Take me away! Oh, hide me somewhere!
Don't let me see anyone — anyone! Oh, what have I done —
what have I done, that anything so dreadful should come to
me.''

''You have done nothing, Stella, except a little folly,
childish folly, that meant nothing. Will you let her alone,
please? You have done enough harm here. It was you who
brought those — those very vulgar young men to this house.''

Even Stella lifted her tearful face in consternation at Katherine's boldness, and Mrs. Seton uttered a shriek of dismay.

''What next—what next? Vulgar young men! The very
flower of the country, the finest young fellows going. You've
taken leave of your senses, I think. And to this house — oh,
my goodness, what fun it is! — how they will laugh! To
this house———''

''They had better not laugh in our hearing at least. This
house is sacred to those who live in it, and anyone who comes
here with such hideous miserable gossip may be prepared for a
bad reception. Those vulgar cads!'' cried Katherine. ''Oh,
that word is vulgar too, I suppose. I don't care — they are
so if any men ever were, who think they can trifle with a girl's
name and make her father come down—with what? his money
you mean — it would be good sound blows if I were a man.
And for what? to buy the miserable beings off, to shut their
wretched mouths, to——— ''

''Katherine!'' cried Stella, all aglow, detaching herself
from her sister's arms.

''Here's heroics!'' said Mrs. Seton ; but she was overawed
more or less by the flashing eyes and imposing aspect of this
young woman, who was no ''frump'' after all, as appeared,

but a person to be reckoned with—not Stella's duenna, but
something in her own right.   Then she turned to Stella, who
was more comprehensible, with whom a friend might quarrel
and make it up again and no harm done.   "My dear," she
said, "you are the one of this family who understands a little,
who can be spoken to — I shan't notice the rude things your
sister says — I was obliged to tell you, for it's always best to
hear from a friend what is being said about you outside.   You
might have seen yourself boycotted, don't you know? and not
known what it meant.   But, I dare say, if we all stand by you,
you'll not be boycotted for very long.   You don't mean to be
rude, I hope, to your best friends."

"Oh, Lottie! I hope you will stand by me," cried Stella.
"It was all an accident, as sure, as sure——!   I only took
them to the yacht for fun—and then I thought I should like
to see the sails up—for fun.   And then—oh, it was anything
but fun after that!" the girl cried.

"I dare say.   Were you sick? — did you make an exhibition of yourself?   Oh, I shall hear all about it from Algy —
Charlie won't say anything, so he is the one, I suppose.   Don't
forget he's a very bad boy—oh, there isn't a good one between
them!   *I* shouldn't like to be out with them alone.   But
Charlie!   the rows he has had everywhere, the scandals he has
made!   Oh, my dear!   If you go and marry Charlie Somers,
Stella, which you'll have to do, I believe——"

"He is the very last person she shall marry if she will listen
to me!"

"Oh, you are too silly for anything, Katherine," said
Stella, slightly pushing her away.   "You don't know the
world, you are goody-goody.   What do you know about men?
But I don't want to marry anyone.   I want to have my fun.
The sea was dreadful the other night, and I was terribly frightened and thought I was going to be drowned.   But yet it was
fun in a way.   Oh, Lottie, you understand!   One felt it was
such a dreadful thing to happen, and the state papa and everybody would be in!   Still it is very, very impudent to discuss
me like that, as if I had been run away with.   I wasn't in the

least. It was I who wanted to go out. They said the wind was getting up, but I didn't care, I said. 'Let's try.' It was all for fun. And it was fun, after all.''

"Oh, if you take it in that way," said Mrs. Seton, "and perhaps it is the best way just to brazen it out. Say what fun it was for everybody. Don't go in for being pale and having been ill and all that. Laugh at Algy for being such a milksop. You are a clever little thing, Stella. I am sure that is the best way. And if I were you I should smooth down the old cats here — those old cats, you know, that came to the picnic — and throw dust in the eyes of Lady Jane, and then you'll do. I'll fight your battles for you, you may be sure. And then there is Charlie Somers. I wouldn't turn up my nose at Charlie Somers if I were you.''

"He is nothing to me," said Stella. "He has never said a word to me that all the world—that Kate herself—mightn't hear. When he does it'll be time enough to turn up my nose, or not. Oh, what do I care? I don't want to have anybody to stand up for me. I can do quite well by myself, thank you. Kate, why should I sit here in a dressing gown? I am quite well. I want the fresh air and to run about. You are so silly; you always want to pet me and take care of me as if I were a child. I'm going out now with Lottie to have a little run before lunch and see the view.''

"Brava," said Mrs. Seton, "you see what a lot of good I've done her—that is what she wants, shaking up, not being petted and fed with sweets. All right, Stella, run and get your frock on and I'll wait for you. You may be quite right, Miss Tredgold," she said, when Stella had disappeared, " to stand up for your family. But all the same it's quite true what I say.''

"If it is true, it is abominable; but I don't believe it to be true," Katherine cried.

"Well, I don't say it isn't a shame. I've had abominable things said of me. But what does that matter so long as your husband stands by you like a brick, as Tom does? But if I were you, and Charlie Somers really comes forward—it is just as likely he won't, for he ain't a marrying man, he likes his fun like Stella—but if he does come forward——''

'' I hope he will have more sense than to think of such a thing. He will certainly not be well received.''

'' Oh, if you stick to that! But why should you now? If she married it would be the best thing possible for you. You ain't bad looking, and I shouldn't wonder if you were only the age she says. But with Stella here you seem a hundred, and nobody looks twice at you——''

Katherine smiled, but the smile was not without bitterness. '' You are very kind to advise me for my good,'' she said.

'' Oh, you mean I'm very impudent—perhaps I am! But I know what I'm saying all the same. If Charlie Somers comes forward——''

'' Advise him not to do so, you who are fond of giving advice,'' said Katherine, '' for my father will have nothing to say to him, and it would be no use.''

'' Oh, your father!'' said Mrs. Seton with contempt, and then she kissed her hand to Stella, who came in with her hat on ready for the '' run '' she had proposed. '' Here she is as fresh as paint,'' said that mistress of all the elegancies of language—'' what a good 'un I am for stirring up the right spirit! You see how much of an invalid she is now! Where shall we go for our run, Stella, now that you have made yourself look so killing? You don't mean, I should suppose, to waste that toilette upon me?''

'' We'll go and look at the view,'' said Stella, '' that is all I am equal to; and I'll show you where we went that night.''

'' Papa will be ready for his luncheon in half an hour, Stella.''

'' Yes, I know, I know! Don't push papa and his luncheon down my throat for ever,'' cried the girl. She too was a mistress of language. She went out with her adviser arm-in-arm, clinging to her as if to her dearest friend, while Katherine stood in the window, rather sadly, looking after the pair. Stella had been restored to her sister by the half-illness of her

rescue, and there was a pang in Katherine's mind which was
mingled of many sentiments as the semi-invalid went forth
hanging upon her worst friend. Would nobody ever cling
to Katherine as Stella, her only sister, clung to this woman—
this—woman! Katherine did not know what epithet to use.
If she had had bad words at her disposal I am afraid she would
have expended them on Mrs. Seton, but she had not. They
were not in her way. Was it possible this—woman might be
right? Could Stella's mad prank, if it could be called so—
rather her childish, foolish impulse, meaning no harm—tell
against her seriously with anybody in their senses? Katherine could not believe it—it was impossible. The people who
had known her from her childhood knew that there was no
harm in Stella. She might be thoughtless, disregarding everything that came in the way of her amusement, but after all
that was not a crime. She was sure that such old cats as Mrs.
Shanks and Miss Mildmay would never think anything of the
kind. But then there was Lady Jane. Lady Jane was not
an old cat; she was a very important person. When she
spoke the word no dog ventured to bark. But then her kindness to the Tredgold girls had always been a little in the way
of patronage. She was not of their middle-class world. The
side with which she would be in sympathy would be that of
the young men. The escapade in the boat would be to her
their fun, but on Stella's it would not be fun. It would be
folly of the deepest dye, perhaps—who could tell?—depravity.
In fiction—a young woman not much in society instinctively
takes a good many of her ideas from fiction—it had become
fashionable of late to represent wicked girls, girls without soul
or heart, as the prevailing type. Lady Jane might suppose
that Stella, whom she did not know very well, was a girl without soul or heart, ready to do anything for a little excitement
and a new sensation, without the least reflection what would
come of it. Nay, was not that the *rôle* which Stella herself
was proposing to assume? Was it not to a certain extent her
real character? This thought made Katherine's heart ache.
And how if Lady Jane should think she had really compro-

5

mised herself, forfeited, if not her good name, yet the bloom
that ought to surround it? Katherine's courage sank at the
thought. And, on the other hand, there was her father, who
would understand none of these things, who would turn anybody out of his house who breathed a whisper against Stella,
who would show Sir Charles himself the door.

CHAPTER VIII.

It would be absurd to suppose that Mrs. Shanks and Miss Mildmay had not heard the entire story of Stella's escape and all that led up to it, the foolish venture and the unexpected and too serious punishment. They had known all about it from the first moment. They had seen her running down to the beach with her attendants after her, and had heard all about the boat with the new figure-head which Mr. Tredgold had got a bargain and had called after his favourite child. And they had said to each other as soon as they had heard of it, "Mark my words! we shall soon hear of an accident to that boat." They had related this fact in all the drawing-rooms in the neighbourhood with great, but modest, pride when the accident did take place. But they had shown the greatest interest in Stella, and made no disagreeable remarks as to the depravity of her expedition. Nobody had been surprised at this self-denial at first, for no one had supposed that there was any blame attaching to the young party, two out of the three of whom had suffered so much for their imprudence; for Stella's cold and the shock to her nerves had at first been raised by a complimentary doctor almost to the same flattering seriousness as Captain Scott's pneumonia. Now the event altogether had begun to sink a little into the mild perspective of distance, as a thing which was over and done with, though it would always be an exciting reminiscence to talk of—the night when poor Stella Tredgold had been carried out to sea by the sudden squall, "just in her white afternoon frock, poor thing, without a wrap or anything."

This had been the condition of affairs before Mrs. Seton's visit. I cannot tell how it was breathed into the air that the

adventure was by no means such a simple matter, that Stella
was somehow dreadfully in fault, that it would be something
against her all her life which she would have the greatest difficulty in " living down." Impossible to say who sowed this
cruel seed. Mrs. Seton declared afterwards that she had spoken
to no one, except indeed the landlady of the hotel where Captain Scott was lying, and his nurse ; but that was entirely
about Algy, poor boy. But whoever was the culprit, or by
what methods soever the idea was communicated, certain it is
that the views of the little community were completely changed
after that moment. It began to be whispered about in the
little assemblies, over the tea-tables, and over the billiard-tables
(which was worse), that Stella Tredgold's escapade was a very
queer thing after all. It was nonsense to say that she had
never heard of the existence of the *Stella* till that day, when it
was well known that old Tredgold bragged about everything
he bought, and the lot o' money, or the little money he had
given for it ; for it was equally sweet to him to get a great
bargain or to give the highest price that had ever been paid.
That he should have held his tongue about this one thing, was
it likely? And she was such a daring little thing, fond of
scandalising her neighbours ; and she was a little fast, there
could be no doubt; at all events, she had been so ever since
she had made the acquaintance of that Mrs. Seton—that Seton
woman, some people said. Before her advent it only had been
high spirits and innocent nonsense, but since then Stella had
been infected with a love of sensation and had learned to like
the attendance of men—any men, it did not matter whom. If
the insinuation was of Mrs. Seton's making, she was not herself
spared in it.

Mrs. Shanks and Miss Mildmay were by no means the last
to be infected by this wave of opinion. They lived close to
each other in two little houses built upon the hill side, with
gardens in long narrow strips which descended in natural terraces to the level of the high road. They were houses which
looked very weedy and damp in the winter time, being surrounded by verandahs, very useful to soften the summer glow

but not much wanted in October when the wind blew heaps
of withered leaves (if you ventured to call those rays of gold
and crimson withered) under the shelter of their green trellises.
There are few things more beautiful than these same autumn
leaves; but a garden is sadly "untidy," as these ladies la-
mented, when covered with them, flying in showers from somebody else's trees, and accumulating in heaps in the corners of
the verandahs. "The boy," who was the drudge of Mrs.
Shanks' establishment, and "the girl" who filled the same
place in Miss Mildmay's, swept and swept for ever, but did not
succeed in "keeping them down;" and indeed, when these
two ladies stepped outside in the sunny mornings, as often as
not a leaf or two lighted, an undesired ornament upon the frills
of Mrs. Shanks' cap or in the scanty coils of Miss Mildmay's
hair. There was only a low railing between the two gardens
in order not to break the beauty of the bank with its terraces
as seen from below, and over this the neighbours had many
talks as they superintended on either side the work of the boy
and the girl, or the flowering of the dahlias which made a little show on Mrs. Shanks' side, or the chrysanthemums on the
other. These winterly flowers were what the gardens were
reduced to in October, though there were a few roses still to
be found near the houses, and the gay summer annuals were
still clinging on to life in rags and desperation along the bor-
ders, and a few sturdy red geraniums standing up boldly here
and there.

"Have you heard what they are saying about Stella Tredgold?" said the one lady to the other one of these mornings.
Mrs. Shanks had a hood tied over her cap, and Miss Mildmay
a Shetland shawl covering her grey hair.

"Have I heard of anything else?" said the other, shaking
her head.

"And I just ask you, Ruth Mildmay," said Mrs. Shanks,
"do you think that little thing is capable of making up any
plan to run off with a couple of officers? Good gracious, why
should she do such a thing? She can have them as much as
she likes at home. That silly old man will never stop her, but

feed them with the best of everything at breakfast, lunch, and dinner, if they like—and then be astonished if people talk. And as for Katherine—but I have no patience with Katherine,'' the old lady said.

"If it's only a question what Stella Tredgold is capable of,'' answered Miss Mildmay, "she is capable of making the hair stand up straight on our heads—and there is nothing she would like better than to do it.''

"Ah,'' said Mrs. Shanks, "she would find that hard with me ; for I am nearly bald on the top of my head.''

"And don't you try something for it?'' said the other blandly. Miss Mildmay was herself anxiously in search of "something'' that might still restore to her, though changed in colour, the abundance of the locks of her youth.

"I try a cap for it,'' said the other, "which covers everything up nicely. What the eye does not see the heart does not grieve—not like you, Ruth Mildmay, that have so much hair. Did you feel it standing up on end when you heard of Stella's escapade?''

"I formed my opinion of Stella's escapade long ago,'' said Miss Mildmay. "I thought it mad—simply mad, like so many things she does ; but I hoped nobody would take any notice, and I did not mean to be the first to say anything.''

"Well, it just shows how innocent I am,'' said Mrs. Shanks, "an old married woman that ought to know better ! Why, I never thought any harm of it at all ! I thought they had just pushed off a bit, three young fools ! ''

"But why did they push off a bit—that is the question ? They might have looked at the boat ; but why should she go out, a girl with two men ?''

"Well, two was better than one, surely, Ruth Mildmay ! If it had been one, why, you might have said—but there's safety in numbers—besides, one man in a little yacht with a big sail. I hate those things myself,'' said Mrs. Shanks. "I would not put my foot in one of them to save my life. They are like guns which no one believes are ever loaded till they go off and kill you before you know.

" I have no objection to yachting, for my part. My Uncle Sir Ralph was a great yachtsman. I have often been out with him. The worst of these girls is that they've nobody to give them a little understanding of things—nobody that knows. Old Tredgold can buy anything for them, but he can't tell them how to behave. And even Katherine, you know——"

" Oh, Katherine—I have no patience with Katherine. She lets that little thing do whatever she pleases."

" As if any one could control Stella, a spoilt child if ever there was one ! May I ask you, Jane Shanks, what you intend to do ? "

" To do ? " cried Mrs. Shanks, her face, which was a little red by nature, paling suddenly. She stopped short in the very act of cutting a dahlia, a large very double purple one, into which the usual colour of her cheeks seemed to have gone.

" Oh, for goodness' sake take care of those earwigs," cried Miss Mildmay. " I hate dahlias for that—they are always full of earwigs. When I was a little child I thought I had got one in my ear. You know the nursery-maids always say they go into your ear. And the miserable night I had ! I have never forgotten it. There is one on the rails, I declare."

" Are we talking of earwigs—or of anything more important ? " Mrs. Shanks cried.

" There are not many things more important, I can tell you, if you think one has got into your ear. They say it creeps into your brain and eats it up—and all sorts of horrible things. I was talking of going to the Cliff to see what those girls were about, and what Stella has to say for herself."

" To the Cliff ! " Mrs. Shanks said.

" Well," said her neighbour sharply, " did you mean to give them up without even asking what they had to say for themselves ? "

" I—give them up ?—I never thought of such a thing. You go so fast, Ruth Mildmay. It was only yesterday I heard of this talk, which never should have gone from me. At the worst it's a thing that might be gossiped about ; but to give them up——"

"You wouldn't, I suppose," said Miss Mildmay sternly, "countenance depravity—if it was proved to be true."

"If what was proved to be true? What is it they say against her?" Mrs. Shanks cried.

But this was not so easy to tell, for nobody had said anything except the fact which everybody knew.

"You know what is said as well as I do," said Miss Mildmay. "Are you going? Or do you intend to drop them? That is what I want to know."

"Has any one dropped them, yet?" her friend asked. There was a tremble in her hand which held the dahlias. She was probably scattering earwigs on every side, paying no attention. And her colour had not yet come back. It was very rarely that a question of this importance came up between the two neighbours. "Has Lady Jane said anything?" she asked in tones of awe.

"I don't know and I don't care," cried Miss Mildmay boldly; for, maiden lady as she was, and poor, she was one of those who did not give in to Lady Jane. "For my part, I want to hear more about it before I decide what to do."

"And so should I too," said Mrs. Shanks, though still with bated breath. "Oh, Ruth Mildmay, I do not think I could ever have the heart! Such a little thing, and no mother, and such a father as Mr. Tredgold! I think it is going to rain this afternoon. I should not mind for once having the midge if you will share it, and going to call, and see what we can see."

"I will share the midge if you like. I have other places where I must call. I can wait for you outside if you like, or I might even go in with you, for five minutes," Miss Mildmay said severely, as if the shortness of that term justified the impulse. And they drove out accordingly, in the slumbrous afternoon, when most people were composing themselves comfortably by the side of their newly-lighted fires, comforting themselves that, as it had come on to rain, nobody would call, and that they were quite free either to read a book or to nod over it till tea-time. It rained softly, persistently, quietly, as the midge drove along amid a mingled shower of water-drops and falling leaves. The leaves were like bits of gold, the water-drops sparkled on the glass of the windows. All was soft, weeping, and downfall, the trees standing fast through the mild rain, scattering, with a sort of forlorn pleasure in it, their old glories off them. The midge stumbled along, jolting over the stones, and the old ladies seated opposite—for it held only one on each side—nodded their heads at each other, partly because they could not help it, partly to emphasise their talk. "That little thing! to have gone wrong at her age! But girls now were not like what they used to be—they were very different—not the least like what we used to be in our time."

"Here is the midge trundling along the drive and the old cats coming to inquire. They are sure to have heard everything that ever was said in the world," cried Stella, "and they are coming to stare at me and find out if I look as if I felt it. They shall not see me at all, however I look. I am not going to answer to them for what I do."

"Certainly not," said Katherine. "If that is what they have come for, you had better leave them to me."

"I don't know, either," said Stella, "it rains, and nobody else will come. They might be fun. I shall say everything I can think of to shock them, Kate."

"They deserve it, the old inquisitors," cried Kate, who was more indignant than her sister; "but I think I would not, Stella. Don't do anything unworthy of yourself, dear, whatever other people may say."

"Oh! unworthy of myself!—I don't know what's worthy of myself—nothing but nonsense, I believe. I should just like, however, for fun, to see what the old cats have to say."

The old cats came in, taking some time to alight from the midge and shake out their skirts in the hall. They were a little frightened, if truth must be told. They were not sure of their force against the sharp little claws sheathed in velvet of the little white cat-princess, on whom they were going to make an inquisition, whether there was any stain upon her coat of snow.

"We need not let them see we've come for that, or have heard anything," Mrs. Shanks whispered in Miss Mildmay's ear.

"Oh, I shall let them see!" said the fiercer visitor; but nevertheless she trembled too.

They were taken into the young ladies' room, which was on the ground floor, and opened with a large window upon the lawn and its encircling trees. It was perhaps too much on a level with that lawn for a house which is lived in in autumn and winter as well as summer, and the large window occupied almost one entire side of the room. Sometimes it was almost too bright, but to-day, with the soft persistent rain pouring down, and showers of leaves coming across the rain from time to time, as if flying frightened before every puff of air, the effect of the vast window and of the white and gold furniture was more dismal than bright. There was a wood fire, not very bright either, but hissing faintly as it smouldered, which did not add much to the comfort of the room. Katherine was working at something as usual—probably something of no importance—but it was natural to her to be occupied, while it was natural for Stella to do nothing. The visitors instinctively remarked the fact with the usual approval and disapproval.

"Katherine, how do you do, my dear? We thought we were sure to find you at home such a day. Isn't it a wet day? raining cats and dogs; but the midge is so good for that, one is so sheltered from the weather. Ruth Mildmay thought it was just the day to find you; Jane Shanks was certain you would be at home. Ah, Stella, you are here too!" they said both together.

"Did you think I shouldn't be here too?" said Stella. — "I am always here too. I wonder why you should be surprised."

"Oh, indeed, Stella! We know that is not the case by any means. If you were always with Katherine, it would be very, very much the better for you. You would get into no scrapes if you kept close to Katherine," Mrs. Shanks said.

"Do I get into scrapes?" cried Stella, tossing her young head. "Oh, I knew there would be some fun when I saw the midge coming along the drive! Tell me what scrapes I have got into. I hope it is a very bad one to-day to make your hair stand on end.''

'' My dear, you know a great deal better than we can tell you what things people are saying,'' said Miss Mildmay. '' I did not mean to blurt it out the first thing as Jane Shanks has done. It is scarcely civil, I feel—perhaps you would yourself have been moved to give us some explanation which would have satisfied our minds—and to Katherine it is scarcely polite.''

'' Oh, please do not mind being polite to me!'' cried Katherine, who was in a white heat of resentment and indignation, her hands trembling as she threw down her work. And Stella, that little thing, was completely at her ease! '' If there is anything to be said I take my full share with Stella, whatever it may be.'' And then there was a little pause, for tea was brought in with a footman's instinct for the most dramatic moment. Tea singularly changed the face of affairs. Gossip may be exchanged over the teacups; but to come fully prepared for mortal combat, and in the midst of it to be served by your antagonist with a cup of tea, is terribly embarrassing. Katherine, being excited and innocent, would have left it there with its fragrance rising fruitlessly in the midst of the fury melting the assailants' hearts; but Stella, guilty and clever, saw her advantage. Before she said anything more she sprang up from her chair and took the place which was generally Katherine's before the little shining table. Mr. Tredgold's tea was naturally the very best that could be got for money, and had a fragrance which was delightful; and there were muffins in a beautiful little covered silver dish, though October is early in the season for muffins. '' I'll give you some tea first,'' cried the girl, '' and then you can come down upon me as much as you please.''

And it was so nice after the damp drive, after the jolting of the midge, in the dull and dreary afternoon! It was more than female virtue was equal to, to refuse that deceiving cup. Miss Mildmay said faintly: '' None for me, please. I am

going on to the——'' But before she had ended this asser-
tion she found herself, she knew not how, with a cup in her
hand.

"Oh, Stella, my love,'' cried Mrs. Shanks, "what tea
yours is! And oh, how much sweeter you look, and how
much better it is, instead of putting yourself in the way of a
set of silly young officers, to sit there smiling at your old
friends and pouring out the tea!''

Miss Mildmay gave a little gasp, and made a motion to put
down the cup again, but she was not equal to the effort.

"Oh, it is the officers you object to!'' cried Stella. "If
it was curates perhaps you would like them better. I love the
officers! they are so nice and big and silly. To be sure, curates are silly also, but they are not so easy and nice about it.''

Miss Mildmay's gasp this time was almost like a choke.
"Believe me,'' she said, "it would be much better to
keep clear of young men. You girls now are almost as bad
as the American girls, that go about with them everywhere—
worse, indeed, for it is permitted there, and it is not permitted
here.''

"That makes it all the nicer,'' cried Stella; "it's delightful because it's wrong. I wonder why the American girls do
it when all the fun is gone out of it!''

"Depend upon it,'' said Miss Mildmay, "it's better to
have nothing at all to do with young men.''

"But then what is to become of the world?'' said the culprit gravely.

"Stella!'' cried Katherine.

"It is quite true. The world would come to an end—
there would be no more——''

"Stella, Stella!''

"I think you are quite right in what you said, Jane
Shanks,'' said Miss Mildmay. "It is a case that can't be
passed over. It is——''

"I never said anything of the sort,'' cried Mrs. Shanks,
alarmed. "I said we must know what Stella had to say for
herself——''

"And so you shall," said Stella, with a toss of her saucy head. "I have as much as ever you like to say for myself. There is nothing I won't say. Some more muffin, Mrs. Shanks—one little other piece. It is so good, and the first of the season. But this is not enough toasted. Look after the tea, Katherine, while I toast this piece for Miss Mildmay. It is much nicer when it is toasted for you at a nice clear fire."

"Not any more for me," cried Miss Mildmay decisively, putting down her cup and pushing away her chair.

"You cannot refuse it when I have toasted it expressly for you. It is just as I know you like it, golden brown and hot! Why, here is another carriage! Take it, take it, dear Miss Mildmay, before some one else comes in. Who can be coming, Kate—this wet day?"

They all looked out eagerly, speechless, at the pair of smoking horses and dark green landau which passed close to the great window in the rain. Miss Mildmay took the muffin mechanically, scarcely knowing what she did, and a great consternation fell upon them all. The midge outside, frightened, drew away clumsily from the door, and the ladies, both assailed and assailants, gazed into each other's eyes with a shock almost too much for speech.

"Oh, heavens," breathed Mrs. Shanks, "do you see who it is, you unfortunate children? It is Lady Jane herself—and how are you going to stand up, you little Stella, before Lady Jane?"

"Let her come," said Stella defiant, yet with a hot flush on her cheeks.

And, indeed, so it happened. Lady Jane did not pause to shake out her skirts, which were always short enough for all circumstances. Almost before the footman, who preceded her with awe, could open the door decorously, she pushed him aside with her own hand to quicken his movements, Lady Jane herself marched squarely into the expectant room.

CHAPTER IX.

LADY JANE walked into the room squarely, with her short
skirts and her close jacket. She looked as if she were quite
ready to walk back the four miles of muddy road between
her house and the Cliff. And so indeed she was, though she
had no intention of doing so to-day. She came in, pushing
aside the footman, as I have said, who was very much frightened of Lady Jane. When she saw the dark figures of Mrs.
Shanks and Miss Mildmay sitting against the large light of the
window, she uttered a suppressed sound of discontent. It
might be translated by an " Oh," or it might be translated,
as we so often do as the symbol of a sound, by a " Humph."
At all events, it was a sound which expressed annoyance.
" You here ! " it seemed to say; but Lady Jane afterwards
shook hands with them very civilly, it need not be said. For
the two old cats were very respectable members of society,
and not to be badly treated even by Lady Jane.

" That was your funny little carriage, I suppose," she
said, when she had seated herself, " stopping the way."

" Was it stopping the way? " cried Mrs. Shanks, " the
midge? I am astonished at Mr. Perkins. We always give
him the most careful instructions; but if he had found one of
the servants to gossip with, he is a man who forgets everything one may say."

" I can't undertake what his motives were, but he was in
the way, blocking up the doors," said Lady Jane; " all the
more astonishing to my men and my horses, as they were
brought out, much against their will, on the full understanding that nobody else would be out on such a day."

" It is a long way to Steephill," said Miss Mildmay, " so

that we could not possibly have known Lady Jane's intentions, could we, Jane Shanks? or else we might have taken
care not to get into her way."

" Oh, the public roads are free to every one," said Lady
Jane, dismissing the subject. " What rainy weather we have
had, to be sure ! Of course you are all interested in that
bazaar; if it goes on like this you will have no one, not a
soul to buy; and all the expense of the decorations and so
forth on our hands."

" Oh, the officers will come over from Newport," said Miss
Mildmay; " anything is better than nothing. Whatever has
a show of amusement will attract the officers, and that will
make the young ladies happy, so that it will not be thrown
away."

" What a Christian you are ! " said Lady Jane. " You
mean it is an ill wind that blows nobody good. I have
several cousins in the garrison, but I don't think I should care
so much for their amusement as all that."

" Was there ever a place," said Mrs. Shanks, with a certain tone of humble admiration, which grated dreadfully upon
her companion, " in which you had not a number of cousins, Lady Jane? They say the Scotch are the great people
for having relatives everywhere, and my poor husband was
a Scotchman; but I'm sure he had not half so many as
you."

Lady Jane answered curtly with a nod of her head and went
on. " The rain is spoiling everything," she said. " The
men, of course, go out in spite of it when they can, but they
have no pleasure in their work, and to have a shooting party
on one's hands in bad weather is a hard task. They look at
you as if it were your fault, as if you could order good
weather as easily as you can order luncheon for them at the
cover side."

" Dear me, that is not at all fair, is it, Ruth Mildmay ? In
my poor husband's lifetime, when we used to take a shooting
regularly, I always said to his friends, ' Now, don't look reproachfully at me if it's bad weather. We can't guarantee

the weather.   You ought to get so many brace if you have good luck.   We'll answer for that.' "

"You were a bold woman," said Lady Jane; "so many brace without knowing if they could fire a gun or not ! That's a rash promise.   Sir John is not so bold as that, I can tell you.   He says, ' There's a bird or two about if you can hit 'em.'   Katherine, you may as well let me see those things of ' yours for my stall.   It will amuse me a little this wet day."

"They are all upstairs, Lady Jane."

"Well, I'll go upstairs.   Oh, don't let me take you away from your visitors.   Stella, you can come with me and show them ; not that I suppose you know anything about them."

"Not the least in the world," said Stella very clearly.   Her face, so delicately tinted usually, and at present paler than ordinary, was crimson, and her attitude one of battle.   She could propitiate and play with the old cats, but she dare not either cajole or defy Lady Jane.

"Then Katherine can come, and I can enjoy the pleasure of conversation with you after.   Shall I find you still here," said Lady Jane, holding out her hand graciously to the other ladies, "when I come downstairs again ? "

"Oh, we must be going——"

Mrs. Shanks was interrupted by Miss Mildmay's precise tones.   "Probably you will find *me* here, Lady Jane; and I am sure it will be a mutual pleasure to continue the conversation which——"

"Then I needn't say good-bye," said the great lady calmly, taking Katherine by the arm and pushing the girl before her.   Stella stood with her shoulders against the mantel-piece, very red, watching them as they disappeared.   She gave the others an angry look of appeal as the door closed upon the more important visitor.

"Oh, I wish you'd take me away with you in the midge ! " she cried.

"Ah, Stella," cried Mrs. Shanks, shaking her head, "the times I have heard you making your fun of the midge !   But in a time of trouble one finds out who are one's real friends."

Miss Mildmay was softened too, but she was not yet disposed to give in. She had not been able to eat that special muffin which Stella had re-toasted for her. Lady Jane, in declining tea curtly with a wave of her hands, had made the tea-drinkers uncomfortable, and especially had arrested the eating of muffins, which it is difficult to consume with dignity unless you have the sympathy of your audience. It was cold now, quite cold and unappetizing. It lay in its little plate with the air of a thing rejected. And Miss Mildmay felt it was not consistent with her position to ask even for half a cup of hot tea.

" It has to be seen," she said stiffly, " what friends will respond to the appeal ; everybody is not at the disposal of the erring person when and how she pleases. I must draw a line——"

" What do you say I have done, then ? " cried Stella, flushing with lively wrath. " Do you think I went out in that boat on purpose to be drowned or catch my death ? Do you think I wanted to be ill and sea-sick and make an exhibition of myself before two men ? Do you think I wanted them to see me *ill ?* Goodness ! " cried Stella, overcome at once by the recollection and the image, " could you like a man—especially if he was by way of admiring you, and talking nonsense to you and all that—to see you *ill* at sea ? If you can believe that you can believe anything, and there is no more for me to say."

The force of this argument was such that Miss Mildmay was quite startled out of her usual composure and reserve. She stared at Stella for a moment with wide-opened eyes.

" I did not think of that," she said in a tone of sudden conviction. " There is truth in what you say—certainly there is truth in what you say."

" Truth in it ! " cried the girl. " If you had only seen me—but I am very thankful you didn't see me—leaning over the side of that dreadful boat, not minding what waves went over me ! When you were a girl and had men after you, oh, Miss Mildmay, I ask you, would you have chosen to have them to see you *then ?* "

6

Miss Mildmay put the plate with the cold muffin off her
knees. She set down her empty cup. She felt the solemnity
of the appeal.

"No," she said, "if you put it to me like that, Stella, I
am obliged to allow I should not. And I may add," she went
on, looking round the room as if to a contradictory audience,
"I don't know any woman who would ; and that is my opinion, whatever anybody may say." She paused a moment with
a little triumphant air of having conducted to a climax a potent argument, looking round upon the baffled opponents. And
then she came down from that height and added in soft tones
of affectionate reproach : "But why did you go out with them
at all, Stella? When I was a girl, as you say, and had—I
never, never should have exposed myself to such risks, by going out in a boat with——"

"Oh, Miss Mildmay," cried Stella, "girls were better in
your time. You have always told us so. They were not perhaps so fond of—fun; they were in better order; they had
more—more— " said the girl, fishing for a word, which Mrs.
Shanks supplied her with by a movement of her lips behind
Miss Mildmay's back—"disciplined minds," Stella said with
an outburst of sudden utterance which was perilously near a
laugh.

"And you had a mother, Ruth Mildmay ? " said the plot-
ter behind, in tender notes.

"Yes ; I had a mother—an excellent mother, who would
not have permitted any of the follies I see around me. Jane
Shanks, you have conquered me with that word. Stella, my
dear, count on us both to stand by you, should that insolent
woman upstairs take anything upon her. Who is Lady Jane,
I should like to know? The daughter of a new-made man
—coals, or beer, or something ! A creation of this reign !
Stella, this will teach you, perhaps, who are your true friends."

And Miss Mildmay extended her arms and took the girl to
her bosom. Stella had got down on her knees for some reason of her own, which girls who are fond of throwing themselves about may understand, and therefore was within reach

of this unexpected embrace, and I am afraid laughed rather than sobbed on Miss Mildmay's lap; but the slight heaving of her shoulders in that position had the same effect, and sealed the bargain. The two ladies lingered a little after this, hoping that Lady Jane might come down. At least Miss Mildmay hoped so. Mrs. Shanks would have stolen humbly out to get into the midge at a little distance along the drive, not to disturb the big landau with the brown horses which stood large before the door. But Miss Mildmay would have none of that; she ordered the landau off with great majesty, and waved her hand indignantly for Perkins to "come round," as if the midge had been a chariot, a manœuvre which Stella promoted eagerly, standing in the doorway to see her visitors off with the most affectionate interest, while the other carriage paced sullenly up and down.

In the meantime Lady Jane had nearly completed her interview with Katherine in the midst of the large assortment of trumpery set out in readiness for the bazaar. "Oh, yes, I suppose they'll do well enough," she said, turning over the many coloured articles into which the Sliplin ladies had worked so many hours of their lives with careless hands. "Mark them cheap; the people here like to have bargains, and I'm sure they're not worth much. Of course, it was not the bazaar things I was thinking of. Tell me, Katherine, what is all this about Stella? I find the country ringing with it. What has she done to have her name mixed up with Charlie Somers and Algy Scott—two of the fastest men one knows? What has the child been doing? And how did she come to know these men?"

"She has been doing nothing, Lady Jane. It is the most wicked invention. I can tell you exactly how it happened. A little yacht was lying in the harbour, and they went up to papa's observatory, as he calls it, to look at it through his telescope, and papa himself was there, and he said——"

"But this is going very far back, surely? I asked you what Stella was doing with these men."

"And I am telling you," cried Katherine, red with indignation. "Papa said it was his yacht, which he had just bought, and they began to argue and bet about who it was from whom he had bought it, and he would not tell them; and then Stella said——"

"My dear Katherine, this elaborate explanation begins to make me fear——"

"Stella cried: 'Come down and look at it, while Kate orders tea.' You know how careless she is, and how she orders me about. They ran down by our private gate. It was to settle their bet, and I had tea laid out for them—it was quite warm then—under the trees. Well," said Katherine, pausing to take breath, "the first thing I saw was a white sail moving round under the cliff while I sat waiting for them to come back. And then papa came down screaming that it was the *Stella*, his yacht, and that a gale was blowing up. And then we spent the most dreadful evening, and darkness came on and we lost sight of the sail, and I thought I should have died and that it would kill papa."

Her breath went from her with this rapid narrative, uttered at full speed to keep Lady Jane from interrupting. What with indignation and what with alarm, the quickening of her heart was such that Katherine could say no more. She stopped short and stood panting, with her hand upon her heart.

"And at what hour," said Lady Jane icily, "did they come back?"

"Oh, I can't tell what hour it was. It seemed years and years to me. I got her back in a faint and wet to the skin, half dead with sickness and misery and cold. Oh, my poor, poor little girl! And now here are wicked and cruel people saying it is her fault. Her fault to risk her life and make herself ill and drive us out of our senses, papa and me!"

"Oh, Stella would not care very much for her papa and you, so long as she got her fun. So it was as bad as that, was it—a whole night at sea along with these two men? I could not have imagined any girl would have been such a fool."

"I will not hear my sister spoken of so. It was the men who were fools, or worse, taking her out when a gale was rising. What did she know about the signs of a gale? She thought of nothing but two minutes in the bay, just to see how the boat sailed. It was these men.''

'' What is the use of saying anything about the men? I dare say they enjoyed it thoroughly. It doesn't do them any harm. Why should they mind? It is the girl who ought to look out, for it is she who suffers. Good Heavens, to think that any girl should be such a reckless little fool !''

'' Stella has done nothing to be spoken of in that way.''

'' Oh, don't speak to me !'' said Lady Jane. '' Haven't I taken you both up and done all I could to give you your chance, you two? And this is my reward. Stella has done nothing? Why, Stella has just compromised herself in the most dreadful way. You know what sort of a man Charlie Somers is? No, you don't, of course. How should you, not living in a set where you were likely to hear? That's the worst, you know, of going out a little in one *monde* and be- longing to another all the time.''

''I don't know what you mean, Lady Jane,'' cried Kath- erine, on the edge of tears.

'' No ; there's no need you should know what I mean. A girl, in another position, that got to know Charlie Somers would have known more or less what he was. You, of course, have the disadvantages of both—acquaintance and then igno- rance. Who introduced Charlie Somers to your sister? The blame lies on her first of all.''

'' It was—they were all—at the hotel, and Stella thought it would be kind to ask Mrs. Seton to a picnic we were giv- ing——''

''Lottie Seton !'' cried Lady Jane, sitting down in the weakness of her consternation. '' Why, this is the most ex- traordinary thing of all !''

'' I see nothing extraordinary in the whole business,'' said Katherine, in a lofty tone.

'' Oh, my dear Katherine, for goodness' sake don't let me have any more of your innocent little-girlishness. Of course you see nothing ! You have no eyes, no sense, no—— Lottie Seton !—she to give over two of her own men to a pretty, silly, reckless little thing like Stella, just the kind for them! Well, that is the last thing I should have expected. Why, Lottie Seton is nothing without her tail. If they abandon her she is lost. She is asked to places because she is always sure to be able to bring a few men. What they can see in her nobody knows, but there it is—that's her faculty. And she actually gave over two of her very choicest——''

" You must excuse me, Lady Jane," said Katherine, " if I don't want to hear any more of Mrs. Seton and her men. They are exceedingly rude, stupid, disagreeable men. You may think it a fine thing for us to be elevated to the sphere in which we can meet men like Sir Charles Somers. I don't think so. I think he is detestable. I think he believes women to exist only for the purpose of amusing him and making him laugh, like an idiot, as he is !''

Lady Jane sat in her easy-chair and looked sardonically at the passion of the girl, whose face was crimson, whose voice was breaking. She was, with that horrible weakness which a high-spirited girl so resents in herself, so near an outbreak of crying that she could scarcely keep the tears within her eyes. The elder lady looked at her for some time in silence. The sight troubled her a little, and amused her a little also. It occurred to her to say, " You are surely in love with him yourself," which was her instinct, but for once forbore, out of a sort of awed sense that here was a creature who was outside of her common rules.

" He is not an idiot, however," she said at last. " I don't say he is intellectual. He does think, perhaps, that women exist, &c. So do most of them, my dear. You will soon find that out if you have anything to do with men. Still, for a good little girl, I have always thought you were nice, Katherine. It is for your sake more than hers that I feel inclined to do that silly little Stella a good turn. How could she be such a little fool ? Has she lived on this cliff half her life and doesn't know when a gale's coming on ? The more shame to her, then ! And I don't doubt that instead of being ashamed

she is quite proud of her adventure. And I hear, to make
things worse, that Algy Scott went and caught a bad cold over
it. That will make his mother and all her set furious with the
girl, and say everything about her. He's not going to die—
that's a good thing. If he had, she need never have shown
her impertinent little nose anywhere again. Lady Scott's an
inveterate woman. It will be bad enough as it is. How are
we to get things set right again ?"

"It is a pity you should take any trouble," said Katherine; "things are quite right, thank you. We have quite
enough in what you call our own *monde*."

"Well, and what do you find to object to in the word? It
is a very good word ; the French understand that sort of thing
better than we do. So you have quite enough to make you
happy in your own *monde ?* I don't think so—and I know
the world in general better than you do. And, what is more,
I am very doubtful indeed whether Stella thinks so."

"Oh, no," cried a little voice, and Stella, running in, threw
herself down at Lady Jane's feet, in the caressing attitude which
she had so lately held in spite of herself at Miss Mildmay's.
"Stella doesn't think so at all. Stella will be miserable if
you don't take her up and put things right for her, dear Lady
Jane. I have been a dreadful little fool. I know it, I know
it ; but I didn't mean it. I meant nothing but a little—fun.
And now there is nobody who can put everything right again
but you, and only you."

CHAPTER X.

LADY JANE THURSTON was a fine lady in due place and time; but on other occasions she was a robust countrywoman, ready to walk as sturdily as any man, or to undertake whatever athletic exercise was necessary. When she had gone downstairs again, and been served with a cup of warm tea (now those old cats were gone), she sent her carriage off that the horses might be put under shelter, not to speak of the men, and walked herself in the rain to the hotel, where the two young men were still staying, Captain Scott being as yet unable to be moved. It was one of those hotels which are so pretty in summer, all ivy and clematis, and balconies full of flowers. But on a wet day in October it looked squalid and damp, with its open doorway traversed by many muddy footsteps, and the wreaths of the withered creepers hanging limp about the windows. Lady Jane knew everybody about, and took in them all the interest which a member of the highest class—quite free from any doubt about her position—is able to take with so much more ease and naturalness than any other. The difference between the Tredgolds, for instance, and Mrs. Black of the hotel in comparison with herself was but slightly marked in her mind. She was impartially kind to both. The difference between them was but one of degree; she herself was of so different a species that the gradations did not count. In consequence of this she was more natural with the Blacks at the hotel than Katherine Tredgold, though in her way a Lady Bountiful, and universal friend, could ever have been. She was extremely interested to hear of Mrs. Black's baby, which had come most inopportunely, with a sick gentleman in the house, at least a fortnight before it was expected, and went upstairs to see the mother and administer a word or two of rebuke to the precipitate infant before she proceeded on her own proper errand. "Silly little thing, to rush into this rain sooner than it could help," she said, "but mind you don't do the same, my dear woman. Never trouble your head about the sick gentleman. Don't stir till you have got up your strength." And then she marched along the passages to the room in which Algy and Charlie sat, glum and tired to death, looking out at the dull sky and the raindrops on the window. They had invented a sort of sport with those same raindrops, watching them as they ran down and backing one against the other. There had just been a close race, and Algy's man had won to his great delight, when Lady Jane's sharp knock came to the door ; so that she went in to the sound of laughter pealing forth from the sick gentleman in such a manner as to reassure any anxious visitor as to the state of his lungs, at least.

"Well, you seem cheerful enough," Lady Jane said.

"Making the best of it," said Captain Scott.

"How do, Lady Jane ? I say, Algy, there's another starting. Beg pardon, too excitin' to stop. Ten to one on the little fellow. By George, looks as if he knew it, don't he now ! Done this time, old man—— "

"Never took it," said Algy, with a kick directed at his friend. "Shut up ! It's awfully kind of you coming to see a fellow—in such weather—Lady Jane ! "

"Yes," she said composedly, placing herself in the easiest chair. "It would be kind if I had come without a motive — but I don't claim that virtue. How are you, by the way ? Better, I hope."

"Awfully well—as fit as a——, but they won't let me budge in this weather. I've got a nurse that lords it over me, and the doctor, don't you know ?—daren't stir, not to save my life."

"And occupying your leisure with elevating pastimes," said Lady Jane.

"Don't be hard on a man when he's down—nothing to do," said Sir Charles. "Desert island sort of thing—Algy

educating mouse, and that sort of thing; hard lines upon
me.''

"Does he know enough?'' said Lady Jane with a polite air
of inquiry. "I am glad to find you both,'' she added, "and
not too busy evidently to give me your attention. How did
you manage, Algy, to catch such a bad cold?''

"Pneumonia, by Jove,'' the young man cried, inspired by
so inadequate a description.

"Well, pneumonia—so much the worse—and still more foolish for you who have a weak chest. How did you manage to
do it? I wonder if your mother knows, and why is it I don't
find her here at your bedside?''

"I say, don't tell her, Lady Jane; it's bad enough being
shut up here, without making more fuss, and the whole thing
spread all over the place.''

"What is the whole thing?'' said Lady Jane.

"Went out in a bit of a yacht,'' said Sir Charles, "clear
up a bet, that was why we did it. Caught in a gale—my
fault, not Algy's—says he saw it coming—I——''

"You were otherwise occupied, Charlie——''

"Shut up!'' Sir Charles was the speaker this time, with a
kick in the direction of his companion in trouble.

"I am glad to see you've got some grace left,'' said Lady
Jane. "Not you, Algy, you are beyond that—I know all
about it, however. It was little Stella Tredgold who ran away
with you—or you with her.''

Algy burst into a loud laugh. Sir Charles on his part said
nothing, but pulled his long moustache.

"Which is it? And what were the rights of it? and was
there any meaning in it? or merely fun, as you call it in your
idiotic way?''

"By Jove!'' was all the remark the chief culprit made.
Algy on his sofa kicked up his feet and roared again.

"Please don't think,'' said Lady Jane, "that I am going
to pick my words to please you. I never do it, and especially
not to a couple of boys whom I have known since ever they
were born, and before that. What do you mean by it, if it is

you, Charlie Somers ? I suppose, by Algy's laugh, that he is
not the chief offender this time. You know as well as I do
that you're not a man to take little girls about. I suppose you
must have sense enough to know that, whatever good opinion
you may have of yourself. Stella Tredgold may be a little fool,
but she's a girl I have taken up, and I don't mean to let her
be compromised. A girl that knew anything would have
known better than to mix up her name with yours. Now
what is the meaning of it ? You will just be so good as to inform me."

" Why, Cousin Jane, it was all the little thing herself."

" Shut up ! " said Sir Charles again, with another kick at
Algy's foot.

" Well ! " said Lady Jane, very magisterially. No judge
upon the bench could look more alarming than she. It is true
that her short skirts, her strong walking shoes, her very sever-
est hat and stiff feather that would bear the rain, were not so
impressive as flowing wigs and robes. She had not any of the
awe-inspiring trappings of the Law ; but she was law all the
same, the law of society, which tolerates a great many things,
and is not very nice about motives nor forbidding as to details,
but yet draws the line—if capriciously—sometimes, yet very
definitely, between what can and what cannot be done.

" Well," came at length hesitatingly through the culprit's
big moustache. " Don't know, really—have got anything
to say—no meaning at all. Bet to clear up—him and me ;
then sudden thought—just ten minutes—try the sails. No
harm in that, Lady Jane," he said, more briskly, recovering
courage, " afterwards gale came on ; no responsibility," he
cried, throwing up his hands.

" Fact it was she that was the keenest. I shan't shut up,"
cried Algy ; " up to anything, that little thing is. Never
minded a bit till it got very bad, and then gave in, but never
said a word. No fault of anybody, that is the truth. But
turned out badly—for me——" .

" And worse for her," said Lady Jane—" that is, without
me ; all the old cats will be down upon the girl " (which was

not true, the reader knows). " She is a pretty girl, Char-lie.''

Sir Charles, though he was so experienced a person, coloured faintly and gave a nod of his head.

"Stunner, by Jove!'' said Algy, "though I like the little plain one better,'' he added in a parenthesis.

"And a very rich girl, Sir Charles,'' Lady Jane said.

This time a faint " O—Oh '' came from under the big moustache.

" A *very* rich girl. The father is an old curmudgeon, but he is made of money, and he adores his little girl. I believe he would buy a title for her high and think it cheap.''

" Oh, I say ! '' exclaimed Sir Charles, with a colour more pronounced upon his cheek.

"Yours is not anything very great in that way,'' said the remorseless person on the bench, " but still it's what he would call a title, you know ; and I haven't the least doubt he would come down very handsomely. Old Tredgold knows very well what he is about.''

" Unexpected,'' said Sir Charles, "sort of serious jaw like this. Put it off, if you don't mind, till another time.''

" No time like the present,'' said Lady Jane. " Your father was a great friend of mine, Charlie Somers. He once proposed to me—very much left to himself on that occasion, you will say—but still it's true. So I might have been your mother, don't you see. I know your age, therefore, to a day. You are a good bit past thirty, and you have been up to nothing but mischief all your life.''

" Oh, I say now ! '' exclaimed Sir Charles again.

" Well, now here is a chance for you. Perhaps I began without thinking, but now I'm in great earnest. Here is really a chance for you. Stella's not so nice as her sister, as Algy there (I did not expect it of him) has the sense to see : but she's much more in your way. She is just your kind, a reckless little hot-headed—all for pleasure and never a thought of to-morrow. But that sort of thing is not so risky when you have a good fortune behind you, well tied down. Now,

Charlie, listen to me. Here is a capital chance for you; a man at your age, if he is ever going to do anything, should stop playing the fool. These boys even will soon begin to think you an old fellow. Oh, you needn't cry out! I know generations of them, and I understand their ways. A man should stop taking his fling before he gets to thirty-five. Why, Algy there would tell you that, if he had the spirit to speak up."

"I'm out of it," said Algy. "Say whatever you like, it has nothing to do with me."

"You see," said Lady Jane, with a little flourish of her hand, "the boy doesn't contradict me; he daren't contradict me, for it's truth. Now, as I say, here's a chance for you. Abundance of money, and a very pretty girl, whom you like." She made a pause here to emphasise her words. "Whom—you—like. Oh, I know very well what I'm saying. I am going to ask her over to Steephill and you can come too if you please; and if you don't take advantage of your opportunities, Sir Charles, why you have less sense than even I have given you credit for, and that is a great deal to say."

"Rather public, don't you think, for this sort of thing? Go in and win, before admiring audience. Don't relish exhibition. Prefer own way."

This Sir Charles said, standing at the window, gazing out, apparently insensible even of the raindrops, and turning his back upon his adviser.

"Well, take your own way. I don't mind what way you take, so long as you take my advice, which is given in your very best interests, I can tell you. Isn't the regiment ordered out to India, Algy?" she said, turning quickly upon the other. "And what do you mean to do?"

"Go, of course," he said—"the very thing for me, they say. And I'm not going to shirk either; see some sport probably out there."

"And Charlie?" said Lady Jane. There was no apparent connection between her previous argument and this question, yet the very distinct staccato manner in which she said these words called the attention.

Sir Charles, still standing by the window with his back to Lady Jane, once more muttered, "By Jove!" under his breath, or under his moustache, which came to the same thing.

"Oh, Charlie! He'll exchange, I suppose, and get out of it; too great a swell for India, he is. And how could he live out of reach of Pall Mall?"

"Well, I hope you'll soon be able to move, my dear boy; if the weather keeps mild and the rain goes off you had better come up to Steephill for a few days to get up your strength."

"Thanks, awf'lly," said Captain Scott. "I will with pleasure; and Cousin Jane, if that little prim one should be there——"

"She shan't, not for you, my young man, you have other things to think of. As for Charlie, I shall say no more to him; he can come too if he likes, but not unless he likes. Send me a line to let me know."

Sir Charles accompanied the visitor solemnly downstairs, but without saying anything until they reached the door, where to his surprise no carriage was waiting.

"Don't mean to say you walked—day like this?" he cried.

"No; but the horses and the men are more used to take care of themselves; they are to meet me at the Rectory. I am going there about this ridiculous bazaar. You can walk with me, if you like," she said.

He seized a cap from the stand and lounged out after her into the rain. "I say—don't you know?" he said, but paused there and added no more.

"Get it out," said Lady Jane.

After a while, as he walked along by her side, his hands deep in his pockets, the rain soaking pleasantly into his thick tweed coat, he resumed: "Unexpected serious sort of jaw that, before little beggar like Algy—laughs at everything."

"There was no chance of speaking to you alone," said Lady Jane almost apologetically.

"Suppose not. Don't say see my way to it. Don't deny, though—reason in it."

" And inclination, eh ? not much of one without the other, if I am any judge.''

" First-rate judge, by Jove ! '' Sir Charles said.

And he added no more. But when he took leave of Lady Jane at the Rectory he took a long walk by himself in the rain, skirting the gardens of the Cliff and getting out upon the downs beyond, where the steady downfall penetrated into him, soaking the tweed in a kind of affectionate natural way as of a material prepared for the purpose. He strolled along with his hands in his pockets and the cap over his eyes as if it had been a summer day, liking it all the better for the wetness and the big masses of the clouds and the leaden monotone of the sea. It was all so dismal that it gave him a certain pleasure ; he seemed all the more free to think of his own concerns, to consider the new panorama opened before him, which perhaps, however, was not so new as Lady Jane supposed. She had forced open the door and made him look in, giving all the details ; but he had been quite conscious that it had been there before, within his reach, awaiting his inspection. There were a great many inducements, no doubt, to make that fantastic prospect real if he could. He did not want to go to India, though indeed it would have been very good for him in view of his sadly reduced finances and considerably affected credit in both senses of that word. He had not much credit at headquarters, that he knew ; he was not what people called a good officer. No doubt he would have been brave enough had there been fighting to do, and he was not disliked by his men, his character of a '' careless beggar '' being quite as much for good as for evil among those partial observers ; but his credit in higher regions was not great. Credit in the other sense of the word was a little failing too, tradesmen having a wonderful *flair* as to a man's resources and the rising and falling of his account at his bankers. It would do him much good to go to India and devote himself to his profession ; but then he did not want to go. Was it last of all or first of all that another motive came in, little Stella herself to wit, though she broke down so much in her attempts to imitate Lottie Seton's

ways, and was not amusing at all in that point of view?
Stella had perhaps behaved better on that impromptu yachting
trip than she was herself aware.   Certainly she was far more
guilty in the beginning of it than she herself allowed.   But
when the night was dark and the storm high, she had—what
had she done?   Behaved very well and made the men admire
her pluck, or behaved very badly and frightened them—I cannot tell ; anyhow, she had been very natural, she had done and
said only what it came into her head to say and to do, without
any affectation or thought of effect ; and the sight of the little
girl, very silly and yet so entirely herself, scolding them, up-
braiding them, though she was indeed the most to blame, yet
bearing her punishment not so badly after all and not without
sympathy for them, had somehow penetrated Charles Somers'
very hardened heart.   She was a nice little girl—she was a
very pretty little girl—she was a creature one would not tire
of even if she was not amusing like Lottie Seton.   If a man
was to have anything more to do with her, it was to be hoped
she never would be amusing like Lottie Seton.   He paced
along the downs he never knew how long, pondering these
questions ; but he was not a man very good at thinking.   In
the end he came to no more than a very much strengthened
conviction that Stella Tredgold was a very pretty little girl.

CHAPTER XI.

IT shut the mouths of all the gossips, or rather it afforded a new but less exciting subject of comment, when it was known that Stella Tredgold had gone off on a visit to Steephill. I am not sure that Mrs. Shanks and Miss Mildmay did not feel themselves deceived a little. They had pledged themselves to Stella's championship in a moment of enthusiasm, stimulated thereto by a strong presumption of the hostility of Lady Jane. Miss Mildmay in particular had felt that she had a foeman worthy of her steel, and that it would be an enterprise worth her while to bring the girl out with flying colours from any boycotting or unfriendly action directed by the great lady of the district; and to find that Stella had been taken immediately under Lady Jane's wing disturbed her composure greatly. There was great talk over the railing between the ladies, and even, as it became a little too cold for these outdoor conferences, in the drawing-rooms in both houses, under the shade of the verandah which made these apartments a little dark and gloomy at this season of the year. But I must not occupy the reader's time with any account of these talks, for as a matter of fact the ladies had committed themselves and given their promise, which, though offended, they were too high-minded to take back. It conduced, however, to a general cooling of the atmosphere about them, that what everybody in Sliplin and the neighbourhood now discussed was not Stella's escapade, but Stella's visit to Steephill, where there was a large party assembled, and where her accomplices in that escapade were to be her fellow-guests. What did this mean was now the question demanded? Had Lady Jane any intentions in respect to Stella? Was there "anything between" her and either of

7

these gentlemen ?   But this was a question to which no one as
yet had any reply.

Stella herself was so much excited by the prospect that all
thought of the previous adventure died out of her mind.
Save at a garden party, she had never been privileged to enter
Lady Jane's house except on the one occasion when she and
Katherine stayed all night after a ball ; and then there were
many girls besides themselves, and no great attention paid to
them.   But to be the favoured guest, almost the young lady
of the house, among a large company was a very different
matter.   Telegrams flew to right and left—to dressmakers, mil-
liners, glovers, and I don't know how many more.   Stevens, the
maid, whom at present she shared with Katherine, but who was,
of course, to accompany her to Steephill as her own separate
attendant, was despatched to town after the telegrams with
more detailed and close instructions.   The girl shook off all
thought both of her own adventure and of her companions in
it.   She already felt herself flying at higher game.   There was
a nephew of Lady Jane's, a young earl, who, it was known,
was there, a much more important personage than any trumpery baronet.   This she informed her father, to his great delight, as he gave her his paternal advice with much unction
the evening before she went away.

" That's right, Stella," he said, " always fly at the highest—
and them that has most money.   This Sir Charles, I wager
you anything, he is after you for your fortune.   I dare say he
hasn't a penny.   He thinks he can come and hang up his hat
and nothing more to do all his life.   But he'll find he's a bit
mistaken with me."

" It isn't very nice of you, papa," said Stella, " to think I
am only run after because I have money—or because you have
money, for not much of it comes to me."

" Ain't she satisfied with her allowance ? " said the old
gentleman, looking over Stella's head at her elder sister.
" It's big enough.   Your poor mother would have dressed
herself and me and the whole family off half of what that
little thing gets through.   It is a deal better the money should

be in my hands, my pet. And if any man comes after you,
you may take your oath he shan't have you cheap. He'll
have to put down shillin' for shillin', I can tell you. You
find out which is the one that has the most money, and go for
him. Bad's the best among all them new earls and things,
but keep your eyes open, Stella, and mark the one that's best
off.'' Here he gave utterance to a huge chuckle. '' Most
people would think she would never find that out ; looks as
innocent as a daisy, don't she, Katie ? But she's got the old
stuff in her all the same.''

''I don't know what you call the old stuff,'' said Stella,
indignant; ''it must be very nasty stuff. What does your
horrid money do for me ? I have not half enough to dress on,
and you go over my bills with your spectacles as if I were
Simmons, the cook. If you had a chest full of diamonds and
rubies, and gave us a handful now and then, that is the kind
of richness I should like ; but I have no jewels at all,'' cried
the girl, putting up her hand to her neck, which was encircled
by a modest row of small pearls ; ''and they will all be in
their diamonds and things.''

Mr. Tredgold's countenance fell a little. '' Is that true ? ''
he said. '' Katie, is that true ? ''

'' Girls are not expected to wear diamonds,'' said Katie ;
'' at least, I don't think so, papa.''

'' Oh, what does she know ? That's all old-fashioned
nowadays. Girls wear just whatever they can get to wear, and
why shouldn't girls wear diamonds ? Don't you think I
should set them off better than Lady Jane, papa ? '' cried
Stella, tossing her young head.

Mr. Tredgold was much amused by this question; he
chuckled and laughed over it till he nearly lost his breath.
'' All the difference between parchment and white satin, ain't
there, Katie ? Well, I don't say as you mightn't have some
diamonds. They're things that always keep their value. It's
not a paying investment, but, anyhow, you're sure of your
capital. They don't wear out, don't diamonds. So that's
what you're after, Miss Stella. Just you mind wnat you're

about, and don't send me any young fool without a penny in
his pocket, but a man that can afford to keep you like you've
been kept all your life.   And I'll see about the jewels,'' Mr.
Tredgold said.

The consequence of this conversation was that little Stella
appeared at Steephill, notwithstanding her vapoury and girlish toilettes of white chiffon and other such airy fabrics, with
a *rivière* of diamonds sparkling round her pretty neck, which,
indeed, did them much greater justice than did Lady Jane.
Ridiculous for a little girl, all the ladies said—but yet impressive more or less, and suggestive of illimitable wealth on
the part of the foolish old man, who, quite unaware what was
suitable, bedizened his little daughter like that.   And Stella
was excited by her diamonds and by the circumstances, and
the fact that she was the youngest there, and the most fun ;
for who would expect fun from portly matrons or weather-
beaten middle age, like Lady Jane's?   To do her justice, she
never or hardly ever thought, as she might very well have
done, that she was the prettiest little person in the party.
On the contrary, she was a little disposed to be envious of
Lady Mary, the niece of Lady Jane and sister of the Earl,
who was not pretty in the least, but who was tall, and had a
figure which all the ladies' maids, including Stevens, admired
much.   ''Oh, if you only was as tall as Lady Mary, Miss
Stella,'' Stevens said.   ''Oh, I wish as you had that kind of
figger—her waist ain't more than eighteen inches, for all as
she's so tall.''   Stella had felt nearly disposed to cry over her
inferiority.   She was as light as a feather in her round and
blooming youth, but she was not so slim as Lady Mary.   It
was a consolation to be able to say to herself that at least she
was more fun.

Lady Mary, it turned out, was not fun at all ; neither most
surely was the young Earl.   He talked to Stella, whom, and
her diamonds, he approached gravely, feeling that the claims
of beauty were as real as those of rank or personal importance,
and that the qualification of youth was as worthy of being
taken into consideration as that of age, for he was a philoso-

pher about University Extension, and the great advantage it was to the lower classes to share the culture of those above them.

"Oh, I am sure I am not cultured at all," cried Stella. "I am as ignorant as a goose. I can't spell any big words, or do any of the things that people do."

"You must not expect to take me in with professions of ignorance," said the Earl with a smile. "I know how ladies read, and how much they do nowadays—perhaps in a different way from us, but just as important."

"Oh, no, no," cried Stella; "it is quite true, I can't spell a bit," and her eyes and her diamonds sparkled, and a certain radiance of red and white, sheen of satin, and shimmer of curls, and fun and audacity, and youth, made a sort of atmosphere round her, by which the grave youth, prematurely burdened by the troubles of his country and the lower classes, felt dazzled and uneasy, as if too warm a sun was shining full upon him.

"Where's a book?" cried Algy Scott, who sat by in the luxury of his convalescence. "Let's try; I don't believe any of you fellows could spell this any more than Miss Stella— here you are—sesquipedalian. Now, Miss Tredgold, there is your chance."

Stella put her pretty head on one side, and her hands behind her. This was a sort of thing which she understood better than University Extension. "S-e-s," she began, and then broke off. "Oh, what is the next syllable? Break it down into little, quite little syllables—*quip*—I know that, q-u-i-p. There, oh, help me, help me, someone!" There was quite a crush round the little shining, charming figure, as she turned from one to another in pretended distress, holding out her pretty hands. And then there were several tries, artificially unsuccessful, and the greatest merriment in the knot which surrounded Stella, thinking it all "great fun." The Earl, with a smile on his face which was not so superior as he thought, but a little tinged by the sense of being "out of it," was edged outside of this laughing circle, and Lady Mary came and placed her arm within his to console him. The brother and sister lingered for a moment looking on with a disappointed chill, though they were so superior; but it became clear to his lordship from that moment, though with a little envy in the midst of the shock and disapproval, that Stella Tredgold, unable to spell and laughing over it with all those fellows, was not the heroine for him.

Lady Jane, indeed, would have been both angry and disappointed had the case turned out otherwise; for her nephew was not poor and did not stand in need of any *mésalliance*, whereas she had planned the whole affair for Charlie Somers' benefit and no other. And, indeed, the plan worked very well. Sir Charles had no objection at all to the *rôle* assigned him. Stella did not require to be approached with any show of deference or devotion; she was quite willing to be treated as a chum, to respond to a call more curt than reverential. "I say, come on and see the horses." "Look here, Miss Tredgold, let's have a stroll before lunch." "Come along and look at the puppies." These were the kind of invitations addressed to her; and Stella came along tripping, buttoning up her jacket, putting on a cap, the first she could find, upon her fluffy hair. She was *bon camarade*, and did not "go in for sentiment." It was she who was the first to call him Charlie, as she had been on the eve of doing several times in the Lottie Seton days, which now looked like the age before the Flood to this pair.

"Fancy only knowing you through that woman," cried Stella; "and you should have heard how she bullied me after that night of the sail!"

"Jealous," said Sir Charles in his moustache. "Never likes to lose any fellow she knows."

"But she was not losing you!" cried Stella with much innocence. "What harm could it do to her that you spent one evening with—anyone else?"

"Knows better than that, does Lottie," the laconic lover said.

"Oh, stuff!" cried Stella. "It was only to make herself disagreeable. But she never was any friend of mine."

"Not likely. Lottie knows a thing or two. Not so soft as all that. Put you in prison if she could—push you out of her way."

"But I was never in her way," cried Stella.

At which Sir Charles laughed loud and long. "Tell you what it is—as bad as Lottie. Can't have you talk to fellows like Uppin'ton. Great prig, not your sort at all. Call myself your sort, Stella, eh? Since anyhow you're mine."

"I don't know what you mean by your sort," Stella said, but with downcast eyes.

"Yes, you do—chums—always get on. Awf'lly fond of you, don't you know? Eh? Marriage awf'l bore, but can't be helped. Look here! Off to India if you won't have me," the wooer said.

"Oh, Charlie!"

"Fact; can't stand it here any more—except you'd have me, Stella."

"I don't want," said Stella with a little gasp, "to have any one—just now."

"Not surprised," said Sir Charles, "marriage awf'l bore. Glad regiment's ordered off; no good in England now. Knock about in India; get knocked on the head most likely. No fault of yours—if you can't cotton to it, little girl."

"Oh, Charlie! but I don't want you to go to India," Stella said.

"Well, then, keep me here. There are no two ways of it," he said more distinctly than usual, holding out his hand.

And Stella put her hand with a little hesitation into his. She was not quite sure she wanted to do so. But she did not want him to go away. And though marriage was an awf'l bore, the preparations for it were "great fun." And he was her sort—they were quite sure to get on. She liked him better than any of the others, far better than that prig, Uffington, though he was an earl. And it would be nice on the whole to be called my Lady, and not Miss any longer. And Charlie was very nice; she liked him far better than any of the others. That was the refrain of Stella's thoughts as she turned over in her own room all she had done. To be married at twenty is pleasant too. Some girls nowadays do not marry till thirty or near it, when they are almost decrepit. That was what would happen to Kate; if, indeed, she ever married at all. Stella's mind then jumped to a consideration of the wedding presents and who would give her—what, and then to her own appearance in her wedding dress, walking down the aisle of the old church. What a fuss all the Stanleys would be in about the decorations; and then there were the bridesmaids to be thought of. Decidedly the preliminaries would be great fun. Then, of course, afterwards she would be presented and go into society—real society—not this mere country house business. On the whole there was a great deal that was desirable in it, all round.

"Now have over the little prim one for me," said Algy Scott. "I say, cousin Jane, you owe me that much. It was I that really suffered for that little thing's whim—and to get no good of it; while Charlie—no, I don't want this one, the little prim one for my money. If you are going to have a dance to end off with, have her over for me."

"I may have her over, but not for you, my boy," said Lady Jane. "I have the fear of your mother before my eyes, if you haven't. A little Tredgold girl for my Lady Scott! No, thank you, Algy, I am not going to fly in your mother's face, whatever you may do."

"Somebody will have to fly in her face sooner or later," Algy said composedly; "and, mind you, my mother would like to tread gold as well as any one."

"Don't abandon every principle, Algy. I can forgive anything but a pun."

"It's such a very little one," he said.

And Lady Jane did ask Katherine to the dance, who was very much bewildered by the state of affairs, by her sister's engagement, which everybody knew about, and the revolution which had taken place in everything, without the least intimation being conveyed to those most concerned. Captain Scott's attentions to herself were the least of her thoughts. She was impatient of the ball—impatient of further delay. Would it all be so easy as Stella thought? Would the old man, as they called him, take it with as much delight as was expected? She pushed Algy away from her mind as if he had been a fly in the great preoccupations of her thoughts.

CHAPTER XII.

"Bravo, Charlie !" said Lady Jane. "I never knew any-thing better or quicker done. My congratulations ! You have proved yourself a man of sense and business. Now you've got to tackle the old man."

"Nothin' of th' sort," said Sir Charles, with a dull blush covering all that was not hair of his countenance. "Sweet on little girl. Like her awf'lly ; none of your business for me."

"So much the better, and I respect you all the more ; but now comes the point at which you have really to show your-self a hero and a man of mettle—the old father———"

Sir Charles walked the whole length of the great drawing-room and back again. He pulled at his moustache till it seemed likely that it might come off. He thrust one hand deep into his pocket, putting up the corresponding shoulder. "Ah !" he said with a long-drawn breath, "there's the rub." He was not aware that he was quoting any one, but yet would have felt more or less comforted by the thought that a fellow in his circumstances might have said the same thing before him.

"Yes, there's the rub indeed," said his sympathetic but amused friend and backer-up. "Stella is the apple of his eye."

"Shows sense in that."

"Well, perhaps," said Lady Jane doubtfully. She thought the little prim one might have had a little consideration too, being partially enlightened as to a certain attractiveness in Katherine through the admiration of Algy Scott. "Any-how, it will make it all the harder. But that's doubtful too. He will probably like his pet child to be Lady Somers, which sounds very well. Anyhow, you must settle it with him at once. I can't let it be said that I let girls be proposed to in my house, and that afterwards the men don't come up to the scratch."

" Not my way," said Sir Charles. " Never refuse even it were a harder jump than that."

" Oh, you don't know how hard a jump it is till you try," said Lady Jane. But she did not really expect that it would be hard. That old Tredgold should not be pleased with such a marriage for his daughter did not occur to either of them. Of course Charlie Somers was poor ; if he had been rich it was not at all likely that he would have wanted to marry Stella ; but Lady Somers was a pretty title, and no doubt the old man would desire to have his favourite child so distinguished. Lady Jane was an extremely sensible woman, and as likely to estimate the people round her at their just value as anybody I know ; but she could not get it out of her head that to be hoisted into society was a real advantage, however it was accomplished, whether by marriage or in some other way. Was she right ? was she wrong ? Society is made up of very silly people, but also there the best are to be met, and there is something in the Freemasonry within these imaginary boundaries which is attractive to the wistful imagination without. But was Mr. Tredgold aware of these advantages, or did he know even what it was, or that his daughters were not in it ? This was what Lady Jane did not know. Somers, it need not be said, did not think on the subject. What he thought of was that old Tredgold's money would enable him to marry, to fit out his old house as it ought to be, and restore it to its importance in his county, and, in the first place of all, would prevent the necessity of going to India with his regiment. This, indeed, was the first thing in his mind, after the pleasure of securing Stella, which, especially since all the men in the house had so flattered and ran after her, had been very gratifying to him. He loved her as well as he understood love or she either. They were on very equal terms.

Katherine did not give him any very warm reception when the exciting news was communicated to her; but then Katherine was the little prim one, and not effusive to any one. "She is always like that," Stella had said—"a stick! but she'll stand up for me, whatever happens, all the same."

"I say," cried Sir Charles alarmed—"think it'll be a hard job, eh? with the old man, don't you know?"

"You will please," said Stella with determination, "speak more respectfully of papa. I don't know if it'll be a hard job or not—but you're big enough for that, or anything, I hope."

"Oh, I'm big enough," he said; but there was a certain faltering in his tone.

He did not drive with the two girls on their return to the Cliff the morning after the ball, but walked in to Sliplin the five miles to pull himself together. He had no reason that he knew of to feel anxious. The girl—it was by this irreverent title that he thought of her, though he was so fond of her— liked him, and her father, it was reported, saw everything with Stella's eyes. She was the one that he favoured in everything. No doubt it was she who would have the bulk of his fortune. Sir Charles magnanimously resolved that he would not see the other wronged—that she should always have her share, whatever happened. He remembered long afterwards the aspect of the somewhat muddy road, and the hawthorn hedges with the russet leaves hanging to them still, and here and there a bramble with the intense red of a leaf lighting up the less brilliant colour. Yes, she should always have her share! He had a half-conscious feeling that to form so admirable a resolution would do him good in the crisis that was about to come.

Mr. Tredgold stood at the door to meet his daughters when they came home, very glad to see them, and to know that everybody was acquainted with the length of Stella's stay at Steephill, and the favour shown her by Lady Jane, and de- lighted to have them back also, and to feel that these two pretty creatures—and especially the prettiest of the two—were his own private property, though there were no girls like them, far or near. "Well," he said, "so here you are back again—

glad to be back again I'll be bound, though you've been among all the grandees! Nothing like home, is there, Stella, after all?'' (He said 'ome, alas! and Stella felt it as she had never done before.) '' Well, you are very welcome to your old pa. Made a great sensation, did you, little 'un, diamonds and all? How did the diamonds go down, eh, Stella? You must give them to me to put in my safe, for they're not safe, valuable things like that, with you.''

'' Dear papa, do you think all that of the diamonds?'' said Stella. '' They are only little things—nothing to speak of. You should have seen the diamonds at Steephill. If you think they are worth putting in the safe, pray do so; but I should not think of giving you the trouble. Well, we didn't come back to think of the safe and my little *rivière*, did we, Kate? As for that, the pendant you have given her is handsomer of its kind, papa.''

'' Couldn't leave Katie out, could I? when I was giving you such a thing as that?'' said Mr. Tredgold a little confused.

'' Oh, I hope you don't think I'm jealous,'' cried Stella. '' Kate doesn't have things half nice enough. She ought to have them nicer than mine, for she is the eldest. We amused ourselves very well, thank you, papa. Kate couldn't move without Algy Scott after her wherever she turned. You'll have him coming over here to make love to you, papa.''

'' I think you might say a word of something a great deal more important, Stella.''

'' Oh, let me alone with your seriousness. Papa will hear of that fast enough, when you know Charlie is—— I'm going upstairs to take off my things. I'll bring the diamonds if I can remember,'' she added, pausing for a moment at the door and waving her hand to her father, who followed her with delighted eyes.

'' What a saucy little thing she is!'' he said. '' You and I have a deal to put up with from that little hussy, Katie, haven't we? But there aren't many like her all the same, are there? We shouldn't like it if we were to lose her. She keeps everything going with her impudent little ways.''

"You are in great danger of losing her, papa. There is a man on the road——"

"What's that—what's that, Katie? A man that is after my Stella? A man to rob me of my little girl? Well, I like 'em to come after her, I like to see her with a lot at her feet. And who's this one? The man with a handle to his name?"

"Yes; I suppose you would call it a handle. It was one of the men that were out in the boat with her—Sir Charles——"

"Oh!" said Mr. Tredgold, with his countenance falling. "And why didn't the t'other one—his lordship—come forward? I don't care for none of your Sir Charleses—reminds me of a puppy, that name."

"The puppies are King Charles's, papa. I don't know why the Earl did not come forward; because he didn't want to, I suppose. And, indeed, he was not Stella's sort at all."

"Stella's sort! Stella's sort!" cried the old man. "What right has Stella to have a sort when she might have got a crown to put on her pretty head. Coronet? Yes, I know; it's all the same. And where is this fellow? Do you mean that you brought him in my carriage, hiding him somewhere between your petticoats? I will soon settle your Sir Charles, unless he can settle shilling to shilling down."

"Sir Charles is walking," said Katherine; "and, papa, please to remember that Stella is fond of him, she is really fond of him; she is—in love with him. At least I think so, otherwise—— You would not do anything to make Stella unhappy, papa?"

"You leave that to me," said the old man; but he chuckled more than ever.

Katherine did not quite understand her father, but she concluded that he was not angry—that he could not be going to receive the suitor unfavourably, that there was nothing to indicate a serious shock of any kind. She followed Stella upstairs, and went into her room to comfort her with this assurance; for which I cannot say that Stella was at all grateful.

"Not angry? Why should he be angry?" the girl cried. "Serious? I never expected him to be serious. What could he find to object to in Charlie? I am not anxious about it at all.''

Katherine withdrew into her own premises, feeling herself much humbled and set down. But somehow she could not make herself happy about that chuckle of Mr. Tredgold's. It was not a pleasant sound to hear.

Sir Charles Somers felt it very absurd that he should own a tremor in his big bosom as he walked up the drive, all fringed with its rare plants in every shade of autumn colour. It was not a long drive, and the house by no means a "place," but only a seaside villa, though (as Mr. Tredgold hoped) the costliest house in the neighbourhood. The carriage had left fresh marks upon the gravel, which were in a kind of a way the footsteps of his beloved, had the wooer been sentimental enough to think of that. What he did think of was whether the old fellow would see him at once and settle everything before lunch, comfortably, or whether he would walk into a family party with the girls hanging about, not thinking it worth while to take off their hats before that meal was over. There might be advantage in this. It would put a little strength into himself, who was unquestionably feeling shaky, ridiculous as that was, and would be the better, after his walk, of something to eat ; and it might also put old Tredgold in a better humour to have his luncheon before this important interview. But, on the other hand, there was the worry of the suspense. Somers did not know whether he was glad or sorry when he was told that Mr. Tredgold was in his library, and led through the long passages to that warm room which was at the back of the house. A chair was placed for him just in front of the fire as he had foreseen, and the day, though damp, was warm, and he had heated himself with his long walk.

"Sit down, sit down, Sir Charles," said the old gentleman, whose writing-table was placed at one side, where he had the benefit of the warmth without the glare of the fire. And he leant amicably and cheerfully across the corner of the table, and said, "What can I do for you this morning?" rubbing his hands. He looked so like a genial money-lender before

the demands of the borrower are exposed to him, that Sir
Charles, much more accustomed to that sort of thing than to
a prospective father-in-law, found it very difficult not to propose, instead of for Stella, that Mr. Tredgold should do him a
little bill.   He got through his statement of the case in a most
confused and complicated way.   It was indeed possible, if it
had not been for the hint received beforehand, that the old
man would not have picked up his meaning ; as it was, he listened patiently with a calm face of amusement, which was the
most aggravating thing in the world.

"Am I to understand," he said at last, " that you are making me a proposal for Stella, Sir Charles?   Eh ?   It is for
Stella, is it, and not for any other thing ?   Come, that's a good
thing to understand each other.   Stella is a great pet of mine.
She is a very great pet.   There is nobody in the world that I
think like her, or that I would do so much for."

"M' own feelings—to a nicety—but better expressed," Sir
Charles said.

"That girl has had a deal of money spent on her, Sir
Charles, first and last; you wouldn't believe the money that
girl has cost me, and I don't say she ain't worth it.   But she's
a very expensive article and has been all her life.   It's right
you should look that in the face before we get any forwarder.
She has always had everything she has fancied, and she'll cost
her husband a deal of money, when she gets one, as she has
done me."

This address made Somers feel very small, for what could he
reply ?   To have been quite truthful, the only thing he could
have said would have been, "I hope, sir, you will give her so
much money that it will not matter how expensive she is ; "
but this he could not say.   "I know very well," he stam-
mered, "a lady—wants a lot of things ;—hope Stella—will
never—suffer, don't you know ?—through giving her to me."

Ah, how easy it was to say that !   But not at all the sort of
thing to secure Stella's comfort, or her husband's either, which,
on the whole, was the most important of the two to Sir Charles.

"That's just what we've got to make sure of," said old

Tredgold, chuckling more than ever. There was no such joke
to the old man as this which he was now enjoying. And he
did not look forbidding or malevolent at all. Though what
he said was rather alarming, his face seemed to mean nothing
but amiability and content. " Now, look here, Sir Charles,
I don't know what your circumstances are, and they would be
no business of mine, but for this that you've been telling me ;
you young fellows are not very often flush o' money, but you
may have got it tied up, and that sort of thing. I don't give
my daughter to any man as can't count down upon the table
shillin' for shillin' with me." This he said very deliberately,
with an emphasis on every word ; then he made a pause, and,
putting his hand in his pocket, produced a large handful of
coins, which he proceeded to tell out in lines upon the table
before him. Sir Charles watched him in consternation for a
moment, and then with a sort of fascination followed his example. By some happy chance he had a quantity of change
in his pocket. He began with perfect gravity to count it out
on his side, coin after coin, in distinct rows. The room was
quite silent, the air only moved by the sound of a cinder falling now and then on the hearth and the clink of the money
as the two actors in this strange little drama went on with the
greatest seriousness counting out coin after coin.

When they had both finished they looked up and met each
other's eyes. Then Mr. Tredgold threw himself back in his
chair, kicking up his cloth-shod feet. " See," he cried, with
a gurgle of laughter in his throat, " that's the style for me."

He was pleased to have his fine jest appreciated, and doubly
amused by the intense and puzzled gravity of his companion's
face.

" Don't seem to have as many as you," Sir Charles said.
" Five short, by Jove."

" Shillin's don't matter," said the old man ; " but suppose
every shillin' was five thousand pounds, and where would you
be then ? eh ? perhaps you would go on longer than I could.
What do I know of your private affairs ? But that's what the
man that gets Stella will have to do—table down his money,

8

cent for cent, five thousand for five thousand, as I do. I know
what my little girl costs a year.   I won't have her want for
anything, if it's ever so unreasonable ; so, my fine young man,
though you've got a handle to your name, unless you can show
the colour of your money, my daughter is not for you."

Sir Charles Somers's eyes had acquired a heavy stare of astonishment and consternation.   What he said in his disappointment and horror he did not himself know—only one part of it
fully reached the outer air, and that was the unfortunate words,
" money of her own."

" Money of her own ! " cried old Tredgold.   " Oh, yes, she's
got money of her own—plenty of money of her own—but not
to keep a husband upon.   No, nor to keep herself either.   Her
husband's got to keep her, when she gets one.   If I count out
to the last penny of my fortune he's got to count with me.   I'll
give her the equal.   I'll not stint a penny upon her ; but give
my money or her money, it's all the same thing, to keep up
another family, her husband and her children, and the whole
race of them—no, Sir Charles Somers," cried Mr. Tredgold,
hastily shuffling his silver into his pocket, " that's not good
enough for me."

Saying which he jumped up in his cloth shoes and began to
walk about the room, humming to himself loudly something
which he supposed to be a tune.   Sir Charles, for his part, sat
for a long time gazing at his money on the table.   He did not
take it up as Tredgold had done.   He only stared at it va-
cantly, going over it without knowing, line by line.   Then
he, too, rose slowly.

" Can't count with you," he said.   " Know I can't.
Chance this—put down what I put down—no more.   Got to
go to India in that case.   Never mind, Stella and I——"

" Don't you speak any more of Stella.   I won't have it.
Go to India, indeed—my little girl !   I will see you—further
first.   I will see you at the bottom of the sea first !   No.   If
you can count with me, something like, you can send your
lawyer to me.   If you can't, do you think I'm a man to put
pounds again' your shillin's ?   Not I !   And I advise you just

to give it up, Sir Charles Somers, and speak no more about Stella to me.''

It was with the most intense astonishment that Charlie Somers found himself out of doors, going humbly back along that drive by which he had approached so short a time before, as he thought, his bride, his happiness, and his luncheon. He went dismally away without any of them, stupefied, not half conscious what had happened; his tail more completely between his legs, to use his own simile, than whipped dog ever had. He had left all his shillings on the table laid out in two shining rows. But he did not think of his shillings. He could not think. His consternation made him speechless both in body and in soul.

It was not till late in the afternoon, when he had regained his self-command a little, that he began to ask himself the question, What would Stella do? Ah, what would Stella do? That was another side of the question altogether.

CHAPTER XIII.

THERE was great consternation at Steephill when Somers came back, not indeed so cowed as when he left the Cliff, but still with the aspect more or less of a man who had been beaten and who was extremely surprised to find himself so. He came back, to make it more remarkable, while the diminished party were still at luncheon, and sat down humbly in the lowest place by the side of the governess to partake of the mutton and rice pudding which Lady Jane thought most appropriate when the family was alone. Algy was the only stranger left of all the large party which had dispersed that morning, the few remaining men having gone out to shoot; and to Algy, as an invalid, the roast mutton was of course quite appropriate.

" What luck ! without even your lunch ! " they cried out— Algy with a roar (the fellow was getting as strong as an elephant) of ridicule and delight.

" As you see," said Sir Charles with a solemnity which he could not shake off. The very governess divined his meaning, and that sharp little Janey—the horrid little thing, a mite of fourteen. " Oh, didn't Stella ask you to stay to lunch ? Didn't they give you anything to eat after your walk ? " that precocious critic cried. And Sir Charles felt with a sensation of hatred, wishing to kill them all, that his own aspect was enough to justify all their jokes. He was as serious as a mustard-pot; he could not conjure up a laugh on his face ; he could not look careless and indifferent or say a light word. His tail was between his legs ; he felt it, and he felt sure that everybody must see it, down to the little boys, who, with spoonfuls of rice suspended, stared at him with round blue eyes ; and he dared not say, " Confound the little beggars ! " before Lady Jane.

"What is the matter?" she asked him, hurrying him after luncheon to her own room away from the mocking looks of the governess—she too mixing herself up with it!—and the gibes of Algy. "For goodness' sake," she cried, "don't look as if you had been having a whipping, Charlie Somers! What has been done to you? Have you quarrelled with Stella on the way?"

Sir Charles walked to the window, pulling his moustache, and stood there looking out, turning his back on Lady Jane. A window is a great resource to a man in trouble. "Old man turned me off," he said.

"What? *What?* The old man turned you off? Oh!" cried Lady Jane in a tone of relief; "so long as it was only the old man!"

Sir Charles stood by the window for some time longer, and then he turned back to the fire, near which Lady Jane had comfortably seated herself. She was much concerned about him, yet not so much concerned as to interfere with her own arrangements—her chair just at the right angle, her screen to preserve her from the glare. She kept opening and looking at the notes that lay on her table while she talked to him.

"Oh, old Tredgold," she said. "He was bound to object at first. About money, I suppose? That of course is the only thing he knows anything about. Did he ask you what you would settle upon her? You should have said boldly, 'Somerton,' and left him to find out the rest. But I don't suppose you had the sense to stop his mouth like that. You would go and enter into explanations."

"Never got so far," said Sir Charles. "He that stopped my mouth. Game to lay down pound for pound with him, or else no go."

"Pound for pound with him!" cried Lady Jane in consternation. She was so much startled that she pushed back her chair from her writing-table, and so came within the range of the fire and disorganized all her arrangements. "Now I think of it," she said, "(pull that screen this way, Charlie) I have heard him say something like that. Pound for pound

with him! Why, the old——" (she made a pause without
putting in the word as so many people do), "is a millionaire!"

Sir Charles, who was standing before the fire with his back
to it, in the habitual attitude of Englishmen, pulled his moustache again and solemnly nodded his head.

"And who does he think," cried Lady Jane, carried away
by her feelings, "that could do *that* would ever go near him
and his vulgar, common—— Oh, I beg your pardon, Charlie,
I am sure!" she said.

"No pardon needed. Know what you mean," Somers said
with a wave of his hand.

"Of course," said Lady Jane with emphasis, "I don't
mean the girls, or else you may be sure I never should have
taken them out or had them here." She made a little pause
after this disclaimer, in the heat of which there was perhaps
just a little doubt of her own motives, checked by the reflection
that Katherine Tredgold at least was not vulgar, and might
have been anybody's daughter. She went on again after a
moment. "But he is an old—— Oh! I would not pay the
least attention to what he said; he was bound to say that sort
of thing at first. Do you imagine for a moment that any man
who could do *that* would please Stella? What kind of man
could do that? Only perhaps an old horror like himself,
whom a nice girl would never look at. Oh! I think I should
be easy in my mind, Charlie, if I were you. It is impossible,
you know! There's no such man, no such *young* man. Can
you fancy Stella accepting an old fellow made of money? I
don't believe in it for a moment," said Lady Jane.

"Old fellows got sons—sometimes," said Sir Charles, "City
men, rolling in money, don't you know?"

"One knows all those sort of people," said Lady Jane;
"you could count them on your fingers; and they go in for
rank, &c., not for other millionaires. No, Charlie, I don't see
any call you have to be so discouraged. Why did you come
in looking such a whipped dog? It will be all over the island
in no time and through the regiment that you have been refused

by Stella Tredgold. The father's nothing. The father was quite sure to refuse. Rather picturesque that about laying down pound for pound, isn't it? It makes one think of a great table groaning under heaps of gold."

"Jove!" said Sir Charles. "Old beggar said shillin' for shillin'. Had a heap of silver—got it like a fool—didn't see what he was driving at—paid it out on the table." He pulled his moustache to the very roots and uttered a short and cavernous laugh. "Left it there, by Jove!—all my change," he cried; "not a blessed thruppenny to throw to little girl at gate."

"Left it there?" said Lady Jane—"on the table?" Her gravity was overpowered by this detail. "Upon my word, Charlie Somers, for all your big moustache and your six feet and your experiences, I declare I don't think there ever was such a simpleton born."

Somers bore her laughter very steadily. He was not unused to it. The things in which he showed himself a simpleton were in relation to the things in which he was prematurely wise as three to a hundred; but yet there were such things. And he was free to acknowledge that leaving his seventeen shillings spread out on the millionaire's table, or even taking the millionaire's challenge *au pied de la lettre*, was the act of a simpleton. He stood tranquilly with his back to the fire till Lady Jane had got her laugh out. Then she resumed with a sort of apology:

"It was too much for me, Charlie. I could not help laughing. What will become of all that money, I wonder? Will he keep it and put it to interest? I should like to have seen him after you were gone. I should like to have seen him afterwards, when Stella had her knife at his throat, asking him what he meant by it. You may trust to Stella, my dear boy. She will soon bring her father to reason. He may be all sorts of queer things to you, but he can't stand against her. She can twist him round her little finger. If it had been Katherine I should not have been so confident. But Stella—he never has refused anything to Stella since ever she was born."

"Think so, really?" said Somers through his moustache. He was beginning to revive a little again, but yet the impression of old Tredgold's chuckling laugh and his contemptuous certainty was not to be got over lightly. The gloom of the rejected was still over him.

"Yes, I think so," said Lady Jane. "Don't, for Heaven's sake, go on in that hang-dog way. There's nothing happened but what was to be expected. Of course, the old curmudgeon would make an attempt to guard his money-bags. I wish I were as sure of a company for Jack as I am of Stella's power to do anything she likes with her father. But if you go down in this way at the first touch——"

"No intention of going down," said Sir Charles, piqued. "Marry her to-morrow—take her out to India—then see what old beggar says."

"That, indeed," cried Lady Jane—"that would be a fine revenge on him! Don't propose it to Stella if you don't want her to accept, for she would think it the finest fun in the world."

"By George!" Somers said, and a smile began to lift up the corners of his moustache.

"That would bring him to his senses, indeed," Lady Jane said reflectively; "but it would be rather cruel, Charlie. After all, he is an old man. Not a very venerable old man, perhaps; not what you would call a lovely old age, is it? but still—— Oh, I think it would be cruel. You need not go so far as that. But we shall soon hear what Stella says."

And it very soon was known what Stella said. Stella wrote in a whirlwind of passion, finding nothing too bad to say of papa. An old bull, an old pig, were the sweetest of the similes she used. She believed that he wanted to kill her, to drag her by the hair of her head, to shut her up in a dungeon or a back kitchen or something. She thought he must have been changed in his sleep, for he was not in the very least like her own old nice papa, and Kate thought so too. Kate could not understand it any more than she could. But one thing was certain—that, let papa say what he would or do what he

would, she (Stella) never would give in. She would be true,
whatever happened. And if she were locked up anywhere she
would trust in her Charlie to get her out. All her trust was
in her Charlie, she declared. She had got his money, his
poor dear bright shillings, of which papa had robbed him, and
put them in a silk bag, which she always meant to preserve
and carry about with her. She called it Charlie's fortune.
Poor dear, dear Charlie; he had left it all for her. She knew
it was for her, and she would never part with it, never! This
whirlwind of a letter amused Charlie very much; he did not
mind letting his friends read it. They all laughed over it, and
declared that she was a little brick, and that he must certainly
stick to her whatever happened. The old fellow was sure to
come round, they all said; no old father could ever stand out
against a girl like that. She had him on toast, everybody
knew.

These were the encouraging suggestions addressed to Sir
Charles by his most intimate friends, who encouraged him
still more by their narratives of how Lottie Seton tossed her
head and declared that Charlie Somers had been waiting all
along for some rich girl to drop into his mouth. He had
always had an *arrière pensée*, she cried (whatever that might
be), and had never been at all amusin' at the best of times.
He was very amusin' now, however, with Stella's letter in his
pocket and this absorbing question to discuss. The whole
regiment addressed itself with all the brain it possessed to the
consideration of the subject, which, of course, was so much
the more urgent in consequence of the orders under which it
lay. To go or not to go to India, that was the rub, as Charlie had said. Stella only complicated the question, which had
been under discussion before. He did not want to go; but
then, on the other hand, if he remained at home, his creditors
would be rampant and he would be within their reach, which
would not be the case if he went to India. And India meant
double pay. And if it could be secured that Stella's father
should send an expedition after them to bring them back
within a year, then going to India with Stella as a companion

would be the best fun in the world. To go for a year was
one thing, to go as long as the regiment remained, doing ordinary duty, was quite another. Everybody whom he consulted, even Lady Jane, though she began to be a little frightened by the responsibility, assured him that old Tredgold
would never hold out for a year. Impossible! an old man in
shaky health who adored his daughter. "Doubt if he'll give
you time to get on board before he's after you," Algy said.
"You'll find telegrams at Suez or at Aden or somewhere,"
said another; and a third chaunted (being at once poetical
and musical, which was not common in the regiment) a verse
which many of them thought had been composed for the
occasion:

> " Come back, come back," he cried in grief
>   Across the stormy water,
> " And I'll forgive your Highland chief,
>   My daughter, O my daughter!"

"Though Charlie ain't a Highland chief, you know," said
one of the youngsters. "If it had been Algy, now!"

All these things worked very deeply in the brain of Sir
Charles Somers, Baronet. He spent a great deal of time thinking of them. A year in India would be great fun. Stella,
for her part, was wild with delight at the thought of it. If it
could but be made quite clear that old Tredgold, dying for the
loss of his favourite child, would be sure to send for her!
Everybody said there was not a doubt on the subject. Stella,
who ought to know, was sure of it; so was Lady Jane, though
she had got frightened and cried, "Oh, don't ask me!"
when importuned the hundredth time for her opinion. If a
fellow could only be quite sure! Sometimes a chilling vision
of the "old beggar" came across Charlie's mind, and the
courage began to ooze out at his fingers' ends. That old fellow did not look like an old fellow who would give in. He
looked a dangerous old man, an old man capable of anything.
Charles Somers was by no means a coward, but when he remembered the look which Mr. Tredgold had cast upon him,
all the strength went out of him. To marry an expensive wife

who had never been stinted in her expenses and take her out
to India, and then find that there was no relenting, remorse-
ful father behind them, but only the common stress and strain
of a poor man's life in a profession, obliged to live upon his
pay! What should he do if this happened? But everybody
around him assured him that it could not, would not happen.
Stella had the old gentleman " on toast." He could not live
without her; he would send to the end of the world to bring
her back; he would forgive anything, Highland chief or whoever it might be. Even Lady Jane said so. "Don't ask me
to advise you," that lady cried. "I daren't take the responsibility. How can I tell whether Stella and you are fond
enough of each other to run such a risk? Old Mr. Tredgold?
Oh, as for old Mr. Tredgold, I should not really fear any last-
ing opposition from him. He may bluster a little, he may try
to be overbearing, he may think he can frighten his daughter.
But, of course, he will give in. Oh, yes, he will give in.
Stella is everything to him. She is the very apple of his eye.
It is very unjust to Katherine I always have said, and always
will say. But that is how it is. Stella's little finger is more
to him than all the rest of the world put together. But please,
please don't ask advice from me!"

Sir Charles walked up and down the room, the room at
Steephill, the room at the barracks, wherever he happened to
be, and pulled his moustache almost till the blood came. But
neither that intimate councillor, nor his fellow-officers, nor
his anxious friends gave him any definite enlightenment. He
was in love, too, in his way, which pushed him on, but he
was by no means without prudence, which held him back. If
old Tredgold did not break his heart, if he took the other
one into Stella's place—for to be sure Katherine was his
daughter also, though not equal to Stella! If!—it is a little
word, but there is terrible meaning in it. In that case what
would happen? He shuddered and turned away from the
appalling thought.

CHAPTER XIV.

"KATE, Kate, Kate!" cried Stella. All had been quiet between the two rooms connected by that open door. Katherine was fastening the ribbon at her neck before the glass. This made her less ready to respond to Stella's eager summons; but the tone of the third repetition of her name was so urgent that she dropped the ends of the ribbon and flew to her sister. Stella was leaning half out of the open window. "Kate," she cried—"Kate, he has sent him away!"

"Who is sent away?" cried Katherine, in amazement.

Stella's answer was to seize her sister by the arm and pull her half out of the window, endangering her equilibrium. Thus enforced, however, Katherine saw the figure of Sir Charles Somers disappearing round the corner of a group of trees, which so entirely recalled the image, coarse yet expressive, of a dog with its tail between its legs, that no certainty of disappointment and failure could be more complete. The two girls stared after him until he had disappeared, and then Stella drew her sister in again, and they looked into each other's eyes for a moment. Even Stella the unsubduable was cowed; her face was pale, her eyes round and staring with astonishment and trouble; the strength was all taken out of her by bewilderment. What did it mean? Papa, papa, he who had denied her nothing, who had been the more pleased the more costly was the toy which she demanded! Had Charlie offended him? Had he gone the wrong way to work? What could he possibly have done to receive a rebuff from papa?

"Of course I shall not stand it," Stella cried, when she had recovered herself a little. "He shall not have much

peace of his life if he crosses me. You let him dance upon
you, Kate, and never said a word—though I don't suppose you
cared, or surely you would have stood out a little more than
you did. But he shan't dance upon me—he shall soon find
out the difference. I am going to him at once to ask what
he means.'' She rushed towards the door, glowing anew with
courage and spirit, but then suddenly stopped herself, and
came running back, throwing herself suddenly on Katherine's
shoulders.

"Oh, Kate, why should parents be so hard,'' she said,
shedding a few tears—'' and so hypocritical ! '' she exclaimed,
rousing herself again—'' pretending to be ready to do everything, and then doing nothing ! ''

"Oh, hush, Stella ! '' cried Katherine, restraining her ;
"there is nothing you have wanted till now that papa has
not done.''

"What ! '' cried the girl indignantly. "Diamonds and
such wretched things.'' She made a gesture as if to pull
something from her throat and throw it on the floor, though
the diamonds, naturally, at this hour in the morning, were not
there. "But the first thing I really want — the only thing —
oh, let me go, Kate, let me go and ask him what he means ! ''

"Wait a little,'' said Katherine—'' wait a little ; it may
not be as bad as we think ; it may not be bad at all. Let us
go down as if nothing had happened. Perhaps Sir Charles has
only—gone—to fetch something.''

"Like that ? '' cried Stella ; and then a something of the
ridiculous in the drooping figure came across her volatile mind.
He was so like, so very like, that dog with his tail between his
legs. She burst out into a laugh. "Poor Charlie, oh, poor
Charlie ! he looked exactly like—but I will pay papa for
this,'' the girl cried.

"Oh, not now,'' said Katherine. "Remember, he is an
old man—we must try not to cross him but to soothe him.
He may have been vexed to think of losing you, Stella. He
may have been—a little sharp ; perhaps to try to—break it
off—for a time.''

" And you think he might succeed, I shouldn't wonder,"
Stella cried, tossing her head high.   To tell the truth, Katherine was by no means sure that he might not succeed.   She
had not a great confidence in the depth of the sentiment
which connected her sister and Sir Charles.   She believed that
on one side or the other that tie might be broken, and that it
would be no great harm.   But she made no reply to Stella's
question.   She only begged her to have patience a little, to
make no immediate assault upon her father.   " You know the
doctor said he must be very regular — and not be disturbed—
in his meals and things."

" Oh, if it is lunch you are thinking of ! " cried Stella, with
great disdain ; but after a little she consented to take things
quietly and await the elucidation of events.   The meal that followed was not, however, a very comfortable meal.   Mr. Tredgold
came in with every evidence of high spirits, but was also nervous, not knowing what kind of reception he was likely to meet
with.   He was as evidently relieved when they seated themselves
at table without any questions, but it was a relief not unmingled
with excitement.   He talked continuously and against time,
but he neither asked about their visit as he usually did, nor
about the previous night's entertainment, nor Stella's appearance nor her triumphs.   Stella sat very silent at her side of the
table.   And Katherine thought that her father was a little afraid.
He made haste to escape as soon as the luncheon was over, and
it was not a moment too soon, for Stella's excitement was no
longer restrainable.   " What has he said to Charlie—what has
he done to him ? " she cried.   " Do you think he would dare
send him away for good and never say a word to me ?   What
is the meaning of it, Kate ?   You would not let me speak,
though it choked me to sit and say nothing.   Where is my
Charlie ? and oh, how dared he, how dared he, to send him
away ? "

Katherine suggested that he might still be lingering about
waiting for the chance of seeing one of them, and Stella darted
out accordingly and flew through the grounds, in and out of the
trees, with her uncovered head shining in the sun, but came

back with no further enlightenment. She then proceeded imperiously to her father's room ; where, however, she was again
stopped by the butler, who announced that master was having
his nap and was not to be disturbed. All this delayed the explanation and prolonged the suspense, which was aggravated,
as in so many cases, by the arrival of visitors. "So you have
got back, Stella, from your grand visit ? Oh, do tell us all
about it ! " It was perhaps the first fiery ordeal of social difficulty to which that undisciplined little girl had been exposed.
And it was so much the more severe that various other sentiments came in—pride in the visit, which was so much greater
a privilege than was accorded to the ordinary inhabitants of
Sliplin ; pride, too, in a show of indifference to it, desire to
make her own glories known, and an equally strong desire to
represent these glories as nothing more than were habitual and
invariable. In the conflict of feeling Stella was drawn a little
out of herself and out of the consideration of her father's un-
imaginable behaviour. Oh, if they only knew the real climax
of all those eager questions ! If only a hint could have been
given of the crowning glory, of the new possession she had acquired, and the rank to which she was about to be elevated !

Stella did not think of "a trumpery baronet" now. It was
the Earl whom she thought trumpery, a creation of this reign,
as Miss Mildmay said, whereas the Somers went back to the
Anglo-Saxons. Stella did not know very well who the Anglo-
Saxons were. She did not know that baronetcies are compar-
atively modern inventions. She only knew that to be Lady
Somers was a fine thing, and that she was going to attain that
dignity. But then, papa—who was papa, to interfere with her
happiness? what could he do to stop a thing she had made
up her mind to?—stood in the way. It was papa's fault
that she could not make that thrilling, that tremendous an-
nouncement to her friends. Her little tongue trembled on the
edge of it. At one moment it had almost burst forth. Oh,
how silly to be talking of Steephill, of the dance, of the rides,
of going to the covert side with the sportsmen's luncheon—
all these things which unengaged persons, mere spectators of

life, make so much of—when she had had it in her power to
tell something so much more exciting, something that would
fly not only through Sliplin and all along the coast but over the
whole island before night !   And to think she could not tell it
—must not say anything about it because of papa !

Thus Stella fretted through the afternoon, determined, however, to "have it out with papa" the moment her visitors were
gone, and not, on the whole, much afraid.   He had never
crossed her in her life before.   Since the time when Stella
crying for it in the nursery was enough to secure any delight
she wanted, till now, when she stood on the edge of life and
all its excitements, nothing that she cared for had ever been
refused her.   She had her little ways of getting whatever she
wanted.   It was not that he was always willing or always
agreed in her wishes; if that had been so, the prospect before
her would have been more doubtful; but there were things
which he did not like and had yet been made to consent to
because of Stella's wish.   Why should he resist her now for
the first time?   There was no reason in it, no probability in
it, no sense.   He had been able to say No to Charlie—that
was quite another thing.   Charlie was very nice, but he was
not Stella, though he might be Stella's chosen ; and papa had,
no doubt, a little spite against him because of that adventure
in the yacht, and because he was poor, and other things.
But Stella herself, was it possible that papa could ever hold
head against her, look her in the face and deny her anything?
No, certainly no !   She was going over this in her mind while
the visitors were talking, and even when she was giving them '
an account of what she wore.   Her new white, and her diamonds—what diamonds !   Oh, hadn't they heard?   A *rivière*
that papa had given her ; not a big one, you know, like an
old lady's—a little one, but such stones, exactly like drops of
dew !   As she related this, her hopes—nay, certainties—
sprang high.   She had not needed to hold up her little finger to
have those jewels—a word had done it, the merest accidental
word.   She had not even had the trouble of wishing for them.
And to imagine that he would be likely to cross her now !

"Stella! Stella! where are you going?" Katherine cried.

"I am going—to have it out with papa." The last visitor
had just gone; Stella caught the cloth on the tea-table in the
sweep of her dress, and disordered everything as she flew by.
But Katherine, though so tidy, did not stop to restore things
to their usual trimness. She followed her sister along the
passage a little more slowly, but with much excitement too.
Would Stella conquer, as she usually did? or, for the first time
in her life, would she find a blank wall before her which
nothing could break down? Katherine could not but remember the curt intimation which had been given to her that
James Stanford had been sent away and was never to be spoken
of more. But then she was not Stella—she was very different
from Stella; she had always felt even (or fancied) that the
fact that James Stanford's suit had been to herself and not to
Stella had something to do with his rejection. That anyone
should have thought of Katherine while Stella was by! She
blamed herself for this idea as she followed Stella flying
through the long and intricate passages to have it out with
papa. Perhaps she had been wrong, Katherine said to herself.
If papa held out against Stella this time, she would feel sure
she had been wrong.

Stella burst into the room without giving any indication of
her approach, and Katherine went in behind her—swept in
the wind of her going. But what they saw was a vacant
room, the fire purring to itself like a cat, with sleepy little
starts and droppings, a level sunbeam coming in broad at one
window, and on the table two lines of silver money stretched
along the dark table-cloth and catching the eye. They were
irregular lines—one all of shillings straight and unbroken, the
other shorter, and made up with a half-crown and a sixpence.
What was the meaning of this? They consulted each other
with their eyes.

"I am coming directly," said Mr. Tredgold from an inner
room. The door was open. It was the room in which his
safe was, and they could hear him rustling his paper, putting
in or taking out something. "Oh, papa, make haste! I am

waiting for you," Stella cried in her impatience. She could scarcely brook at the last moment this unnecessary delay.

He came out, but not for a minute more ; and then he was wiping his lips as if he had been taking something to support himself; which indeed was the case, and he had need of it. He came in with a great show of cheerfulness, rubbing his hands. " What, both of you ? " he said, " I thought it was only Stella.   I am glad both of you are here.   Then you can tell me——"

" Papa, I will tell you nothing, nor shall Kate, till you have answered my question.   What have you done to Charlie Somers ?   Where is he ? where have you sent him ? and how —how—how da—how could you have sent him away ? "

" That's his money," said the old gentleman, pointing to the table.   " You'd better pick it up and send it to him ; he might miss it afterwards.   The fool thought he could lay down money with me ; there's only seventeen shillings of it," said Mr. Tredgold contemptuously—" not change for a sovereign !   But he might want it.   I don't think he had much more in his pocket, and I don't want his small change ; no, nor nobody else's.   You can pick it up and send it back."

" What does all this mean ? " asked Stella in imperious tones, though her heart quaked she could scarcely tell why. " Why have you Charlie Somers's money on your table ? and why—why, have you sent him away ? "

Mr. Tredgold seated himself deliberately in his chair, first removing the newspaper that lay in it, folding that and placing it carefully on a stand by his side.   " Well, my little girl," he said, also taking off his spectacles and folding them before he laid them down, " that's a very easy one to answer. I sent him away because he didn't suit me, my dear."

" But he suited me," cried Stella, " which is surely far more important."

" Well, my pet, you may think so, but I don't.   I gave him my reasons.   I say nothing against him—a man as I know nothing of, and don't want to know.   It's all the same who you send to me ; they'll just hear the same thing.   The

man I give my little girl to will have to count out shillin' for
shillin' with me. That fellow took me at my word, don't
you see ?—took out a handful of money and began to count it
out as grave as a judge. But he couldn't do it, even at that.
Seventeen shillings ! not as much as change for a sovereign,"
said Mr. Tredgold with a chuckle. " I told him as he was an
ass for his pains. Thousand pound for thousand pound down,
that's my rule ; and all the baronets in the kingdom—or if
they were dukes for that matter—won't get me out of that."

" Papa, do you know what you are saying ? " Stella was so
utterly bewildered that she did not at all know what she was
saying in the sudden arrest of all her thoughts.

" I think so, pet ; very well indeed, I should say. I'm a
man that has always been particular about business arrangements. Business is one thing ; feelings, or so forth, is another. I never let feelings come in when it's a question of
business. Money down on the table—shillin's, or thousands,
which is plainer, for thousands, and that's all about it ; the
man who can't do that don't suit me."

Stella stood with two red patches on her cheeks, with her
mouth open, with her eyes staring before the easy and com-
placent old gentleman in his chair. He was, no doubt, conscious of the passion and horror with which she was regarding
him, for he shifted the paper and the spectacles a little nervous-
ly to give himself a countenance ; but he took no notice otherwise, and maintained his easy position—one leg crossed over
the other, his foot swinging a little—even after she burst forth.

" Papa, do you say this to me—to *me ?* And I have given
him my word, and I love him, though you don't know what
that means. Papa, can you look me in the face—me, Stella,
and dare to say that you have sent my Charlie away ? "

" My dear," said Mr. Tredgold, " he ain't your Charlie,
and never will be. He's Sir Charles Somers, Bart., a fine
fellow, but I don't think we shall see him here again, and I
can look my little Stella quite well in the face."

He did not like to do it, though. He gave her one glance,
and then turned his eyes to his paper again.

"Papa," cried Stella, stamping her foot, "I won't have it! I shall not take it from you! Whatever you say, he shall come back here. I won't give him up, no, not if you should shut me up on bread and water—not if you should put me in prison, or drag me by the hair of my head, or kill me! which, I think, is what you must want to do."

"You little hussy! You never had so much as a whipping in your life, and I am not going to begin now. Take her away, Katie. If she cries till Christmas she won't change me. Crying's good for many things, but not for business. Stella, you can go away."

"Oh, papa, how can you say Stella, and be so cruel!" Stella threw herself down suddenly by his side and seized his hand, upon which she laid down her wet cheek. "You have always done everything for Stella. Never—never has my papa refused me anything. I am not used to it. I can't bear it! Papa, it is *me* whose heart you are breaking. Papa, *me!* Stella, it is Stella!"

"Kate, for goodness' sake take her away. It is no use. She is not going to come over me. Stella's a very good name for anything else, but it's not a name in business. Go away, child. Take her away. But, Katie, if there's anything else she would like now, a new carriage, or a horse, or a bracelet, or a lot of dresses, or anything—anything in that way——"

Stella drew herself up to her full height; she dried her eyes; she turned upon her father with that instinct of the drama which is so strong in human nature. "I scorn all your presents; I will take nothing—nothing, as long as I live, you cruel, cruel father," she cried.

Later, when Mr. Tredgold had gone out in his Bath-chair for his afternoon "turn," Stella came back very quietly to his room and gathered up poor Charlie's shillings. She did not know very much about the value of money, though she spent so much; indeed, if she had ever felt the need of it it was in this prosaic form of a few shillings. She thought he might want them, poor Charlie, whom she had not the faintest intention of giving up, whatever papa might say.

CHAPTER XV.

But Stella neither shuddered nor hesitated. She was in the highest spirits, flying everywhere, scarcely touching the ground with her feet. "Oh, yes ! I'm engaged to Sir Charles," she said to all her friends. "Papa won't hear of it, but he will have to give in."

"Papas always give in when the young people hold out," said some injudicious sympathiser.

"Don't they?" cried Stella, giving a kiss to that lady. She was not in the least discouraged. There was a great deal of gaiety going on at the time, both in the village (as it was fashionable to call the town of Sliplin) and in the county, and Stella met her Charlie everywhere, Mr. Tredgold having no means, and perhaps no inclination, to put a stop to this. He did not want to interfere with her pleasures. If she liked to dance and "go on" with that fellow, let her. She should not marry him ; that was all. The old gentleman had no wish to be unkind to his daughter. He desired her to have her fling like the rest, to enjoy herself as much as was possible ; only for this one thing he had put down his foot.

"When is that confounded regiment going away?" he asked Katherine.

"Dear papa," Katherine replied, "won't you think it over again? Charlie Somers has perhaps no money, but Stella is very fond of him, and he of——"

"Hold your tongue !" said old Tredgold. "Hold your confounded tongue ! If I don't give in to her, do you think it"—with a dash—"likely that I will to you?"

Katherine retreated very quickly, for when her father began to swear she was frightened. He did not swear in an ordinary way, and visions of apoplexy were associated to her with oaths. Stella did not care. She would have let him swear as long as he liked, and paid no attention. She went to her parties almost every night, glittering in her *rivière* of diamonds and meeting Sir Charles everywhere. They had all the airs of an engaged couple, people said. And it was thought quite natural, for nobody believed that old Tredgold would stand out. Thus, no one gave him any warning of what was going on. The whole island was in a conspiracy on behalf of the lovers. Nor was it like any other abetting of domestic insurrection, for the opinion was unanimous that the father would give in. Why, Stella could do anything with him. Stella was his favourite, as he had shown on every possible occasion. Everybody knew it, even Katherine, who made no struggle against the fact. To think of his having the strength of mind really to deny Stella anything! It was impossible. He was playing with her a little now, only for the pleasure of being coaxed and wheedled, many people thought. But when the time came, of course he would give in. So Stella thought, like everybody else. There was nobody but Katherine and, as I have said, Somers himself who did not feel quite sure. As time went on, the two ladies who went to all the parties and saw everything —the two old cats, Mrs. Shanks and Miss Mildmay—had many consultations on the subject over the invisible rail of separation between their gardens. It was a very bright October, and even the beginning of the next dreary month was far milder than usual, and in the mornings, when the sun shone, these ladies were still to be found on their terraces, caressing the last remnants of their flowers, and cutting the last chrysanthemums or dahlias.

"Stella danced every dance last night with that Sir Charles," Miss Mildmay said.

"But she always does, my dear; and why shouldn't she, when she is going to marry him?"

There was really no answer to this, which was so well ascertained a fact, and which everybody knew.

"But I wonder if old Mr. Tredgold knows how much they

are together! As he never goes out himself, it is so easy to keep him deceived. I wonder, Jane Shanks,'' said Miss Mildmay, '' whether you or I should say a word?''

'' You may say as many words as you please, Ruth Mildmay; but I shan't,'' cried the other. '' I would not interfere for the world.''

'' I am not the least afraid of interfering,'' Miss Mildmay said; and she succeeded in persuading her friend to go out in the midge once more, and call at the Cliff, on an afternoon when the girls were known to be out of the way.

'' We ought, I am sure, to congratulate you, Mr. Tredgold. We heard that you did not approve, and, of course, it must be dreadful for you to think of losing Stella; but as it is going on so long, we feel, at last, that the engagement must be true.''

'' What engagement?'' said the old man. He liked to amuse himself with the two old cats. He put his newspaper away and prepared to '' get his fun out of them.''

'' Oh, the engagement between Stella and Sir Charles,'' said Mrs. Shanks, with bated breath.

'' Oh! they're engaged, are they?'' he said, with that laugh which was like an electrical bell.

'' Dear Mr. Tredgold, it is given out everywhere. They are for ever together. They dance every dance with one another.''

'' Confounded dull, I should think, for my little girl. You take my word, she'll soon tire of that,'' he said.

'' Oh, but she does not tire of it; you don't go out with them, you don't see things. I assure you they are always together. If you don't approve of it, Mr. Tredgold, indeed—indeed you should put a stop to it. It isn't kind to dear Stella.''

'' Oh, stop, stop, Ruth Mildmay!'' cried Mrs. Shanks. '' Stella knows very well just how far she can go. Stella would never do anything that was displeasing to her dear papa. May I pour out the tea for you, dear Mr. Tredgold, as the girls are not in?''

Mr. Tredgold gave the permission with a wave of his hand, and hoped that Miss Mildmay would say just as much as she pleased.

" I like to know what my girls do when they're out," he said. " I like to know that Stella is enjoying herself. That's what they go out for. Just to get themselves as much pleasure as is to be had, in their own way."

" But you would not wish them to compromise themselves," said Miss Mildmay. " Oh, I wouldn't interfere for the world. But as you don't go out with them you ought to be told. I do hope you approve of Sir Charles, Mr. Tredgold. He is a nice young man enough. He has been a little fast ; but so have they all ; and he is old enough now to have more sense. I am sure he will make you a very good son-in-law. So long as you approve——"

" I approve of my little girl enjoying herself," said the old man. " Bring some more muffins, John ; there's plenty in the house, I hope. I know why you won't take that piece, Miss Mildmay, because it is the last in the plate, and you think you will never be married." He accompanied this with a tremendous tinkle of a laugh, as if it were the greatest joke in the world.

Miss Mildmay waved her hand with dignity, putting aside the foolish jest, and also putting aside the new dish of muffins, which that dignity would not permit her to touch.

" The question is," she said, " not my marriage, which does not concern you, Mr. Tredgold, but dear Stella's, which does."

" Mr. Tredgold is so fond of his joke," Mrs. Shanks said.

" Yes, I'm fond of my joke, ain't I ? I'm a funny man. Many of the ladies call me so. Lord ! I like other people to have their fun too. Stella's welcome to hers, as long as she likes. She's a kitten, she is ; she goes on playin' and springin' as long as anybody will fling a bit of string at her. But she's well in hand all the same. She knows, as you say, just how far to go."

" Then she has your approval, we must all presume," said Miss Mildmay, rising from her chair, though Mrs. Shanks had not half finished her tea.

" Oh, she's free to have her fun," Mr. Tredgold said.

What did it mean, her fun ? This question was fully dis-

cussed between the two ladies in the midge. Marriage is no
fun, if it comes to that, they both agreed, and the phrase was
very ambiguous ; but still, no man in his senses, even Mr. Tredgold, could allow his young daughter to make herself so con-
spicuous if he did not mean to consent in the end.

" I am very glad to hear, Stella, that it is all right about
your marriage," Mrs. Shanks said next time she met the girls.
" Your papa would not say anything very definite ; but still,
he knows all about it, and you are to take your own way, as
he says."

" Did he say I was to have my own way ? " said Stella, in
a flush of pleasure.

" At least, he said the same thing. Yes, I am sure that was
what he meant. He was full of his jokes, don't you know ?
But that must have been what he meant ; and I am sure I
wish you joy with all my heart, Stella, dear."

Stella went dancing home after this, though Katherine
walked very gravely by her side.

" I knew papa would give in at last. I knew he never
would stand against me, when he knew I was in earnest this
time," she cried.

" Do you think he would tell Mrs. Shanks, after sending
off both of us, and frightening me ? "

" You are so easily frightened," cried Stella. " Yes, I
shouldn't wonder at all if he told Mrs. Shanks. He likes the
two old cats ; he knows they will go and publish it all over
the place. He would think I should hear just as soon as if
he had told me, and so I have. I will run in and give him a
kiss, for he is a dear old soul, after all."

Stella did run in and gave her father a tumultuous kiss, and
roused him out of a nap.

" Oh, papa, you dear, you old darling—you best papa in
the world ! " she cried.

Mr. Tredgold felt a little cross at first, but the kiss and the
praises were sweet to him. He put his arms round her as she
stood over him.

" What have I done now ? " he said, with his tinkling laugh.

"You have done just what I wanted most—what it was dearest of you to do," she cried.   "Mrs. Shanks told me. You told her, of course, dear papa, because you knew it would be published directly all over the place."

"Oh, the two old cats!" he said, tinkling more than ever. "That's what they made of it, is it?   I said you might have your fun, my dear.   You are free to have your fun as much as ever you like.   That's what I said, and that's what I shall say as long as you're amusing yourself, Stella.   You can have your fling; I shan't stop you.   Enjoy yourself as long as you can, if that's what you like," he said.

"Oh, papa, what do you mean—what do you mean?" cried Stella.   "Don't you mean, dear papa," she continued, with renewed caresses, putting her arms round his neck, pressing his bald head upon her breast, "that you'll let Charlie come— that he needn't go to India, that we are to be married, and that you'll give us your blessing, and—and everything?   That is what you mean, isn't it, dear papa?"

"Don't strangle me, child," he said, coughing and laughing.   "There's such a thing, don't you know? as to be killed with kindness.   I've told you what I'll do, my dear," he continued.   "I shall let you have your fun as long as ever you like. You can dance with him down to the very ship's side, if you please.   That won't do any harm to me, but he don't set a foot in this house unless he's ready to table pound for pound with me.   Where's his shillin's, by the way, Katie?   He ought to have had his shillin's; he might have wanted them, poor man.   Ah, don't strangle me, I tell you, Stella!"

"I wish I could!" cried Stella, setting her little teeth. "You deserve it, you old dreadful, dreadful——"

"What is she saying, Kate?   Never mind; it was swearing or something, I suppose—all the fault of those old cats, not mine.   I said she should have her swing, and she can have her swing and welcome.   That's what she wants, I suppose. You have always had your fun, Stella.   You don't know what a thing it is to have your fun and nobody to oppose you.   I never had that in my life.   I was always pulled up sharp.

Get along now, I want my nap before dinner; but mind, I
have said all I'm going to say. You can have your fun, and
he can table down pound for pound with me, if he has the
money—otherwise, not another word. I may be a funny man,"
said Mr. Tredgold, " but when I put my foot down, none of
you will get it up again, that's all I have got to say."

" You are a very hard, cruel, tyrannical father," said Stella, "and you never will have any love from anyone as long
as you live ! "

" We'll see about that," he said, with a grimace, preparing
to fling his handkerchief over his head, which was his way
when he went to sleep.

" Oh, papa !—oh, dear papa ! Of course I did not mean
that. I want no fling and no fun, but to settle down with
Charlie, and to be always ready when you want me as long as
I live."

" You shall settle down with some man as I approve of, as
can count down his hundreds and his thousands on the table,
Stella. That's what you are going to do."

" Papa, you never would be so cruel to me, your little
Stella ? I will have no man if I have not Charlie—never,
never, if he had all the money in the world."

" Well, there's no hurry ; you're only twenty," he said,
blinking at her with sleepy eyes. " I don't want to get rid
of you. You may give yourself several years to have your fun
before you settle down."

Stella, standing behind her father's bald and defenceless
head, looked for a minute or two like a pretty but dreadful
demon, threatening him with a raised fist and appalling looks.
Suddenly, however, there came a transformation scene—her
arms slid round his neck once more ; she put her cheek against
his bald head. " Papa," she said, her voice faltering between
fury and the newly-conceived plan, which, in its way, was
fun, " you gave me a kind of an alternative once. You said,
if I didn't have Charlie——"

" Well ? " said the old man, waking up, with a gleam of
amusement in his eyes.

" I could have—you said it yourself—anything else I liked,"
said Stella, drooping over the back of his chair. Was she
ashamed of herself, or was she secretly overcome with something, either laughter or tears ?

" Stella," cried Katherine, " do come away now and let
papa rest." The elder sister's face was full of alarm, but for
what she was frightened she could scarcely herself have said.

" Let her get it out," cried Mr. Tredgold. " Speak up,
Stella, my little girl ; out with it, my pet. What would it
like from its papa ? "

" You said I might have anything I liked—more diamonds,
a lot of new dresses——"

" And so you shall," he said, chuckling, till it was doubtful if he would ever recover his breath. " That's my little
girl down to the ground—that's my pet ! That's the woman
all over—just the woman I like ! You shall have all that—
diamonds ? Yes, if I'd to send out to wherever they come
from. And frocks ? As many as you can set your face to.
Give me a kiss, Stella, and that's a bargain, my dear."

" Very well, papa," said Stella, with dignity, heaving a
soft sigh. " You will complete the parure, please ; a handsome pendant, and a star for my hair, and a bracelet—*but*
handsome, really good, fit for one of the princesses."

" As good as they make 'em, Stella."

" And I must have them," she said languidly, " for that
ball that is going to be given to the regiment before they go
away. As for the dresses," she added, with more energy,
" papa, I shall fleece you—I shall rob you ! I will order
everything I take a fancy to—everything that is nice, everything that is dear. I shall ruin you ! " she cried, clapping
her hands together with a sound like a pistol-shot over his
head.

Through all this the tinkling of his laugh had run on. It
burst out now and had a little solo of its own, disturbed by a
cough, while the girls were silent and listened. " That's the
sort of thing," he cried. " That's my Stella—that's my pet !
Ruin me ! I can stand it. Have them as dear as they're

made. I'll write for the diamonds to-night; and you shall go to the ball all shinin' from head to foot, my Stella—that's what you've always been since you were born—my little star!''

Then she pulled the handkerchief over his head, gave him a kiss through it, and hurried away.

" Oh, Stella, Stella ! '' cried Katherine under her breath. She repeated the words when they had gone into their own room. Stella, flushed and excited, had thrown herself upon the stool before the piano and began to play wildly, with jars and crashes of sound. " Oh, Stella, how dared you do such a thing? How dared you barter away your love, for he is your love, for diamonds and frocks? Oh, Stella, you are be-having very, very badly. I am not fond of Charles Somers ; but surely, if you care for him at all, he is worth more than that. And how dared you—how dared you sell him—to papa ? ''

But Stella said never a word. She went on playing wild chords and making crashes of dreadful sound, which, to Kath-erine, who was more or less a musician, were beyond bear-ing. She seized her sister's arm after a moment and stopped her almost violently. " Stop that, stop that, and answer me ! '' she cried.

" Don't you like my music, Kate ? It was all out of my own head—what you call improvising. I thought you would like me to go to the piano for comfort. So it is an ease to one's mind—it lets the steam off,'' cried Stella with a last crash, louder and more discordant than the others. Then she abandoned the piano and threw herself down in a chair.

" Wasn't that a funny talk I had with papa ? You may tell Charlie, if you like, it will amuse him so. They would all think it the most glorious. I shall tell it to everybody when I am on the——''

Here Stella stopped, and gave her sister a half-inquiring, half-malicious look, but found no response in Katherine's grieved eyes.

" I don't know what you mean, Stella,'' she said. " If you

mean what papa thinks, it is the most odious, humiliating bargain ; if you mean something else, it is—but I can't say what
it is, for I don't know what you mean.   You are going to be
a traitor one way or else another, either to Charlie or to papa.
I don't know which is worse, to break that man's heart (for
he is fond of you) by throwing him over at the last moment,
or to steal papa's money and break his heart too.''

"You needn't trouble yourself so much about people's
hearts, Kate.   How do you know that Charlie would have me
if he thought papa wouldn't give in ?   And, as for papa's
heart, he would only have to give in, and then all would be
right.   It isn't such a complicated matter as you think.   You
are so fond of making out that things are complicated.   I
think them quite simple.   Papa has just to make up his mind
which he likes best, me or his money.   He thinks he likes his
money best.   Well, perhaps later he will find he doesn't, and
then he has only got to change.   Where's the difficulty ?   As
for me, you must just weave webs about me as long as you
please.   I am not complicated—not a bit.   I shall do what I
like best.   I am not sure even now which I like best, but I
shall know when the time comes.   And in the meantime I am
laying up all the best evidence to judge from.   I shall send
Stevens up to town for patterns to-morrow.   I shall get the
very richest and the very dearest things that Madame has or
can get.   Oh,'' cried the girl, clapping her hands with true
enjoyment, " what fun it will be ! ''

CHAPTER XVI.

EVERYTHING now began to converge towards the great ball which was to be given in Sliplin to the regiment before it went off to India. It was in its little way something like that great Brussels ball which came before Waterloo. They were to embark next morning, these heroic soldiers. If they were not going to fight, they were at least going to dare the dangers of the deep in a troop-ship, which is not comfortable ; and they were fully impressed with their own importance as the heroes of the moment. Lady Jane was at the head of the undertaking, along with certain other magnates of the neighbourhood. Without them I doubt whether the Sliplin people proper would have felt it necessary to give the Chestnuts a ball ; the officers had never been keen about the village parties. They had gone to the Cliff, where everything smelt of gold, but they had not cared for those little entertainments— for lawn tennis in the summer and other mild dissipations at which their presence would have been an excitement and delight. So that the good people in Sliplin had looked rather coldly upon the suggestion at first. When it was settled, however, and the greatness of the event was realised, the Sliplin people warmed up into interest. A ball is a ball, however it is brought about.

Mr. Tredgold subscribed liberally, and so of course Stella and Katherine had been "in it" from the very first. They took the greatest interest in the decorations, running up and down to the great hall in which it was to be held, and superintending everything. Mrs. Shanks and Miss Mildmay also looked in a great many times in a day, and so did many other of the Sliplin ladies, moved at last to "take an interest" when it was no longer possible that it should cost them any-thing.

" I hear they have plenty of money for everything—too much indeed—so it is just as well that we did not come forward. If we had come forward I don't know what the lists would have risen to. As it is, I hear there is almost too much. Mr. Tredgold insists upon champagne—oceans of champagne. I am sure I hope that the young men will behave properly. I don't approve of such rivers of wine. If they are fond of dancing, surely they can enjoy their dancing without that."

This is a very general opinion among the ladies of country towns, and gives a fine disinterested aspect to the pursuit of dancing for its own sake ; but no doubt the Chestnuts liked it better when there were oceans of champagne.

It had been known all along in the place that Stella Tred-gold meant to surpass herself on this occasion, which was a matter calling forth much astonishment and speculation among her friends. It was also known, more or less, that Sir Charles Somers had made his proposals to her father and had been re-fused. All his own friends were well aware of the fact, and it was not to be supposed that it should be a secret at Sliplin. Sir Charles had been refused by Mr. Tredgold because he had no money, not by Stella, who was very much in love with him, everybody said, as he was with her. It was enough to see them together to be convinced of that. And yet she meant to be the gayest of the gay at the ball on the eve of parting with him ! Some of the girls expected and hoped that evidences of a broken heart would be visible even under the lovely white dress and wonderful diamonds in which she was understood to be going to appear. So ridiculous for a girl of her age to wear diamonds, the elder ladies said ; and they did not think there would be any evidences of a broken heart. " She has no heart, that little thing ; Lord Uffington will be there, and she will go in for him, now that Sir Charles has failed." It must be admitted it was strange that she should show so much delight in this ball and proclaim her intention of being dressed more gorgeously than she had ever been in her life on the eve of parting with her lover. Was it to leave such an impression on his mind that he never should forget her ? was it to show she didn't care? But nobody could tell. Stella had always been an odd girl, they said, though indeed I do not think that this was true.

She was very much occupied on the day of the ball, still looking after these decorations, and even made a dash across the country in her own little brougham in the morning to get one particular kind of white chrysanthemum which only grew in a cottage garden in the middle of the island. She returned from this wild expedition about noon with the brougham filled with the flowers, and a great air of triumph and excitement. "Wasn't it clever of me?" she cried. "I just remembered. We saw them, don't you recollect, Kate? the last time we were out that way. They were just the things that were wanted for the head of the room. I flew to the stables and called Andrews, and we were there —oh, I can't tell you how soon."

"Nice thing for my horse," said Mr. Tredgold. "He's a young devil, that Andrews boy. I shall give him the sack if he doesn't mind."

"It is my horse," said Stella ; "the brougham's mine, and the boy's mine. You forget what you said, papa."

"There never was an extortioner like this little——" said Mr. Tredgold, chuckling; "drives her horse to death and then feeds him with sugar—just like women—it's what they all do."

"I think," said Katherine, "you might have found some chrysanthemums nearer home."

"But you see I didn't," said Stella, with her usual impatience, breaking into song and tossing her shining head as she walked away.

"Doesn't make much of the parting, and that fellow off to India, does she?" said her father. "I knew how it would be ; I never believe in a girl's swagger, bless you. She's very fond of one man till she sees another. You'll find my lord will make all the running to-night."

10

"And if Lord Uffington should propose for Stella," said Katherine with her grave air, " which I don't think very likely, but, still, from your point of view, papa, would you insist upon the same test with my lord—as you call him—pound for pound on the table as you say, and that sort of thing ? "

"Certainly I should—if he was a Royal Dook," Mr. Tredgold said.

"Then it is a pity," said Katherine; but she said no more, nor would any question bring forth the end of her sentence. She went out and took a walk along the cliff, where there was that beautiful view. It was a very fine day, one of those matchless days of early winter which are perhaps the most beautiful of English weather. The sun was blazing, calling forth the dazzling whiteness of that sharp cliff which was the furthest point to the east, and lighting every wave as with the many coloured facets of a diamond. There were one or two boats out, lying in the light, or moving softly with the slight breeze, which was no more than a little movement in the celestial air—as if suspended between earth and heaven. And to think it was November, that grim month in which everything is dismal ! I don't think Katherine was thinking very much about the view, but she was soothed by it in the multitude of her thoughts.

She was out there again very late, between one and two in the morning, after the ball. Stella had wanted to leave early, and would fain have escaped before her sister. But Katherine balked her in this, without having any particular reason for it. She felt only that when Stella went away she must go too, and that though she had seemed so indifferent there was now a great deal of excitement in Stella's gaiety, which was so unrestrained. They went off accordingly, leaving a crowd of disappointed partners shouting complaints and good-nights after them. When they entered the drive, where a sleepy woman came forth from the lodge to let them in, Katherine noticed a dark figure which stole in with the carriage.

" Who is that ? " she said.

" Oh, Katie, Katie dear, don't say anything ! " cried Stella,

putting a hand upon her mouth. " It is Charlie come to say
good-bye. I must say one little word to him before he goes;
do you think that I am made of stone ? "

" Oh, no, no ! " cried Katherine. " I have been wondering — I thought you had got over — I didn't know what to
think."

" I shall never get over it," said Stella, vehemently. She
was crying with her head against her sister's shoulder. " Oh,
Kate, don't be hard upon me, or say anything ! I must — I
must have one little half hour with Charlie before he goes
away."

" Indeed—indeed, I shall not say anything ! I do feel for
you, Stella. I am sorry for him. But, oh, don't stay long,
dear, it will only prolong the trouble. And it is so late, and
people might say—— "

" How could people say if they didn't know ? And,
Katie," cried her sister, " if you stay here to watch over us,
while I bid him—I mean talk to him yonder—what could anyone say ? Won't it be enough to quench every evil tongue if
you are there ? "

" I suppose it will," said Katherine dubiously.

She got down very dubiously from the brougham, from
which Stella had sprung like an arrow. And Andrews, who
drove the warm little carriage which was Stella's, as he was
more or less Stella's man, turned immediately and drove away,
no doubt to relieve the gatekeeper, who was waiting to close
up after him. A sleepy footman had opened the door, and
stood waiting while Katherine, in her white cloak, lingered in
the porch. The fire was still burning in the hall, and the lamp
bright. Katherine told the man to go to bed, and that she
would herself fasten the door, and then she turned to the glory
of the night, and the lawn, and all the shrubberies, looking
like frosted silver in the moonlight. Stella had disappeared
somewhere among the shadows with her lover. Katherine
heard a faint sound of steps, and thought she could perceive
still a gleam of whiteness among the trees. She stepped out
herself upon the walk. It sounded a little crisp under her foot,

for there was frost in the air.   The moon was glorious, filling
earth and heaven with light, and flinging the blackest shadows
into all the corners.   And the stillness was such that the dropping of one of those last yellow leaves slowly down through the
air was like an event.   She was warmly wrapped up in her fur
cloak, and, though the hour was eerie, the night was beautiful,
and the house with its open door, and the glow of the red fire,
and the light of the lamp, gave protection and fellowship.   All
the rare trees, though sufficiently hardy to bear it, had shrunk
a little before that pennyworth of frost, though it was really
nothing, not enough to bind the moisture in a little hollow of
the path, which Katherine had to avoid as she walked up
and down in her satin shoes.   After a while she heard the little
click of the door at the foot of the steep path which led to the
beach, and concluded that Stella had let her lover out that
way, and would soon join her.   But Katherine was in no
hurry ; she was not cold, and she had never been out, she
thought, in so lovely a night.   It carried her away to many
thoughts ; I will not venture to allege that James Stanford was
not one of them.   It would have been strange if she had not
thought of him in these circumstances.   She had never had the
chance of saying farewell to him ; he had been quenched at
once by her father, and he had not had the spirit to come
back, which, she supposed, Sir Charles had.   He had disappeared and made no sign.   Stella was more lucky than she was
in every way.   Poor Stella ! who must just have gone through
one of the most terrible of separations !   " Partings that press
the life from out young hearts ! "   Who was it that said that ?
But still it must be better to have the parting than that he
should disappear like a shadow without a word, and be no
more seen or heard of—as if he were dead.   And perhaps he
was dead, for anything she knew.

But, what a long time Stella was coming back !   If she
had let him out at that door, she surely should have found her
way up the cliff before now.   Katherine turned in that direction, and stood still at the top of the path and listened, but
could hear nothing.   Perhaps she had been mistaken about the

click of the door. It was very dark in that deep shadow—too dark to penetrate into the gloom by herself without a lantern, especially as, after all, she was not quite sure that Stella had gone that way. She must at least wait a little longer before making any search which might betray her sister. She turned back again, accordingly, along the round of the broad cliff with its feathering edge of tamarisks. Oh, what a wonderful world of light and stillness ! The white cliff to the east shone and flamed in the moonlight ; it was like a tall ghost between the blue sea and the blue sky, both of them so indescribably blue—the little ripple breaking the monotony of one, the hosts of stars half veiled in the superior radiance of the moon diversifying the other. She had never been out on such a beautiful night. It was a thing to remember. She felt that she should never forget (though she certainly was not fond of him at all) the night of Charlie Somers's departure—the night of the ball, which had been the finest Sliplin had ever known.

As Katherine moved along she heard in the distance, beginning to make a little roll of sound, the carriages of the people going away. She must have been quite a long time there when she perceived this ; the red fire in the hall was only a speck now. A little anxious, she went back again to the head of the path. She even ventured a few steps down into the profound blackness. " Stella ! " she cried in a low voice, " Stella ! " Then she added, still in a kind of whisper, " Come back, oh, come back ; it is getting so late."

But she got no reply. There were various little rustlings, and one sound as of a branch that crushed under a step, but no step was audible. Could they be too engrossed to hear her, or was Stella angry or miserable, declining to answer ? Katherine, in great distress, threaded her way back among the trees that seemed to get in her way and take pleasure in striking against her, as if they thought her false to her sister. She was not false to Stella, she declared to herself indignantly ; but this was too long — she should not have stayed so long. Katherine began to feel cold, with a chill that was not of the night. And then there sounded into the clear shining air the stroke of

the hour.   She had never heard it so loud before.   She felt that
it must wake all the house, and bring every one out to see if
the girls had not come back.   It would wake papa, who was
not a very good sleeper, and betray everything.   Three !
" Stella, Stella ! oh, for goodness' sake, don't stay any longer ! " cried Katherine, making a sort of funnel of her two
hands, and sending her voice down into the dark.

After all, she said to herself, presently, three was not late for
a ball.   The rest of the people were only beginning to go
away.   And a parting which might be for ever !   " It may be
for years, and it may be for ever."   The song came into her
mind and breathed itself all about her, as a song has a way of
doing.   Poor things, poor young things ! and perhaps they might
never see each other again.   " Partings that press the life from
out young hearts."   Katherine turned with a sigh and made
a little round of the cliff again, without thinking of the view.
And then she turned suddenly to go back, and looked out upon
the wonderful round of the sea and sky.

There was something new in it now, something that had not
been there before — a tall white sail, like something glorified,
like an angel with one foot on the surface of the waves, and one
high white wing uplifted.   She stood still with a sort of breath-
less admiration and rapture.   Sea and sky had been wonderful
before, but they had wanted just that — the white softly moving sail, the faint line of the boat.   Where was it she had seen
just that before, suddenly coming into sight while she was
watching ?   It was when the *Stella*, when Stella — good heavens ! — the *Stella*, and Stella——

Katherine uttered a great cry, and ran wildly towards the
house.   And then she stopped herself and went back to the
cliff and gazed again.   It might only be a fishing-boat made
into a wonderful thing by the moonlight.   When she looked
again it had already made a great advance in the direction of
the white cliff, to the east ; it was crossing the bay, gliding
very smoothly on the soft waves.   The *Stella* — could it be
the *Stella ?* — and where was her sister ?   She gathered up her
long white dress more securely and plunged down the dark

path towards the beach. The door was locked, there was not
a sound anywhere.

"Stella!" she cried, louder than ever. "Stella! where
are you?" but nobody heard, not even in the sleeping house,
where surely there must be some one waking who could help
her. This made her remember that Stevens, the maid, must
be waking, or at least not in bed. She hurried in, past the
dying fire in the hall, and up the silent stairs, the sleeping
house so still that the creak of a plank under her feet sounded
like a shriek. But there was no Stevens to be found, neither
in the young ladies' rooms where she should have been, nor in
her own ; everything was very tidy, there was not a brush nor
a pocket-handkerchief out of place, and the trim, white bed
was not even prepared for any inhabitant. It was as if it were
a bed of death.

Then Katherine bethought her to go again to the gardener's
wife in the lodge, who had a lantern. She had been woke up
before, perhaps it was less harm to wake her up again (this was
not logical, but Katherine was above logic). Finally, the
woman was roused, and her husband along with her, and the
lantern lighted, and the three made a circle of the shrubberies.
There was nothing to be found there. The man declared that
the door was not only locked but jammed, so that it would be
very hard to open it, and he unhesitatingly swore that it was
the *Stella* which was now gliding round beyond the Bunbridge
cliffs.

"How do you know it is the *Stella*? It might be any
yacht," cried Katherine.

The man did not condescend to make any explanation. " I
just knows it," he said.

It was proved presently by this messenger, despatched in
haste to ascertain, that the *Stella* was gone from the pier, and
there was nothing more to be said.

The sight of these three, hunting in every corner, filling the
grounds with floating gleams of light, and voices and steps no
longer subdued, while the house lay open full of sleep, the
lamp burning in the hall but nobody stirring, was a strange

sight.   At length there was a sound heard in the silent place.
A window was thrown open, a night-capped head was thrust
into the air.

"What the deuce is all this row about?" cried the voice of
Mr. Tredgold.   "Who's there?   Look out for yourselves,
whoever you are; I'm not going to have strangers in my garden at this hour of the night."

And the old man, startled, put a climax to the confusion by
firing wildly into space.   The gardener's wife gave a shriek
and fell, and the house suddenly woke up, with candles moving from window to window, and men and women calling out
in different tones of fury and affright, "Who is there?   Who
is there?"

CHAPTER XVII.

NOT only Sliplin, but the entire island was in commotion next day. Stella Tredgold had disappeared in the night, in her ball dress, which was the most startling detail, and seized the imagination of the community as nothing else could have done. Those of them who had seen her, so ridiculously over-dressed for a girl of her age, sparkling with diamonds from head to foot, as some of these spectators said, represented to themselves with the dismayed delight of excitement that gleaming figure in the white satin dress which many people had re-marked was like a wedding dress, the official apparel of a bride. In this wonderful garb she had stolen away down the dark private path from the Cliff to the beach, and got round somehow over the sands and rocks to the little harbour; and, while her sister was waiting for her on the cold cliff in the moonlight, had put out to sea and fled away—Stella the girl, and *Stella* the yacht, no one knew where. Was it her wedding dress, indeed? or had she, the misguided, foolish creature, flung herself into Charlie Somers's life without any safeguard, trusting to the honour of a man like that, who was a profligate and without honour, as everybody knew.

No one, however, except the most pessimistic—who always exist in every society, and think the worst, and alas! prove in so many cases right, because they always think the worst—believed in this. Indeed, it would be only right to say that nobody believed Stella to have run away to shame. There was a conviction in the general mind that a marriage licence, if not a marriage certificate, had certainly formed part of her baggage; and nobody expected that her father would be able to drag her back "by the hair of her head," as it was believed

the furious old man intended to do. Mr. Tredgold's fury
passed all bounds, it was universally said. He had discharged
a gun into the group on the lawn, who were searching for Stella
in the shrubberies (*most* absurd of them!), and wounded, it
was said, the gardener's wife, who kept the lodge, and who
had taken to her bed and made the worst of it, as such a person would naturally do. And then he had stood at the open
window in his dressing-gown, shouting orders to the people as
they appeared—always under the idea that burglars had got
into the grounds.

" Have the girls come back? Is Stella asleep? Don't let
them disturb my little Stella! Don't let them frighten my
pet," he had cried, while all the servants ran and bobbed
about with lanterns and naked candles, flaring and blowing
out, and not knowing what they were looking for. A hundred details were given of this scene, which no outsider had
witnessed, which the persons involved were not conscious of,
but which were nevertheless true. Even what Katherine said
to her father crept out somehow, though certainly neither he
nor she reported the details of that curious scene.

When she had a little organised the helpless body of servants and told them as far as she could think what to do—which
was for half of them at least to go back to bed and keep quiet;
when she had sent a man she could trust to make inquiries
about the *Stella* at the pier, and another to fetch a doctor for
the woman who considered herself to be dying, though she
was, in fact, not hurt at all, and who made a diversion for
which Katherine was thankful, she went indoors with Mrs.
Simmons, the housekeeper, who was a person of some sense
and not helpless in an emergency as the others were. And
Mrs. Simmons had really something to tell. She informed
Katherine as they went in together through the cold house,
where the candles they carried made faintly visible the confusion of rooms abandoned for the night, with the ashes of last
night's fires in the grate, and last night's occupations in every
chair carelessly pushed aside, and table heaped with news-
papers and trifles, that she had been misdoubting as something

was up with Stevens at least. Stevens was the point at which the story revealed itself to Mrs. Simmons. She had been holding her head very high, the little minx. She had been going on errands and carrying letters as nobody knew where they were to ; and yesterday was that grand she couldn't contain herself, laughing and smiling to herself and dressed up in her very best. She had gone out quite early after breakfast on the day of the ball to get some bit of ribbon she wanted, but never came back till past twelve, when she came in the brougham with Miss Stella, and laughing so with her mistress in her room (you were out, Miss Katherine) as it wasn't right for a maid to be carrying on like that. And out again as soon as you young ladies was gone to the ball, and never come back, not so far as Mrs. Simmons knew. "Oh, I've misdoubted as there was something going on," the housekeeper said. Katherine, who was shivering in the dreadful chill of the house in the dead of night, in the confusion of this sudden trouble, was too much depressed and sick at heart to ask why she had not been told of these suspicions. And then her father's voice calling to her was audible coming down the stairs. He stood at the head of the staircase, a strange figure in his dressing-gown and night-cap, with a candle held up in one hand and his old gun embraced in the other arm.

"Who's there?" he cried, staring down in the darkness. "Who's there? Have you got 'em ?—have you got 'em ? Damn the fellows, and you too, for keeping me waitin' ! " He was foaming at the mouth, or at least sending forth jets of moisture in his excitement. Then he gave vent to a sort of broken shout—"Kath-i-rine ! " astonishment and sudden terror driving him out of familiarity into her formal name.

"Yes, papa, I am coming. Go back to your room. I will tell you everything—or, at least, all I know." She was vaguely thankful in her heart that the doctor would be there, that there would be some one to fall back upon if it made him ill. Katherine seemed by this time to have all feeling deadened in her. If she could only have gone to her own room and lain down and forgotten everything, above all, that

Stella was not there breathing softly within the ever-open door
between! She stopped a moment, in spite of herself, at the
window on the landing which looked out upon the sea, and
there, just rounding the white cliff, was that moving speck of
whiteness sharing in the intense illumination of the moonlight,
which even as she looked disappeared, going out of sight in a
minute as if it had been a cloud or a dream.

"Have they got 'em, Katie? and what were you doing
there at this time of night, out on the lawn in your——
George!" cried the old man—"in your ball finery? Have
you just come back? Why, it's near five in the morning.
What's the meaning of all this? Is Stella in her bed safe?
And what in the name of wonder are you doing here?"

"Papa," said Katherine in sheer disability to enter on the
real subject, "you have shot the woman."

"Damn the woman!" he cried.

"And there were no burglars," she said with a sob. The
cold, moral and physical, had got into her very soul. She
drew her fur cloak more closely about her, but it seemed to
give no warmth, and then she dropped upon her knees by the
cold fireplace, in which, as in all the rest, there was nothing
but the ashes of last night's fire. Mr. Tredgold stood leaning
on the mantel-piece, and he was cold too. He bade her tell
him in a moment what was the matter, and what she had been
doing out of the house at this hour of the night—with a tremulous roar.

"Papa! oh, how can I tell you! It is Stella—Stella——"

"What!" he cried. "Stella ill? Stella ill? Send for
the doctor. Call up Simmons. What is the matter with the
child? Is it anything bad that you look so distracted? Good
Lord—my Stella!"

"Oh, have patience, sir," said Mrs. Simmons, coming in
with wood to make a fire; "there'll be news of her by the
morning—sure there'll be news by the morning. Miss
Katherine have done everything. And the sea is just like a
mill-pond, and her own gentlemen to see to her——"

"The sea?" cried the old man. "What has the sea to do

with my Stella?" He aimed a clumsy blow at the housekeeper, kneeling in front of the fire, with the butt end of the
gun he still had in his hand, in his unreflecting rage. "You
old hag! what do you know about my Stella?" he cried.

Mrs. Simmons did not feel the blow which Katherine di-
verted, but she was wounded by the name, and rose up with
dignity, though not before she had made a cheerful blaze. "I
meant to have brought you some tea, Miss Katherine, but if
Master is going on with his abuse—— He did ought to think
a little bit of *you* as are far more faithful. What do I know—
more than that innocent lamb does of all their goings on?"

"Katie," cried Mr. Tredgold, "put that wretched woman
out by the shoulders. And why don't you go to your sister?
Doesn't Stella go before everything? Have you sent for the
doctor? Where's the doctor? And can't you tell me what
is the matter with my child?"

"If I'm a wretched woman," cried Mrs. Simmons, "I
ain't fit to be at the head of your servants, Mr. Tredgold; and
I'm quite willing to go this day month, sir, for it's a hard
place, though very likely better now Miss Stella's gone. As
for Miss Stella, sir, it's no doctor, but maybe a clergyman as
she is wanting; for she is off with her gentleman as sure as I
am standing here."

Mr. Tredgold gave an inarticulate cry, and felt vaguely for
the gun which was still within his arm; but he missed hold of
it and it fell on the floor, where the loaded barrel went off,
scattering small shot into all the corners. Mrs. Simmons flew
from the room with a conviction, which never left her, that
she had been shot at, to meet the trembling household flocking
from all quarters to know the meaning of this second report.
Katherine, whose nerves were nearly as much shaken as those
of Mrs. Simmons, and who could not shut out from her mind
the sensation that some one must have been killed, shut the
door quickly, she hardly knew why; and then she came back
to her father, who was lying back very pale, and looking as if
he were the person wounded, on the cushions of his great
chair.

" What—what—does she mean ? " he half said, half looked. " Is—is—it true ? "

" Oh, papa !" cried Katherine, kneeling before him, trying to take his hand. " I am afraid, I am afraid—— "

He pushed her off furiously. " You—afraid !" Impossible to describe the scorn with which he repeated this word. " Is it—is it true ? "

Katherine could make no reply, and he wanted none, for thereupon he burst into a roar of oaths and curses which beat down on her head like a hailstorm. She had never heard the like before, nor anything in the least resembling it. She tried to grasp at his hands, which he dashed into the air in his fury, right and left. She called out his name, pulled at his arm in the same vain effort. Then she sprang to her feet, crying out that she could not bear it—that it was a horror and a shame. Katherine's cloak fell from her ; she stood, a vision of white, with her uncovered shoulders and arms, confronting the old man, who, with his face distorted like that of a demoniac, sat volleying forth curses and imprecations. Katherine had never been so splendidly adorned as Stella, but a much smaller matter will make a girl look wonderful in all her whiteness shining, in the middle of the gloom against the background of heavy curtains and furniture, at such a moment of excitement and dismay. It startled the doctor as he came in, as with the effect of a scene in a play. And indeed he had a totally different impression of Katherine, who had always been kept a little in the shade of the brightness of Stella, from that day.

" Well," he said, coming in, energetic but calm, into the midst of all this agitation, with a breath of healthful freshness out of the night, " what is the matter here ? I have seen the woman, Miss Katherine, and she is really not hurt at all. If it had touched her eyes, though, it might have been bad enough. Hullo ! the gun again—gone off of itself this time, eh ? I hope you are not hurt—nor your father."

" We are in great trouble," said Katherine. " Papa has been very much excited. Oh, I am so glad—so glad you have come, doctor ! Papa—— "

"Eh? what's the matter? Come, Mr. Tredgold, you must get into bed—not a burglar about, I assure you, and the man on the alert. What do you say? Oh, come, come, my friend, you mustn't swear."

To think he should treat as a jest that torrent of oaths that had made Katherine tremble and shrink more than anything else that had happened! It brought her, like a sharp prick, back to herself.

"Don't speak to me, d—— you," cried the old man. "D—— you all—d——"

"Yes," said the doctor, "cursed be the whole concern, I know—and a great relief to your mind, I shouldn't wonder. But now there's been enough of that and you must get to bed."

He made Katherine a sign to go away, and she was thankful beyond expression to do so, escaping into her own room, where there was a fire, and where the head housemaid, very serious, waited to help her to undress—"As Stevens, you are aware, Miss Katherine, 'as gone away." The door of the other room was open, the gleam of firelight visible within. Oh, was it possible—was it possible that Stella was not there, that she was gone away without a sign, out on the breadths of the moonlit sea, from whence she might never come again? Katherine had not realised this part of the catastrophe till now. "I think I can manage by myself, Thompson," she said faintly; "don't let me keep you out of bed."

"Oh, there's no question of bed now for us, Miss," said Thompson with emphasis; "it's only an hour or two earlier than usual, that's all. We'll get the more forwarder with our work—if any one can work, with messengers coming and going, and news arriving, and all this trouble about Miss Stella. I'm sure, for one, I couldn't close my eyes."

Katherine vaguely wondered within herself if she were of more common clay than Thompson, as she had always been supposed to be of more common clay than her sister; for she felt that she would be very glad to close her eyes and forget for a moment all this trouble. She said in a faint voice, "We do not know anything about Miss Stella, Thompson, as yet. She may have gone—up to Steephill with Lady Jane.''

"Oh, I know, Miss, very well where she's gone. She's gone to that big ship as sails to-morrow with all the soldiers. How she could do it, along of all those men, I can't think. I'm sure I couldn't do it," cried Thompson. "Oh, I had my doubts what all them notes and messages was coming to, and Stevens that proud she wouldn't speak a word to nobody. Well, I always thought as Stevens was your maid, Miss Katherine, as you're the eldest; but I don't believe she have done a thing for you.''

"Oh, she has done all I wanted. I don't like very much attendance. Now that you have undone these laces, you may go. Thank you very much, Thompson, but I really do not want anything more.''

"I'll go and get you some tea, Miss Katherine," the woman said. Another came to the door before she had been gone a minute. They were all most eager to serve the remaining daughter of the house, and try to pick up a scrap of news, or to state their own views at the same time. This one put in her head at the door and said in a hoarse confidential whisper, "Andrews could tell more about it than most, Miss, if you'd get hold of him.''

"Andrews!" said Katherine.

"He always said he was Miss Stella's man, and he's drove her a many places—oh, a many places—as you never knowed of. You just ast him where he took her yesterday mornin', Miss?''

At this point Thompson came back, and drove the other skurrying away.

When Katherine went back, in the warm dressing-gown which was so comfortable, wrapping her round like a friend, to her father's room, she found the old man in bed, very white and tremulous after his passion, but quiet, though his lips still moved and his cruel little red eyes shone. Katherine had never known before that they were cruel eyes, but the impression came upon her now with a force that made her shiver;

they were like the eyes of a wild creature, small and impotent, which would fain have killed but could not—with a red glare in them, unwinking, fixed, full of malice and fury. The doctor explained to her, standing by the fireplace, what he had done; while Katherine, listening, saw across the room those fiery small eyes watching the conversation as if they could read what it was in her face. She could not take her own eyes away, nor refuse to be investigated by that virulent look.

"I have given him a strong composing draught. He'll go to sleep presently, and the longer he sleeps the better. He has got his man with him, which is the best thing for him; and now about you, Miss Katherine." He took her hand with that easy familiarity of the medical man which his science authorises, and in which there is often as much kindness as science. "What am I to do for you?"

"Oh, nothing, doctor, unless you can suggest something. Oh, doctor, it is of no use trying to conceal it from you—my sister is gone!" She melted suddenly, not expecting them at all, thinking herself incapable of them—into tears.

"I know, I know," he said. "It is a great shock for you, it is very painful; but if, as I hear, he was violently against the marriage, and she was violently determined on it, was not something of the kind to be expected? You know your sister was very much accustomed to her own way."

"Oh, doctor, how can you say that!—as if you took it for granted—as if it was not the most terrible thing that could happen! Eloped, only imagine it! Stella! in her ball dress, and with that man!"

"I hope there is nothing very bad about the man," said the doctor with hesitation.

"And how are we to get her back? The ship sails to-morrow. If she is once carried away in the ship, she will never, never—— Oh, doctor, can I go? who can go? What can we do? Do tell me something, or I will go out of my senses," she cried.

"Is there another room where we can talk? I think he is going to sleep," said the doctor.

11

Katherine, in her distress, had got beyond the power of the terrible eyes on the bed, which still gleamed, but fitfully. Her father did not notice her as she went out of the room. And by this time the whole house was astir—fires lighted in all the rooms—to relieve the minds of the servants, it is to be supposed, for nobody knew why. The tray that had been carried to her room was brought downstairs, and there by the perturbed fire of a winter morning, burning with preternatural vigilance and activity as if eager to find out what caused it, she poured out the hot tea for the doctor, and he ate bread and butter with the most wholesome and hearty appetite—which was again a very curious scene.

The Tredgolds were curiously without friends. There was no uncle, no intimate to refer to, who might come and take the lead in such an emergency. Unless Katherine could have conducted such inquiries herself, or sent a servant, there was no one nearer than the doctor, or perhaps the vicar, who had always been so friendly. He and she decided between them that the doctor should go off at once, or at least as soon as there was a train to take him, to the great ship which was to embark the regiment early that morning, to discover whether Sir Charles Somers was there; while the vicar, whom he could see and inform in the meantime, should investigate the matter at home and at Steephill. The gardener, a trustworthy man, had, as soon as his wife was seen to be " out of danger," as they preferred to phrase it—" scarcely hurt at all," as the doctor said—been sent off to trace the *Stella*, driving in a dog-cart to Bunbridge, which was the nearest port she was likely to put in at. By noon the doctor thought they would certainly have ascertained among them all that was likely to be ascertained. He tried to comfort Katherine's mind by an assurance that no doubt there would be a marriage, that Somers, though he had not a good character, would never—but stopped with a kind of awe, perceiving that Katherine had no suspicion of the possibility of any other ending, and condemning himself violently as a fool for putting any such thought into her head; but he had not put any such thought in her head, which was incapable of it. She had no conception of anything that could be worse than the elopement. He hastened to take refuge in something she did understand. "All this on one condition," he said, "that you go to bed and try to sleep. I will do nothing unless you promise this, and you can do nothing for your sister. There is nothing to be done ; gazing out over the sea won't bring the yacht back. You must promise me that you will try to go to sleep. You will if you try."

"Oh, yes, I will go to sleep," Katherine said. She reflected again that she was of commoner clay than Thompson, who could not have closed an eye.

CHAPTER XVIII.

IT proved not at all difficult to find out everything, or almost everything, about the runaway pair. The doctor's mission, though it seemed likely to be the most important of all, did not produce very much. In the bustle of the embarkation he had found it difficult to get any information at all, but eventually he had found Captain Scott, whom he had attended during his illness, and whom he now sent peremptorily down below out of the cold. "If that's your duty, you must not do it, that's all," he had said with the decision of a medical man, though whether he had secured his point or not, Katherine, ungratefully indifferent to Algy, did not ascertain. But he found that Sir Charles Somers had got leave and was going out with a P. and O. from Brindisi to join his regiment when it should reach India.

"It will cost him the eyes out of his head," Algy said. "Lucky beggar, he don't mind what he spends now."

"Why?" the doctor asked, and was laughed at for not knowing that Charlie had run off with old Tredgold's daughter, who was good for any amount of money, and, of course, would soon give in and receive the pair back again into favour. "Are you so sure of that?" the doctor said. And Algy had replied that his friend would be awfully up a tree if it didn't turn out so. The doctor shook his head in relating this story to Katherine. "I have my doubts," he said; but she knew nothing on that subject, and was thinking of nothing but of Stella herself, and the dreadful thought that she might see her no more.

The vicar, on his side, had been busy with his inquiries too, and he had found out everything with the greatest ease; in the first place from Andrews, the young coachman, who declared that he had always taken his orders from Miss Stella, and didn't know as he was doing no wrong. Andrews admitted very frankly that he had driven his young mistress to the little church, one of the very small primitive churches of the island near Steephill, where the tall gentleman with the dark moustaches had met her, and where Miss Stevens had turned up with a big basketful of white chrysanthemums. They had been in the church about half an hour, and then they had come out again, and Miss Stevens and the young lady had got into the brougham. The chrysanthemums had been for the decoration of the ballroom, as everybody knew. Then he had taken Miss Stevens to meet the last train for Ryde; and finally he had driven his young ladies home with a gentleman on the box that had got down at the gate, but whether he came any further or not Andrews did not know. The vicar had gone on in search of information to Steephill Church, and found that the old rector there, in the absence of the curate—he himself being almost past duty by reason of old age—had married one of the gentlemen living at the Castle to a young lady whose name he could not recollect further than that it was Stella. The old gentleman had thought it all right as it was a gentleman from the Castle, and he had a special licence, which made everything straight. The register of the marriage was all right in the books, as the vicar had taken care to see. Of course it was all right in the books ! Katherine was much surprised that they should all make such a point of that, as if anything else was to be thought of. What did it matter about the register ? The thing was that Stella had run away, that she was gone, that she had betrayed their trust in her, and been a traitor to her home.

But a girl is not generally judged very hardly when she runs away ; it is supposed to be her parents' fault or her lover's fault, and she but little to blame. But when Katherine thought of her vigil on the cliff, her long watch in the moonlight, without a word of warning or farewell, she did not think that Stella was so innocent. Her heart was very sore and wounded by the desertion. The power of love indeed ! Was there no love, then, but one ? Did her home count for

nothing, where she had always been so cherished ; nor her
father, who had loved her so dearly ; nor her sister, who had
given up everything to her ?   Oh, no ; perhaps the sister
didn't matter !   But at least her father, who could not bear
that she should want anything upon which she had set her
heart !   Katherine's heart swelled at the thought of all
Stella's contrivances to escape in safety.   She had carried all
her jewels with her, those jewels which she had partly acquired as the price of abandoning Sir Charles.   Oh, the
treachery, the treachery of it !   She could scarcely keep her
countenance while the gentlemen came with their reports.
She felt her features distorted with the effort to show nothing
but sorrow, and to thank them quietly for all the trouble they
had taken.   She would have liked to stamp her foot, to dash
her clenched hands into the air, almost to utter those curses
which had burst from her father.   What a traitor she had
been !   What a traitor !   She was glad to get the men out of
the house, who were very kind, and wanted to do more if she
would let them—to do anything, and especially to return and
communicate to Mr. Tredgold the result of their inquiries
when he woke from his long sleep.   Katherine said No, no,
she would prefer to tell him herself.   There seemed to be but
one thing she desired, and that was to be left alone.

After this hot fit there came, as was natural, a cold one.
Katherine went upstairs to her own room, the room divided
from that other only by an open door, which they had occupied ever since they were children.   Then her loneliness came
down upon her like a pall.   Even with the thrill of this news in
all her frame, she felt a foolish impulse to go and call Stella—
to tell Stella all about it, and hear her hasty opinion.   Stella
never hesitated to give her opinion, to pronounce upon every
subject that was set before her with rapid, unhesitating de-
cisions.   She would have known exactly what to say on
this subject.   She would have taken the girl's part ; she would
have asked what right a man had because he was your father
to be such a tyrant.   Katherine could hear the very tone in
which she would have condemned the unnatural parent, and

see the indignant gesture with which she would have lifted her head. And now there was nobody, nothing but silence ; the room so vacant, the trim bed so empty and cold and white. It was like a bed of death, and Katherine shivered. The creature so full of impulses and hasty thoughts and crude opinions and life and brightness would never be there again. No, even if papa would forgive—even if he would receive her back, there would be no Stella any more. This would not be her place ; the sisterly companionship was broken, and life could never more be what it had been.

She sat down on the floor in the middle of the desolation and cried bitterly. What should she do without Stella ? Stella had always been the first to think of everything ; the suggestion of what to do or say had always been in her hands. Katherine did not deny to herself that she had often thought differently from Stella, that she had not always accepted either her suggestions or her opinions ; but that was very different from the silence, the absence of that clear, distinct, self-assured little voice, the mind made up so instantaneously, so ready to pronounce upon every subject. Even in this way of looking at it, it will be seen that she was no blind admirer of her sister. She knew her faults as well as anyone. Faults ! she was made up of faults—but she was Stella all the same.

She had cried all her tears out, and was still sitting intent, with her sorrowful face, motionless, in the reaction of excitement, upon the floor, when Simmons, the housekeeper, opened the door, and looked round for her, calling at last in subdued tones, and starting much to see the lowly position in which her young mistress was. Simmons came attended by the little jingle of a cup and spoon, which had been so familiar in the ears of the girls in all their little childish illnesses, when Simmons with the beef-tea or the arrowroot, or whatever it might be, was a change and a little amusement to them, in the dreadful vacancy of a day in bed. Mrs. Simmons, though she was a great personage in the house and (actually) ordered the dinners and ruled over everything, notwithstanding any fond illusions that Katherine might cherish on that subject, had never delegated this care to anyone else, and Katherine knew very well what was going to be said.

"Miss Katherine, dear, sit up now and take this nice beef-tea. I've seen it made myself, and it's just as good as I know how. And you must take something if you're ever to get up your strength. Sit up, now, and eat it as long as it's nice and hot—do!" The address was at once persuasive, imploring, and authoritative. "Sit up, now, Miss Katherine—do!"

"Oh, Simmons, it isn't beef-tea I want this time," she said, stumbling hastily to her feet.

"No," Simmons allowed with a sigh, "but you want your strength kep' up, and there's nothing so strengthening. It'll warm you too. It's a very cold morning and there's no comfort in the house—not a fire burning as it ought to, not a bit of consolation nowhere. We can't all lay down and die, Miss Katherine, because Miss Stella, bless her, has married a very nice gentleman. He ain't to your papa's liking, more's the pity, and sorry I am in many ways, for a wedding in the house is a fine thing, and such a wedding as Miss Stella's, if she had only pleased your papa! It would have been a sight to see. But, dear, a young lady's fancy is not often the same as an old gentleman's, Miss Katherine. We must all own to that. They thinks of one thing and the young lady, bless her, she thinks of another. It's human nature. Miss Stella's pleased herself, she hasn't pleased Master. Well, we can't change it, Miss Katherine, dear; but she's very 'appy, I don't make a doubt of it, for I always did say as Sir Charles was a very taking man. Lord bless us, just to think of it! I am a-calling her Miss Stella, and it's my Lady she is, bless her little heart!"

Though she despised herself for it, this gave a new turn to Katherine's thoughts too. Lady Somers! yes, that was what Stella was now. That little title, though it was not an exalted one, would have an effect upon the general opinion, however lofty might be the theories expressed, as to the insignificance of rank. Rank; it was the lowest grade of anything that could be called rank. And yet it would have a certain effect on the general mind. She was even conscious of feeling it herself, notwithstanding both the indignation and the sorrow in her mind. " My sister, Lady Somers ! " Was it possible that she could say it with a certain pleasure, as if it explained more or less now (a question which had always been so difficult) who the Tredgolds were, and what they were worth in the island. Now Katherine suddenly realised that people would say, " One of the daughters married Sir Charles Somers." It would be acknowledged that in that case the Tredgolds might be people to know. Katherine's pride revolted, yet her judgment recognised the truth of it. And she wondered involuntarily if it would affect her father—if he would think of that?

" Is my father awake yet, Simmons ? " she asked.

" Beginning to stir, Miss Katherine," Dolby said. " How clever they are, them doctors, with their sleeping draffs and things ! Oh, I'm quite opposed to 'em. I don't think as it's right to force sleep or anything as is contrary to the Almighty's pleasure. But to be such nasty stuff, the effeck it do have is wonderful. Your papa, as was so excited like and ready to shoot all of us, right and left, he has slep' like a baby all these hours. And waking up now, Dolby says, like a lamb, and ready for his breakfast."

" I must go to him at once, Simmons," cried Katherine, thrusting back into Simmons's hand the cup and the spoon.

" You won't do nothing of the sort, Miss, if so be as you'll be guided by me. He'll not think of it just at once, and he'll eat his breakfast, which will do him a lot of good, and if he don't see you, why, he'll never remember as anything's up. And then when he comes to think, Dolby will call you, Miss Katherine, if the doctor isn't here first, which would be the best way."

" I think I ought to go to him at once," Katherine said. But she did not do so. It was no pleasant task. His looks when he burst forth into those oaths and curses (though she had herself felt not very long ago as if to do the same might have been a relief to her surcharged and sickened soul), and

when he lay, with his keen small eyes gleaming red with passion, in his bed, looking at her, came back to her with a shudder.   Perhaps she had not a very elevated ideal of a father.
The name did not imply justice or even tenderness to her
mind.   Katherine was well aware that he had never done her
justice all her life.   He had been kind—enough ; but his kindness had been very different from the love he had shown to
Stella.   He had elevated the younger sister over the elder since
ever the children had known how to distinguish between good
and evil.   But still he was papa.   It might be that an uneasy
feeling that she was not proud of her father had visited the
girl's mind more than once, when she saw him among other
men ; but still he was papa just as Stella was Stella, and therefore like no one else, whatever they might say or do.   She
did not like to go to him again, to renew his misery and her
own, to hear him curse the girl whom he had adored, to see
that dreadful look as if of a fiend in his face.   Her own feelings had fallen into a sort of quietude now by means of ex-
haustion, and of the slow, slow moments, which felt every one
of them as if it were an hour.

It was some time longer before she was called.   Mr. Tredgold had got up ; he had made his toilet, and gone down to
his sitting-room, which communicated with his bedroom by a
little private staircase.   And it was only when he was there
that his eyes fell on his clock, and he cried with a start :

"Half-past twelve, and I just come downstairs !   What
does this mean—what does it mean ?   Why wasn't I called at
the right time ? "

"You had a—a restless night, sir," said the man, trembling.
("Oh, where's that Miss Katherine, where's that young person," he said to himself.)

"A restless night !   And why had I a restless night ?   No
supper, eh ?   Never eat supper now.   Girls won't let me.
Hollo !   I begin to remember.   Wasn't there an alarm of
burglars ?   And none of you heard, you deaf fools ; nobody
but me, an old man !   I let go one barrel at them, eh ?
Enough to send them all flying.   Great fun that.   And then

Katherine, Katherine—what do I remember about Katherine? Stopped me before I could do anything, saying there was nobody. Fool, to mind what she said; quite sure there was somebody, eh? Can't you tell me what it was?''

'' Don't know, indeed, sir,'' said the man, whose teeth were chattering with fear.

'' Don't know, indeed! You ought to be ashamed of yourself. Speak out, you fool. Was it burglars——''

'' No, sir. I think not, sir. I—don't know what it was, sir. Something about Miss—— about Miss——''

''About whom?'' the old man cried.

'' Oh, sir, have a little patience—it's all right, it's all right, sir—just Miss Stella, sir, that—that is all right, sir—all safe, sir,'' the attendant cried.

Old Tredgold sat upright in his chair; he put his elbows on the table to support his head. '' Miss Stella!'' he said with a sudden hoarseness in his voice.

And then the man rushed out to summon Katherine, who came quietly but trembling to the call.

He uncovered his face as she came in. It was ghastly pale, the two gleaming points of the eyes glimmering out of it like the eyes of a wild beast. '' Stella, Stella!'' he said hoarsely, and, seizing Katherine by the arm, pressed her down upon a low chair close to him. '' What's all this cock and a bull story?'' he said.

'' Oh, papa!''

He seized her again and shook her in his fury. '' Speak out or I'll—I'll kill you,'' he said.

Her arm was crushed as in an iron vice. Body and soul she trembled before him. '' Papa, let me go or I can say nothing! Let me go!''

He gave her arm one violent twist and then he dropped it. ''What are you afraid of?'' he said, with a gleam of those angry eyes. '' Go on—go on—tell me what happened last night.''

Katherine's narrative was confused and broken, and Mr. Tredgold was not usually a man of very clear intelligence. It must have been that his recollections, sent into the background of his mind by the extreme shock of last night, and by the opiate which had helped him to shake it off, had all the time been working secretly within him through sleeping and waking, waiting only for the outer framework of the story now told him. He understood every word. He took it all up point by point, marking them by the beating of his hand upon the arm of his chair. "That's how it was," he said several times, nodding his head. He was much clearer about it than Katherine, who did not yet realise the sequence of events or that Stella was already Charlie Somers's wife when she came innocently back with her white flowers, and hung about her father at his luncheon, doing everything possible to please him; but he perceived all this without the hesitation of a moment and with apparent composure. "It was all over, then," he said to himself; "she had done it, then. She took us in finely, you and me, Kate. We are a silly lot—to believe what everyone tells us. She was married to a fine gentleman before she came in to us all smiling and pleasant;" and, then, speaking in the same even tone, he suddenly cursed her, without even a pause to distinguish the words.

"Papa, papa!" Katherine cried, almost with a shriek.

"What is it, you little fool? You think perhaps I'll say 'Bless you, my children,' and have them back? They think so themselves, I shouldn't wonder; they'll find out the difference. What about those diamonds that I gave her instead of him—instead of——" And here he laughed, and in the same steady tone bade God curse her again.

"I cannot hear you say that—I cannot, I cannot! Oh, God bless and take care of my poor Stella! Oh, papa, little Stella, that you have always been so fond of——"

Mr. Tredgold's arm started forth as if it would have given a blow. He dashed his fist in the air, then subsided again and laughed a low laugh. "I shan't pay for those diamonds," he said. "I'll send them back, I'll—— And her new clothes that she was to get—God damn her. She can't have taken her clothes, flying off from a ball by night."

" Oh, what are clothes, or money, or anything, in comparison with Stella ! '' Katherine said.

" Not much to you that don't have to pay for them,'' he
said. '' I shan't pay for them. Go and pack up the rags,
don't you hear ? and bring me the diamonds. She thinks
we'll send 'em after her.'' And here the curse again. '' She
shan't have one of them, not one. Go and do what I tell
you, Katie. God damn her and her——''

" Oh, papa, for the sake of everything that is good ! Yes,
I will go—I will go. What does it matter ? Her poor little frocks, her——''

" They cost a deal of money all the same. And bring me
the diamonds,'' Mr. Tredgold said.

And then there suddenly flashed upon Katherine a strange
revelation, a ludicrous tragic detail which did not seem laugh-
able to her, yet was so—— " The diamonds,'' she said
faltering, half turning back on her way to the door.

" Well ! the diamonds ? ''

" Oh, forgive her, forgive her ! She never could have
thought of that ; she never could have meant it. Papa, for
God's sake, forgive her, and don't say—*that* again. She was
wearing them all at the ball. She was in her ball dress. She
had no time to change—she ——''

He seized and shook her savagely as if she had been confessing a theft of her own, and then rose up with his habitual
chuckle in his throat. " George, she's done me,'' he said.
" She's got her fortune on her back. She's—she's a chip of
the old block, after all.'' He dropped down again heavily in
his chair, and then with a calm voice, looking at Katherine,
said tranquilly, " God damn her '' once more.

CHAPTER XIX.

IT was afterwards discovered that Stella had calculated her elopement in a way which justified most perfectly the unwilling applause elicited from her father—that she was a chip of the old block. She had over-decorated herself, as had been remarked, it now appeared, by everybody at the ball, on the night of her flight, wearing all the diamonds she had got from her father as an equivalent for her lover—and other things besides, everything she had that was valuable. It was ridiculous enough to see a girl blazing in all those diamonds; but to have her pearl necklace as well, adjusted as an ornament on her bodice, and bracelets enough to go up almost to the elbow, was more absurd still, and Katherine, it now appeared, was the only person who had not observed this excess of jewellery. She remembered now vaguely that she had felt Stella to be more radiant, more dazzling than ever, and had wondered with a sort of dull ache whether it was want of heart, whether it was over-excitement, or what it was which made her sister's appearance and aspect so brilliant on the very eve of her parting from her lover. "Partings which press the life from out young hearts." How was it possible that she could be so bright, so gay, so full of life, and he going away? She had felt this, but she had not noticed, which was strange, the extraordinary number of Stella's bracelets, or the manner in which her pearls were fastened upon the bosom of her dress. This was strange, but due chiefly perhaps to the fact that Stella had not shown herself, as usual, for her sister's admiration, but had appeared in a hurry rather late, and already wrapped in her cloak.

It was found, however, on examining her drawers, that Stella had taken everything she had which was of any value. It was

also discovered later that she had taken advantage of her
father's permission to get as many new frocks as she pleased—
always to make up for the loss of Charlie—by ordering for
herself an ample *trousseau*, which had been sent to await her to
a London hotel. She had all these things now and the lover
too, which was so brilliant a practical joke that it kept the
regiment in laughter for a year ; but was not so regarded at
home, though Mr. Tredgold himself was not able to refrain
from a certain admiration when he became fully aware of it,
as has been seen. It afflicted Katherine, however, with a dull,
enduring pain in the midst of her longing for her sister and
her sense of the dreadful vacancy made by Stella's absence.
The cheerful calculation, the peaceful looks with which Stella
had hid all her wiles and preparations gave her sister a pang,
not acute but profound—a constant ache which took away all
the spring of her life. Even when she tried to escape from it,
making to herself all those *banal* excuses which are employed
in such circumstances—about love, to which everything is permitted, and the lover's entreaties, to which nothing can be
refused, and the fact that she had to live her own life, not
another's, and was obeying the voice of Nature in choosing for
herself—all these things, which Katherine presented to herself
as consolations, were over and over again refused. If Stella
had run away in her little white frock and garden hat, her sister could have forgiven her ; but the *trousseau*, the maid, the
diamonds, even the old pearls which had been given to both of
them, and still remained the chief of Katherine's possessions—
that Stella should have settled and arranged all that was more
than Katherine could bear. She locked away her own pearls,
with what she felt afterwards to be a very absurd sentiment,
and vowed that she would never wear them again. There
seemed a sort of insult in the addition of that girlish decoration to all her other ornaments. But this, the reader will perceive, was very high-flown on Katherine's part.

A day or two after this tremendous crisis, which, I need not
say, was by far the most delightful public event which had
occurred in Sliplin for centuries, and which moved the very

island to its centre, Lady Jane called with solemnity at the Cliff. Lady Jane was better dressed on this occasion than I believe she had ever been seen to be in the memory of men. She was attired in black brocade with a train, and wore such a mantle as everybody said must have been got for the occasion, since it was like nothing that had ever been seen on Lady Jane's shoulders before. The furs, too, were unknown to Sliplin; perhaps she wore them in more favoured places, perhaps she had borrowed them for the occasion. The reason of all this display was beyond the divination of Katherine, who received her visitor half with the suppressed resentment which she felt she owed to everyone who could be supposed privy to Stella's plans, and half with the wistful longing for an old friend, a wiser and more experienced person, to console herself. Katherine had abandoned the young ladies' room, with all its double arrangements and suggestions of a life that was over. She sat in the large drawing-room, among the costly, crowded furniture, feeling as if, though less expensive, she was but one of them—a daughter needed, like the Italian cabinets, for the due furnishing of the house.

Lady Jane came in, feeling her way between the chairs and tables. It was appropriate that so formal a visit should be received in this formal place. She shook hands with Katherine, who held back visibly from the usual unnecessary kiss. It marked at once the difference, and that the younger woman felt herself elevated by her resentment, and was no longer to be supposed to be in any way at Lady Jane's feet.

"How do you do?" said Lady Jane, carrying out the same idea. "How is your father? I am glad to hear that he has, on the whole, not suffered in health—nor you either, Katherine, I hope?"

"I don't know about suffering in health. I am well enough," the girl said.

"I perceive," said Lady Jane, "by your manner that you identify me somehow with what has happened. That is why I have come here to-day. You must feel I don't come as I usually do. In ordinary circumstances I should probably have

sent for you to come to me. Katherine, I can see that you
think I'm somehow to blame, in what way, I'm sure I don't
know."

"I have never expressed any blame. I don't know that I
have ever thought anyone was to blame—except——"

"Except—except themselves. You are right. They are
very hot-headed, the one as much as the other. I don't mean
to say that he—he is a sort of relation of mine—has not asked
my advice. If he has done so once he has done it a hundred
times, and I can assure you, Katherine, all that I have said has
been consistently 'Don't ask me.' I have told him a hundred
times that I would not take any responsibility. I have said to
him, 'I can't tell how you will suit each other, or whether
you will agree, or anything.' I have had nothing to do with
it. I felt, as he was staying in my house at the time, that you
or your father might be disposed to blame me. I assure you
it would be very unjust. I knew no more of what was going
on on Wednesday last—no more than—than Snap did," cried
Lady Jane. Snap was the little tyrant of the fields at Steephill, a small fox terrier, and kept everything under his control.

"I can only say that you have never been blamed, Lady
Jane. Papa has never mentioned your name, and as for
me——"

"Yes, Katherine, you; it is chiefly you I think of. I am
sure you have thought I had something to do with it."

Katherine made a pause. She was in a black dress. I can
scarcely tell why—partly, perhaps, from some exaggerated
sentiment—actually because Mrs. Simmons, who insisted on
attending to her till someone could be got to replace Stevens,
had laid it out. And she was unusually pale. She had not
in reality "got over" the incident so well as people appeared
to hope.

"To tell the truth," she said, "all the world has seemed
quite insignificant to me except my sister. I have had so
much to do thinking of her that I have had no time for anything else."

12

"That's not very complimentary to people that have taken so great an interest in you." Lady Jane was quite discomposed by having the word insignificant applied to her. She was certainly not insignificant, whatever else she might be.

"Perhaps it is not," Katherine said. "I have had a great deal to think of," she added with a half appeal for sympathy.

"I dare say. Is it possible that you never expected it? Didn't you see that night? All those jewels even might have told their story. I confess that I was vaguely in a great fright; but I thought you must have been in her confidence, Katherine, that is the truth."

"I in her confidence! Did you think I would have helped her to — to — deceive everybody — to — give such a blow to papa?"

"Is it such a blow to your papa? I am told he has not suffered in health. Now I look at you again you are pale, but I don't suppose you have suffered in health either. Katherine, don't you think you are overdoing it a little? She has done nothing that is so very criminal. And your own conduct was a little strange. You let her run off into the dark shrubberies to say farewell to him, as I am told, and never gave any alarm till you saw the yacht out in the bay, and must have known they were safe from any pursuit. I must say that a girl who has behaved like that is much more likely to have known all about it than an outsider like me!"

"I did not know anything about it," cried Katherine— "nothing! Stella did not confide in me. If she had done so—if she had told me——"

"Yes; what would you have done then?" Lady Jane asked with a certain air of triumph.

Katherine looked blankly at her. She was wandering about in worlds not realised. She had never asked herself that question. And yet perhaps her own conduct, her patience in that moonlight scene was more extraordinary in her ignorance than it would have been had she sympathised and known. The question took her breath away, and she had no answer to give.

" If she had told you that she had been married to Charlie Somers that morning ; that he was starting for India next day ; that whatever her duty to her father and yourself might have been (that's nonsense ; a girl has no duty to her sister), her duty to her husband came first then. If she had told you that at the last moment, Katherine, what would you have done ? "

Katherine felt every possibility of reply taken from her. What could she have done ? Supposing Stella that night— that night in the moonlight, which somehow seemed mixed up with everything—had whispered *that* in her ear, instead of the lie about wishing to bid Charlie farewell. What could she have done ; what would she have done ? With a gasp in her throat she looked helplessly at her questioner. She had no answer to make.

" Then how could you blame me ? " cried Lady Jane, throwing off her wonderful furs, loosening her mantle, beginning, with her dress tucked up a little in front, to look more like herself. " What was to be done when they had gone and taken it into their own hands ? You can't separate husband and wife, though, Heaven knows, there are a great many that would be too thankful if you could. But there they were— married. What was to be done ? I made sure when you would insist on driving home with her, Katherine, that she must have told you."

" I was not expected, then, to drive home with her ? " Katherine said sharply. " It was intended that I should know nothing—nothing at all."

" I thought—I sincerely thought," said Lady Jane, hanging her head a little, " that she would have told you then. I suppose she was angry at the delay."

Katherine's heart was very sore. She had been the one who knew nothing, from whom everything had been kept. It had been intended that she should be left at the ball while Stella stole off with her bridegroom ; and her affectionate anxiety about Stella's headache had been a bore, the greatest bore, losing so much time and delaying the escape. And shut up there with her sister, her closest friend, her inseparable com-

panion of so many years, there had not been even a whisper of
the great thing which had happened, which now stood between
them and cut them apart for ever. Katherine, in her life of
the secondary person, the always inferior, had learned unconsciously a great deal of self-repression; but it taxed all her
·powers to receive this blow full on her breast and make no
sign. Her lips quivered a little; she clasped her hands tightly
together; and a hot and heavy moisture, which made everything awry and changed, stood in her eyes.

" Was that how it was ? " she said at last when she had controlled her voice to speak.

" Katherine, dear child, I can't tell you how sorry I am.
Nobody thought that you would feel it——" Lady Jane added
after a moment, " so much," and put out her hand to lay it
on Katherine's tightly-clasped hands.

" Nobody thought of me, I imagine, at all," said Katherine,
withdrawing from this touch, and recovering herself after that
bitter and blinding moment. " It would have been foolish to
expect anything else. And it is perhaps a good thing that I
was not tried—that I was not confided in. I might perhaps
have thought of my duty to my father. But a woman who is
married," she added quickly, with an uncontrollable bitterness,
" has, I suppose, no duties, except to the man whom—who
has married her."

" He must always come first," said Lady Jane with a little
solemnity. She was thunderstruck when Katherine, rising
quickly to her feet and walking about the room, gave vent to
Brabantio's exclamation before the Venetian senators :

> " Look to her, thou : have a quick eye to see.
> She hath deceived her father and may thee."

Lady Jane was not an ignorant woman for her rank and position. She had read the necessary books, and kept up a kind
of speaking acquaintance with those of the day. But it may be
excused to her, a woman of many occupations, if she did not
remember whence this outburst came, and thought it exceed-

ingly ridiculous and indeed of very doubtful taste, if truth
must be told.

" I could not have thought you would be so merciless," she
said severely. " I thought you were a kind creature, almost
too kind. It is easy to see that you have never been touched
by any love-affair of your own."

Katherine laughed—there seemed no other reply to this as-
sumption—and came back and sat down quietly in her chair.

" Was that all, Lady Jane?" she said. " You came to tell
me you had nothing to do with the step my sister has taken,
and then that you knew all about it, and that it was only I who
was left out."

" You are a very strange girl, Katherine Tredgold. I excuse
you because no doubt you have been much agitated, otherwise
I should say you were very rude and impudent." Lady Jane
was gathering on again her panoply of war—her magnificent
town-mantle, the overwhelming furs which actually belonged
to her maid. " I knew nothing about the first step," she said
angrily. " I was as ignorant of the marriage as you were.
Afterwards, I allow, they told me ; and as there was nothing
else to be done—for, of course, as you confess, a woman as
soon as she is married has no such important duty as to her
husband—I did not oppose the going away. I advised them
to take you into their confidence ; afterwards, I allow, for their
sakes, I promised to keep you engaged, if possible, to see that
you had plenty of partners and no time to think."

Katherine was ashamed afterwards to remember how the
prick of injured pride stung her more deeply than even that of
wounded affection. " So," she said, her cheeks glowing crimson, " it was to your artifice that I owed my partners ! But I
have never found it difficult to get partners—without your aid,
Lady Jane ! "

" You will take everything amiss, however one puts it," said
Lady Jane. And then there was a long pause, during which
that poor lady struggled much with her wraps without any
help from Katherine, who sat like stone and saw her difficulties
without lifting so much as a little finger. " You are to be

excused," the elder lady added, " for I do not think you have been very well treated, though, to be sure, poor Stella must have felt there was very little sympathy likely, or she certainly would have confided in you. As for Charlie Somers——" Lady Jane gave an expressive wave of her hand, as if consenting that nothing was to be expected from him; then she dropped her voice and asked with a change of tone, " I don't see why it should make any difference between you and me, Katherine. I have really had nothing to do with it—except at the very last. Tell me now, dear, how your father takes it? Is he very much displeased ? "

" Displeased is a weak word, Lady Jane."

"Well, angry then — enraged — any word you like; of course, for the moment no word will be strong enough."

" I don't think," said Katherine, " that he will ever allow her to enter his house, or consent to see her again."

"Good Heavens ! " cried Lady Jane. " Then what in the world is to become of them? But I am sure you exaggerate —in the heat of the moment; and, of course, Katherine, I acknowledge you have been very badly used," she said.

CHAPTER XX.

KATHERINE was perhaps not in very good condition after
Lady Jane's visit, though that great personage found it, on
the whole, satisfactory, and felt that she had settled the future
terms on which they were to meet in quite a pleasant way—
to receive the first letter which Stella sent her, an epistle
which arrived a day or two later. Stella's epistle was very
characteristic indeed. It was dated from Paris:

" Dearest Kate,—I can't suppose that you have not heard
everything about all that we have done and haven't done. I
don't excuse myself for not writing on the plea that you
couldn't possibly be anxious about me, as you must have
known all this by next morning, but I can't help feeling that
you must have been angry, both you and papa, and I thought
it would perhaps be better just to let you cool down. I know
you have cause to be angry, dear; I ought to have told you,
and it was on my lips all the time; but I thought you might
think it your duty to make a row, and then all our plans
might have been turned upside down. What we had planned
to do was to get across to Southsea in the yacht, and go next
morning by the first train to London, and on here at once,
which, with little divergencies, we carried out. You see we
have never been to say out of reach; but it would have done
you no good to try to stop us, for, of course, from the moment
I was Charlie's wife my place was with him. I know you
never would have consented to such a marriage; but it is
perfectly all right, I can assure you—as good as if it had come
off in St. George's, Hanover Square. And we have had a delightful time. Stevens met me at Southsea with the few things
I wanted (apologies for taking her from you, but you never

made so much use of her as I did, and I don't think you ever
cared for Stevens), and next day we picked up our things at
London. I wish you could see my things, they are beautiful.
I hope papa won't be dreadfully angry that I took him at his
word ; and I am quite frightened sometimes to think what it
will all cost—the most lovely *trousseau* all packed in such nice
boxes—some marked cabin and some—but that's a trifle.
The important thing is that the clothes are charming, just
what you would expect from Madame's tastes. I do hope
that papa will not make any fuss about her bill. They are
not dear at all, for material and workmanship (can you say
workmanship, when it's needlework, and all done by women ?)
are simply splendid. I never saw such beautiful things.

" And so here I am, Kate, a married woman, off to India
with my husband. Isn't it wonderful ? I can't say that I
feel much different myself. I am the same old Stella, always
after my fun. I shouldn't wonder in the least if after a while
Charlie were to set up a way of his own, and think he can
stop me ; but I don't advise him to try, and in the meantime
he is as sweet as sugar and does exactly what I like. It is
nice, on the whole, to be called my Lady, and it is very nice
to see how respectful all the people are to a married person,
as if one had grown quite a great personage all at once. And
it is nicer still to turn a big man round your little finger, even
when you have a sort of feeling, as I have sometimes, that it
may not last. One wonderful thing is that he is always meeting somebody he knows. People in society I believe know
everybody—that is, really everybody who ought to be known.
This man was at school with him, and that man belongs to
one of his clubs, and another was brother to a fellow in his
regiment, and so on, and so on—so we need never be alone
unless we like : they turn up at every corner. Of course, he
knows the ladies too, but this is not a good time in the year
for them, for the grandees are at their country houses and
English people only passing through. We did see one
gorgeous person, who was a friend of his mother's (who is
dead, Heaven be praised !), and to whom he introduced me,

but she looked at me exactly as if she had heard that Charlie
had married a barmaid, with a 'How do you do?' up in
the air—an odious woman. She was, of course, Countess of
Something or Other, and as poor as a Church mouse. Papa
could buy up dozens of such countesses; tell him I said so.

" You will wonder what we are doing knocking about in
Paris when the regiment is on the high seas; but Charlie
could not take me, you know, in a troopship, it would have
been out of the question, and we couldn't possibly have spent
our honeymoon among all those men. So he got his leave
and we are going by a P. and O. boat, which are the best,
and which we pick up at Brindisi, or at Suez, or somewhere.
I am looking forward to it immensely, and to India, which is
full of amusement, everybody tells me. I intend to get all
the fun I can for the next year, and then I hope, I do hope,
dear Katie, that papa may send for us home.

" How is poor dear papa? You may think I am a little
hypocrite, having given him such a shock, but I did really
hope he would see some fun in it—he always had such a sense
of humour. I have thought of this, really, truly, in all I have
done. About the *trousseau* (which everybody thinks the
greatest joke that ever was), and about going off in the yacht,
and all that, I kept thinking that papa, though he would be
very angry, would see the fun. I planned it all for that—
indeed, indeed, Kate, I did, whatever you may think. To
be sure, Charlie went for half in the planning, and I can't
say I think he has very much sense of humour, but, still, that
was in my mind all the time. Was he very, very angry when
he found out? Did you wake him in the night to tell him
and risk an illness? If you did, I think you were very, very
much to blame. There is never any hurry in telling bad
news. But you are so tremendously straightforward and all
that. I hope he only heard in the morning, and had his
good night's rest and was not disturbed. It was delicious this
time in the yacht, as quiet almost as a mill-pond—just a nice
soft little air that carried us across the bay and on to Southsea; such a delightful sail! I ought to have thought of you

promenading about in the cold waiting for me without any
companion, but I really couldn't, dear. Naturally we were too
much taken up with ourselves, and the joy of having got off
so nicely. But I do beg your pardon most sincerely, dear
Katie, for having left you out in the cold, really out in the
cold—without any figure of speech—like that.

"But my thoughts keep going back constantly to dear
papa. You will miss me a little, I hope, but not as he will
miss me. What does he say? Was he very angry? Do you
think he is beginning to come round? Oh, dear Kate, I hope
you take an opportunity when you can to say something nice
to him about me. Tell him Charlie wanted to be married in
London, but I knew what papa would think on this subject,
and simply insisted for his sake that it should be in the little
Steephill Church, where he could go himself, if he liked, and
see the register and make sure that it was all right. And I
have always thought of him all through. You may say it
doesn't look very like it, but I have, I have, Kate. I am
quite sure that he will get very fond of Charlie after a time,
and he will like to hear me called Lady Somers; and now
that my mind is set at rest and no longer drawn this way and
that way by love affairs, don't you know? I should be a
better daughter to him than ever before. Do get him to see
this, Kate. You will have all the influence now that I am
away. It is you that will be able to turn him round your
little finger. And, oh, I hope, I hope, dear, that you will do
it, and be true to me! You have always been such a faithful,
good sister, even when I tried you most with my nonsense.
I am sure I tried you, you being so different a kind from such
a little fool as Stella, and so much more valuable and all that.
Be sure to write to me before we leave Paris, which will be in
a week, to tell me how papa is, and how he is feeling about
me—and, *oh*, do be faithful to us, dear Kate, and make him
call us back within a year! Charlie does not mind about his
profession; he would be quite willing to give it up and settle
down, to be near papa. And then, you see, he has really a
beautiful old house of his own in the country, which he never

could afford to live in, where we could arrange the most charming *appartement,* as the French say, for papa for part of the year.

" Do, dearest Kate, write, write ! and tell me all about the state of affairs.   With Charlie's love,

" Your most affectionate sister,

" STELLA (LADY) SOMERS."

" I have a letter from—Stella, papa," said Katherine the same night.

" Ah ! " he said, with a momentary prick of his ears ; then he composed himself and repeated with the profoundest composure, " God damn her ! " as before.

" Oh, papa, do not say that !   She is very anxious to know how you are, and to ask you—oh, with all her heart, papa—to forgive her."

Mr. Tredgold did not raise his head or show any interest. He only repeated with the same calm that phrase again.

" You have surely something else to say at the mention of her name than that.   Oh, papa, she has done very, very wrong, but she is so sorry—she would like to fling herself at your feet."

" She had better not do that ; I should kick her away like a football," he said.

" You could never be cruel to Stella—your little Stella ! You always loved her the best of us two.   I never came near her in one way nor another."

" That is true enough," said the old man.

Katherine did not expect any better, but this calm daunted her.   Even Stella's absence did not advance her in any way ; she still occupied the same place, whatever happened.   It was with difficulty that she resumed her questions.

" And you will miss her dreadfully, papa.   Only think, those long nights that are coming—how you will miss her with her songs and her chatter and her brightness !   I am only a dull companion," said Katherine, perhaps a little, though not very reasonably, hoping to be contradicted.

"You are that," said her father calmly.

What was she to say? She felt crushed down by this disapproval, the calm recognition that she was nobody, and that
all her efforts to be agreeable could never meet with any response. She did make many efforts, far more than ever Stella
had done. Stella had never taken any trouble; her father's
comfort had in reality been of very little importance to her.
She had pleased him because she was Stella, just as Katherine,
because she was Katherine, did not please him. And what
was there more to be said? It is hard upon the unpleasing
one, the one who never gives satisfaction, but the fact remains.

"You are very plain spoken," said Katherine, trying to
find a little forlorn fun in the situation. "You don't take
much pains to spare my feelings. Still, allowing that to be all
true, and I don't doubt it for a moment, think how dull you
will be in the evenings, papa! You will want Stella a hundred times in an hour, you will always want her. This winter,
of course, they could not come back; but before another
winter, oh, papa, think for your own advantage—do say that
you will forgive her, and that they may come back!"

"We may all be dead and gone before another winter,"
Mr. Tredgold said.

"That is true; but then, on the other hand, we may all be
living and very dull and in great, great need of something to
cheer us up. Do hold out the hope, papa, that you will forgive her, and send for her, and have her back!"

"What is she to give you for standing up for her like
this?" said the old man with his grim chuckling laugh.

"To give—me?" Katherine was so astonished this time
that she could not think of any answer.

"Because you needn't lose your breath," said her father,
"for you'll lose whatever she has promised you. I've only
one word to say about her, and that I've said too often already
to please you—God damn her," her father said.

And Katherine gave up the unequal conflict—for the moment at least. It was not astonishing, perhaps, that she spent

a great deal of her time, as much as the weather would allow,
which now was grim November, bringing up fog from land
and sea, upon the cliff, where she walked up and down sometimes when there was little visible except a grey expanse of
mist behind the feathery tracery of the tamarisk trees ; sometimes thinking of those two apparitions of the *Stella* in the
bay, which now seemed to connect with each other like two
succeeding events in a story, and sometimes of very different
things.   She began to think oftener than she had ever done of
her own lover, he whom she had not had time to begin to
love, only to have a curious half-awakened interest in, at the
time when he was sent so summarily about his business.   Had
he not been sent about his business, probably Katherine might
never have thought of him at all.   It was the sudden fact of
his dismissal and the strange discovery thus made, that there
was one person in the world at least whose mind was occupied
with her and not with Stella, that gave him that hold upon her
mind which he had retained.

She wondered now vaguely what would have happened had
she done what Stella had done?   (It was impossible, because
she had not thought of him much, had not come to any conscious appropriation of him until after he was gone ; but supposing, for the sake of argument, that she had done what Stella
had done).   She would have been cut off, she and he, and
nobody would have been much the worse.   Stella, then, being
the only girl of the house, would have been more serious,
would have been obliged to think of things.   She would have
chosen someone better than Charlie Somers, someone that
would have pleased her father better; and he would have kept
his most beloved child, and all would have been well.   From
that point of view it would perhaps have been better that
Katherine should have done evil that good might come.
Was it doing evil to elope from home with the man you
loved, because your father refused him—if you felt you could
not live without him ?   That is a question very difficult to
solve.   In the first place, Katherine, never having been, let us
say, very much in love herself, thought it was almost immodest

in a woman to say that she could not live without any man. It might be that she loved a man who did not love her, or who loved somebody else, and then she would be compelled, whatever she wished, to live without him. But, on the other hand, there was the well-worn yet very reasonable argument that it is the girl's life and happiness that is concerned, not the parents', and that to issue a ukase like an emperor, or a bull like a pope, that your child must give up the man who alone can make her happy is tyrannical and cruel. You are commanded to obey your parents, but there are limits to that command; a woman of, say, thirty for instance (which to Katherine, at twenty-three, was still a great age), could not be expected to obey like a child; a woman of twenty even was not like a little girl. A child has to do what it is told, whether it likes or not; but a woman—and when all her own life is in question?

Those were thoughts which Katherine pondered much as she walked up and down the path on the cliff. For some time she went out very little, fearing always to meet a new group of interested neighbours who should question her about Stella. She shrank from the demands, from the criticisms that were sometimes very plain, and sometimes veiled under pretences of interest or sympathy. She would not discuss her sister with anyone, or her father, or their arrangements or family disasters, and the consequence was that, during almost the whole of that winter she confined herself to the small but varied domain which was such a world of flowers in summer, and now, though the trees were bare, commanded all the sun that enlivens a wintry sky, and all the aspects of the sea, and all the wide expanse of the sky. There she walked about and asked herself a hundred questions. Perhaps it would have been better for all of them if she had run away with James Stanford. It would have cost her father nothing to part with her; he would have been more lenient with the daughter he did not care for. And Stella would have been more thoughtful, more judicious, if there had been nobody at home behind her to bear the responsibility of common life. And then, Katherine wondered, with a gasp, as to the life that might have been hers had she been James Stanford's wife. She would have gone to India, too, but with no *trousseau*, no diamonds, no gay interval at Paris. She would have had only him, no more, to fill up her horizon and occupy her changed life. She thought of this with a little shiver, wondering—for, to be sure, she was not, so to speak, in love with him, but only interested in him—very curious if it had been possible to know more about him, to get to understand him. It was a singular characteristic in him that it was she whom he had cared for and not Stella. He was the first and only person who had done so—at least, the only man. Women, she was aware, often got on better with her than with her sister; but that did not surprise her, somehow, while the other did impress her deeply. Why should he have singled out her, Katherine, to fall in love with? It showed that he must be a particular kind of man, not like other people. This was the reason why Katherine had taken so much interest in him, thought so much of him all this time, not because she was in love with him. And it struck her with quite a curious impression, made up of some awe, some alarm, some pleasure, and a good deal of abashed amusement, to think that she might, like Stella, have eloped with him—might have been living with him as her sole companion for two or three years. She used to laugh to herself and hush up her line of thinking abruptly when she came to this point, and yet there was a curious attraction in it.

Soon, however, the old routine, although so much changed, came back, the usual visitors came to call, there were the usual little assemblages to luncheon, which was the form of entertainment Mr. Tredgold preferred; the old round of occupations began, the Stanley girls and the others flowed and circled about her in the afternoon, and, before she knew, Katherine was drawn again into the ordinary routine of life.

CHAPTER XXI.

THE company in the house on the cliff was, however, very considerably changed, though the visitors were not much lessened in number. It became, perhaps, more *bourgeois*, certainly more village, than it had been. Stella, a daring, audacious creature, with her beauty, which burst upon the spectators at the first glance, and her absence of all reserve, and her determination to be "in" everything that was amusing or agreeable, had made her way among her social betters as her quieter and more sensitive sister would never have done. Then the prestige which had attached to them because of their wealth and that character of heiress which attracts not only fortune-hunters who are less dangerous, but benevolent match-makers and the mothers and sisters of impecunious but charming young men, had been much dulled and sobered by the discovery that the old father, despised of everybody, was not so easily to be moved as was supposed. This was an astonishing and painful discovery, which Lady Jane, in herself perfectly disinterested and wanting nothing from old Tredgold, felt almost more than anyone. She had not entertained the least doubt that he would give in. She did not believe, indeed, that Stella and her husband would ever have been allowed to leave England at all. She had felt sure that old Tredgold's money would at once and for ever settle all questions about the necessity of going to India with the regiment for Charlie ; that he would be able at once to rehabilitate his old house, and to set up his establishment, and to settle into that respectable country-gentleman life in which all a man's youthful peccadilloes are washed out and forgotten.

Mr. Tredgold's obstinacy was thus as great a blow to Lady Jane as if she herself had been impoverished by it. She felt the ground cut from under her feet, and her confidence in human nature destroyed. If you cannot make sure of a vulgar old father's weakness for his favourite child whom he has spoiled outrageously all her life, of what can you make sure? Lady Jane was disappointed, wounded, mortified. She felt less sure of her own good sense and intuitions, which is a very humbling thing—not to speak of the depreciation in men's minds of her judgment which was likely to follow. Indeed, it did follow, and that at once, people in general being very sorry for poor Charlie Somers, who had been taken in so abominably, and who never would have risked the expenses of married life, and a wife trained up to every extravagance, if he had not felt sure of being indemnified; and, what was still worse, they all agreed he never would have taken such a strong step—for he was a cautious man, was Charlie, notwithstanding his past prodigalities—if he had not been so pushed forward and kept up to the mark by Lady Jane.

The thing that Lady Jane really fell back on as a consolation in the pressure of these painful circumstances was that she had not allowed Algy to make himself ridiculous by any decisive step in respect to the "little prim one," as he called Katherine. This Lady Jane had sternly put down her foot upon. She had said at once that Katherine was not the favourite, that nothing could be known as to how the old man would leave her, along with many other arguments which intimidated the young one. As a matter of fact, Lady Jane, naturally a very courageous woman, was afraid of Algy's mother, and did not venture to commit herself in any way that would have brought her into conflict with Lady Scott, which, rather than any wisdom on her part, was the chief reason which had prevented additional trouble on that score. Poor Charlie Somers had no mother nor any female relation of importance to defend him. Lady Jane herself ought to have been his defence, and it was she who had led him astray. It was not brought against her open-mouthed, or to her face. But she felt that it was in everybody's mind, and that her reputation, or at least her prestige, had suffered.

13

This it was that made her drop the Tredgolds "like a hot potato." She who had taken such an interest in the girls, and superintended Stella's *début* as if she had been a girl of her own, retreated from Katherine as if from the plague. After the way they had behaved to poor dear Charlie Somers and his wife, she said, she could have no more to do with them. Lady Jane had been their great patroness, their only effectual connection with the county and its grandeurs, so that the higher society of the island was cast off at once from Katherine. I do not think she felt it very much, or was even conscious for a long time that she had lost anything. But still it was painful and surprising to her to be dismissed with a brief nod, and " How d'ye do ? " in passing, from Lady Jane. She was troubled to think what she could have done to alienate a woman whom she had always liked, and who had professed, as Katherine knew, to think the elder sister the superior of the younger. That, however, was of course a mere *façon de parler*, for Stella had always been, Katherine reminded herself, the attraction to the house. People might even approve of herself more, but it was Stella who was the attraction—Stella who shocked and disturbed, and amused and delighted everybody about; who was always inventing new things, festive surprises and novelties, and keeping a whirl of life in the place. The neighbours gave their serious approval to Katherine, but she did not amuse them or surprise. They never had to speculate what she would do next. They knew (she said to herself) that she would always do just the conventional proper thing, whereas Stella never could be calculated upon, and had a perpetual charm of novelty. Katherine was not sufficiently enlightened to be aware that Stella's way in its wildness was much the more conventional of the two.

But the effect was soon made very plain. The link between the Tredgolds and the higher society of the island was broken. Perhaps it is conventional, too, to call these good people the higher society, for they were not high society in any sense of the word. There were a great many stupid people among them. Those who were not stupid were little elevated above the other classes except by having more beautiful manners *when they chose.* Generally, they did not choose, and therefore were worse than the humble people because they knew better. Their one great quality was that they were the higher class. It is a great thing to stand first, whatever nation or tribe, or tongue, or sect, or station you may belong to. It is in itself an education: it saves even very stupid people from many mistakes that even clever people make in other spheres, and it gives a sort of habit of greatness—if I may use the words—of feeling that there is nothing extraordinary in brushing shoulders with the greatest at any moment; indeed, that it is certain you will brush shoulders with them, to-day or to-morrow, in the natural course of events. To know the people who move the world makes even the smallest man a little bigger, makes him accustomed to the stature of the gods.

I am not sure that this tells in respect to the poets and painters and so forth, who are what the youthful imagination always fixes on as the flower of noble society. One thinks in maturer life that perhaps one prefers not to come to too close quarters with these, any more than with dignified clergymen, lest some of the bloom of one's veneration might be rubbed off. But one does not venerate in the same way the governors of the world, the men who are already historical; and it is perhaps they and their contemporaries from beyond all the seas, who, naturally revolving in that sphere, give a kind of bigness, not to be found in other spheres, to the highest class of society everywhere. One must account to oneself somehow for the universal pre-eminence of an aristocracy which consists of an enormous number of the most completely commonplace, and even vulgar, individuals. It is not high, but it cannot help coming in contact with the highest. Figures pass familiarly before its eyes, and brush its shoulders in passing, which are wonders and prodigies to other men. One wants an explanation, and this is the one that commends itself to me. Therefore, to be cut off from this higher class is an evil, whatever anyone may say.

Katherine, in her wounded pride and in her youth, did not

allow that she thought so, I need not say.   Her serious little
head was tossed in indignation as scornfully as Stella's would
have been.   She recalled to herself what dull people they were
(which was quite true), and how commonplace their talk,
and asked heaven and earth why she should care.   Lottie
Seton, for instance, with her retinue of silly young men : was
she a loss to anyone?   It was different with Lady Jane,
who was a person of sense, and Katherine felt herself obliged
to allow, different someway—she could not tell how—from
the village ladies.   Yet Lady Jane, though she disapproved
highly of Mrs. Seton, for instance, never would have shut her
out, as she very calmly and without the least hesitation shut
out Katherine, of whom in her heart she did approve.   It
seemed to the girl merely injustice, the tyranny of a prepos-
terous convention, the innate snobbishness (what other word
is there?) of people in what is called society.   And though
she said little, she felt herself dropped out of that outer ledge
of it, upon which Lady Jane's patronage had posed her and
her sister, with an angry pang.   Stella belonged to it now,
because she had married a pauper, a mercenary, fortune-hunt-
ing, and disreputable man ; but she, who had done no harm,
who was exactly the same Katherine as ever, was dropped.

  There were other consequences of this which were more
harmful still.   People who were connected in business with Mr.
Tredgold, who had always appeared occasionally in the house,
but against whom Stella had set her little impertinent face,
now appeared in greater numbers, and with greater assurance
than ever ; and Mr. Tredgold, no longer held under subjection
by Stella, liked to have them.   With the hold she had on the
great people, Stella had been able to keep these others at a
distance, for Stella had that supreme distinction which belongs
to aristocracy of being perfectly indifferent whether she hurt
other people's feelings or not ; but Katherine possessed neither
the one advantage nor the other—neither the hold upon society
nor the calm and indifference.   And the consequence naturally
was that she was pushed to the wall.   The city people came
more and more ; and she had to be kind to them, to receive

them as if she liked it.   When I say she had to do it, I do not
mean that Katherine was forced by her father, but that she
was forced by herself.   There is an Eastern proverb that says
" A man can act only according to his nature."   It was no
more possible for Katherine to be uncivil, to make anyone
feel that he or she was unwelcome, to " hurt their feelings,"
as she would have said, than to read Hebrew or Chinese.

   So she was compelled to be agreeable to the dreadful old
men who sat and talked stocks and premiums, and made still
more dreadful jokes with her father, making him chuckle till
he almost choked ; and to the old women who criticised her
housekeeping, and told her that a little bit of onion (or something else) would improve this dish, or just a taste of brandy
that, and who wondered that she did not control the table
in the servants' hall, and give them out daily what was wanted.
Still more terrible were the sons and daughters who came, now
one, now another ; the first making incipient love to her, the
other asking about the officers, and if there were many balls,
and men enough, or always too many ladies, as was so often
the case.   The worst part of her new life was these visits upon
which she now exercised no control.   Stella had done so.
Stella had said, " Now, papa, I cannot have those old guys of
yours here ; let the men come from Saturday to Monday and
talk shop with you if you like, but we can't have the women,
nor the young ones.   There I set down my foot," and this
she had emphasised with a stamp on the carpet, which was
saucy and pretty, and delighted the old man.   But Mr. Tredgold was no fool, and he knew very well the difference between
his daughters.   He knew that Katherine would not put down
her foot, and if she had attempted to do so, he would have
laughed in her face—not a delighted laugh of acquiescence as
with Stella, but a laugh of ridicule that she could suppose he
would be taken in so easily.   Katherine tried quietly to express to her father her hope that he would not inflict these
guests upon her.   " You have brought us up so differently,
papa," she would say with hesitation, while he replied, " Stuff
and nonsense ! they are just as good as you are."

" Perhaps," said Katherine. " Mrs. Simmons, I am sure, is a much better woman than I am ; but we don't ask her to come in to dinner."

" Hold your impudence ! " her father cried, who was never choice in his expressions. " Do you put my friends on a level with your servants ? " He would not have called them her servants in any other conversation, but in this it seemed to point the moral better.

" They are not so well bred, papa," she said, which was a speech which from Stella would have delighted the old man, but from Katherine it made him angry.

" Don't let me hear you set up such d——d pretensions," he cried. " Who are you, I wonder, to turn up your nose at the Turnys of Lothbury ? There is not a better firm in London, and young Turny's got his grandfather's money, and many a one of your grand ladies would jump at him. If you don't take your chance when you find it, you may never have another, my fine lady. None of your beggars with titles for me. My old friends before all."

This was a fine sentiment indeed, calculated to penetrate the most callous heart ; but it made Katherine glow all over, and then grow chill and pale. She divined what was intended— that there were designs to unite her, now the representative of the Tredgolds, with the heir of the house of Turny. There was do discrepancy of fortune there. Old Turny could table thousand by thousand with Mr. Tredgold, and it was a match that would delight both parties. Why should Katherine have felt so violent a pang of offended pride ? Mr. Turny was no better and no worse in origin than she. The father of that family was her father's oldest friend ; the young people had been brought up with " every advantage "—even a year or two of the University for the eldest son, who, however, when he was found to be spending his time in vanities with other young men like himself—not with the sons of dukes and earls, which might have made it bearable—was promptly withdrawn accordingly, but still could call himself an Oxford man. The girls had been to school in France and in Germany, and had learned their music in Berlin and their drawing in Paris. They were far better educated than Katherine, who had never had any instructor but a humble governess at home. How, then, did it come about that the idea of young Turny having the insolence to think of her should have made Katherine first red with indignation, then pale with disgust? I cannot explain it, neither could she to herself; but so it was. We used to hear a great deal about nature's noblemen in the days of sentimental fiction. But there certainly is such a thing as a natural-born aristocrat, without any foundation for his or her instinct, yet possessing it as potently as the most highly descended princess that ever breathed. Katherine's grandfather, as has been said, had been a respectable linen-draper, while the Turnys sprung from a house of business devoting itself to the sale of crockery at an adjoining corner; yet Katherine felt herself as much insulted by the suggestion of young Turny as a suitor as if she had been a lady of high degree and he a low-born squire. There are more things in heaven and earth than are dreamt of in our philosophy.

Two or three of such suitors crossed her path within a short time. Neither of the sisters might have deserved the attentions of these gentlemen had they been likely to share their father's wealth; but now that the disgrace of one was generally known, and the promotion of the other as sole heiress generally counted upon, this was what happened to Katherine. She was exceedingly civil in a superior kind of way, with an *air noble* that indeed sat very well upon her, and a dignity worthy of a countess at least to these visitors: serious and stately with the mothers, tolerant with the fathers, gracious with the daughters, but altogether unbending with the sons. She would have none of them. Two other famous young heroes of the city (both of whom afterwards married ladies of distinguished families, and who has not heard of Lady Arabella Turny?) followed the first, but with the same result. Mr. Tredgold was very angry with his only remaining child. He asked her if she meant to be an infernal fool too. If so,

she might die in a ditch for anything her father cared, and he
would leave all his money to a hospital.

"A good thing too.   Far better than heaping all your
good money, that you've worked and slaved for, on the head
of a silly girl.   Who are you, I wonder," he said, "to turn
up your dashed little nose?   Why, you're not even a beauty
like the other ; a little prim thing that would never get a
man to look twice at you but for your father's money at your
back.   But don't you make too sure of your father's money
— to keep up your grandeur," he cried.   Nevertheless,
though he was so angry, Mr. Tredgold was rather pleased all
the same to see his girl turn up her nose at his friends' sons.
She was not a bit better than they were—perhaps not so
good.   And he was very angry, yet could not but feel flattered too at the hang-dog looks with which the Turnys and
others went away—" tail between their legs," he said to himself ; and it tickled his fancy and pride, though he was so
much displeased.

CHAPTER XXII.

PERHAPS the village society into which Katherine was now thrown was not much more elevating than the Turnys, &c. ; but it was different. She had known it all her life, for one thing, and understood every allusion, and had almost what might be called an interest in all the doings of the parish. The fact that the old Cantrells had grown so rich that they now felt justified in confessing it, and were going to retire from the bakery and set up as private gentlefolks while their daughter and son-in-law entered into possession of the business, quite entertained her for half an hour while it was being discussed by Miss Mildmay and Mrs. Shanks over their téa. Katherine had constructed for herself in the big and crowded drawing-room, by means of screens, a corner in which there was both a fireplace and a window, and which looked like an inner room, now that she had taken possession of it. She had covered the gilded furniture with chintzes, and the shining tables with embroidered cloths. The fire always burned bright, and the window looked out over the cliff and the fringe of tamarisks upon the sea. The dual chamber, the young ladies' room, with all its contrivances for pleasure and occupation, was shut up, as has been said, and this was the first place which Katherine had ever had of her very own.

She did not work nearly so much for bazaars as she had done in the old Stella days. Then that kind of material occupation (though the things produced were neither very admirable in themselves nor of particular use to anyone) gave a sort of steady thread, flimsy as it was, to run through her light and airy life. It meant something if not much. *Elle fait ses robes*— which is the last height of the good girl's excellence in modern

French—would have been absurd; and to make coats and
cloaks for the poor by Stella's side would have been extremely
inappropriate, not to say that such serious labours are much
against the exquisite disorder of a modern drawing-room,
therefore the bazaar articles had to do.   But now there was no
occasion for the bazaars—green and gilt paper stained her fingers no more.   She had no one to keep in balance ; no one but
herself, who weighed a little if anything to the other side, and
required, if anything, a touch of frivolity, which, to be sure,
the bazaars were quite capable of furnishing if you took them
in that way.   She read a great deal in this retreat of hers ; but
I fear to say it was chiefly novels she read.   And she had not
the least taste for metaphysics.   And anything about Woman,
with a capital letter, daunted her at once.   She was very dull
sometimes—what human creature is not ?—but did not blame
anyone else for it, nor even fate.   She chiefly thought it was
her own fault, and that she had indeed no right to be dull ; and
in this I think she showed herself to be a very reasonable
creature.

  Now that Lady Jane's large landau never swept up to the
doors, one of the most frequent appearances there was that con-
venient but unbeautiful equipage called the midge.   It was not
a vehicle beloved of the neighbourhood.   The gardener's wife,
now happily quite recovered from the severe gunshot wound she
had received on the night of Stella's elopement, went out most
reluctantly, taking a very long time about it, to open the gate
when it appeared.   She wanted to know what was the good of
driving that thing in, as was no credit to be seen anywhere,
when them as used it might just as well have got out outside
the gate and walked. The ladies did not think so at all. They
were very particular to be driven exactly up to the door and
turned half round so that the door which was at the end, not
the side of the vehicle, should be opposite the porch ; and they
would sometimes keep it waiting an hour, a remarkable object
seen from all the windows, while they sat with poor Katherine
and cheered her up.   These colloquies always began with inquiries after her sister.

"Have you heard again from Stella? Where is sne now, poor child? Have you heard of their safe arrival? And where is the regiment to be quartered? And whât does she say of the climate? Does she think it will agree with her? Are they in the plains, where it is so hot, or near the hills, where there is always a little more air?"

Such was the beginning in every case, and then the two ladies would draw their chairs a little nearer, and ask eagerly in half-whispers, "And your papa, Katherine? Does he show any signs of relenting? Does he ever speak of her? Don't you think he will soon give in? He must give in soon. Considering how fond he was of Stella, I cannot understand how he has held out so long."

Katherine ignored as much as she could the latter questions.

"I believe they are in quite a healthy place," she said, "and it amuses Stella very much, and the life is all so new. You know she is very fond of novelty, and there are a great many parties and gaieties, and of course she knows everybody. She seems to be getting on very well."

"And very happy with her husband, I hope, my dear—for that is the great thing after all."

"Do you expect Stella to say that she is not happy with her husband, Jane Shanks? or Katherine to repeat it if she did? All young women are happy with their husbands—that's taken for granted—so far as the world is concerned."

"I think, Ruth Mildmay, it is you who should have been Mrs. Shanks," cried the other, with a laugh.

"Heaven forbid! You may be quite sure that had I ever been tempted that way, I should only have changed for a better, not a worse name."

"Stella," cried Katherine to stop the fray, "seems to get on capitally with Charlie. She is always talking of him. I should think they were constantly together, and enjoying themselves very much indeed."

"Ah, it is early days," Miss Mildmay said, with a shake of her head. "And India is a very dissipated place. There are always things going on at an Indian station that keep people

from thinking.   By-and-by, when difficulties come——   But
you must always stand her friend and keep her before your
father's eyes.   I don't know if Jane Shanks has told you—but
the news is all over the town—the Cantrells have taken that
place, you know, with the nice paddock and garden ; the place
the doctor was after—quite a gentleman's little place.   I forget the name, but it is near the Rectory—don't you know ?—
a little to the right ; quite a gentleman's house.''

"I suppose Mr. Cantrell considers himself a gentleman
now,'' Katherine said, glad of the change of subject.

"Why, he's a magistrate,'' said Mrs. Shanks, "and could
buy up the half of us—isn't that the right thing to say when a
man has grown rich in trade ? ''

"It is a thing papa says constantly,'' said Katherine; "and
I suppose, as that is what has happened to himself——''

"O my dear Katherine ! you don't suppose that for one
moment ! fancy dear Mr. Tredgold, with his colossal fortune
—a merchant prince and all that—compared to old Cantrell,
the baker !   Nobody could ever think of making such a comparison ! ''

"It just shows how silly it is not to make up your mind,''
said Miss Mildmay.   "I know the doctor was after that house
—much too large a house for an unmarried man, I have always said, but it was not likely that he would think anything
of what I said—and now it is taken from under his very nose.
The Cantrells did not take long to make up their minds !
They go out and in all day long smiling at each other.   I believe they think they will quite be county people with that
house.''

"It is nice to see them smiling at each other—at their age
they were just as likely to be spitting fire at each other.   I
shall call certainly and ask her to show me over the house.   I
like to see such people's houses, and their funny arrangements
and imitations, and yet the original showing through all the
same.''

"And does George Cantrell get the shop?'' Katherine
asked.   She had known George Cantrell all her life—better

than she knew the young gentlemen who were to be met at Steephill and in whom it would have been natural to be interested. " He was always very nice to us when we were little," she said.

" Oh, my dear child, you must not speak of George Cantrell. He has gone away somewhere—nobody knows where. He fell in love with his mother's maid-of-all-work—don't you know ?—and married her and put the house of Cantrell to shame. So there are no shops nor goodwills for George. He has to work as what they call a journeyman, after driving about in his nice cart almost like a gentleman."

" I suppose," said Miss Mildmay, " that even in the lower classes grades must tell. There are grades everywhere. When I gave the poor children a tea at Christmas, the carpenter's little girls were not allowed to come because the little flower-woman's children were to be there."

" For that matter we don't know anything about the doctor's grade, Ruth Mildmay. He might be a baker's son just like George for anything we know."

" That is true," said the other. " You can't tell who anybody is nowadays. But because he is a doctor—which I don't think anything of as a profession—none of my belongings were ever doctors, I know nothing about them—he might ask any girl to marry him—anybody——"

" Surely, his education makes some difference," Katherine said.

" Oh, education ! You can pick up as much education as you like at any roadside now. And what does that kind of education do for you ?—walking hospitals where the worst kind of people are collected together, and growing familiar with the nastiest things and the most horrible ! Will that teach a man the manners of a gentleman ? " Miss Mildmay asked, raising her hands and appealing to earth and heaven.

At this point in the conversation the drawing-room door opened, and someone came in knocking against the angles of the furniture.

" May I announce myself ? " a voice said. " Burnet—

Dr., as I stand in the directory. John was trying to catch
the midge, which had bolted, and accordingly I brought myself in. How do you do, Miss Katherine ? It is very cold
outside.''

" The midge bolted ! " both the ladies cried with alarm,
rushing to the window.

" Nothing of the sort," cried Mrs. Shanks, who was the
more nimble. " It is there standing as quiet as a judge.
Fancy the midge bolting ! "

" Oh, have they got it safe again ? " he said. " But you
ladies should not drive such a spirited horse."

" Fancy——" Mrs. Shanks began, but the ground was cut
from under her feet by her more energetic friend.

" Katherine," she said, " you see what a very good example this is of what we were saying. It is evident the doctor
wants us to bolt after the midge—if you will forgive me using
such a word."

" On the contrary," said the doctor, " I wish you to give
me your advice, which I am sure nobody could do better. I
want you to tell me whether you think the Laurels would be
a good place for me to set up my household gods."

" The Laurels ! oh, the Laurels——" cried Mrs. Shanks,
eager to speak, but anxious at the same time to spare Dr. Burnet's feelings.

" The Cantrells have bought the Laurels," said Miss Mildmay, quickly, determined to be first.

" The Cantrells—the bakers ! " he cried, his countenance
falling.

" Yes, indeed, the Cantrells, the bakers—people who know
their own mind, Dr. Burnet. They went over the house yesterday, every corner, from the drawing-room to the dustbin ;
and they were delighted with it, and they settled everything
this morning. They are going to set up a carriage, and, in
short, to become county people—if they can," Miss Mildmay
said.

" They are very respectable," said Mrs. Shanks. " Of
course, Ruth Mildmay is only laughing when she speaks of

county people—but I should like to ask her, after she has got
into it, to show me the house.''

''The Cantrells—the bakers ! '' cried Dr. Burnet, with a
despair which was half grotesque, '' in *my* house ! This is a
very dreadful thing for me, Miss Katherine, though I see that
you are disposed to laugh. I have been thinking of it for
some time as my house. I have been settling all the rooms,
where this was to be and where that was to be.'' Here he
paused a moment, and gave her a look which was startling,
but which Katherine, notwithstanding her experience with
the Turnys, etc., did not immediately understand. And
then he grew a little red under his somewhat sunburnt weather-beaten complexion, and cried—'' What am I to do? It
unsettles everything. The Cantrells ! in my house.''

'' You see, it doesn't do to shilly-shally, doctor,'' said Miss
Mildmay. '' You should come to the point. While you
think about it someone else is sure to come in and do it.
And the Cantrells are people that know their own minds.''

'' Yes, indeed,'' he said—'' yes, indeed,'' shaking his head.
'' Poor George—they know their own minds with a ven-
geance. That poor fellow now is very likely to go to the
dogs.''

'' No ; he will go to London,'' said the other old lady.
'' I know some such nice people there in the same trade, and
I have recommended him to them. You know the people,
Katherine—they used to send us down such nice French
loaves by the parcel post, that time when I quarrelled with
the old Cantrells, don't you remember, about——''

'' I don't think there is any other house about Sliplin that
will suit you now, Dr. Burnet,'' said Miss Mildmay. '' You
will have to wait a little, and keep on the look-out.''

'' I suppose so,'' he said dejectedly, thrusting his hands
down to the depths of his pockets, as if it were possible that
he should find some consolation there.

And he saw the two ladies out with great civility, putting
them into the midge with a care for their comfort which melted
their hearts.

" I should wait a little now, if I were you," said Miss Mild-may, gripping his hand for a moment with the thin old fin-gers, which she had muffled up in coarse woollen gloves drawn on over the visiting kid. " I should wait a little, since you have let this chance slip."

" Do you think so ? " he said.

" Ruth Mildmay," said Mrs. Shanks, when they had driven away. " This is not treating me fairly. There is something private between you and that young man which you have never disclosed to me."

" There is nothing private," said Miss Mildmay. " Do you think I'm an improper person, Jane Shanks ? There is noth-ing except that I've got a pair of eyes in my head."

Dr. Burnet went slowly back to the drawing-room, where Katherine had promised him a cup of tea. His step sounded differently, and when he knocked against the furniture the sound was dull. He looked a different man altogether. He had come in so briskly, half an hour before, that Katherine was troubled for him.

" I am afraid you are very much disappointed about the house," she said.

" Yes, Miss Katherine, I am. I had set my heart on it somehow—and on other things connected with it," he said.

She was called Miss Katherine by everybody in consequence of the dislike of her father to have any sign of superiority over her sister shown to his eldest daughter. Miss Katherine and Miss Stella meant strict equality. Neither of them was ever called Miss Tredgold.

" I am very sorry," she said, with her soft sympathetic voice.

He looked at her, and she for a moment at him, as she gave him his cup of tea. Again she was startled, almost confused, by his look, but could not make out to herself the reason why. Then she made a little effort to recover herself, and said, with a half laugh, half shiver, " You are thinking how we once took tea together in the middle of the night."

" On that dreadful morning ? " he said. " No, I don't

know that I was, but I shall never forget it. Don't let me
bring it back to your mind."

"Oh, it doesn't matter. I think of it often enough. And
I don't believe I ever thanked you, Dr. Burnet, for all you did
for me, leaving everything to go over to Portsmouth, you that
are always so busy, to make those inquiries—which were of so
little good—and explaining everything to the Rector, and
sending him off too."

"And his inquiries were of some use, though mine were
not," he said. "Well, we are both your very humble servants, Miss Katherine : I will say that for him. If Stanley
could keep the wind from blowing upon you too roughly he
would do so, and it's the same with me."

Katherine looked up with a sudden open-eyed glance of
pleasure and gratitude. "How very good of you to say that !"
she cried. "How kind, how beautiful, to think it ! It is true
I am very solitary now. I haven't many people to feel for me.
I shall always be grateful and happy to think that you have so
kind a feeling for me, you two good men."

"Oh, as for the goodness," he said. And then he remembered Miss Mildmay's advice, and rubbed his hands over his
eyes as if to take something out of them which he feared was
there. Katherine sat down and looked at him very kindly,
but her recollection was chiefly of the strong white teeth with
which he had eaten the bread-and-butter in the dark of the
winter morning after *that* night. It was the only breakfast he
was likely to have, going off as he did on her concerns, and he
had been called out of his bed in the middle of the night, and
had passed a long time by her father's bedside. All these
things made the simple impromptu meal very necessary ; but
still she had kept the impression on her mind of his strong
teeth taking a large bite of the bread-and-butter, which was
neither sentimental nor romantic. This was about all that
passed between them on that day.

14

CHAPTER XXIII.

THE village society in Sliplin was not to be despised, especially by a girl who had no pretensions, like Katherine. When a person out of the larger world comes into such a local society, it is inevitable that he or she should look upon it with a more or less courteous contempt, and that the chief members should condole with him or her upon the inferiority of the new surroundings, and the absence of those intellectual and other advantages which he or she is supposed to have tasted in London, for example. But, as a matter of fact, the intellectual advantages are much more in evidence on the lower than on the higher ground. Lady Jane, no doubt, had her own particular box from Mudie's and command of all the magazines, &c., at first hand; but then she read very little, having the Mudie books chiefly for her governess, and glancing only at some topic of the day, some great lady's predilections on Society and its depravity, or some fad which happened to be on the surface for the moment, and which everybody was expected to be able to discuss. Whereas the Sliplin ladies read all the books, vying with each other who should get them first, and were great in the *Nineteenth Century* and the *Fortnightly*, and all the more weighty periodicals. They were members of mutual improvement societies, and of correspondence classes, and I don't know all what. Some of them studied logic and other appalling subjects through the latter means, and many of them wrote modest little essays and chronicles of their reading for the press. When the University Extension Lectures were set up quite a commotion was made in the little town. Mr. Stanley, the rector, and Dr. Burnet were both on the committee, and everybody went to hear the lectures. They were one year on the History of the Merovingians, and another year on Crockery—I mean Pottery, or rather Ceramic Art—and a third upon the Arctic Circle. They were thus calculated to produce a broad general intelligence, people said, though it was more difficult to see how they extended the system of the Universities, which seldom devote themselves to such varied studies. But they were very popular, especially those which were illustrated by the limelight.

All the ladies in Sliplin who had any respect for themselves attended these lectures, and a number read up the subjects privately, and wrote essays, the best of which were in their turn read out at subsequent meetings for the edification of the others. I think, however, these essays were rarely appreciated except by the families of the writers. But it may be easily perceived that a great deal of mental activity was going on where all this occurred.

The men of the community took a great deal less trouble in the improvement of their minds—two or three of them came to the lectures, a rather shame-faced minority amid the ranks of the ladies, but not one, so far as I have heard, belonged to a mutual improvement society, or profited by a correspondence class, or joined a Reading Union. Whether this was because they were originally better educated, or naturally had less intellectual enthusiasm, I cannot tell. In other places it might have been supposed to be because they had less leisure ; but that was scarcely to be asserted in Sliplin, where nobody, or hardly anybody, had anything to do. There was a good club, and very good billiard tables, which perhaps supplied an alternative ; but I would not willingly say anything to the prejudice of the gentlemen, who were really, in a general way, as intelligent as the ladies, though they did so much less for the improvement of their minds. Now, the people whom Katherine Tredgold had met at Steephill did none of these things —the officers and their society as represented by Charlie Somers and Algy Scott, and their original leader, Mrs. Seton, were, it is needless to state, absolutely innocent of any such efforts. Therefore Katherine, as may be said, had gained rather than lost by being so much more drawn into this intellectually active circle when dropped by that of Lady Jane.

The chief male personages in this society were certainly the doctor and the clergyman. Curates came and curates went, and some of them were clever and some the reverse; but Mr. Stanley and Dr. Burnet went on for ever. They were of course invariably of all the dinner parties, but there the level of intelligence was not so high—the other gentlemen in the town and the less important ones in the country coming in as a more important element. But in the evening parties, which were popular in Sliplin during the winter, and the afternoon-tea parties which some people, who did not care to go out at night, tried hard to introduce in their place, they were supreme. It was astonishing how the doctor, so hard-worked a man, managed to find scraps of time for so many of these assemblages. He was never there during the whole of these symposia. He came very late or he went away very early, he put in half an hour between two rounds, or he ran in for ten minutes while he waited for his dog-cart. But the occasions were very rare on which he did not appear one time or another during the course of the entertainment. Mr. Stanley, of course, was always on the spot. He was a very dignified clergyman, though he had not risen to any position in the Church beyond that of Rector of Sliplin. He preached well, he read well, he looked well, he had not too much to do; he had brought up his motherless family in the most beautiful way, with never any entanglement of governesses or anything that could be found fault with for a moment. Naturally, being the father of a family, the eldest of which was twenty-two, he was not in his first youth; but very few men of forty-seven looked so young or so handsome and well set up. He took the greatest interest in the mental development of the Sliplin society, presiding at the University Extension as well as all the other meetings, and declaring publicly, to the great encouragement of all the other students, that he himself had "learned a great deal" from the Merovingians lectures and the Ceramic lectures, and those on the Arctic regions.

Mr. Stanley had three daughters, and a son who was at Cambridge; and a pretty old Rectory with beautiful rooms, and everything very graceful and handsome about him. The young people were certainly a drawback to any matrimonial aspirations on his part; but it was surmised that he entertained them all the same. Miss Mildmay was one of the people who was most deeply convinced on this subject. She had an eye which could see through stone walls in this particular. She knew when a man conceived the idea of asking a woman to marry him before he knew it himself. When she decided that a thing was to be (always in this line) it came to pass. Her judgment was infallible. She knew all the signs—how the man was being wrought up to the point of proposing, and what the woman's answer was going to be—and she took the keenest interest in the course of the little drama. It was only a pity that she had so little exercise for her faculty in that way, for there were few marriages in Sliplin. The young men went away and found their wives in other regions; the young women stayed at home, or else went off on visits where, when they had any destiny at all, they found their fate. It was therefore all the more absorbing in its interest when anything of the kind came her way. Stella's affair had been outside her orbit, and she had gained no advantage from it; but the rector and the doctor and Katherine Tredgold were a trio that kept her attention fully awake.

There was a party in the Rectory about Christmas, at which all Sliplin was present. It was a delightful house for a party. There was a pretty old hall most comfortably warmed—which is a rare attraction in halls—with a handsome oak staircase rising out of it, and a gallery above which ran along two sides. The drawing-room was also a beautiful old room, low, but large, with old furniture judiciously mingled with new, and a row of recessed windows looking to the south and clothed outside with a great growth of myrtle, with pink buds still visible at Christmas amid the frost and snow. Inside it was bright with many lamps and blazing fires; and there were several rooms to sit in, according to the dispositions of the guests—the hall where the

young people gathered together, the drawing-rooms to which
favoured people went when they were bidden to go up higher,
and Mr. Stanley's study, where a group of sybarites were always
to be found, for it was the warmest and most luxurious of all.
The hall made the greatest noise, for Bertie was there with
various of his own order, home, like himself, for Christmas,
and clusters of girls, all chattering at the tops of their voices,
and urging each other to the point of proposing a dance, for
which the hall was so suitable, and quite large enough.   The
drawing-room was full of an almost equally potent volume of
sound, for everybody was talking, though the individual voices
might be lower in tone.   But in the study it was more or less
quiet.   The Rector himself had taken Katherine there to show
her some of his books.   "It would be absurd to call them
priceless," he said, "for any chance might bring a set into
the market, and then, of course, a price would be put upon
them, varying according to the dealer's knowledge and the
demand; but they are rare, and for a poor man like me to
have been able to get them at all is—well, I think that, with
all modesty, it is a feather in my cap; I mean, to get them at
a price within my means."

"It is only people who know that ever get bargains, I
think," Katherine said, in discharge of that barren duty of
admiration and approval on subjects we do not understand,
which makes us all responsible for many foolish speeches.   Mr.
Stanley's fine taste was not quite pleased with the idea that his
last acquisition was a bargain, but he let that pass.

"Yes; I think that, without transgressing the limits of
modesty, I may allow that to be the case.   It holds in everything; those who know what a friend is attain to the best
friends; those who can appreciate a noble woman——"

"Oh!" said Katherine, a little startled, "that is carrying
the principle perhaps too far.   I was thinking of china, you
know, and things of that sort—when you see an insignificant
little pot which you would not give sixpence for, and suddenly
a connoisseur comes in who puts down the sixpence in a great
hurry and carries it off rejoicing—and you hear afterwards that

it was priceless, too, though not, of course," she added apologetically, " like your books."

" Quite true, quite true," said the Rector blandly ; " but I maintain my principle all the same, and the real prize sometimes stands unnoticed while some rubbish is chosen instead. I hope," he added in a lower tone, " that you have good news from your sister, Miss Katherine, and at this season of peace and forgiveness that your father is thinking a little more kindly——"

" My father says very little on the subject," Katherine said. She knew what he did say, which nobody else did, and the recollection made her shiver. It was very concise, as the reader knows.

" We must wait and hope—he has such excellent—perceptions," said the Rector, stumbling a little for a word, " and so much—good sense—that I don't doubt everything will come right." Then he added, bending over her, " Do you think that I could be of any use ? " He took her hand for a moment, half fatherly in his tender sympathy. " Could I help you, perhaps, to induce him——"

" Oh, no, no ! " cried Katherine, drawing her hand away ; her alarm, however, was not for anything further that the Rector might say to herself, but in terror at the mere idea of anyone ever hearing what Mr. Tredgold said.

" Ah, well," he said with a sigh, " another time—perhaps another time." And then by way of changing the subject Katherine hurried off to a little display of drawings on the table. Charlotte Stanley, the Rector's eldest daughter, had her correspondence class like the other ladies ; but it was a Drawing Union. She was devoted to art. She had made little drawings since ever she could remember in pencil and in slate-pencil, and finally in colour. Giotto could not have begun more spontaneously ; and she was apt to think that had she been taken up as Giotto was, she, too, might have developed as he did. But short of that the Drawing Union was her favourite occupation. The members sent little portfolios about from one to another marked by pretty fictitious names. Char-

lotte signed herself Fenella, though it would have been difficult
to tell why; for she was large and fair. The portfolio, with
all the other ladies' performances, was put out to delight the
guests, and along with that several drawings of her own. She
came up hastily to explain them, not, perhaps, altogether to
her father's satisfaction, but he yielded his place with his
usual gentleness.

"We send our drawings every month," said the young art-
ist, "and they are criticised first and then sent round. Mr.
Strange, of the Water Colour Society, is our critic. He is
quite distinguished; here is his little note in the corner.
'Good in places, but the sky is heavy, and there is a want of
atmospheric effect'—that is Fair Rosamond's. Oh, yes, I
know her other name, but we are not supposed to mention
them; and this is one of mine—see what he says: 'Great improvement, shows much desire to learn, but too much stippling and great hardness in parts.' I confess I am too fond of
stippling," Charlotte said. "And then every month we have
a composition. 'The Power of Music' was the subject last
time — that or 'Sowing the Seed.' I chose the music.
You will think, perhaps, it is very simple." She lifted a
drawing in which a little child in a red frock and blue pina-
fore stood looking up at a bird of uncertain race in a cage.
"You see what he says," Charlotte continued—"'Full of
good intention, the colour perhaps a little crude, but there is
much feeling in the sketch.' Now, feeling was precisely
what I aimed at," she said.

Katherine was no judge of drawing any more than she was
of literature, and though the little picture did not appeal to
her (for there were pictures at the Cliff, and she had lived in
the same room with several Hunts and one supreme scrap of
Turner—bought a bargain on the information that it was a
safe investment many years ago—and therefore had an eye
more cultivated than she was aware of) she was impressed by
her friend's achievement, and thought it was a great thing to
employ your time in such elevated ways. Evelyn, who was
only seventeen and very frolicsome, wrote essays for the Mu-

tual Improvement Society. This filled Katherine, who did nothing particular, with great respect. She found a little knot of them consulting and arguing what they were to say in the next paper, and she was speechless with admiration. Inferior ! Lady Jane did not think much of the Sliplin people. She had warned the girls in the days of her ascendency not to "mix themselves up" with the village folk, not to conduct themselves as if they belonged to the nobodies. But Lady Jane had never, Katherine felt sure, written an essay in her life. She had her name on the Committee of the University Extension centre at Sliplin, but she never attended a lecture. She it was who was inferior, she and her kind : if intellect counted for anything, surely, Katherine thought, the intellect was here.

And then Dr. Burnet, came flying in, bringing a gust of fresh air with him. Though he had but a very short time to spare, he made his way to her through all the people who detained him. " I am glad to see you here ; you don't despise the village parties," he said.

" Despise them !—but I am not nearly good enough for them. I feel so small and so ignorant—they are all thinking of so many things—essays and criticisms and I don't know what. It is they who should despise me."

" Oh, I don't think very much of the essays—nor would you if you saw them," Dr. Burnet said.

" I tell you all," said Miss Mildmay, " though you are so grand with your theories and so forth, it is the old-fashioned girls who know nothing about such nonsense that the gentlemen like best."

" The gentlemen—what gentlemen ? " said Katherine, not at all comforted by this side of the question, and, indeed, not very clear what was meant.

" Oh, don't pretend to be a little fool," said Miss Mildmay. She was quite anxious to promote what she considered to be Katherine's two chances—the two strings she had to her bow—but to put up with this show of ignorance was too much for her. She went off angrily to where her companion sat, yawning a little over an entertainment which depended so entirely for its success upon whether you had someone nice to talk to or not. "Kate Tredgold worries me," she said. "She pretends she knows nothing, when she is just as well up to it as either you or I."

"I am up to nothing," said Mrs. Shanks; "I only know what you say; and I don't believe Mr. Tredgold would give his daughter and only heiress to either of them——if Stella is cut off, poor thing——"

"Stella will not be cut off," said Miss Mildmay. "Mark my words. He'll go back to her sooner or later; and what a good thing if Katherine had someone to stand by her before then!"

"If you saw two straws lying together in the road you would think there was something between them," cried Mrs. Shanks, yawning more than ever. "Oh, Ruth Mildmay, fancy our being brought out on a cold night and having to pay for the Midge and all that, and nothing more in it than to wag our heads at each other about Katherine Tredgold's marriage, if it ever comes off!"

"Let me take you in to supper," said the rector, approaching with his arm held out.

And then Mrs. Shanks felt that there was compensation in all things. She was taken in one of the first, she said afterwards; not the very first—she could not expect that, with Mrs. Barry of Northcote present, and General Skelton's wife. The army and the landed gentry naturally were first. But Miss Mildmay did not follow till long after—till the doctor found her still standing in a corner, with that grim look of suppressed scorn and satirical spectatorship with which the proud neglected watch the vulgar stream pressing before them.

"Have you not been *in* yet?" the doctor said.

"No," said Miss Mildmay. "You see, I am not young to go with the girls, nor married to go with the ladies who are at the head of society. I only stand and look on."

"That is just my case," said Dr. Burnet. "I am not young to go with the girls, nor married to disport myself with Mrs.

Barry or such magnates. Let us be jolly together, for we are both in the same box."

" Don't you let that girl slip through your fingers," said Miss Mildmay solemnly, as she went " in " on his arm.

" Will she ever come within reach of my fingers? " the doctor said, shaking his head.

" You are not old, like that Stanley man ; you've got no family dragging you back. I should not stand by if I were you, and let her be seduced into this house as the stepmother! " said Miss Mildmay with energy.

" Don't talk like that in the man's house. He is a good man, and we are just going to eat his sandwiches."

" If there are any left," Miss Mildmay said.

CHAPTER XXIV.

THUS it will be seen that Katherine's new position as the only daughter of her father was altogether like a new beginning of life, though she had been familiar with the place and the people for years. Stella had been the leader in everything, as has been said. When she went to a party at the Rectory, she turned it into a dance or a romp at once, and kept the Drawing Union and the Mutual Improvement Society quite in the background. Even the books which for a year or two back the rector would have liked to show Katherine privately, beguiling her into separate talks, had been thrust aside necessarily when Katherine was imperiously demanded for Sir Roger de Coverley or a round game. Therefore these more studious and elevated occupations of the little community came upon her now with the force of a surprise. Her own home was changed to her also in the most remarkable way. Stella was not a creature whom anyone fully approved of, not even her sister. She was very indifferent to the comfort and wishes of others; she loved her own amusement by whatever way it could be best obtained. She was restrained by no scruples about the proprieties, or the risk—which was one of Katherine's chief terrors—of hurting other people's feelings. She did what she liked, instantaneously, recklessly, at any risk. And her father himself, though he chuckled and applauded and took a certain pride in her cleverness even when she cheated and defied him, did not pretend to approve of Stella; but she carried her little world with her all the same. There was a current, a whirl of air about her rapid progress. The stiller figures were swept on with her whether they liked it or not; and, as a matter of fact, they generally did like it when fairly afloat upon that quick-flowing, rippling, continuous stream of youth and life.

But now that all this movement and variety had departed nothing could be imagined more dull than Mr. Tredgold's house on the Cliff. It was like a boat cast ashore—no more commotion of the sea and waves, no more risk of hurricane or tempest, no need to shout against the noise of a cyclone, or to steer in the teeth of a gale. It was all silent, all quiet, nothing to be done, no tides to touch the motionless mass or tinkle against the dull walls of wood. When Katherine received her guests from the city, she felt as if she were showing them over a museum rather than a house. " This is the room we used to sit in when my sister was at home ; I do not use it now." How often had she to say such words as these ! And when the heavy tax of these visits had been paid she found herself again high and dry, once more stranded, when the last carriage had driven away.

But the rush of little parties and festivities about Christmas, when all the sons and brothers were at home, into which she was half forced by the solicitations of her neighbours, and half by her own forlorn longing to see and speak to somebody, made a not unwelcome change. The ladies in Sliplin, especially those who had sons, had always been anxious to secure the two Miss Tredgolds, the two heiresses, for every entertainment, and there was nothing mercenary in the increased attention paid to Katherine. She would have been quite rich enough with half her father's fortune to have fulfilled the utmost wishes of any aspirant in the village. The doctor and the rector had both thought of Katherine before there was any change in her fortunes—at the time when it was believed that Stella would have the lion's share of the money, as well as, evidently, of the love. In that they were quite unlike the city suitors, who only found her worth their while from the point of view of old Tredgold's entire and undivided fortune. Indeed, it is to be feared that Sliplin generally would have been overawed by the greatness of her heiresshood had it grasped this idea. But still nobody believed in the disinheriting of Stella, They believed

that she would be allowed to repent at leisure of her hasty
marriage, but never that she would be finally cut off.   The
wooing of the rector and that of the doctor had only reached
an acuter stage because now Katherine was alone.   They felt
that she was solitary and downcast, and wanted cheering and a
companion to indemnify her for what she had lost, and this
naturally increased the chances of the fortunate man who should
succeed.

Mr. Stanley would (perhaps) have been alarmed at the idea
of offering the position of stepmother to his children to Mr.
Tredgold's sole heiress ; although he would not, perhaps, have
thought that in justice to his family he could have asked her to
share his lot had it not been evident that she must have her
part of her father's fortune.   He was a moderate man—modest,
as he would himself have said—and he had made up his mind
that Katherine in Stella's shadow would have made a perfect
wife for him.   Therefore he had been frightened rather than
elated by the change in her position ; but with the consciousness of his previous sentiments, which were so disinterested, he
had got over that, and now felt that in her loneliness a proposal such as he had to make might be even more agreeable
than in other circumstances.   The doctor was in something of
the same mind.   He was not at all like Turney and Company.
He felt the increased fortune to be a drawback, making more
difference between them than had existed before, but yet met
this difficulty like a man, feeling that it might be got over.
He would probably have hesitated more if she had been cut off
without a shilling as Stella was supposed, but never believed,
to be.

Neither of these gentlemen had any idea of that formula
upon which Mr. Tredgold stood.   The money on the table,
thousand for thousand, would have been inconceivable to them.
Indeed, they did not believe, notwithstanding the experience of
Sir Charles Somers, that there would be much difficulty in deal-
ing with old Tredgold.   He might tie up his money, and these
good men had no objection—they did not want to grasp at her
money.   Let him tie it up !   They would neither of them have

opposed that. As to further requirements on his part they were
tranquil, neither of them being penniless, or in the condition,
they both felt, to be considered fortune-hunters at all. The
curious thing was that they were each aware of the other's sentiments, without hating each other, or showing any great
amount of jealousy. Perhaps the crisis had not come near
enough to excite this; perhaps it was because they were
neither of them young, and loved with composure as they did
most things; yet the doctor had some seven years the advantage of the rector, and was emphatically a young man still,
not middle-aged at all.

It was partly their unconscious influence that drew Katherine
into the way of life which was approved by all around her.
The doctor persuaded her to go to the ambulance class, which
she attended weekly, very sure that she never would have had
the courage to apply a tourniquet or even a bandage had a real
emergency occurred. "Now, Stella could have done it," she
said within herself. Stella's hands would not have trembled,
nor her heart failed her. It was the rector who recommended
her to join the Mutual Improvement Society, offering to look
over her essays, and to lend her as many books as she might
require. And it was under the auspices of both that Katherine
appeared at the University Extension Lectures, and learned
all about the Arctic regions and the successive expeditions that
had perished there. "I wish it had been India," she said on
one occasion; "I should like to know about India, now that
Stella is there."

"I don't doubt in the least that after Christmas we might
get a series on India. It is a great, a most interesting subject; what do you think, Burnet?"

Burnet entirely agreed with him. "Nothing better," he
said; "capital contrast to the ice and the snow."

And naturally Katherine was bound to attend the new
series which had been so generously got up for her. There
were many pictures and much limelight, and everybody was
delighted with the change.

"What we want in winter is a nice warm blazing sun, and

not something colder than we have at home," cried Mrs. Shanks.

And Katherine sat and looked at the views and wondered where Stella was, and then privately to herself wondered where James Stanford was, and what he could be doing, and if he ever thought now of the old days. There was not very much to think of, as she reflected when she asked herself that question ; but still she did ask it under her breath.

" Remember, Miss Katherine, that all my books are at your service," said the rector, coming in to the end of the drawing-room where Katherine had made herself comfortable behind the screens ; " and if you would like me to look at your essay, and make perhaps a few suggestions before you send it in——"

" I was not writing any essay. I was only writing to—my sister," said Katherine.

" To be sure. It is the India mail day, I remember. Excuse me for coming to interrupt you. What a thing for her to have a regular correspondent like you! You still think I couldn't be of any use to say a word to your father? You know that I am always at your disposition. Anything I can do——"

" You are very good, but I don't think it would be of any use." Katherine shivered a little, as she always did at the dreadful thought of anyone hearing what her father said.

" I am only good to myself when I try to be of use to you," the rector said, and he added, with a little vehemence, " I only wish you would understand how dearly I should like to think that you would come to me in any emergency, refer to me at once, whatever the matter might be——"

" Indeed, Mr. Stanley, I understand, and I do," she said, raising her eyes to his gratefully. " You remember how I appealed to you that dreadful time, and how much—how much you did for us ? "

" Ah, you sent Burnet to me," he said, " that's not exactly the same. Of course, I did what I could ; but what I should like would be that you should come with full confidence to tell me anything that vexes you, or to ask me to do anything you want done, like——"

"I know," she said. "Like Charlotte and Evelyn. And, indeed, I should, indeed I will—trust me for that."

The rector drew back, as if she had flung in his face the vase of clear water which was waiting on the table beside her for the flowers she meant to put in it. He gave an impatient sigh and walked to the window, with a little movement of his hands which Katherine did not understand.

"Oh, has it begun to snow?" she said, for the sky was very grey, as if full of something that must soon overflow and fall, and everybody had been expecting snow for twenty-four hours past.

"No, it has not begun to snow," he said. "It is pelting hailstones—no, I don't mean that; nothing is coming down as yet—at least, out of the sky. Perhaps I had better leave you to finish your letter."

"Oh, there is no hurry about that. There are hours yet before post-time, and I have nearly said all I have to say. I have been telling her I am studying India. It is a big subject," Katherine said. "And how kind you and Dr. Burnet were, getting this series of lectures instead of another for me—though I think everybody is interested, and the pictures are beautiful with the limelight."

"I should have thought of it before," said the rector. "As for Burnet, he wanted some scientific series about evolution and that sort of thing. Medical men are always mad after science, or what they believe to be such. But as soon as I saw how much you wished it——"

"A thing one has something to do with is always so much the more interesting," Katherine said, half apologetically.

"I hope you know that if it were left to me I should choose only those subjects that you are interested in."

"Oh, no," cried Katherine, "not so much as that. You are so kind, you want to please and interest us all."

"Kindness is one thing; but there are other motives that tell still more strongly." The rector went to and from the

15

window, where Katherine believed him to be looking out for
the snow, which lingered so long, to the table, where she still
trifled with her pen in her hand, and had not yet laid it down
to put the flowers which lay in a little basket into water.
The good clergyman was more agitated than he should have
thought possible. Should he speak ? He was so much wound
up to the effort that it seemed as if it must burst forth at any
moment, in spite of himself; but, on the other hand, he was
afraid lest he might precipitate matters. He watched her
hands involuntarily every time he approached her, and then
he said to himself that when she had put down the pen and
begun to arrange the flowers, he would make the plunge, but
not till then. That should be his sign.

It was a long time before this happened. Katherine held
her pen as if it had been a shield, though she was not at all
aware of the importance thus assigned to it. She had a certain
sense of protection in its use. She thought that if she kept up
the fiction of continuing her letter Mr. Stanley would go away ;
and somehow she did not care for him so much as usual to-day.
She had always had every confidence in him, and would have
gone to him at any time, trusting to his sympathy and kindness ; but to be appealed to to do this, as if it were some new
thing, confused her mind. Why, of course she had faith in
him, but she did not like the look with which he made that
appeal. Why should he look at her like that ? He had
known her almost all her life, and taught her her Catechism
and her duty, which, though they may be endearing things, are
not endearing in that way. If Katherine had been asked in what
way, she would probably have been unable to answer ; but yet in
her heart she wished very much that Mr. Stanley would go away.

At last, when it seemed to her that this was hopeless—that
he would not take the hint broadly furnished by her unfinished
letter—she did put down the pen, and, pushing her writing-
book away, drew towards her the little basket of flowers from
the conservatory, which the gardener brought her every day.
They were very waxen and winterly, as flowers still are in Jan-
uary, and she took them up one by one, arranging them so as

to make the most of such colour as there was. The rector had turned at the end of his little promenade when she did so, and came back rapidly when he heard the little movement. She was aware of the quickened step, and said, smiling, " Well, has the snow begun at last ? "

" There is no question of snow," he said hurriedly, and Katherine heard with astonishment the panting of his breath, and looked up—to see a very flushed and anxious countenance directed towards her. Mr. Stanley was a handsome man of his years, but his was a style which demanded calm and composure and the tranquillity of an even mind to do it justice. He was excited now, which was very unbecoming; his cheeks were flushed, his lips parted with hasty breathing. " Katherine," he said, " it is something much more important than—any change outside." He waved his hand almost contemptuously at the window, as if the snow was a slight affair, not worth mentioning. " I am afraid," he said, standing with his hand on the table looking down upon her, yet rather avoiding her steady, half-wondering look, " that you are too little self-conscious to have observed lately—any change in me."

" I don't know," she said faltering, looking up at him ; " is there anything the matter, really ? I have thought once or twice —that you looked a little disturbed."

It flashed into her mind that there might be something wrong in the family, that Bertie might have been extravagant, that help might be wanted from her rich father. Oh, poor Mr. Stanley ! if his handsome stately calm should be disturbed by such a trouble as that ? Katherine's look grew very kind, very sympathising as she looked up into his face.

" I have often, I am sure, looked disturbed. Katherine, it is not a small matter when a man like me finds his position changed in respect to—one like yourself—by an overmastering sentiment which has taken possession of him he knows not how, and which he is quite unable to restrain."

" Rector ! " cried Katherine astonished, looking up at him with even more feeling than before. " Mr. Stanley ! have I done anything ? "

" That shows," he cried, with something like a stamp of his foot and an impatient movement of his hand, " how much I have to contend with.　You think of me as nothing but your clergyman—a—a sort of pedagogue—and your thought is that he is displeased—that there is something he is going to find fault with——"

" No," she said.　" You are too kind to find fault ; but—— I am sure I never neglect anything you say to me.　Tell me what it is—and I—I will not take offence.　I will do my very best——"

" Oh, how hard it is to make you understand !　You put me on a pedestal—whereas it is you who——　Katherine ! do you know that you are not a little girl any longer, but a woman, and a—most attractive one ?　I have struggled against it, knowing that was not the light in which I can have appeared to you, but it's too strong for me.　I have come to tell you of a feeling which has existed for years on my part—and to ask you—if there is any possibility, any hope, to ask you—to marry me——"　The poor rector ! his voice almost died away in his throat.　He put one knee to the ground—not, I need not say, with any prayerful intention, but only to put himself on the same level with her, with his hands on the edge of her table, and gazed into her face.

" To——　What did you say, Mr. Stanley ? " she asked, with horror in her eyes.

" Don't be hasty, for the sake of heaven !　Don't condemn me unheard.　I know all the disparities, all the——　But, Katherine, my love for you is more than all that.　I have been trying to keep it down for years.　I said, to marry me—to marry me, my dear and only——"

" Do you mean that you are on your knees to me, a girl whom you have catechised ? " cried Katherine severely, holding her head high.

The rector stumbled up in great confusion to his feet. " No, I did not mean that.　I was not kneeling to you.　I was only——　Oh, Katherine, how small a detail is this ! God knows I do not want to make myself absurd in your eyes. I am much older than you are. I am—but your true lover notwithstanding—for years ; and your most fond and faithful—— Katherine ! if you will be my wife——''

'' And the mother of Charlotte and Bertie ! '' said Katherine, looking at him with shining eyes. '' Charlotte is a year younger than I am. She comes between Stella and me ; and Bertie thinks he is in love with me too. Is it *that* you come and offer to a girl, Mr. Stanley ? Oh, I know. Girls who are governesses and poor have it offered to them and are grateful. But I am as well off as you are. And do you think it likely that I would want to change my age and be my own mother for the sake of—what ? Being married ? I don't want to be married. Oh, Mr. Stanley, it is wicked of you to confuse everything—to change all our ways of looking at each other—to——'' Katherine almost broke down into a torrent of angry tears, but controlled herself for wrath's sake.

The rector stood before her with his head down, as sorely humiliated a man as ever clergyman was. '' If you take it in that light, what can I say ? I had hoped you would not take it in that light. I am not an old man. I have not been accustomed to—apologise for myself,'' he said, with a gleam of natural self-assertion. He, admired of ladies for miles round —to the four seas, so to speak—on every hand. He could have told her things ! But the man was *digne ;* he was no traitor nor ungrateful for kindness shown him. '' If you think, Katherine, that the accident of my family and of a very early first marriage is so decisive, there is perhaps nothing more to be said. But many men only begin life at my age ; and I think it is ungenerous—to throw my children in my teeth— when I was speaking to you—of things so different——''

'' Oh, Mr. Stanley,'' cried Katherine, subdued, '' I am very, very sorry. I did not mean to throw—anything in your teeth. But how could anyone forget Charlotte and Bertie and Evelyn and the rest ? Do you call them an accident—all the family ? '' Katherine's voice rose till it was almost shrill in .the thought of this injury to her friends. '' But I only think of you as their father and my clergyman—and always very, very kind," she said.

The flowers had never yet got put into the water. She had thrown them down again into the basket. The empty vase stood reproachfully full and useless, reflecting in its side a tiny sparkle of the firelight ; and the girl sitting over them, and the man standing by her, had both of them downcast heads, and did not dare to look at each other. This group contin- ued for a moment, and then he moved again towards the win- dow. " It has begun at last," he said in a strange changed tone. " It is snowing fast."

And the rector walked home in a blinding downfall, and was a white man, snow covered, when he arrived at home, where his children ran out to meet him, exclaiming at his beard which had grown white, and his hair, which, when his hat was taken off, exhibited a round of natural colour fringed off with ends of snow. The family surrounded him with chat- terings and caresses, pulling off his coat, unwinding his scarf, shaking off the snow, leading him into the warm room by the warm fire, running off for warm shoes and everything he could want. An accident ! The accident of a family ! He sub- mitted with a great effort over himself, but in his heart he would have liked to push them off, the whole band of them, into the snow.

CHAPTER XXV.

IT will perhaps be thought very unfeeling of Katherine to have received as she did this unlooked for elderly lover. All Sliplin, it is true, could have told her for some time past that the Rector was in love with her, and meant to make her an offer, and Miss Mildmay believed that she had been aware of it long before that. But it had never occurred to Katherine that the father of Charlotte and Gerard was occupied with herself in any way, or that such an idea could enter his mind. He had heard her say her catechism! He had given Charlotte in her presence the little sting of a reproof about making a noise, and other domestic sins which Katherine was very well aware she was intended to share. In the *douceurs* which, there was no denying, he had lately shed about, she had thought of nothing but a fatherly intention to console her in her changed circumstances ; and to think that all the time this old middle-aged man, this father of a family, had it in his mind to make her his wife ! Katherine let her flowers lie drooping, and paced up and down the room furious, angry even with herself. Forty-five is a tremendous age to three-and-twenty ; and it was the first time she had ever received a proposal straight in the face, so to speak. Turny and Company had treated with her father, but had retreated from before her own severe aspect when she gave it to be seen how immovable she was. And to think that her first veritable proposal should be this—a thing that filled her with indignation ! What ! did the man suppose for a moment that she, his daughter's friend, would marry him ? Did all men think that a girl would do anything to be married ?—or what did they think ?

Katherine could not realise that Mr. Stanley to the Rector was not at all the same person that he was to her. The Rector thought himself in the prime of life, and so he was. The children belonged to him and he was accustomed to them, and did not, except now and then, think them a great burden ; but himself was naturally the first person in his thoughts. He knew that he was a very personable man, that his voice was considered beautiful, and his aspect (in the pulpit) imposing. His features were good, his height was good, he was in full health and vigour. Why shouldn't he have asked anybody to marry him ? The idea that it was an insult to a girl never entered his mind. And it was no insult. He was not even poor or in pursuit of her wealth. No doubt her wealth would make a great difference, but that was not in the least his motive, for he had thought of her for years. And in his own person he was a man any woman might have been proud of. All this was very visible to him.

But to Katherine it only appeared that Mr. Stanley was forty-five, that he was the father of a girl as old as herself, and of a young man, whom she had laughed at, indeed, but who also had wished to make love to her. What would Gerard say? This was the first thing that changed Katherine's mood, that made her laugh. It brought in a ludicrous element. What Charlotte would say was not half so funny. Charlotte would be horrified, but she would probably think that any woman might snatch at a man so admired as her father, and the fear of being put out of her place would occupy her and darken her understanding. But the thought of Gerard made Katherine laugh and restored her equilibrium. Strengthened by this new view she came down from her pinnacle of indignation and began to look after the things she had to do. The snow went on falling thickly, a white moving veil across every one of the windows ; the great flickering flakes falling now quickly, now slowly, and everything growing whiter and whiter against the half-seen grey of the sky. This whiteness shut in the house, encircling it as with a flowing mantle. Nobody would come near the house that afternoon, nobody would come out that could help it—not even the midge was likely to appear along the white path. The snow made an end of visitors, and Katherine felt herself shut up within it, condemned not to hear any voice or meet with any incident for the rest of the day. It was not a cheering sensation. She finished her letter to Stella, and paused and wondered whether she should tell her what had happened ; but she fortunately remembered that a high standard of honour forbade the disclosure of secrets like this, which were the secrets of others as well as her own. She had herself condemned from that high eminence with much indignation the way in which other girls blazoned such secrets. She would not be like one of them. And besides, Stella and her husband would laugh and make jokes in bad taste and hold up the Rector to the laughter of the regiment, which would not be fair though Katherine was so angry with him. When she had finished her letter she returned to the flowers, and finally arranged them as she had intended to do long ago. And then she went and stood for a long time at the window watching the snow falling. It was very dull to see nobody, to be alone, all alone, for all these hours. There was a new novel fresh from Mudie's on the table, which was always something to look forward to ; but even a novel is but a poor substitute for society when you have been so shaken and put out of your *assiette* as Katherine had been by a personal incident. Would she have told anyone if anyone had come ? She said to herself, " No, certainly not." But as she was still thrilling and throbbing all over, and and felt it almost impossible to keep still, I cannot feel so sure as she was that she would not have followed a multitude to do evil, and betrayed her suitor's secret by way of relieving her own mind. But I am sure that she would have felt very sorry had she done so as soon as the words were out of her mouth.

She had seated herself by the fire and taken up her novel, not with the content and pleasure which a well-conditioned girl ought to exhibit at the sight of a new story in three volumes (in which form it is always most welcome, according

to my old-fashioned ideas) and a long afternoon to enjoy it
in, but still with resignation and a pulse beating more quietly
—when there arose sounds which indicated a visit after all.
Katherine listened eagerly, then subsided as the footsteps
and voices faded again, going off to the other end of the
house.

" Dr. Burnet to see papa," she said half with relief, half
with expectation. She had no desire to see Dr. Burnet. She
could not certainly to him breathe the faintest sigh of a revelation, or relieve her mind by the most distant hint of anything that had happened. Still, he was somebody. It was
rather agreeable to give him tea. The bread and butter disappeared so quickly, and it had come to be such a familiar
operation to watch those strong white teeth getting through
it. Certainly he had wonderful teeth. Katherine gave but
a half attention to her book, listening to the sounds in the
house. Her father's door closed, he had gone in, and then
after a while the bell rang and the footsteps became audible
once more in the corridor. She closed her book upon her
hand wondering if he would come this way, or—— He was
coming this way ! She pushed her chair away from the hearth,
feeling that, what with the past excitement and the glow of the
fire, her cheeks were ablaze.

But Dr. Burnet did not seem to see this when he came in.
She had gone to the window by that time to look out again
upon the falling snow. It was falling, falling, silent and white
and soft, in large flakes like feathers, or rather like white
swan's down. He joined her there and they stood looking
at it together, and saying to each other how it seemed to close
round the house and wrap everything up as in a downy mantle.

" I like to see it," the doctor said, " which is very baby-
ish, I know. I like to see that flutter in the air and the great
soft flakes dilating as they fall. But it puts a great stop to
everything. You have had no visitors, I suppose, to-day ? "

" Oh, yes, before it came on," said Katherine ; and then
she added in a voice which she felt to be strange even while
she spoke, " The Rector was here."

That was all — not another word did she say; but Dr. Burnet gave her a quick look, and he knew as well as the reader knows what had happened. The Rector, then, had struck his blow. No doubt it was by deliberate purpose that he had chosen a day threatening snow, when nobody was likely to interrupt him. And he had made his explanation and it had not been well received. The doctor divined all this and his heart gave a jump of pleasure, though Katherine had not said a word, and indeed had not looked at him, but stood steadily with a blank countenance in which there was nothing to be read, gazing out upon the snow. Sometimes a blank countenance displays more than the frankest speech.

" He is a handsome man—for his time of life," Dr. Burnet said, he could not tell why.

" Yes ? " said Katherine, as if she were waiting for further evidence ; and then she added, " It is droll to think of that as being a quality of the Rector—just as you would say it of a boy."

" Do you think that handsome is as handsome does, Miss Katherine ? I should not have expected that of you. I always thought you made a great point of good looks."

" I like nice-looking people," she said, and in spite of herself gave a glance aside at the doctor, who in spite of those fine teeth and very good eyes and other points of advantage, could not have been called handsome by the most partial of friends.

" You are looking at me," he said with a laugh, " and the reflection is obvious, though perhaps it is only my vanity that imagines you to have made it. I am not much to brag of, I know it. I am very 'umble. A man who knows he is good-looking must have a great advantage in life to begin with. It must give him so much more confidence wherever he makes his appearance—at least for the first time."

" Do you think so ? " she said. " I should think one would forget it so quickly, both the possessor himself and those who look at him. If people are *nice* you think of that and not of their beauty, unless——''

" Unless what, Miss Katherine? You can't think how interesting this talk is to me. Tell me something on which an ugly man can rest and take courage. You are thinking of John Wilkes' famous saying that he only wanted half-an-hour's start of the handsomest man——"

" Who was John Wilkes?" said Katherine with the serenest ignorance. "I suppose one of the men one ought to know; but then I know so little. After a year of the Mutual Improvement Society——"

" Don't trouble about that," cried the doctor, " but my ambulance classes are really of the greatest use. I do hope you will attend them. Suppose there was an accident before your eyes—on the lawn there, and nobody within reach—what should you do?"

" Tremble all over and be of use to nobody," Katherine said with a shudder.

" That is just what I want to obviate—that is just what ought to be obviated. You, with your light touch and your kind heart and your quick eye——"

" Have I a quick eye and a light touch?" said Katherine with a laugh; " and how do you know? It is understood that every girl must have a kind heart. On the whole, I would rather write an essay, I think, than be called upon to render first aid. My hand is not at all steady if my touch is light."

She lifted one of the vases as she spoke to change its position and her hand shook. He looked at it keenly, and she, not thinking of so sudden a test, put down the vase in a hurry with a wave of colour coming over her face.

" That's not natural, that's worry, that's excitement," Dr. Burnet said.

" The outlook is not very exciting, is it?" cried Katherine; " one does not come in the way of much excitement at Sliplin, and I have not even seen Miss Mildmay and Mrs. Shanks. No, it is natural, doctor. So you see how little use it would be to train me. Come to the fire and have some tea."

"I must not give myself this pleasure too often," he said. "I find myself going back to it in imagination when I am out in the wilds. It is precious cold in my dog-cart facing the wind, Miss Katherine. I say to myself, Now the tea is being brought in in the drawing-room on the Cliff, now it is being poured out. I smell the fragrance of it driving along the bitter downs; and then I go and order some poor wretch the beastliest draught that can be compounded to avenge myself for getting no tea."

"You should give them nothing but nice things, then, when you do have tea—as now," said Katherine.

He came after her to where the little tea-table shone and sparkled in the firelight, and took from her hand the cup of tea she offered him, and stood with his back to the fire holding it in his hand. His groom was driving his dog-cart round and round the snowy path, crossing the window from time to time, a dark apparition amid the falling of the snow. What the thoughts of the groom might be, looking in through the great window on this scene of comfort, the figure of Katherine in her pretty dress and colour stooping over the table, and his master behind standing against the firelight with his cup of tea, nobody asked. Perhaps he was making little comparisons as to his lot, perhaps only thinking of the time when he should be able to thrust his hands into his pockets and the doctor should have the reins. Yet Dr. Burnet did not ignore his groom. "There," he said, "is fate awaiting me. This time she has assumed the innocent form of John Dobbs, my groom. I have got ten miles to drive, there and back, to see Mrs. Crumples, who could do perfectly well without me, and then to the Chine for a moment to ascertain if the new man there has digested his early dinner, and then to Steephill to look after the servants' hall. I am not good enough, except on an emergency, for the family or Lady Jane."

"I would not go more, then, if it is only for the servants' hall," cried Katherine.

"Why not?" he said. "I consider Mrs. Cole, the cook, is quite as valuable a member of society as Lady Jane. The world would not come to an end if Lady Jane were absent for a day, or laid up, but it would very nearly—at Steephill—if anything happened to the cook.''

"You said you were 'umble, Dr. Burnet, and I did not believe you. I see that you are really so, now.''

"Ah, there I disagree with you,'' he said, a little flush on his face. "I am 'umble about my personal appearance, but I only don't mind with Lady Jane. She thinks of me merely as the general practitioner from Sliplin, which shows she doesn't know anything—for I am more than a general practitioner.''

"I know,'' cried Katherine quickly, half with a generous desire not to leave him to sing his own praises, and half with a wondering scorn that he should think it worth the while; "you will be a great physician one of these days.''

"I hope so,'' he said quietly. Then, after a while, "But I am still more than that; at least, what would seem more in Lady Jane's eyes. I am not a doctor only, Miss Katherine. I have not such a bad little estate behind me. My uncle has it now, but I'm the man after him; and a family a good deal better known than the Uffingtons, who are not a century old.'' He said this with a little excitement, and a flourish in his hand of the teaspoon with which he had been stirring his tea.

Jim Dobbs, driving past the window, white with snow, yet looking like a huge blackness in the solidity of the group, he and his high coat and his big horse amid the falling feathers, caught the gesture and wondered within himself what the doctor could be about; while Katherine, looking up at him from the tea-table, was scarcely less surprised. Why should he tell her this? Why at all? Why now? The faint wonder in her look made Dr. Burnet blush.

"What a fool I am! As if you cared about that,'' he said with a stamp of his foot, in impatience with himself, and shame.

"Oh, yes, I care about it. I am glad to hear of it. But— Dr. Burnet, let me give you another cup of tea.''

" But," he said, " you think what have I to do with the man's antecedents ? You see I want you to know that I can put my foot forward sometimes—like——'' he paused for a moment and laughed, putting down his cup hastily. " No more ! No more! I must tear myself from this enchanted cliff, or Jim Dobbs will mistake the window for the stable door—like my elderly friend, Miss Katherine," he said over his shoulder as he went away.

Like—his elderly friend ? Who was his elderly friend, and what did the doctor mean ? Katherine watched from the window while Burnet got into his dog-cart and whirled away at a very different pace from that of his groom. She could not see this from her window, but listened till the sounds died away, looking out upon the snow. What a fascination that snow had, falling, falling, without any dark object now to disturb its absolute possession of the world ! Katherine stood for a long time watching before she went back to her novel, which was only when the lamps were brought in, changing the aspect of the place. Did she care for Dr. Burnet's revelations, or divine the object of them ? In the first place not at all; in the second, I doubt whether she took the trouble to ask herself the question.

CHAPTER XXVI.

But though Dr. Burnet had been 'umble about his position at Steephill, and considered himself only as the physician of the servants' hall, he was not invaribly left in that secondary position. On this particular snowy evening, when master and horse and man were all eager to get home in view of the drifting of the snow, which was already very deep, and the darkness of the night, which made it dangerous, Lady Jane—who was alone at Steephill, i.e. without any house party, and enjoying the sole society of Sir John, her spouse, which was not lively—bethought herself that she would like to consult the doctor. She did not pretend that she had more than a cold, but then a cold may develop into anything, as all the world knows. It was better to have a talk with Dr. Burnet than not to say a word to anybody, and to speak of her cold rather than not to speak at all. Besides, she did want to hear something of old Tredgold, and whether Katherine was behaving well, and what chance there might be for Stella. The point of behaviour in Katherine about which Lady Jane was anxious was whether or not she was keeping her sister's claims before her father—her conduct in other respects was a matter of absolute indifference to her former patroness.

"I have not been in Sliplin for quite a long time," she said. "It may be a deficiency in me, but, you know, I don't very much affect your village, Dr. Burnet."

"No; few people do; unless they want it, or something in it," the doctor said as he made out his prescription, of which I think *eau sucrée*, or something like it, was the chief ingredient.

"I don't know what I should want in it or with it," said

Lady Jane with a touch of impatience. And then she added, modifying her tone, "Tell me about the Tredgolds, Dr. Burnet. How is the old man? Not a very satisfactory patient, I should think—so fond of his own way; especially when you have not Stella at hand to make him amenable."

"He is not a bad patient," said Dr. Burnet. "He does not like his own way better than most old men. He allows himself to be taken good care of on the whole."

"Oh, I am glad to hear so good an opinion of him. I thought he was very headstrong. Now, you know, I don't want you to betray your patient's secrets, Dr. Burnet."

"No," he said; "and it wouldn't matter, I fear, if you did," he continued after a pause; "but I know no secrets of the Tredgolds, so I am perfectly safe——"

"That's rather rude," said Lady Jane, "but of course it's the right thing to say; and of course also you know all about Stella and her elopement and the dreadful disappointment. I confess, for my own part, I did not think he could stand out against her for a day."

"He is a man who knows his own mind very clearly, Lady Jane."

"So it appears. And will he hold out, do you think, till the bitter end? Can Katherine do nothing? Couldn't she do something if she were to try? I mean for those poor Somers—they are great friends of mine. He is, you know, a kind of relation. And poor Stella! Do tell me, Dr. Burnet, do you think there is no hope? Couldn't you do something yourself? A doctor at a man's bedside has great power."

"It is not a power I would ever care to exercise," Dr. Burnet said.

"Oh, you are too scrupulous! And when you consider how poor they are, doctor!—really badly off. Why, they have next to nothing! The pay, of course, is doubled in India, but beyond that—— Think of Charlie Somers living on his pay! And then there is, Stella the most expensive little person, accustomed to every luxury you can think of, and never used to deny herself anything. It is extremely hard

16

lines for them, certain as they were that her father—— Oh, I
can't help thinking, Dr. Burnet, that Katherine could do
something if she chose."

" Then you may be quite at ease, Lady Jane, for I am sure she
will choose—to do a hardness to anyone, let alone her sister——"

" Ah, Dr. Burnet," cried Lady Jane, shaking her head, " it
is so difficult to tell in what subtle forms self-interest will get
in.　Now there is one thing that I wish I could see as a way
of settling the matter.　I should like to see Katherine Tredgold married to some excellent, honourable man.　Oh, I am
not without sources of information.　I have heard a little bird
here and there.　What a good thing if there was such a man,
who would do poor little Stella justice and give her her share !
Half of Mr. Tredgold's fortune would be a very handsome
fortune.　It would make all the difference to—say, a rising
professional man."

Dr. Burnet pretended to make a little change in the prescription he had been writing.　His head was bent over the
writing-table, which was an advantage.

" I have no doubt half of Mr. Tredgold's fortune would be
very nice to have," he said, " but unfortunately Miss Katherine is not married, nor do I know who are the candidates for
her hand."

" I assure you," said Lady Jane, " if there was such a
person I should take care to do everything I could to further
his views.　I have not seen much of Katherine lately, but I
should make a point of asking her and him to meet here.
There is nothing I would not do to bring such a thing about,
and—and secure her happiness, you know.　You will scarcely
believe it, but it is the truth, that Katherine was always the
one I liked best."

What a delightful, satisfactory, successful lie one can sometimes tell by telling the truth.　Dr. Burnet, who loved Katherine Tredgold, was touched by this last speech—there was the
ring of sincerity in the words ; and though Lady Jane had
not in the least the welfare of Katherine in her head at this
moment, still, these words were undoubtedly true.

He sat for some time making marks with the pen on the paper before him, and Lady Jane was so much interested in his reply that she did not press for it, but sat quite still, letting him take his time.

" Have you any idea," he said, making as though he were about to alter the prescription for the third time, " on what ground Mr. Tredgold refused Sir Charles Somers, who was not ineligible as marriages go ? " His extreme coolness, and the slight respect with which he spoke had a quite subduing influence upon Lady Jane. " Was it—for his private character, perhaps ? "

" Nothing of the sort," cried Lady Jane. " Do you know Charlie Somers is a cousin of mine, Dr. Burnet ? "

" That," said the doctor, " though an inestimable advantage, would not save him from having had—various things said about him, Lady Jane."

" No," she said with a laugh. " I acknowledge it. Various things have been said of him. The reason given was simply ludicrous. I don't know if Charlie invented it — but I don't think he was clever enough to invent it. It was something about putting money down pound for pound, or shilling for shilling, or some nonsense, and that he would give Stella to nobody that couldn't do that. On the face of it that is folly, you know."

" I am not so sure that it is folly. I have heard him say something of the kind ; meaning, I suppose, that any son-in-law he would accept would have to be as wealthy as himself."

" But that is absolute madness, Dr. Burnet ! Good heavens ! who that was as rich as old Tredgold could desire to be old Tredgold's son-in-law ? It is against all reason. A man might forgive to the girls who are so nice in themselves that they had such a father ; but what object could one as rich as himself—— Oh ! it is sheer idiocy, you know."

" Not to him ; and he, after all, is the person most concerned," said Dr. Burnet, with his head cast down and rather a dejected look about him altogether. The thought was not cheerful to himself any more than to Lady Jane, and as a matter of fact he had not realised it before.

"But it cannot be," she cried, "it cannot be ; it is out of the question. Oh, you are a man of resource ; you must find our some way to baffle this old curmudgeon. There must, there must," she exclaimed, "be some way out of it, if you care to try."

"Trying will not invent thousands of pounds, alas ! nor can the man who has the greatest fund of resource but no money do it anyhow," said Dr. Burnet sententiously. "There may be a dodge——"

"That is what I meant. There must be a dodge to—to get you out of it," she cried.

"It is possible that the man whose existence you divine might not care to get a wife—if she would have him to begin with—by a dodge, Lady Jane."

"Oh, rubbish ! " cried the great lady, "we are not so high-minded as all that. I am of opinion that in that way any-thing, everything can be done. Charlie Somers is a fool and Stella another ; but to a sensible pair with an understanding between them and plenty of time to work—and an old sick man," Lady Jane laid an involuntary emphasis on the word sick—then stopped and reddened visibly, though her counte-nance was rather weather-beaten and did not easily show.

"A sick man—to be taken advantage of ? No, I think that would scarcely do," he said. "A sensible pair with an un-derstanding, indeed—but then the understanding—there's the difficulty."

"No," cried Lady Jane, anxiously cordial to wipe away the stain of her unfortunate suggestion. "Not at all—the most natural thing in the world—where there is real feeling, Dr. Burnet, on one side, and a lonely, sensitive girl on the other——"

"A lonely, sensitive girl," he repeated. And then he looked up in Lady Jane's face with a short laugh—but made no further remark.

Notwithstanding the safeguard of her complexion, Lady

Jane this time grew very red indeed ; but having nothing to say for herself, she was wise and made no attempt to say it. And he got up, having nothing further to add by any possibility to his prescription, and put it into her hand.

" I must make haste home," he said, " the snow is very blinding, and the roads by this time will be scarcely distinguishable."

" I am sorry to have kept you so long—with my ridiculous cold, which is really nothing. But Dr. Burnet," she said, putting her hand on his sleeve, " you will think of what I have said. Let justice be done to those poor Somers. Their poverty is something tragic. They had so little expectation of anything of the kind."

" It is most unlikely that I can be of any use to them, Lady Jane," he said a little stiffly, as he accepted her outstretched hand.

Perhaps Lady Jane had more respect for him than ever before. She held his prescription in her hand and looked at it for a moment.

" I think I'll take it," she said to herself as if making a heroic resolution. She had really a little cold.

As for the doctor, he climbed up into his dog-cart and took the reins from the benumbed hands of Jim, who was one mass of whiteness now instead of the black form sprinkled over with flakes of white which he had appeared at the Cliff. It was a difficult thing to drive home between the hedges, which were no longer visible, and with the big snow-flakes melting into his eyes and confusing the atmosphere, and he had no time to think as long as he was still out in the open country, without even the lights of Sliplin to guide him. It was very cold, and his hands soon became as benumbed as Jim's, with the reins not sensible at all through his big gloves to his chilled fingers.

" I think we should turn to the left, here ? " he said to Jim, who answered " Yessir," with his teeth chattering, " or do you think it should perhaps be to the right ? "

Jim said " Yessir," again, dull to all proprieties.

If Jim had been by himself he would probably have gone to sleep, and allowed the mare to find her own way home, which very likely she would have done ; but Dr. Burnet could not trust to such a chance.   To think much of what had been said to him was scarcely possible in these circumstances.   But when the vague and confused glimmer of the Sliplin lights through the snow put his mind at rest, it cannot but be said that Dr. Burnet found a great many thoughts waiting to seize hold upon him.   He was not perhaps surprised that Lady Jane should have divined his secret.   He had no particular desire to conceal it, and though he did not receive Lady Jane's offer with enthusiasm, he could not but feel that her friendship and assistance would be of great use to him—in fact, if not with Katherine, at least with other things.   It would be good for him professionally, even this one visit, and the prescription for Lady Jane, not for Mrs. Cole, which must be made up at the chemist's, would do him good.   A man who held the position of medical attendant at Steephill received a kind of warrant of skill from the fact, which would bring other patients of distinction.   When Dr. Burnet got home, and got into dry and comfortable clothes, and found no impatient messenger awaiting him, it was with a grateful sense of ease that he gave himself up to the study of this subject by the cheerful fire.   His mind glanced over the different suggestions of Lady Jane, tabulating and classifying them as if they had been scientific facts.   There was that hint about the old sick man, which she had herself blushed for before it was fully uttered, and at which Dr. Burnet now grinned in mingled wrath and ridicule.   To take advantage of an old sick man— as being that old man's medical attendant and desirous of marrying his daughter—was a suggestion at which Burnet could afford to laugh, though fiercely, and with an exclamation not complimentary to the intentions of Lady Jane.   But there were other things which required more careful consideration.

Should he follow these other suggestions, he asked himself? Should he become a party to her plan, and get her support,

and accept the privileges of a visitor at her house as she had
almost offered, and meet Katherine there, which would probably be good for Katherine in other ways as well as for himself? There was something very tempting in this idea, and
Dr. Burnet was not mercenary in his feeling towards Katherine, nor indisposed to do "justice to Stella" in the almost
incredible case that it ever should be in his power to dispose
of Mr. Tredgold's fortune. He could not help another short
laugh to himself at the absurdity of the idea. He to dispose of
Mr. Tredgold's fortune! So many things were taken for
granted in this ridiculous hypothesis. Katherine's acceptance
and consent for one thing, of which he was not at all sure.
She had evidently sent the Rector about his business, which
made him glad, yet gave him a little thrill of anxiety too,
for, though he was ten years younger than the Rector, and had
no family to encumber him, yet Mr. Stanley, on the other
hand, was a handsome man, universally pleasing, and perhaps
more desirable in respect to position than an ordinary country
practitioner—a man who dared not call his body, at least,
whatever might be said of his soul, his own ; and who had as
yet had no opportunity of distinguishing himself. If she repulsed the one so summarily, would she not have in all probability the same objections to the other? At twenty-three a
man of thirty-five is slightly elderly as well as one of forty-
seven.

Supposing, however, that Katherine should make no objection, which was a very strong step for a man who did not in
the least believe that at the present moment she had even
thought of him in that light—there was her father to be taken
into account. He had heard Mr. Tredgold say that about
the thousand for thousand told down on the table, and he had
heard it from the two ladies of the midge ; but without, perhaps, paying much attention or putting any great faith in it.
How could he table thousand for thousand against Mr. Tredgold? The idea was ridiculous. He had the reversion of
that little, but ancient, estate in the North, of which he had
been at such pains to inform Katherine; and he had a little

money from his mother ; and his practice, which was a good
enough practice, but not likely to produce thousands for some
time at least to come.   He had said there might be a dodge—
and, as a matter of fact, there had blown across his mind a
suggestion of a dodge, how he might perhaps persuade his
uncle to "table" the value of Bunhope on his side.   But
what was the value of Bunhope to the millions of old Tredgold?   He might, perhaps, say that he wanted nothing more
with Katherine than the equivalent of what he brought ; but
he doubted whether the old man would accept that compromise.
And certainly, if he did so, there could be no question of
doing justice to Stella out of the small share he would have of
her father's fortune.   No ; he felt sure Mr. Tredgold would
exact the entire pound of flesh, and no less ; that he would no
more reduce his daughter's inheritance than her husband's
fortune, and that no dodge would blind the eyes of the acute,
businesslike old man.

This was rather a despairing point of view, from which Dr.
Burnet tried to escape by thinking of Katherine herself, and
what might happen could he persuade her to fall in love with
him.   That would make everything so much more agreeable ;
but would it make it easier?   Alas ! falling in love on Stella's
part had done no good to Somers ; and Stella, though now cast
off and banished, had possessed a far greater influence over her
father than Katherine had ever had.   Dr. Burnet was by no
means destitute of sentiment in respect to her.   Indeed, it is
very probable that had Katherine had no fortune at all he would
still have wished, and taken earlier more decisive steps, to make
her aware that he wished to secure her for his wife ; but the
mere existence of a great fortune changes the equilibrium of
everything.   And as it was there, Dr. Burnet felt that to lose
it, if there was any possible way of securing it, would be a
great mistake.   He was the old man's doctor, who ought to
be grateful to him for promoting his comfort and keeping him
alive ; and he was Katherine's lover, and the best if not the
only one there was.   And he had free access to the house at
all seasons, and a comfortable standing in the drawing-room as

well as in the master's apartment. Surely something must be made of these advantages by a man with his eyes open, neglecting no opportunity. And, on the other hand, there was always the chance that old Tredgold might die, thus simplifying matters. The doctor's final decision was that he would do nothing for the moment, but wait and follow the leading of circumstances; always keeping up his watch over Katherine, and endeavouring to draw her interest, perhaps in time her affections, towards himself—while, on the other hand, it would commit him to nothing to accept Lady Jane's help, assuring her that—in the case which he felt to be so unlikely of ever having any power in the matter—he would certainly do "justice to Stella" as far as lay in his power.

When he had got to this conclusion the bell rang sharply, and, alas! Dr. Burnet, who had calculated on going to bed for once in comfort and quiet, had to face the wintry world again and go out into the snow.

CHAPTER XXVII.

KATHERINE'S life at Sliplin was in no small degree affected by the result of the Rector's unfortunate visit. How its termination became known nobody could tell. No one ventured to say "She told me herself," still less, "He told me." Yet everybody knew. There were some who had upheld that the Rector had too much respect for himself ever to put himself in the position of being rejected by old Tredgold's daughter ; but even these had to acknowledge that this overturn of everything seemly and correct had really happened. It was divined, perhaps, from Mr. Stanley's look, who went about the parish with his head held very high, and an air of injury which nobody had remarked in him before. For it was not only that he had been refused. That is a privilege which no law or authority can take from a free-born English girl, and far would it have been from the Rector's mind to deny to Katherine this right ; but it was the manner in which it had been exercised which gave him so deep a wound. It was not as the father of Charlotte and Evelyn that Mr. Stanley had been in the habit of regarding himself, nor that he had been regarded. His own individuality was too remarkable and too attractive, he felt with all modesty, to lay him under such a risk ; and yet here was a young woman in his own parish, in his own immediate circle, who regarded him from that point of view, and who looked upon his proposal as ridiculous and something like an insult to her youth. Had she said prettily that she did not feel herself good enough for such a position, that she was not worthy—but that she was aware of the high compliment he had paid her, and never would forget it—which was the thing that any woman with a due sense of fitness would have said,

he might have forgiven her. But Katherine's outburst of indignation, her anger to have been asked to be the stepmother
of Charlotte and Evelyn her playfellows, her complete want of
gratitude or of any sense of the honour done her, had in-
flicted a deep blow upon the Rector. That he should be scorned
as a lover seemed to him impossible, that a woman should be
so insensible to every fact of life. He did not get over it for
a long time, nor am I sure that he ever did get over it; not
the disappointment, which he bore like a man, but the sense
of being scorned. So long as he lived he never forgave Katherine that insult to his dearest feelings.

And thus Katherine's small diversions were driven back into
a still narrower circle. She could not go to the Rectory, where
the girls were divided between gratitude to her for not having
turned their life upside down, and wrath against her for not
having appreciated papa; nor could she go where she was
sure to meet him, and to catch his look of offended pride and
wounded dignity. It made her way very hard for her to have
to think and consider, and even make furtive enquiries
whether the Stanleys would be there before going to the mild-
est tea party. When Mrs. Shanks invited her to meet Miss
Mildmay, she was indeed safe. Yet even there Mr. Stanley
might come in to pay these ladies a call, or Charlotte appear
with her portfolio of drawings, or Evelyn fly in for a moment
on her way to the post. She went even to that very mild entertainment with a quiver of anxiety. The great snowstorm
was over which had stopped everything, obliterating all the
roads, and making the doctor's dog-cart and the butcher's
and baker's carts the only vehicles visible about the country—
which lay in one great white sheet, the brilliancy of which
made the sea look muddy where it came up with a dull colour
upon the beach. Everything, indeed, looked dark in comparison with that dazzling cloak of snow, until by miserable
human usage the dazzling white changed into that most squalid
of all squalid things, the remnant of a snowstorm in England,
drabbled by all kinds of droppings, powdered with dust of
smoke and coal, churned into the chillest and most dreadful

of mud. The island had passed through that horrible phase
after a brief delicious ecstasy of skating, from which poor
Katherine was shut out by the same reasons already given, but
now had emerged green and fresh, though cold, with a sense
of thankfulness which the fields seemed to feel, and the birds
proclaimed better and more than the best of the human inhabitants could do.

The terrace gardens of Mrs. Shanks and Miss Mildmay shone
with this refreshed and brightened greenness, and the prospect from under the verandah of their little houses was restored to its natural colour. The sea became once more the
highest light in the landscape, the further cliffs were brown,
the trees showed a faint bloom of pushing buds and rising sap,
and glowed in the light of the afternoon sun near its setting.
Mrs. Shanks' little drawing room was a good deal darkened
by its little verandah, but when the western sun shone in, as it
was doing, the shade of the little green roof was an advantage
even in winter; and it was so mild after the snow that the
window was open, and a thrush in a neighbouring shrubbery had begun to perform a solo among the bushes, exactly,
as Mrs. Shanks said, like a fine singer invited for the entertainment of the guests.

" It isn't often you hear a roulade like that," she said.   " I
consider Miss Sherlock was nothing to it."   Miss Sherlock
was a professional lady who had been paying a visit in Sliplin,
and who at afternoon teas and evening parties, being very kind
and ready to " oblige," had turned the season into a musical
one, and provided for the people who were so kind as to in-
vite her, an entertainment almost as cheap as that of the thrush
in Major Toogood's shrubbery.

" I hope the poor thing has some crumbs," said Miss Mildmay.   " I always took great pains to see that there was plenty
of bread well peppered put out for them during the snow."

" Was Miss Sherlock so very good?" said Katherine.   " I
was unfortunate, I never heard her, even at her concert.   Oh,
yes, I had tickets—but I did not go."

" That is just what we want to talk to you about, my dear

Katherine. Fancy a great singer in Sliplin, and the Cliff not represented, not a soul there. Oh, if poor dear Stella had but been here, she would not have stayed away when there was anything to see or hear."

" Yes, I am a poor creature in comparison," said Katherine, " but you know it isn't nice to go to such places alone."

" If there was any need to go alone ! You know we would have called for you in the midge any time ; but that's ridiculous for you with all your carriages ; it would have been more appropriate for you to call for us. Another time, Katherine, my dear——"

" Oh, I know how kind you are ; it was not precisely for want of some one to go with."

" Jane Shanks," said Miss Mildmay, " what is the use of pretences between us who have known the child all her life? It is very well understood in Sliplin, Katherine, that there must be some motive in your seclusion. You have some reason, you cannot conceal it from us who know you, for shutting yourself up as you do."

" What reason ? Is it not a good enough reason that I am alone now, and that to be reminded of it at every moment is— oh, it is hard," said Katherine, tears coming into her eyes. " It is almost more than I can bear."

" Dear child ! " Mrs. Shanks said, patting her hand which rested on the table. " We shouldn't worry her with questions, should we ? " But there was no conviction in her tone, and Katherine, though her self-pity was quite strong enough to bring that harmless water to her eyes, was quite aware not only that she did not seclude herself because of Stella, but also that her friends were not in the least deceived.

" I ask no questions," said Miss Mildmay, " I hope I have a head on my shoulders and a couple of eyes in it. I don't require information from Katherine ! What I've got to say is that she mustn't do it. Most girls think very little of refusing a man ; sometimes they continue good friends, sometimes they don't. When a man sulks it shows he was much in earnest, and is really a compliment. But to stay at home morning and night because there is a man in the town who is furious with you for not marrying him ; why, that's a thing that is not to be allowed to go on, not for a day——''

'' Nobody has any right to say that there is any man whom——''

'' Oh, don't redden up, Katherine, and flash your eyes at me ! I have known you since you were *that* high, and I don't care a brass button what you say. Do you think I don't know all about you, my dear ? Do you think that there's a thing in Sliplin which I don't know or Jane Shanks doesn't know ? Bless us, what is the good of us, two old cats, as I know you call us——''

'' Miss Mildmay ! '' cried Katherine ; but as it was perfectly true, she stopped there and had not another word to say.

'' Yes, that's my name, and *her* name is Mrs. Shanks ; but that makes no difference. We are the two old cats. I have no doubt it was to Stella we owed the title, and I don't bear her any malice nor you either. Neither does Jane Shanks. We like you, on the contrary, my dear ; but if you think you can throw dust in our eyes—— Why, there is the Rector's voice through the partition asking for me.''

'' Oh,'' said Katherine, '' I must go, really I must go ; this is the time when papa likes me to go to him. I have stayed too long, I really, really must go now——''

'' Sit down, sit down, dear. It is only her fun. There is nobody speaking through the partition. ˙ The idea ! Sliplin houses are not very well built, but I hope they are better than that.''

'' I must have been mistaken,'' said Miss Mildmay grimly. '' I believe after all it is only Jane Shanks' boy ; he has a very gruff manly voice, though he is such a little thing, and a man's voice is such a rarity in these parts that he deceives me. Well, Katherine, the two old cats hear everything. If it does not come to me it comes to *her*. My eyes are the sharpest, I think, but she hears the best. You can't take us in. We ᴋnow pretty well all that has happened to you, though you

have been so very quiet about it. There was that young city
man whom you wouldn't have, and I applaud you for it. But
he'll make a match with somebody of much more consequence
than you. And then there is poor Mr. Stanley. The Stanleys are as thankful to you as they can be, and well they may.
Why, it would have turned the whole place upside down. A
young very rich wife at the Rectory and the poor girls turned
out of doors. It just shows how little religion does for some
people."

"Oh, stop! stop!" cried Mrs. Shanks. "What has his
religion to do with it? It's not against any man's religion to
fall in love with a nice girl."

"Please don't say any more on this subject," cried Katherine; "if you think it's a compliment to me to be fallen in
love with—by an old gentleman!—— But I never said a
word about the Rector. It is all one of your mistakes. You
do make mistakes sometimes, Miss Mildmay. You took little
Bobby's voice for—a clergyman's." It gave more form to the
comparison to say a clergyman than merely a man.

"So I did," said Miss Mildmay, "that will always be
remembered against me; but you are not going to escape,
Katherine Tredgold, in that way. I shall go to your father,
if you don't mind, and tell him everything, and that you are
shutting yourself up and seeing nobody, because of—— Well,
if it is not because of that, what is it? It is not becoming, it
is scarcely decent that a girl of your age should live so much
alone."

"Please let me go, Mrs. Shanks," said Katherine. "Why
should you upbraid me? I do the best I can; it is not my
fault if there is nobody to stand by me."

"We shall all stand by you, my dear," said Mrs. Shanks,
following her to the door, "and Ruth Mildmay is never so
cross as she seems. We will stand by you, in the midge or
otherwise, wherever you want to go. At all times you may be
sure of us, Katherine, either Ruth Mildmay or me."

But when the door was closed upon Katherine Mrs. Shanks
rushed back to the little drawing-room, now just sinking into

greyness, the last ray of the sunset gone. "You see," she cried, " it's all right, I to——"

But she was forestalled with a louder "I told you so!" from Miss Mildmay; "didn't I always say it?" that lady concluded triumphantly. Mrs. Shanks might begin the first, but it was always her friend who secured the last word.

Katherine walked out into the still evening air, a little irritated, a little disgusted, and a little amused by the offer of these two chaperons and the midge to take her about. She had to walk through the High Street of Sliplin, and everybody was out at that hour. She passed Charlotte Stanley with her portfolio under her arm, who would probably have rushed to her and demanded a glance at the sketches even in the open road, or that Katherine should go in with her to the stationer's to examine them at her ease on the counter; but who passed now with an awkward bow, having half crossed the road to get out of her way, yet sending a wistful smile nevertheless across what she herself would have called the middle distance. "Now what have I done to Charlotte?" Katherine said to herself. If there was anyone who ought to applaud her, who ought to be grateful to her, it was the Rector's daughters. She went on with a sort of rueful smile on her lips, and came up without observing it to the big old landau, in which was seated Lady Jane. Katherine was hurrying past with a bow, when she was suddenly greeted from that unexpected quarter with a cry of "Katherine! where are you going so fast?" which brought her reluctantly back.

"My dear Katherine! what a long time it is since we have met," said Lady Jane.

"Yes," said Katherine sedately. "That is very true, it is a long time."

"You mean to say it is my fault by that tone! My dear, you have more horses and carriages, and a great deal more time and youth and all that than I. Why didn't you come to see me? If you thought I was huffy or neglectful, why didn't you come and tell me so? I should have thought that was the right thing to do."

" I should not have thought it becoming,'' cried Katherine, astonished by this accost, " from me to you. I am the youngest and far the humblest———''

" Oh, fiddlesticks-! '' cried the elder lady, " that's not true humility, that's pride, my dear. I was an old friend ; and though poor dear Stella always put herself in the front, you know it was you I liked best, Katherine. Well, when will you come, now ? Come and spend a day or two, which will be extremely dull, for we're all alone; but you can tell me of Stella, as well as your own little affairs.''

" I don't know that I can leave papa,'' Katherine said, with a little remnant of that primness which had been her distinction in Captain Scott's eyes.

" Nonsense ! He will spare you to me,'' said Lady Jane with calm certainty. " Let me see, what day is this, Tuesday ? Then I will come for you on Saturday. You can send over that famous little brougham with your maid and your things, and keep it if you like, for we have scarcely anything but dog-carts, except this hearse. Saturday ; and don't show bad breeding by making any fuss about it,'' Lady Jane said.

Katherine felt that the great lady was right, it would have been bad breeding ; and then her heart rose a little in spite of herself at the thought of the large dull rooms at Steephill in which there was no gilding, nor any attempt to look finer than the most solid needs of life demanded, and where Lady Jane conducted the affairs of life with a much higher hand than any of the Sliplin ladies. After being so long shut up in Sliplin, and now partly out of favour in it, the ways of Lady Jane seemed bigger, the life more easy and less self-conscious, and she consented with a little rising of her heart. She was a little surprised that Lady Jane, with her large voice, should have shouted a cordial greeting to the doctor as he passed in his dog-cart. " I am going to write to you,'' she cried, nodding her head at him ; but no doubt this was about some little ailment in the nursery, for with Katherine, a young lady going on a visit to Steephill, what could it have to do ?

17

CHAPTER XXVIII.

The doctor had made himself a very important feature in Katherine's life during those dull winter days. After the great snowstorm, which was a thing by which events were dated for long after, in the island, and which was almost coincident with the catastrophe of the Rector; he had become more frequent in his visits to Mr. Tredgold and consequently to the tea-table of Mr. Tredgold's lonely daughter. While the snow lasted, and all the atmospheric influences were at their worst, it stood to reason that an asthmatical, rheumatical, gouty old man wanted more looking after than usual; and it was equally clear that a girl a little out of temper and out of patience with life, who was disposed to shut herself up and retire from the usual amusements of her kind, would also be much the better for the invasion into her closed-up world of life and fresh air in the shape of a vigorous and personable young man, who, if not perhaps so secure in self-confidence and belief in his own fasci-nations as the handsome (if a little elderly) Rector, had not generally been discouraged by the impression he knew himself to have made. And Katherine had liked those visits, that was undeniable; the expectation of making a cup of tea for the doctor had been pleasant to her. The thought of his white strong teeth and the bread and butter which she never got 'out of her mind, was now amusing, not painful; she had seen him so often making short work of the little thin slices provided for her own entertainment. And he told her all that was go-ing on, and gave her pieces of advice which his profession warranted. He got to know more of her tastes, and she more of his in this way, than perhaps was the case with any two young people in the entire island, and this in the most simple, the most natural way. If there began to get a whisper into the air of Dr. Burnet's devotion to his patient on the Cliff and its possible consequences, that was chiefly because the doctor's inclinations had been suspected before by an observant public. And indeed the episode of the Rector had afforded it too much entertainment to leave the mind of Sliplin free for further remark in respect to Katherine and her proceedings. And Mr. Tredgold's asthma accounted for everything in those more frequent visits to the Cliff. All the same, it was impossible that there should not be a degree of pleasant intimacy and much self-revelation on both sides during these half hours, when, wrapped in warmth and comfort and sweet society, Dr. Burnet saw his dog-cart promenading outside in the snow or during the deeper miseries of the thaw, with the contrast which enhances present pleasure. He became himself more and more interested in Katherine, his feelings towards her being quite genuine, though perhaps enlivened by her prospects as an heiress. And if there had not been that vague preoccupation in Katherine's mind concerning James Stanford, the recollection not so much of him as of the many, many times she had thought of him, I think it very probable indeed that she would have fallen in love with the doctor; indeed, there were moments when his image pushed Stanford very close, almost making that misty hero give way. He was a very misty hero, a shadow, an outline, indefinite, never having given much revelation of himself; and Dr. Burnet was very definite, as clear as daylight, and in many respects as satisfactory. It would have been very natural indeed that the one should have effaced the other.

Dr. Burnet did not know anything of James Stanford. He thought of Katherine as a little shy, a little cold, perhaps from the persistent shade into which she had been cast by her sister, unsusceptible as people say; but he did not at all despair of moving her out of that calm. He had thought indeed that there were indications of the internal frost yielding, before his interview with Lady Jane. With Lady Jane's help he thought there was little doubt of success. But even that security made him cautious. It was evident that she was a girl with whom one must not attempt to go too fast. The Rector had tried to carry the fort by a *coup de main,* and he had perished ingloriously in the effort. Dr. Burnet drew himself in a little after he acquired the knowledge of that event, determined not to risk the same fate. He had continued his visits but he had been careful to give them the most friendly, the least lover-like aspect, to arouse no alarms. When he received the salutation of Lady Jane in passing, and her promise that he should hear from her, his sober heart gave a bound, which was reflected unconsciously in the start of the mare making a dash forward by means of some magnetism, it is to be supposed conveyed to her by the reins from her master's hand—so that he had to exert himself suddenly with hand and whip to reduce her to her ordinary pace again. If the manœuvre had been intentional it would have been clever as showing his skill and coolness in the sight of his love and of his patroness. It had the same effect not being intentional at all.

I am not sure either whether it was Lady Jane's intention to enhance the effect of Dr. Burnet by the extreme dulness of the household background upon which she set him, so to speak, to impress the mind of Katherine. There was no party at Steephill. Sir John, though everything that was good and kind, was dull ; the tutor, who was a young man fresh from the University, and no doubt might have been very intellectual or very frivolous had there been anything to call either gifts out, was dull also because of having little encouragement to be anything else. Lady Jane indeed was not dull, but she had no call upon her for any exertion ; and the tone of the house was humdrum beyond description. The old clergyman dined habitually at Steephill on the Sunday evenings, and he was duller still, though invested to Katherine with a little interest as the man who had officiated at her sister's marriage. But he could not be got to recall the circumstance distinctly, nor to master the fact that this Miss Tredgold was so closely related to the young lady whom he had made into Lady Somers. " Dear ! dear ! to think of that ! " he had said when the connection had been explained to him, but what he meant by that exclamation nobody knew. I think it very likely that Lady Jane herself was not aware how dull her house was when in entire repose, until she found it out by looking through the eyes of a chance guest like Katherine. "What in thunder did you mean by bringing that poor girl here to bore her to death, when there's nobody in the house?" Sir John said, whose voice was like a westerly gale. "Really, Katherine, I did not remember how deadly dull we were," Lady Jane said apologetically. "It suits us well enough—Sir John and myself; but it's a shame to have asked you here when there's nobody in the house, as he says. And Sunday is the worst of all, when you can't have even your needlework to amuse you. But there are some people coming to dinner to-morrow." Katherine did her best to express herself prettily, and I don't think even that she felt the dulness so much as she was supposed to do. The routine of a big family house, the machinery of meals and walks and drives and other observances, the children bursting in now and then, the tutor appearing from time to time tremendously *comme il faut*, and keeping up his equality, Sir John, not half so careful, rolling in from the inspection of his stables or his turnips with a noisy salutation, "You come out with me after lunch, Miss Tredgold, and get a blow over the downs, far better for you than keeping indoors." And then after that blow on the downs, afternoon tea, and Mr. Montgomery rubbing his hands before the fire, while he asked, without moving, whether he should hand the kettle. All this was mildly amusing, in the proportion of its dulness, for a little while. We none of us, or at least few of us, feel heavily this dull procession of the hours when it is our own life ; when it is another's, our perceptions are more clear.

"But there are people coming to dinner to-morrow," Lady Jane said. There was something in the little nod she gave, of satisfaction and knowingness, which Katherine did not understand or attempt to understand. No idea of Dr. Burnet was associated with Steephill. She was not aware that he was on visiting terms there—he had told her that he attended the servants' hall—so that it was with a little start of surprise that,

raising her eyes from a book she was looking at, she found him
standing before her, holding out his hand as the guests gathered before dinner.   The party was from the neighbourhood
—county, or, at least, country people—and when Dr. Burnet
was appointed to take Katherine in to dinner, that young
lady, though she knew the doctor so well and liked him so
much, did not feel that it was any great promotion.   She
thought she might have had somebody newer, something that
belonged less to her own routine of existence, which is one of
the mistakes often made by very astute women of the world
like Lady Jane.   There was young Fortescue, for instance, a
mere fox-hunting young squire, not half so agreeable as Dr.
Burnet, whom Katherine would have preferred.   " He is an
ass ; he would not amuse her in the very least," Lady Jane
had said.   But Sir John, who was not clever at all, divined
that something new, though an ass, would have amused Katherine more.   Besides, Lady Jane had her motives, which she
mentioned to nobody.

   Dr. Burnet did the very best for himself that was possible.
He gave Katherine a report of her father, he told her the last
thing that had transpired at Sliplin since her departure, he informed her who all the people were at table, pleased to let her
see that he knew them all.   " That's young Fortescue who
has just come in to his estate, and he promises to make ducks
and drakes of it," Dr. Burnet said.   Katherine looked across
the table at the young man thus described.   She was not responsible for him in any way, nor could it concern her if he
did make ducks and drakes of his estate, but she would have
preferred to make acquaintance with those specimens of the
absolutely unknown.   A little feeling suddenly sprang up in
her heart against Dr. Burnet, because he was Dr. Burnet and
absolutely above reproach.   She would have sighed for Dr.
Burnet, for his quick understanding and the abundance he had
to say, had she been seated at young Fortescue's side.

   After dinner, when she had talked a little to all the ladies
and had done her duty, Lady Jane caught Katherine's hand
and drew her to a seat beside herself, and then she beckoned

to Dr. Burnet, who drew a chair in front of them and sat down, bending forward till his head, Katherine thought, was almost in Lady Jane's lap. "I want," she said, "Katherine, to get Dr. Burnet on our side—to make him take up our dear Stella's interests as you do, my dear, and as in my uninfluential way I should like to do too."

"How can Dr. Burnet take up Stella's interests?" cried Katherine, surprised and perhaps a little offended too.

"My dear Katherine, a medical man has the most tremendous opportunities—all that the priest had in old times, and something additional which belongs to himself. He can often say a word when none of the rest of us would dare to do so. I have immense trust in a medical man. He can bring people together that have quarrelled, and—and influence wills, and—do endless things. I always try to have the doctor on my side."

"Miss Katherine knows," said Dr. Burnet, trying to lead out of the subject, for Lady Jane's methods were entirely, on this occasion, too straightforward, "that the medical man in this case is always on her side. Does not Mrs. Swanson, Lady Jane, sing very well? I have never heard her. I am not very musical, but I love a song."

"Which is a sign that you are not musical. You are like Sir John," said Lady Jane, as if that was the worst that could be said. "Still, if that is what you mean, Dr. Burnet, you can go and ask her, on my part. He is very much interested in you all, I think, Katherine," she added when he had departed on this mission. "We had a talk the other day—about you and Stella and the whole matter. I think, if he ever had it in his power, that he would see justice done her, as you would yourself."

"He is very friendly, I daresay," said Katherine, "but I can't imagine how he could ever have anything in his power."

"There is no telling," Lady Jane said. "I think he is quite a disinterested man, if any such thing exists. Now, we must be silent a little, for, of course, Mrs. Swanson is going to sing; she is not likely to neglect an opportunity. She has a good voice, so far as that goes, but little training. It is just the thing that pleases Sir John. And he has planted himself between us and the piano, bless him! now we can go on with our talk. Katherine, I don't think you see how important it is to surround your father with people who think the same as we do about your poor sister."

"No," said Katherine, "it has not occurred to me; my father is not very open to influence."

"Then do you give up Stella's cause? Do you really think it is hopeless, Katherine?"

"How could I think so?" cried the girl with a keen tone in her voice which, though she spoke low, was penetrating, and to check which, Lady Jane placed her hand on Katherine's hand and kept it there with a faint "shsh." "You know what I should instantly do," she added, "if I ever had it in my power."

"Dear Katherine! but your husband might not see it in that light."

"He should—or he should not be—my husband," said Katherine with a sudden blush. She raised her eyes unwillingly at this moment and caught the gaze of Dr. Burnet, who was standing behind the great bulk of Sir John, but with his face towards the ladies on the sofa. Katherine's heart gave a little bound, half of affright. She had looked at him and he at her as she said the words. An answering gleam of expression, an answering wave of colour, seemed to go over him (though he could not possibly hear her) as she spoke. It was the first time that this idea had been clearly suggested to her, but now so simply, so potently, as if she were herself the author of the suggestion. She was startled out of her self-possession. "Oh," she cried with agitation, "I like her voice! I am like Sir John; let us listen to the singing." Lady Jane nodded her head, pressed Katherine's hand, and did what was indeed the first wise step she had taken, stepped as noiselessly as possible to another corner, where, behind her fan, she could talk to a friend more likely to respond to her sentiments and left Dr. Burnet to take her place.

"Is this permitted? It is too tempting to be lost," he said in a whisper, and then he too relapsed into silence and attention. Katherine, I fear, did not get any clear impression of the song. Her own words went through her head, involuntarily, as though she had touched some spring which went on repeating them: "My husband—my husband." Her white dress touched his blackness as he sat down beside her. She drew away a little, her heart beating loudly, in alarm, mingled with some other feeling which she could not understand, but he did not say another word until the song was over, and all the applause, and the moment of commotion in which the singer returned to her seat, and the groups of the party changed and mingled. Then he said suddenly, "I hope you will not think, Miss Katherine, that I desired Lady Jane to drag me in head and shoulders to your family concerns. I never should have been so presumptuous. I do trust you will believe that."

"I never should have thought so, Dr. Burnet," said Katherine, faltering with that commotion which was she hoped entirely within herself and apparent to no one. Then she added as she assured her voice, "It would not have been presumptuous. You know so much of us already, and of *her*, and took so much part———"

"I am your faithful servant," he said, "ready to be sent on any errand, or to take any part you wish, but I do not presume further than that." Then he rose quickly, as one who is moved by a sudden impulse. "Miss Katherine, will you let me take you to the conservatory to see Lady Jane's great aloe? They used to say it blossomed only once in a hundred years."

"But that's all nonsense, you know," said Mr. Montgomery the tutor; "see them all about the Riviera at every corner. Truth, they kill 'emselves when they're about it."

"Which comes to the same thing. Will you come?" said Dr. Burnet, offering his arm.

"But, my dear fellow, Miss Tredgold has seen it three or four times," said this very unnecessary commentator.

" Never mind.   She has not seen what I am going to show her," said the doctor with great self-possession.   Lady Jane followed them with her eyes as they went away into the long conservatory, which was famous in the islands and full of lofty palms and tropical foliage.   Her middle-aged bosom owned a little tremor ; was he going to put it to her, then and there ? Lady Jane had offered assistance, even co-operation, but this prompt action took away her breath.

" I should like to see the aloe, too," said the lady by her side.

" So you shall, presently," said Lady Jane, " but we must not make a move yet, for there is Lady Freshwater going to sing.   Mr. Montgomery, ask Lady Freshwater from me whether she will not sing us one of her delightful French songs.   She has such expression, and they are all as light as air—of course, not serious music.   Look at Sir John, he is pleased, but he likes it better when it is English, and he can make out the words.   He is a constant amusement when he talks of music —and he thinks he understands it, poor dear."

She kept talking until she had watched Lady Freshwater to the piano, and heard her begin.   And then Lady Jane felt herself entitled to a little rest.   She kept one eye on the con- servatory to see that nobody interrupted the botanical exposi- tion which was no doubt going on there.   Would he actually propose—on the spot, all at once, with the very sound of the conversation and of Lady Freshwater's song in their ears? Was it possible that a man should go so fast as that ?   Now that it had come to this point Lady Jane began to get a little compunctious, to ask herself whether she might not have done better for Katherine than a country doctor, without distinc- tion, even though he might have a wealthy uncle and a family place at his back ?   Old Tredgold's daughter was perhaps too great a prize to be allowed to drop in that commonplace way. On the other hand, if Lady Jane had exerted herself to get Katherine a better match, was it likely that a man—if a man of our *monde*—would have consented to such an arrangement about Stella as Dr. Burnet was willing to make ?   If the fortune had been Stella's, Lady Jane was quite certain that Charlie Somers would have consented to no such settlement. And after all, would not Katherine be really happier with a man not too much out of her own *monde*, fitted for village life, knowing all about her, and not likely to be ashamed of his father-in-law? With this last argument she comforted her heart.

And Katherine went into the conservatory to see the aloe, which that malevolent tutor declared she had already seen so often, with her heart beating rather uncomfortably, and her hand upon Dr. Burnet's arm.

CHAPTER XXIX.

But though Lady Jane had so fully made up her mind to it, and awaited the result with so much excitement, and though Katherine herself was thrilled with an uneasy consciousness, and Dr. Burnet's looks gave every sanction to the idea, he did not on that evening under the tall aloe, which had begun to burst the innumerable wrappings of its husk, in the Steephill conservatory, declare his love or ask Katherine to be his wife. I cannot tell the reason why—I think there came over him a chill alarm as to how he should get back if by any accident his suit was unsuccessful. It was like the position which gave Mr. Puff so much trouble in the *Critic*. He could not "exit praying." How was he to get off the stage? He caught the eyes of an old lady who was seated near the conservatory door. They were dull eyes, with little speculation in them, but they gave a faint glare as the two young people passed; and the doctor asked himself with a shudder, How could he meet their look when he came back if——? How indeed could he meet anybody's look—Lady Jane's, who was his accomplice, and who would be very severe upon him if he did not succeed, and jolly Sir John's, who would slap him on the shoulder and shout at him in his big voice? His heart sank to his boots when he found himself alone with the object of his affections amid the rustling palms. He murmured something hurriedly about something he wanted to say to her, but could not here, where they were liable to interruption at any moment, and then he burst into a display of information about the aloe which was very astounding to Katherine. She listened, feeling the occasion *manqué*, with a sensation of relief. I think it quite probable that in the circumstances, and amid the tremor of sympathetic excitement derived from Lady Jane, and the general tendency of the atmosphere, Katherine might have accepted Dr. Burnet. She would probably have been sorry afterwards, and in all probability it would have led to no results, but I think she would have accepted him that evening had he had the courage to put it to the touch ; and he, for his part, would certainly have done it had he not been seized with that tremor as to how he was to get off the stage.

He found it very difficult to explain this behaviour to Lady Jane afterwards, who, though she did not actually ask the question, pressed him considerably about the botanical lecture he had been giving.

" I have sat through a French *café chantant* song in your interests, with all the airs and graces," she said with a look of disgust, " to give you time."

" Yes, I know," said Dr. Burnet—it was at the moment of taking his leave, and he knew that he must soon escape, which gave him a little courage—" you have done everything for me —you have been more than kind, Lady Jane."

" But if it is all to come to nothing, after I had taken the trouble to arrange everything for you ! "

" It was too abrupt," he said, " and I funked it at the last. How was I to get back under everybody's eyes if it had not come off ? "

" It would have come off," she said hurriedly, under her breath, with a glance at Katherine. Then, in her usual very audible voice, she said, " Must you go so early, Dr. Burnet ? Then good-night ; and if your mare is fresh take care of the turning at Eversfield Green."

He did not know what this warning meant, and neither I believe did she, though it was a nasty turning. And then he drove away into the winter night, with a sense of having failed, failed to himself and his own expectations, as well as to Lady Jane's. He had not certainly intended to take any decisive step when he drove to Steephill, but yet he felt when he left it that the occasion was *manqué*, and that he had perhaps risked everything by his lack of courage. This is not a pleasant

thought to a man who is not generally at a loss in any circumstances, and whose ways have generally, on the whole, been
prosperous and successful.   He was a fool not to have put it to
the touch, to be frightened by an old lady's dull eyes which
probably would have noticed nothing, or the stare of the company which was occupied by its own affairs and need not have
suspected even that his were at a critical point.   Had he been
a little bolder he might have been carrying home with him a
certainty which would have kept him warmer than any great-
coat ; but then, on the other hand, he might have been de-
parting shamed and cast down, followed by the mocking
glances of that assembly, and with Rumour following after him
as it followed the exit of the Rector, breathing among all the
gossips that he had been rejected ; upon which he congratu-
lated himself that he had been prudent, that he had not exposed himself at least so far.   Finally he began to wonder, with
a secret smile of superiority, how the Rector had got off the
scene ?   Did he " exit praying " ?—which would at least have
been suitable to his profession.   The doctor smiled grimly
under his muffler ; he would have laughed if it had not been
for Jim by his side, who sat thinking of nothing, looking out
for the Sliplin lights and that turning about which Lady Jane
had warned his master.   If it had not been for Jim, indeed,
Dr. Burnet, though so good a driver, would have run the mare
into the bank of stones and roadmakers' materials which had
been accumulated there for the repair of the road.   " Exit
praying " ?—no, the Rector, to judge from his present aspect
of irritated and wounded pride, could not have done that.
" Exit cursing," would have been more like it.   The doctor
did burst into a little laugh as he successfully steered round the
Eversfield corner, thanks to the observation of his groom, and
Jim thought this was the reason of the laugh.   At all events,
neither the praying nor the cursing had come yet for Dr.
Burnet, and he was not in any hurry.   He said to himself that
he would go and pay old Tredgold a visit next morning, and
tell him of the dinner party at Steephill and see how the land
lay.

I cannot tell whether Mr. Tredgold had any suspicion of the motives which made his medical man so very attentive to him, but he was always glad to see the doctor, who amused him, and whose vigorous life and occupation it did the old gentleman good to see.

"Ah, doctor, you remind me of what I was when I was a young man—always at it night and day. I didn't care not a ha'penny for pleasure ; work was pleasure for me—and makin' money," said the old man with a chuckle and a slap on the pocket where, metaphorically, it was all stored.

"You had the advantage over me, then," the doctor said.

"Why, you fellows must be coining money," cried the patient; "a golden guinea for five minutes' talk ; rich as Creosote you doctors ought to grow—once you get to the top of the tree. Must be at the top o' the tree first, I'll allow— known on 'Change, you know, and that sort of thing. You should go in for royalties, doctor ; that's the way to get known."

"I should have no objection, Mr. Tredgold, you may be sure, if the royalties would go in for me ; but there are two to be taken into account in such a bargain."

"Oh, that's easily done," said the old man. "Stand by when there's some accident, doctor—there's always accidents ; and be on the spot at the proper time."

"Unless I were to hire someone to get up the accident— Would you go so far as to recommend that ?"

Old Tredgold laughed and resumed the former subject. "So you took my Katie in to dinner ? Well, I'm glad of that. I don't approve of young prodigals dangling about my girls ; they may save themselves the trouble. I've let 'em know my principles, I hope, strong enough. If I would not give in to my little Stella, it stands to reason I won't for Kate. So my Lady Jane had best keep her fine gentlemen to herself."

"You may make your mind quite easy, sir," said the doctor ; "there were nothing but county people, and very heavy county people into the bargain."

" County or town, I don't think much of 'em," said old Tredgold ; " not unless they can table their money along-side of me ; that's my principle, Dr. Burnet — pound for pound, or you don't get a daughter of mine. It's the only safe principle. Girls are chiefly fools about money ; though Stella wasn't, mind you—that girl was always a chip o' the old block. Led astray, she was, by not believing I meant what I said — thought she could turn me round her little finger. That's what they all think," he said with a chuckle, " till they try—till they try."

" You see it is difficult to know until they do try," said Dr. Burnet ; " and if you will excuse me saying it, Mr. Tred-gold, Miss Stella had every reason to think she could turn you round her little finger. She had only to express a wish———"

" I don't deny it," said the old man with another chuckle —" I don't deny it. Everything they like—until they come to separatin' me from my money. I'll spend on them as much as any man ; but when it comes to settlin', pound by pound— you've heard it before."

" Oh yes, I've heard it before," the doctor said with a half groan, " and I suppose there are very few men under the cir-cumstances———"

" Plenty of men ! Why there's young Fred Turny—fine young fellow—as flashy as you like with his rings and his pins, good cricketer and all that, though I think it's nonsense, and keeps a young fellow off his business. Why, twice the man that Somers fellow was ! Had him down for Stella to look at, and she as good as turned him out of the house. Oh, she was an impudent one ! Came down again the other day, on spec, looking after Katie ; and bless you, she's just as bad, hanker-ing after them military swells, too, without a copper. I'm glad to know my Lady Jane understands what's what and kept her out of their way."

" There were only county people—young Fortescue, who has a pretty estate, and myself."

" Oh, *you* don't count," said old Mr. Tredgold; " we

needn't reckon you. Young Fortescue, eh? All land, no money. Land's a very bad investment in these days. I think I'll have nothing to do with young Fortescue. Far safer money on the table; then you run no risks.''

'' Young Fortescue is not a candidate, I believe,'' said Dr. Burnet with a smile much against the grain.

'' A candidate for what?—the county? I don't take any interest in politics except when they affect the market. Candidate, bless you, they're all candidates for a rich girl! There's not one of 'em, young or old, but thinks ' That girl will have a lot money.' Why, they tell me old Stanley—old enough to be her father—has been after Katie, old fool !'' the old man said.

Dr. Burnet felt himself a little out of countenance. He said, '' I do not believe, sir, for a moment, that the Rector, if there is any truth in the rumour, was thinking of Miss Katherine's money.''

'' Oh, tell that to the—moon, doctor ! I know a little better than that. Her money? why it's her money everybody is thinking of. D'ye think my Lady Jane would pay her such attention if it wasn't for her money? I thought it was all broken off along of Stella, but she thinks better luck next time, I suppose. By George !'' cried the old man, smiting the table with his fist, '' if she brings another young rake to me, and thinks she'll get over me——By George, doctor ! I've left Stella to taste how she likes it, but I'd turn the other one—that little white proud Katie—out of my house.'' There was a moment during which the doctor held himself ready for every emergency, for old Tredgold's countenance was crimson and his eyes staring. He calmed down, however, quickly, having learned the lesson that agitation was dangerous for his health, and with a softened voice said, '' You, now, doctor, why don't you get married ? Always better for a doctor to be married. The ladies like it, and you'd get on twice as well with a nice wife.''

'' Probably I should,'' said Dr. Burnet, '' but perhaps, if the lady happened to have any money——''

18

"Don't take one without," the old man interrupted.

"I should be considered a fortune-hunter, and I shouldn't like that."

"Oh, you!" said Mr. Tredgold, "you don't count—that's another pair of shoes altogether. As for your young Fortescue, I should just like to see him fork out, down upon the table, thousand for thousand. If he can do that, he's the man for me."

" 'You don't count!' What did the old beggar mean by that?" Dr. Burnet asked himself as he took the reins out of Jim's hand and drove away. Was it contempt, meaning that the doctor was totally out of the question? or was it by any possibility an encouragement with the signification that he as a privileged person might be permitted to come in on different grounds? In another man's case Dr. Burnet would have rejected the latter hypothesis with scorn, but in his own he was not so sure. What was the meaning of that sudden softening of tone, the suggestion, "You, now, doctor, why don't you get married?" almost in the same breath with his denunciation of any imaginary pretender? Why was he (Burnet) so distinctly put in a different category? He rejected the idea that this could mean anything favourable to himself, and then he took it back again and caressed it, and began to think it possible. *You* don't count. Why shouldn't he count? *He* was not a spendthrift like Charlie Somers; *he* was not all but bankrupt; on the contrary, he was well-to-do and had expectations. He was in a better position than the young military swells whom Mr. Tredgold denounced; he was far better off than the Rector. Why shouldn't he count? unless it was meant that the rule about those pounds on the table, &c., did not count where he was concerned, that he was to be reckoned with from a different point of view. The reader may think this was great folly on Dr. Burnet's part, but when you turn over anything a hundred times in your mind it is sure to take new aspects not seen at first. And then Mr. Tredgold's words appeared to the doctor's intelligence quite capable of a special interpretation. He was, as a matter of fact,

www.ingramcontent.com/pod-product-compliance
Lightning Source LLC
Chambersburg PA
CBHW020818260626
47169CB00003B/720